HIGH PRAISE FOR THE NINA REILLY NOVELS BY PERRI O'SHAUGHNESSY

PRESUMPTION OF DEATH

"A very good and exciting legal thriller [that] is also so much more . . . Perri O'Shaughnessy will appeal to readers who love John Grisham."
—*Midwest Book Review*

"Nina Reilly['s] pedal-to-the-metal approach to cases provides armchair thrills on just about every other page. . . . Perfect summer reading fare."
—*Forth Worth Star Telegram*

"Counselor Nina Reilly keeps on . . . getting better."
—*Kirkus Reviews* (starred review)

"A vivid read." —*Houston Chronicle*

"Well-rounded and likable characters [are] set against a richly developed backdrop of some of the loveliest country in the world." —*Publishers Weekly*

"The protagonists are well-rounded and engaging, the legal issues are clarified for the layman, and the pace is relentless." —*BookPage*

UNFIT TO PRACTICE

PRESUMPTION OF DEATH

PERRI O'SHAUGHNESSY

A DELL BOOK

PRESUMPTION OF DEATH
A Dell Book

PUBLISHING HISTORY
Delacorte hardcover edition published August 2003
Dell mass market edition / May 2004

Published by
Bantam Dell
A Division of Random House, Inc.
New York, New York

ISBN 0-440-24087-5

Manufactured in the United States of America
Published simultaneously in Canada

OPM 10 9 8 7 6 5 4 3 2 1

To Peter von Mertens, Ardyth Brock,
Nita Piper, Sherry Jenks,
Mary Ann Robnett, Elizabeth Blair,
Jane Fuller, Joan Westlund,
Joanna Tamer, Helga Gerdes,
and Joyce Lindsey
—steadfast friends

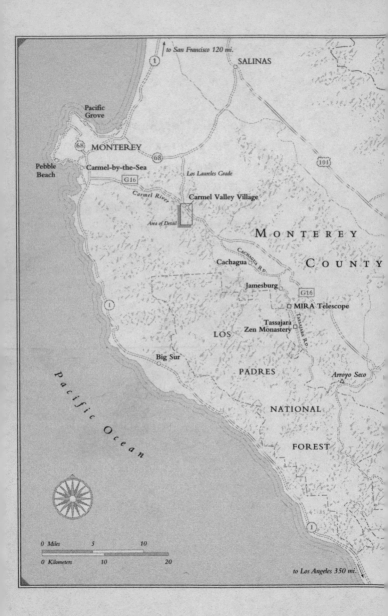

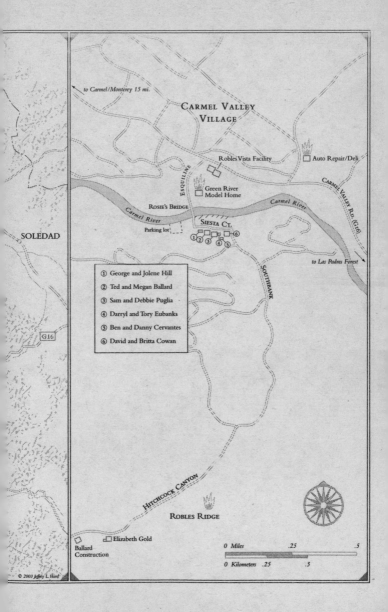

PRESUMPTION OF DEATH

PROLOGUE

"A little noiseless noise among the leaves."
—KEATS

PICTURE IT: A moonless summer night filling a hollow sky, glossy unblinking stars; under this, the rolling brown summits of the Robles Ridge; under this, the dry rattling of the leaf-tops of clustering oaks; and beneath all this, in the deep forest that slopes even farther down toward Steinbeck's pastures of heaven, two young men, hunting.

In soft clothes that did not rustle, one behind the other, they moved in a line between gnarled tree trunks.

To the west, distantly, out of sight, the Pacific Ocean lay black under the sky and poured itself out onto the shore, then drained back into itself with a soft rush. Up the mountain above them somewhere, their prey must be softly crunching like a big buck over the dense dry carpet of dead brush.

They hunted along a steep wooded trail below where it widened to an open saddle before continuing up rocky slopes to the summit, hunting as their ancestors of the Washoe tribe had hunted for tens of thousands of years, following with ancient purpose a spirit moving through the darkness.

But this spirit was no animal.

"Shut up, Willis," Danny whispered, then darted to a new tree, his tall shape merging into utter blackness.

"Don't call me that. Only my mother calls me that." Wish followed Danny, puffing, admiring his headlong confidence and quiet feet. "What am I doing wrong, any-way?" he asked once he had picked his way across the brief clearing and stood pressed against the boulder with Danny.

"Something plops every time you step."

"Oh. The camera. It's slung over my . . ."

"And you sound like an ox. What have you got on your feet?"

"Hey, these are my new Doc Martens. I showed them to you. Remember? I paid a hundred twenty bucks for these. . . ."

"They sound like weed whackers. Pick up your feet. Shh. I hear something."

An owl made a low percussive sound. Above them, bats whooshed through the air like dry leaves. No sound, no echo of the sound they sought. A light rippling liquid fell onto Wish's 49ers hat. Wish tore it off and hit it softly against a tree. "Bat guano falling through the branches, that's all I hear," he whispered.

He looked up at a rift between the treetops where the Milky Way spread like silver buckshot across the sky.

"Is he gone?"

Danny didn't answer. He dropped silently into a crouch. Unlike Wish, whose father hadn't been around when he was growing up and whose mother worked in town, Danny had been brought up to know the wilderness. Danny was the leader here, but then, Danny had always been the leader. So Wish crouched too.

Danny's hand clenched his shoulder. For a moment they listened to the woods, heads thrust forward, nostrils spread. A hot little breeze lifted and dropped Wish's lank hair. Danny gave him a push. "Feel that?" he said in a low voice. "That wind?"

"Kinda warm for June."

"Listen!"

"No, I . . ." Wish stopped talking. He cupped a hand around his ear. He heard a new sound. Singing, like cicadas. No.

Crackling.

"Fire!" Wish breathed. "He set one up there!"

"Uh huh," Danny said in a quiet, tight voice. He stood up, favoring his left knee like always, licked the tips of his fingers, and held them up. "The wind is going to take it down this side of the slope. Now, look, Wish. He's got to come down this side. There isn't any other way down. Can't bushwhack in the dark, it's way too steep. He's gonna come down right past us."

"There are houses down here!"

"We'll get him. Then we'll call for help."

"I don't like this."

"We're not giving up. I know what I'm doing. Don't I always?"

Not at all, Wish thought. Just about never. His mom said Danny made less sense than a pinochle card. What his mom couldn't appreciate was Danny as a force of nature. His energy pulled you along like a big wind. Wish felt excited, just being around him, blowing this way and that, never knowing what lay ahead. And here they were again, in trouble, like always when he let Danny have his way.

They would get out of it somehow, he thought, come fire, earthquake, or landslide. You could depend on Danny for one thing: a screwed-up, hairy outcome, but somehow, you survived.

Around them, other creatures stirred in their holes, disturbed, sniffing in the bush. Wish caught a whiff of smoke, pleasant and woody, like the fires in the cabin in winter back at Markleeville. "Fire, Danny. This is serious. We need to call the fire department. You got a mobile phone?"

"Not hardly."

Though Danny didn't ask, Wish offered, "Mine's in the van, still hooked to the car charger." He waited hopelessly for Danny to give him the okay to get going back down the hill to the street.

"We're close," Danny said. "He's up there, I can feel it. Give him a minute. He'll come tearing down."

Too afraid to pretend patience, Wish flapped his long arms. "Haven't you ever seen those shows? Where fire like, blows up in people's faces? Where even firefighters get trapped? We gotta make like Bambi and Thumper and get outta here!"

Ignoring him, Danny peered into the darkness above them, up the trail that rose another few hundred feet of scrambly sandy dirt to the saddle they couldn't see. The trail climbed steeply up the east flank of the ridge. The breeze had turned gusty and blew across Wish's cheek. Coming this way, his mind recorded automatically. Up higher, jittery reds, oranges, and yellows jerked down the hill in fits and starts like rush-hour traffic, accelerating in bursts. "Could he stay up on the saddle?" said Wish. "It's more open up there."

"Yeah, sit there and get burned up," Danny said, disgusted. "He's not that stupid. Unless maybe he doesn't care and wants to go out in a blaze of glory."

"He might try to go uphill instead of down. There's a trail that runs just below the summit."

"He might. But he's got a car down there on Southbank."

"He won't leave his car," Wish said to reassure himself.

"We stay put," Danny decided. "Listen. He comes down this way, and we're ready. He'll have a flashlight, and we'll spot him first. Then, before he sees us, we shoot him. We slide behind those rocks and trap him trying to get to his car. We shoot, then we let him go."

"But—"

Danny got up, and Wish followed him behind the biggest of the rocks off the trail. Another time, Wish wouldn't have gone near those tumbled rocks with their dark caverns where mountain lions might hide. Flashing his light all around behind the rock and seeing no yellow eyes reflecting back, he picked up a cudgel-like branch, then lowered himself beside Danny, who continued to watch the trail. They could see where it curved around toward them.

What if this guy didn't try to run after they shot him?

Birds fluttered invisibly into darkness. Gusts of heat blew down the mountain. A hell was starting up there.

Wish looked up. Harsh white haze blotted out the stars. A brushing sound, then thuds—somewhere up there branches dropped in erratic drumbeats. The primitive sounds moved through him, pinging like poison darts, making his body shake and his mind fall to pieces.

"He's coming," Danny whispered. "I can smell him."

"Danny, we got to go."

"You want to bail on me? Now, when I need you? I should have expected it. C'mon, don't panic on me, man."

"I'm going, Danny."

"Do what you want," Danny said. "Go. But"—a note of desperation entered his voice—"please don't go yet. A coupla minutes, okay? That's all we need. Okay?"

Wish said nothing.

"The guy is going to come down. It's a matter of seconds! I need this!" Danny said. "We both do!"

A wavering glow advanced down the mountain toward them.

"Three minutes," Wish said.

Two deer burst out of the bush, making Wish's heart stop, and pounded past them along the trail. "It's moving fast," Wish said. There were people down below. "Danny."

"What?"

"We could climb down to the street and catch him at his car, if it's really down there. Shoot him there."

"One hundred thousand dollars," Danny said. "One hundred thousand buckaroos. Remember why we're here. Worth some risk, right? This way, we can't miss." He reached into his shirt pocket and popped a handful of barbecued sunflower seeds into his mouth. Danny ate when he was nervous: jelly beans, candy, seeds. "No more hitting up the family for five bucks to go to town. No more sleeping on the couch."

"Danny—feel that heat! Take a look up there. It's like— a wave of fire coming down. It's almost on top of us." Wish tried to compress his dread into reasonable-sounding words.

"Now, you listen, Wishywashy. You stay here until I say go. You owe me this—"

Old business at a time like this. Just like Danny to resort to emotional blackmail or anything else that might work to get what he wanted. "We have to warn those people below."

"Keep down," Danny ordered, voice urgent. Lifting his head slowly above the slab of rock he froze, nose pointing, eyes big.

His own eyes burning and straining, Wish straightened and peered up the trail. How could Danny see anything through that dust and smoke?

By now the fire had moved close enough for them to feel the whomps as it jumped from tree to tree, setting each one off. Leaves flared red like blue match tops side by side in a box. Branches cracked. Trees tottered and collapsed. Hot wind roared.

Wish had never been so frightened. Shaking behind Danny, he wished to God he had stayed home when Danny came by with this crazy idea, he wished he had listened to his mother, he wished he had stayed back in Tahoe, where it was safe.

A line of trees exploded. Against the light of their dying, Wish thought he saw a figure standing on the curve of the trail. Was that someone watching the fire?

"Hey!" Danny pointed. "See that over there?"

"You see somebody?" Wish asked.

"There he is! That's him!"

"Where?" Wish asked, untangling his camera. "Point. I can't see anything."

"There!"

Wish flipped a button, turning his camera on. He raised it. Dust and flying cinders blew into his eyes. He wasted a second wiping the lens. Putting an eye to the lens he saw nothing but liquid fire coming his way. Blinded by the intensity of the blaze, he pressed the telephoto button, aimed, and shot toward the burning trees. He shot as many times in as many directions as he could.

Out of memory to shoot any more photos, he popped out the memory card and pushed it into his pocket and reloaded, circling the site again. "He's gone, Danny. Oh, man. I'm sorry. I can't see. I don't . . ."

But Danny was up, stomping around in the rocks, black eyes burning as orange as the flames. Smoke billowed white clouds across the clearing. He coughed. "Big surprise! You missed him!"

Wish swung into a wide arc, snapping pictures, flashing ugly hard white futilely into the hellish glow of the woods on fire.

"See him? See him now? No, of course not! Because you missed him! All right, we'll catch up with him."

Wish grabbed for Danny's arm. "This is the end, Danny," he said. "It's over!"

"The end?" Danny stood still as a totem, wrathful, sweating, his eyes narrow against the smoke.

"We'll catch him some other time. We'll die if we don't get out of here!" Wish pulled at him. Danny didn't budge. "Let's go, let's go, let's go!"

"But it's not done yet. It's not over yet. We'll catch up with him. He's stupid, he saw us and he's hiding somewhere."

"I'm going, and you're going with me!"

Orange flames flowed like lava above them, toward them, inexorable. They would both burn if they didn't leave instantly, and finally even Danny seemed to realize that. They took off through the woods, away from treetops that blazed and blew like palms in a tropical sunset.

Wish, running behind Danny, peeled off his jacket and

T-shirt, and wrapped them around his waist. At some point he noticed he'd dropped the camera.

When he straightened up, Danny was gone, and what was worse, what was so much worse, was that he was surrounded by a ring of flame higher than the highest tree. "Danny!" he yelled, choking on smoke. Had he run off to catch the guy on his own? The woods, the wind, the inferno, swallowed his words. The hillside roared its death cries. How had the fire moved so fast?

Now, the trail forgotten, he ran blindly downward. He scraped past branches, stumbling over fallen trees, screaming and chittering like the jackrabbits and deer and chipmunks, running with them, unable to see through the smoke and past the dense band of heat, a million candles blazing all around him. The sky was on fire. He ran toward . . . what? The road? Death?

He fell. Down in the dirt, still ahead of the roaring wind and fire, he tried to think. He called again, gasping for air. He stood up on the strong legs that had hiked so many Sierra trails with Danny, and found them wobbly. Should he crawl, stay low? He didn't know. He felt too clumsy to run and too panicky to think.

When his head came up, he heard a shout. And there he was, Danny, climbing up through the trees, wheezing, calling to him, reaching out his big knobby hand.

"You—where did you—!"

"Take it easy," said Danny. "Follow me." He pulled Wish forward.

Wish held back.

"Calm down. Follow me."

"There's fire over there, actual flames, see that? And this smoke. I can barely see you. I can't breathe!"

"Trust me, Willis. I've got a plan." For a moment the smoke cleared and Wish saw Danny at his most crazed. Holding arms with singed hair over their foreheads against the burning tree limbs, they moved back out onto the trail. No need for the flashlight anymore—Wish had dropped it in the rocks anyway. They rushed downward, sliding, sweating, panting, reckless, hell-bent toward the road.

"Don't stop," Danny commanded when Wish slowed.

"Just one second—can't breathe—"

"Run or it'll catch us. We're almost back to the road—"

"I don't see—any—freaking—road—" Each word a seared, heaving breath—

Death flew low over their heads in a ragged blazing cloak, setting fires wherever it touched down. They ducked. "Another hundred feet," Danny said. "Follow me." And Danny walked through trees, wiggling his fingers. "We got it made now, ol' buddy, ol' pal. Follow Danny, now." Danny moved on ahead, a tall half-lit figure.

Wish took one stumbling step toward him.

And saw several things. Danny, disappearing into the white soup. A wall of fire rearing up like a tsunami in front, bigger than Wish, ready to take him down.

And then two blackened hands reaching out from behind the tree trunk right next to him, holding up a big sharp rock with white stipples and granite lines. He saw the fingers raise it up. He saw the rock crash down toward him.

Wish lurched to one side. He howled, but the noise he made got lost in the belligerent, ripping, tearing fire. Losing his balance, he toppled to the ground.

PART ONE

*And I chiefly use my charm
On creatures that do people harm.*

1

NINA REILLY WIPED her goggles and watched Paul swim. He stroked smoothly, kicking underwater, moving up and down the lane without stopping, like a pacing porpoise. He wore his yellow snorkel and goggles, and she could hear his lungs laboring when he came close.

Enjoying the pattern of the water on the ceiling of the condo-association pool, she returned to backstroking in another lane. Pull hard back with the arms, keep the legs stiff, and windmill that water. The two of them were going nowhere, but it felt like lovemaking, the cool slap of the water he churned up, the water rippling back to him, a water bed without the plastic.

She touched the wall. He turned at the far end. As he swam down the lane she had the strangest feeling about him, as if the pale watery creature before her solidified before her eyes. Hanging on to the rough concrete wall of the pool, she thought, he might swim toward me with that silly yellow snorkel for the rest of my life. How many years do I have left? Forty years, if I get lucky? She was in her mid-thirties, Paul was over forty. How long did they have? A lifetime? A summer?

Well, that's what I came down here to find out, she said to herself.

He hit the wall and came up grinning, goggles fogged up. "Done?" he said. Then, "What's the matter?"

"Nothing."

"Your face says different."

"I'm trying to see the future."

"What do you see?" He pulled himself over until his face was inches from hers, his hazel eyes reddened by the chlorine, the lashes beaded, the water making rivulets along his nose, red lines across his forehead and cheeks from the goggles.

"You."

"That is the correct answer. As your reward, I will sing you a song I just made up." He pulled himself onto the edge of the pool and, legs dangling, sang in a gravelly voice:

I am the creature from the lagoon
You're a blond coed starin' at the moon
I'll rise up drippin', a scary sight
Baby, are you ready, it's love-monster night—

"Like it?"

She hung in the water, her eyes at his ankle level. Tilting her head back and holding the wall with both hands, she let her gaze move boldly up his body, the strong pale thighs, the tight stomach with a little hangover of flesh at the waist, the sensitive nipples and broad shoulders. She said, "Are you going to wear your snorkel when you rise up?"

"I'll do whatever it takes."

"It won't take much." A look passed between them, and Nina reached over and squeezed his big toe.

"Let's wrap up in our towels and get back home," Paul said.

She mantled up onto the side of the pool, rested her knee on the concrete, stood, and adjusted her swimsuit bottom. Paul brought her the striped blue towel and they walked outside, down the path beside the bougainvillaea, below the neighbors' balconies. In the misty late afternoon they saw lights come on as people came home from work. A line of birds sat quietly in the branches of the oaks, paired off mostly, looking around. Peter Jennings pronounced the news in fatherly fashion from somebody's living room.

Paul hadn't even locked the door to his condo. Inside, in the hall with the bokhara rug that led to the living room, he said, "How was it? The future?"

"Blurry."

He said seriously, "You know, this could go on forever or a day. Either one is okay."

"No, a day wouldn't be okay."

"You going to make me a declaration, Nina? Finally?" He folded his arms so the biceps bulged, Mr. Clean in a baggy wet pair of red trunks in his narrow hallway, and waited for her to tell him she was ready to link up her short time on earth with his. The conversations lately had been skidding into turns like these. Paul needed something from her, a formal statement, a closing of the box lid.

She couldn't do that for him, unfortunately. "You can have the first shower," she said, offering what she could.

"You are being oblique."

"You can even use my loofah."

"That's fine. We'll just continue to drift on the seas of uncertainty. Until the sun becomes a supernova and the seas all dry up."

Nina said, "I'll definitely say something before then. Just go get dressed. I'll watch the sun go down on the balcony."

"And get the fish marinating," Paul reminded her.

"Sure."

But he hesitated. He could see that she had a problem and he wanted to fix it. "The rash bothering you?"

"Yes. Go on, now."

"I told you, you can go in and get a shot," Paul said, still trying to fix the wrong problem. "You wouldn't feel so irritable."

They had been quiet at dinner. Now they held each

other in Paul's platform bed, under the red-and-yellow Hudson Bay blanket.

A seashell night-light in the bathroom glowed dimly. Under the covers, her nightgown was pushed up to her waist. Her ankles, rear end, and forearms itched like fury. Damn right she was irritable.

She had a grand case of poison oak, predator of the Central California hills, because, oblivious to it, she had gone hiking behind the condo last week. She had no one to blame but herself, which irritated her even more.

And all of this specific irritation had wrapped itself around a general core of irritation within her. Although Paul did not intend it, circumstance had made of her the girlfriend who lives out of the suitcase in the corner. She had no home anymore, only his home, his street, his doors, his walls. She floated in his pool.

Living together was a revelation. Paul kept guns all over the house and a locked gun case in the car trunk; she hated that. His study was full of high-tech equipment she couldn't identify. He was physically exhausting; he worked out religiously at his gym, ran, played tennis, went rock-climbing, even played darts at his favorite bar. He cooked and loved to drive and he listened to jazz until late into the night. He had way too much vigor for her; he made her feel like a slug.

She liked to read all day, swim a bit, have a walk around the neighborhood with Hitchcock. She was a news junkie, loved to shop on the Net, enjoyed sitting at the kitchen table taking notes for that law-journal article she would write someday.

They weren't kids, and melding their lifestyles didn't come easy. And sometimes, damn right again, she found this irritating.

But she wasn't ready to say these things, so instead she sat up and searched the nightstand for her cream and said, "I told you, I got a shot of prednisone when I was a kid when I had it bad. The next morning I couldn't get out of bed, and my dad called the doctor. Oh, he said, steroids can cause muscle weakness. I couldn't stand up, my legs wouldn't hold me. I had to lie down for a week."

"It cured the rash, didn't it?"

Nina finished applying the hydrocortisone cream, slowly screwed the lid on, and set it on the table. That question of his pushed her irritation to a new flaming height.

Paul lay on his back, the sheet pulled up to his hairy chest, his hands entwined behind his head, revealing armpits covered with the same curling golden hair she loved so much, observing her. His smooth skin was a reproach, and his self-assurance needed a good kick in the rear.

"Do what you want," he said, too late. When he began rubbing her back, she pulled away.

Her dog, Hitchcock, stirred on the rug, stretched and got up and padded into the far corner of the bedroom, sensing gnarly human vibes, looking for peace.

Nina said, lapsing into self-pity, "I feel like a crocodile."

"It's not that bad and it's not catching, honey. And I can't see it in the dark."

She thought, if this love affair ends in a day I won't be able to take it, that's the truth. I've been through enough. But I can't live like this either.

"This will never work," she blurted out.

"Whoa," Paul said. "I thought we were having fun. What catastrophe just happened that I missed?"

"I'm not cut out to be half of a couple. I'm a solitary person." She scratched her forearm.

Paul said in a soothing tone, "Right now, we're together. Right now, we're good."

He reached out a hand and stroked her hip prize-filly style. At least this part of her anatomy had no rash. His touch calmed her. The prickling of her skin seemed less intense.

She felt her blood heating up, rising to the surface of her skin as he continued to massage, moving from her hip down to her thigh. His hand slipped around to her front and his fingers cruised into the danger zone. "Look," he said, "all that wine you drank tonight dehydrated you and makes the rash feel worse. You'll feel better in the morning."

"Grr." Nina pushed off his hand and jumped out of bed. "Leave my drinking habits out of this." She marched around the cold bedroom, arms crossed, thinking dark thoughts. Was there some secret smooth path between men and women that she had yet to discover?

Paul got up on his elbow to watch her. "C'mon back," he said. "Bedtime."

She didn't answer.

"Don't make me get out of bed. One."

The warning, issued in Paul's husky, determined voice, aroused physical reactions, warmth and wetness.

"Two."

Against the white of the sheet, his skin appeared darker than usual. He had an end-of-the-day roughness on his cheeks.

"Not till I'm good and ready!"

"I'll get you good and ready. Two and a half."

"No!"

Paul flung back the covers. "You're asking for it," he said. He jumped out of bed. Nina slid open the screen and rushed out to the deck, Hitchcock joyous at her heels.

Outside, bright stars. Wide oaks studding dark hills. Sage scent. A motorcycle's red light winking on Carmel Valley Road. She stood at the wood railing, back to Paul, wondering what he would do next.

Excited.

He put his arms around her from behind and pressed against her. "I'm sorry, honey," he said. "Whatever I did or said, I'm sorry." Then he mumbled some things about how he loved her, and the universe realigned in that shifty way it has. The anti-itch cream began working and the self-pity dissipated, because he was pressing insistently now, hard and ready.

His skin felt hot in the moist cool air. She let him lower her to the plastic chaise lounge and push up the nightgown and then she locked lips with him. He had hard lips, not the smooshy kind, lips that made definite demands.

Leaves crackled under her on the plastic strapping, marking her, but she was past caring. The Summer Triangle spread across the sky above her half-closed eyes and how unimaginably distant blazed that inferno of stars in the blacklit storm of energies—

"Ah!"

"Oh!"

"Uh!"

The light next door went on. The curious Mr. Mitts, Paul's elderly neighbor, had awakened. The head of his fat tabby appeared on his windowsill, ears pricked, and Hitchcock made a hopeless run for it, barking and snarling and waking up the whole place.

"In we go," Paul whispered. He carried her in.

Paul lay drowsy beside her, his breath thickened into a burr.

"Paul?"

"Mmm."

"Are you awake?"

"No."

"Good night, sweetheart."

Paul didn't answer.

"You know"—she opened her eyes and let the moonlight fill them, let herself talk—"I've been thinking some more about why I left Tahoe. I wanted to be with you, I really did. I needed time off from law. I was wrung dry. We both know that."

No response from his side of the bed.

She sat up in bed and reached for her cream. "I've been here at your place for three weeks. Bob's gone to Europe for the summer, I rented my house at Tahoe, and another lawyer is running my office up there. Pieces of me are strewn all over the place."

She thought about that for a while, punching her pillow, searching for just the right angle to rest her head. "Paul? I can't stand that for long. Have you ever read about the shamans who go through a ceremony of being blasted apart? Metaphorically, I mean. And then they reassemble as new people. They have some guidance, though. Traditions and dogmas. I don't have any guidance at all, and smithereens of me are drifting around. What kind of new person am I becoming?"

He turned as though he heard her and laid a muscular arm over her chest, and the declaration he had asked for earlier launched itself silently in her head. She thought, Even though you're too aggressive and you want to control me, I love you. But, Paul, I'm afraid you want a sidekick. I can't be just a sidekick. I fought too hard to be autonomous, free.

Free, such a rare state for a woman. *Autonomous*. A word too seldom linked with the word *woman*.

She felt herself turning as moody as a three-year-old whose ice cream had fallen off the cone. Damn it, she thought, touching a finger to his tanned cheek. I do sort of want to be your doggone sidekick, at the same time.

What happens now?

She spiraled down into anxious dreams.

The last one went like this: She was back in court at Tahoe, dressed up, made up, sharp, making a closing argument in a murder case. The ladies and gents of the jury watched intently as she held up her arm and scratched her forearm meaningfully, one time only.

Somehow in this dream logic everybody in the courtroom knew that one scratch meant, he's innocent. The jury members lifted their skinny legs and prepared to scratch back.

Just then the door opened and a lawyer named Jeffrey Riesner came in wearing an Armani suit. He looked bewildered. Nina remembered that he was dead and his face began to cave in and she ran out the back. The forest closed around her and she ran on until she came to a rock wall. She could hear his peculiar breathing behind her so she scrabbled up to a high ledge.

He flew up after her like a wasp, to throw her off and kill her—

She woke up, breathing hard, pushing the button on her watch to make it light up. Almost 6:00 A.M. Thursday morning had begun. The phone was ringing.

2

"WUH?" PAUL SAID. He removed his arm from where it had come to rest on her chest.

Outside the sliding doors to the deck, ghostly fog, lit palely by a young sun somewhere above. On Nina's right, Paul lay on his back and went back to snoring. On her left, on a bedside table just big enough for a lamp, a pair of glasses, water, and a book, the phone continued to ring. She reached for it. It fell to the floor.

Paul put a pillow over his head while Nina leaned as far down as she could without falling out of the bed, collected the mouthpiece, and flicked on the lamp.

A muffled growl came from the right, and through the phone, a familiar voice. "It's me."

"Sandy?" She knew the voice, but in her new surroundings it jarred.

"Forget me already?"

"Of course not." Sandy Whitefeather had been Nina's secretary in her law office at South Lake Tahoe, but this summer was doing some kind of work with the federal government at the Bureau of Indian Affairs, something to do with the rights of the Washoe tribe, her people.

At the moment, decaffeinated, Nina couldn't recall details. "Where are you?"

"D.C."

"It's dawn here."

"Not too early for the police to call."

Groggy, squinting at her watch, Nina said, "You've joined the police?"

"Right, I'm the new attorney general. Wake up, we have to talk. The police called me."

"From South Lake Tahoe?" She pulled herself up and propped her back against the headboard. "What do they want?"

"Not Tahoe. Monterey County Sheriff."

"Oh." What in the world? "Why would the sheriff's office call you?"

"You won't believe this," Sandy said, then stopped.

"Won't believe . . . what?"

"Heard about some local fires?"

They had been in the paper all week, the devastating early fires of California. Spring this year had brought drought and with it, fire. Thousands of acres of scourge, hundreds of millions in damage. Last night, right before falling asleep, they had listened to an analysis on NPR. "Yeah."

"Some near you? In Carmel Valley?"

"Now you mention it, yes. Three arson fires in the last month, right? What is it, Sandy?"

"Tuesday night was the third one. Easy to tell it was arson, they found evidence of kerosene. There was a victim this time."

Nina thought about the dead man in her dream. All the fright of the night flowed back. It's going to be someone I know, she thought to herself, and she gritted her teeth and said, "Go on."

"They say," Sandy said. She paused. "They say the body might be Willis."

"Wish? No!" Her lungs expelled their breath, and she held a fist to her heart. "No!"

Sandy's son was spending the summer in the area working at Paul's investigative firm. He lived with roommates in a house Nina owned in Pacific Grove.

"Well, is he there?" Sandy asked. Her usually deadpan

voice held something new and vulnerable and huge and overwhelming in it. Motherhood.

"No," she told Sandy. "What—"

"Did you see him last night?"

"No."

"Huh. Joseph thought maybe you had him there." Joseph was Wish's father, probably holding down the fort at the ranch in Markleeville during Sandy's travels. They had animals there, and, besides, after a long journey that had lasted for years, Joseph seldom left their ranch now.

"Let me think," Nina said rapidly. "Wait. He asked to take the rest of the week off from the office. Paul mentioned it. Why do"—in spite of her dry mouth, Nina swallowed—"the police think it's Wish?"

"He went up the Robles Ridge above Carmel Valley Village Tuesday night with another boy. Fire burned fifteen acres on the ridge. His roommates say he didn't come home that night or last night either. The arson team found a body. That's why."

Oh, no, no, no. Paul stirred. "What's going on?" he asked.

"No fear," Sandy continued. "It isn't him."

Funny how that phrase, *no fear,* the logo on a baseball cap, a phrase Nina so connected to her own son, struck down all her defenses. "What do you mean?"

"It isn't him."

"Did they ask you to come here and identify him?"

"Oh, I'm coming, but I know what I know."

As if Sandy could see her across the three thousand miles, Nina nodded. Then she said painfully, "How do you know?"

Silence ate at the line. Sandy finally said, "I'm his mother. I know. I would feel it if he was gone. No noise strikes the house. I can say his name. Some other things that you're not going to understand. Anyway. I want you to find him."

"We will."

"Is Paul there?"

Nina handed the phone to Paul. "It's bad," she whispered. "That fire in Carmel Valley we heard about in the news last night? They found a body and . . . they think it's Wish."

Paul took the phone from her. The sheet fell off his naked body, but he didn't notice. "What's going on?" he asked. And then, *uh huh, uh huh*s followed many times before he hung up. He jumped from the bed, strode over to the sliding doors, and opened them. Damp air flowed in. He breathed deeply.

"What do we do now?" she asked.

"He was supposed to be at Tahoe with his father. Sounds like he never made it."

"I said good-bye to him at the office on Tuesday night. Paul . . . if he's dead?"

"We deal with what we have right now. Sandy believes he's alive."

"She's three thousand miles away," Nina said.

"We're here. Let's get going."

After dressing and a quick bite, they drove to the sheriff's office in Salinas. Along the road farmworkers were picking late strawberries. The Salinas Valley was one of the richest agricultural areas in the world, lying between the southern coast ranges and the Pacific. Farmers raised lettuce, artichokes, grapes, and thirty other crops in the fields along the river. They were in the land of the California missions, and not too long ago the workers bending over the rows of plants would have been mission Indians, not Latinos.

The fields ended abruptly and town began. In an old art deco building courtesy of WPA workers in the 1930s, the main offices for the enormous County of Monterey had just opened for business. The deputy on duty sent them along to check with the county arson investigator for details about the fire. "Coroner's not done with the body yet. You can't see it."

The summer's usual cool ocean breezes hadn't made it this far inland yet, leaving a hot sun in charge this early Thursday morning. The heat made Nina sweat, so she peeled off her sweater before going inside the nearby building that housed the fire investigator's office.

A young girl at a desk in the entryway had just told them they were out of luck, when in blew David Crockett, a perspiring, huffing man in his late thirties with curly black thinning hair, wearing running shoes and sweats. He gave them a piercing look and took Paul's ID.

"Right. I remember you from Monterey Police, Paul. You broke open that warehouse-fraud case in Seaside." He shook his hand. "You're on your own now, I hear."

"Have been for years. Good to see you again, too, Davy. Thought you were headed to Sacramento."

"I've been up there for the past two years. Been assigned down here only a few days."

Paul looked at him. "Excellent job on that triple homicide in Roseville last year. I'd like to talk some more about that case sometime. The evidence trail your people established was outstanding. Got him what he deserved. Death row's too kind for bastards like him."

"Thanks." Crockett sat them down to wait in an undecorated wood-paneled office. "Give me five seconds," he said, and left. They heard the sound of water running somewhere outside.

"What do you think of him?" Nina asked.

"He's dogged. Resourceful. He stays calm."

"High praise. Did you two get along?"

"I was working my way out of the police force by then and not in the best of moods. So let's put it this way, I hope I have since earned his respect."

"Well, any relationship you have, exploit it, okay?"

"Do what I can," said Paul.

Crockett came back, cheeks freshly scrubbed, decked out in creased navy slacks, a dress shirt, and tie.

"Jane, bring us some coffee," he said to the young woman at the desk in front.

"Okay." Judging by the downturn in her red lips, she did not relish this part of her job.

"Three sugars," he commanded.

A few moments later Jane entered with a water-spattered tray containing a stained thermos, three cups, a bowl gunked with blobs of dried sugar, and a spoon that she picked up and dried with the tail of her blouse before returning to the tray.

"Now, that's service, Janie," Crockett said heartily. When she had closed the door, he said, "She's a trainee. Some kind of chip on her shoulder. We shall see. Yes, we shall see." He tapped his pen on the desk, and his eyes seemed to bore through the door Janie had gone through.

"How'd you end up here?" Paul asked. The small talk was making Nina impatient, but the men needed to establish common grounds and attitudes.

Crockett poured himself a cup and swallowed it. "After I left Monterey, I worked for the sheriff's department in Salinas, then went on to Sacramento. I'm with a special arson-investigation unit here in Monterey County. I like it. Good people here."

"Glad to hear it."

"How about you? How do you like being out on your own?"

"It's a lonely old world, working alone, but there are compensations."

"I see that there are," Crockett said, inclining his head toward Nina, who was scratching her ankle. "This your secretary?"

"My name is Nina Reilly. I'm an attorney," Nina said. "Excuse me for interrupting, but we don't have time to chat. As you know, Mr. van Wagoner is an investigator. We understand you have a victim in the Tuesday fire and a tentative ID on a young man named Willis Whitefeather. We're friends, we're worried, and we'd like to see the victim."

Crockett had turned his whole body toward her in the chair. "I see. You're an attorney, are you?"

"Mr. Whitefeather's mother is out of state and can't get here today. She asked us to come in and talk with you. Apparently she was told . . . a victim of the Tuesday-night Robles Ridge fire might be her son."

Crockett studied her some more, then rustled around on his desk for some papers. "Yes. I talked with Mrs. Whitefeather last night. She's still planning to fly in?"

"Yes, but maybe we can clear things up immediately if we see the victim, although I understand that isn't possible at the moment?" Nina said.

Crockett nodded. "Seeing the body may not clear things up. It was badly burned."

"What's the basis of the ID?"

"Simple logic. He's been missing since Tuesday night, and the last people to see him, his roommates, called in yesterday to report him missing. They heard the news reports and got alarmed because the last time they saw him was Tuesday night, and he was on his way with a friend into the hills above Carmel Valley Village. They read about the fire and decided to report it. The body was found by the sheriff's posse, a mounted patrol out of the Salinas station on Wednesday about noon. They do rescues up there in the backwoods, get into places cars won't go. Some of the area was still too hot to search as of yesterday."

"You went up there too?"

"Yes," he said. "And I'll be going back up this afternoon."

"What about the friend who went up there with Wish? Why aren't you assuming it's him?" Nina said. Paul put his hand on her arm, lightly, but she knew what he meant. He was warning her not to be so intense. Crockett had seen Paul's movement. His eyes missed nothing.

Just as lightly, just as definitely, Nina shrugged off Paul's hand.

"Could be him," Crockett said. "But we don't have a missing-persons report on him. That's the difference. The friend's name is Daniel Cervantes. Mrs. Whitefeather gave us the name after she heard the roommates said it was a young man named Danny. We're still trying to get a local address on him. Ring any bells? Danny Cervantes?"

Nina and Paul shook their heads.

"Childhood friends, Mrs. Whitefeather said. Guess they're both Native Americans from the Tahoe area."

"Wish is a member of the Washoe tribe. He was raised near Lake Tahoe."

"He's, what, twenty-one?"

"Yes," Nina said.

"Going to college up there, I understand. And working for you this summer, Paul, am I right?"

"Right."

"Was he working on a case on Tuesday night? Anything to do with the fires?"

"No."

"You sure about that?"

"I'm sure. What are you getting at, Davy?"

Crockett shifted again in his black chair, which looked like a standard-issue back-torture instrument. "Because the roommates told me he took a backpack, camera, water, that sort of thing. Just wondering if you might know why he would go up the mountain there, since you worked with him."

"I don't know," Paul said. Nina was getting nervous.

She said, giving Paul a warning look, "We understand this fire might have been set, that there have been a couple of suspicious fires in that area."

"That's right. Clear arsons. Kerosene all over the place. The local officials decided they needed someone to coordinate all the information coming in. I'm the liaison. I work with the agencies that are involved, and that can be a lot of bureaucracies, the police, the fire department, the sheriff's department, the state, the park service, the FBI . . . you familiar with the crime of arson?"

"We'd like to hear whatever you can tell us," Paul said.

"I can tell you generally that one of the first things we look for is motive."

Crockett stood up and pointed to a huge aerial photograph of Monterey County on the wall beside his desk.

"Here, here, and here," he said thoughtfully, pointing with his pencil to three spots on the map about fifteen miles inland from Carmel. "Those are the sites. You familiar with Carmel Valley Village?"

"I grew up here on the coast," Nina said. "When I think of the Village, I think of flies buzzing, yellow grass, open spaces. Old cottages along the river."

"Those old cottages are going fast, replaced by million-dollar mansions. Carmel Valley's a hot real-estate market these days. Really hot. So we have to consider what the fires are aimed at, as I said. The first one took out a model home and some construction equipment on a subdivision site near the Carmel River. Twelve homes and a big condo unit were planned for that one."

"I think I read about that project," Nina said. "Didn't they evict some handicapped people from the site?"

"Evict, that's not really the word. There's an old converted motel at the top of the site called Robles Vista. Used now as a state handicapped facility. Has to be torn down anyway, the place is falling apart. The occupants have been offered alternate housing. Most of them haven't moved yet.

"The second fire occurred at the new café right in the Village. It almost got away from the firefighters, and the elementary school next door would have gone up fast. A local character, a woman named Ruthie, was sleeping in the lot outside in her car about three A.M. and smelled it. She may have seen the arsonists. Two people in a car. Dangerous fire, could have burned down half the Village. The shop was gutted.

"The third fire, on Tuesday night, burned fifteen acres above the Village on Robles Ridge, all woods, and came within a hair of several brand-new homes up there. Big homes, spectacular views of the Valley."

"So you think the motive had to do with stopping new development in the Village?"

Crockett shrugged. "It's an obvious starting point. It could still be something else, revenge, insurance, punk kids playing nasty games. But the targets look like new homes and businesses."

"Wish wouldn't be involved in anything like that," Nina said.

"Did you know Mr. Whitefeather was antidevelopment?"

"What? You are way off base. He's not involved. He's not a local. He's not an ecoterrorist. He wants to be a cop!"

"How well did you know him, Ms. Reilly?"

"I know him extremely well, Mr. Crockett." The friendly conversation between Paul and Davy had moved into Mr. Crockett and Ms. Reilly.

"Then you know he participated in the protest last weekend against development interests in the Valley with some local Native Americans?"

Nina remembered Wish leaving Paul's office a few days earlier. "I gotta go early, Paul," he had said. "I promised to drive. People are depending on me."

"There were hundreds of people at that rally," she said, "plus free food."

Crockett shrugged.

"So he was out there exercising his constitutional rights," Nina went on. "It's a big leap from a rally to three rural arson fires in a place he's visiting, where he has no vested interest. What did the police do at that rally, film it and run people's IDs? I thought that went out with the Cold War."

"Well, there's his arrest at age thirteen for arson, that makes us sit up straight. The charges were dropped and the whole thing was put down to a prank. Still, that's not something we can overlook."

"But how would you know that? Records on juvenile offenders are sealed in California," Nina said, trying to hide her dismay at hearing this information.

"I know a few people," Crockett said, looking first at Paul, then staring at the map on the wall. "We don't miss much."

"But that's illegal," Nina said, leaning forward.

She felt like getting into it with Crockett. But before she could, he said casually, "And as I said, he told his roommates he was going up Robles Ridge. That conversation took place about three hours before the first 911 call about the fire. He and the other young man headed up there. Two people, like the witness saw before. Happens sometimes that during the course of a felony one of the perpetrators gets hurt. Makes even a lawyer think, doesn't it?"

"I just hate to see you wasting time and taxpayer money, Mr. Crockett." But she was shaken.

"You have a card to give me, Ms. Reilly? Where's your office?"

While Nina was trying to figure out how to respond to this, Crockett's phone buzzed, and Crockett raised a hand and picked it up. Hanging up, he told them, "The autopsy should be completed by three this afternoon. I told the coroner's office you could go in and attempt an ID. If you promise me you'll call me right after and let me know how it went."

"You got it," Paul said. They got up to leave.

"You do have a card?" Crockett said, standing up with them, his impassive face looking down at Nina.

She gave him the poker face right back. "Not on me," she said. "Call Mr. van Wagoner if you need to get in touch with me."

"Good to see you again, Paul," Crockett said, and the two men shook hands. "I'll be waiting to hear."

She had been rendered invisible. She slunk into the passenger seat of Paul's Mustang and they cruised out of the parking lot. She was thinking, when an attorney has no office and no card, no staff and no clients, maybe she'd better not announce that she's an attorney.

But then, what was she?

"What's the sound of a lawyer falling in the forest?" she asked Paul. "If there's no one there to hear it?"

Paul neatly turned north onto the on-ramp to Highway 1.

"It sounds like a long argument slowly dying out," he said.

Nina laughed.

"So where's your aunt Helen's place?"

"Not far. Over the hill, just past the Pebble Beach turnoff."

"Maybe he'll be there," Paul said, as if to himself. Cypresses and pines pressed against the highway. They turned onto 68 and wound through the views of golf courses and ocean, the fog bank ragged off the distant horizon, like cotton batting leaking from the edge of a faded blue quilt.

3

NINA AND PAUL bumped onto the cracked asphalt driveway of the wooden bungalow in Pacific Grove on Pine Avenue. Aunt Helen had died years earlier and left the place to Nina, and the welcome mat in front and the rhododendron bushes on either side of the entryway dated from Aunt Helen's time, along with one of the few pines left on Pine, an eighty-foot listing Norfolk pine that someday soon would fall on the neighbors' roof and bankrupt Nina. But she couldn't bear to cut it down yet.

Pacific Grove lay at the tip of the Monterey Peninsula, jutting right out into the Pacific, and never got hot. The sea breeze produced clean, tangy air.

Through the open shutters Nina could see someone walking back and forth, and her heart gave a lurch: Wish? Or one of the roommates?

To herself she called the twins who had originally leased the house from her the Boyz in the Hood. Dustin and Tustin Quinn both studied computer science at the California State University at the old Fort Ord and no doubt had a promising future, but after all, what she cared about was the present, and when they had come to Paul's condo to talk to Nina about the rental ad, she had almost turned them down. She didn't want a couple of scruffy male students, she wanted a sweet lady who looked like Aunt Helen, would cultivate an herb garden, and scrub the floor each morning in the predawn.

Unfortunately, only students wanted to rent the place. Built in the twenties, the whole house was heated by a single wall fixture in the living room. The stove had been old in Aunt Helen's time, and there were no hookups for a washer or dryer. You had to cart the dirty clothes to the Washeteria in town. Apparently, elderly gardening ladies chose to live in more modern digs because none applied.

The Boyz had rented the place in May, hoping to stay through the summer and possibly fall. In early June Wish had moved in with them for the summer. Nina had suggested it, knowing the twins would welcome the help with the rent. Wish seemed to like them.

One of the Boyz now trotted out to meet them, shirtless, wearing baggy shorts and fat-tongued athletic shoes, no socks, a backward baseball hat on his head, a bottle of Gatorade in his hand. "My tenant," Nina told Paul as he slammed the front door.

"Hey." The young man nodded to them and blocked their way. He was stocky, buzz cut, and earnest, with a round pink face and round mouth. "How's it going, Nina? Dus is just finishing up the sweeping. We wanted to clean up before you got here."

So Dusty was dusting. "Hi, Tustin," she said. "This is Paul van Wagoner."

"Good to meet you. Any word about Wish?"

"No sign of him." The fast swish of a broom mixed with the yelp of Eminem's 2002 CD drifted through the open window. When Nina had lived there, right after Aunt Helen had passed on, it had been sea lions yelping from the kelp beds a few hundred yards off that she heard, but new millennia bring new kinds of song.

She had rented the house out ever since, and now she saw with landlord's angst that the white paint was faded and peeling in places, and the roof was minus some shingles. "We're sorry to raise up a storm if he's just gone home to Tahoe or something . . ." Tustin was saying.

"No, you did right to call," Paul said. "He hasn't been home. We talked to his mother."

Tustin really wanted to get the story out, or else he was delaying their entry while Dustin madly cleaned up, Nina couldn't decide which. He launched into it, standing right there in the yard with the white picket fence.

"I don't even want to think about him and that fire. We were watching TV when his buddy showed up. Gave him a beer, invited him to dinner. Danny is his name. He was dressed like he was posted on a mission to Iraq or something. He takes Wish aside to tell him something he doesn't want us to hear, then he says to Wish, 'Man, you want in or not? You wanna be broke forever?'

"Well, at the mention of money, Wish's eyes lit up. I have to admit Dus and I wanted to know what was going on, but Danny and Wish went into his room. I heard him ask Wish, 'You still got your camera?' Wish said 'Yeah, but I gotta go to Tahoe tomorrow. I don't think this is such a good idea.' He was reluctant, you know?"

"Wait a minute," Paul said, holding up a hand to slow him down. "What's not a good idea?"

Tustin shrugged. "Who knows? They shut the door. All I know is, he was pushing Wish to go somewhere. Told him he could be home that night—this was Tuesday—in plenty of time to pack for Tahoe.

"We could hear them arguing. Wish wasn't up for it. And then Danny's voice, loud, insisting, talking some more about money. He had an accusatory tone, like, 'You turned on me, man, you're such a wuss.' Then it would get quiet in there, like they were whispering.

"My brother and I went into the living room and sat down to watch the baseball game on TV and eat our pot pies. Wish and Danny came out, and Wish acted embarrassed. He had his backpack and we said, like, where you headed, man? He just shook his head, but when Danny went into the can Wish motioned to me to come into the kitchen and said, 'Listen. I'm going to Robles Ridge. Okay? Just in case anything happens.'

" 'What's going to happen?' I said, but he just shook his head."

Dustin finally appeared at the front door. He gave some signal to his brother, who said, "We can go in now." They mounted the three steps to the welcome mat. Dustin, in scruffy cutoffs and bare feet, held the screen open for them. "Hey."

"Hey." Inside, to Nina's relief, aside from scuffs on the hardwood, dirty fingerprints around the light switches, and overlooked dustballs in the corners, the main room looked okay. However, closed doors to the two bedrooms beckoned. She resolved to have a look before they left. She sat down on the sprung couch with Paul.

Dustin, who acted the householder while his brother did duty as the greeter, went into the kitchen and she heard the fridge door open. In a minute he came back with Gatorade for all. Nina was hungry. Gatorade would do. She unscrewed the top.

"So what's the news?" Dustin said, getting right to it after the introductions.

"No news," Paul said. The Boyz looked at each other and shook their heads.

"Tustin was telling us about Danny's visit," Nina said. "Go ahead. But maybe you could turn down the music?"

Dustin went over to the stereo and Eminem stopped cleaning out his closet and dissing his mama over Dr. Dre's menacing arrangement. She thought of Bob's complaints when she made him clean out *his* closet. Maybe he too would become famous someday from telling the world about his mean mom.

"Yeah. So. Where was I? Right, Wish says, 'Robles Ridge, just in case.' "

Dustin broke in, "So Tus says, 'You better tell us more than that,' just as this loser Danny came back into the kitchen, and this made Danny bullshit."

"Told us to fuck off," Tustin added, "only he was less polite."

"What a poser," Dustin said.

"Drugs?" Paul asked.

"He didn't stagger or laugh a lot or smell funny and his pupils were normal-sized."

"We looked," Tustin added.

"I could see Danny and Wish went way back. At one point Danny was going on like, 'See, the whole cop-school thing, that's to prove you're not afraid. But you are, aren't you, Willis?'"

"And then they left." Dustin took a long swig of Gatorade. A few pounds heavier than his brother, he had apple cheeks and a more innocent air. Nina could see the Boyz in a few years in identical suits, staring at computer screens through identical glasses, juggling mortgages and families, saving consumer capitalism.

The Boyz came from Rhodes, Iowa. She wondered where they would end up.

Paul had been taking notes. He took over. "Describe what they were wearing."

"Danny had on a camouflage jacket, like I said," Tustin replied. "Jeans. He wore the shirt buttoned up, and I had the impression he had a lot of stuff in his pockets. I asked him if he was Army, but he said he got the jacket up at the Moss Landing military-surplus store. I didn't really think he was even ex-military, not with the ponytail."

"Shoes?"

"Sorry, I never noticed. Wish was wearing his Doc Martens, I remember that. The only reason I noticed Wish's boots was he talked about buying them, how expensive they were. He thought about it for a long time. . . ."

"What else did Danny wear?"

The twins looked at each other and shrugged. "I think the T-shirt under the jacket was white. I could see the neck part," Tustin said.

"What did his teeth look like?"

"Teeth. He wasn't a smiler. Why do you ask?" Dustin said. "Oh. Dental records. Damn. Of course. Danny's missing too, is that it? And the firebug, it could be he's the victim. But you only have the one victim. Well, Wish and Danny are both tall and skinny, although I'd say Danny's more muscular. Both Indian-looking."

"Native American–looking," Tustin said.

"Danny's hair is longer."

"I don't know where Danny is," Paul said. "He may not be missing. Any idea where he lives?"

The Boyz shook their heads. Dustin said, "But they talked about Danny's uncle. His name was—"

"Ben," Tustin said.

"That's it, Ben. He called him *Tío*. Seems like Wish knew him too."

"Did you hear the last name Cervantes?"

" 'Fraid not."

"Still, that'll help."

Dustin and Tustin nodded several times.

Nina went on, "What kind of camera did Wish take with him?"

"A Canon. Digital, with a megazoom lens. He just bought it at Costco with some birthday money and his first paycheck."

"What was Wish wearing?"

"Uh, denims. Denim jacket. I don't know what underneath. Same old Bob Marley T-shirt as always, I guess," Tustin said.

"He's a good guy," Dustin said. "Quiet and no creepy habits."

"Let's check his room," Paul said, getting up. Tustin led the way down the short dark hall. Nina's memories of the place flooded up, Aunt Helen and her mother cooking on Easter Sunday in the kitchen, Nina years later carrying Bob from the bedroom when he woke up coughing with a high fever one night, through that very hall, out to the rattletrap Chevy she drove then, and the doctor saying he had pneumonia . . . those had been desperate times. She put her hand on Paul's broad back in front of her.

They crowded into the smaller bedroom at the rear of the house, Bob's kindergarten bedroom. Wish had taken down the blinds over the window in back and left the window open. Sunflower heads waved through it from the tiny overgrown backyard and the room felt swept by air.

Wish's bookshelf, full of the thick textbooks on criminal justice he had studied the previous year, sat in one corner. Aunt Helen's old upholstered chair in a yellow-and-green flower pattern sat in the other, and there was just room for a conference table squeezed along the wall, stacked high with auto tools, comic books, CDs and DVDs and a DVD player under the tiny TV.

In the closet, T-shirts, ten or twelve of them, folded on the upper shelf, an empty duffel on the floor, and several plaid flannel shirts that Nina recognized from Tahoe.

The room smelled like Wish, a dusty outdoors smell, the scent of a living breathing person, and this even more than his shirts frightened Nina. Wish might really be dead. He had been her friend, a cheerful, innocent, eager spirit in her life, too young to be an equal, too old to be a son. Paul too seemed moved. He searched with irritable, feverish efficiency, running his hands over the shirts, checking pockets, unfolding cuffed pants, pushing behind baskets on the closet shelf, searching.

"Nothing," he said.

Nina, at the conference table, said, "Here's his organizer." Sandy had given him one of those leather notebooks full of index tabs and pockets for his twenty-first birthday. In gold letters on the cover she read, "Willis Whitefeather." She opened it. Tabs for addresses, calendars, notes, expenses. Flipping through it, she saw many small crabbed notes and doodles.

She turned to the addresses and looked under the C's and D's.

"Got it," she said. "A phone number with the name *Danny* right beside it."

Paul came over and wrote it down. He said to the Boyz, "We're going to borrow this."

"Paul, it might be evidence. Maybe we should just shut the door and leave it—"

"Put it in your purse," Paul said. Nina opened her mouth and closed it. She put the organizer in her purse.

They said a few reassuring words to the Boyz and went outside. Nina held her heavy purse protectively, as though Wish's life were in there. She was thinking that Sandy would want the organizer. Wish had left so little behind.

They stopped at the Bookshelf on Lighthouse for coffee. Nina leafed through the book.

"What else is in there?" Paul said, bringing coffees and a sandwich for Nina.

"Remember how he draws on his notes? He's worse than I am," Nina said. She showed him a penciled sketch of a sunflower. "He must have been lying on his bed and just picked up his pencil and drew this. I saw the flower outside his window. He can't be dead, Paul."

"He can't. What else?"

"Well, on the calendar for this week, an eye appointment. I remember he was saying he thought he needed glasses. That's it."

"No girlfriend down here yet, I guess. I saw a photo of Brandy Taylor on the bookshelf."

Thinking of Wish's attraction to a young witness a few months before, Nina felt even worse. Wish had been downright noble about reconciling Brandy with her fiancé.

"He got pulled in casually by his friend," she said. "He just went along for the ride. Who knows what Danny told him? He couldn't have known there would be a fire." She swallowed some of her tuna sandwich and opened the notebook to the tab marked Notes.

"Oh, Paul. He wrote down some self-improvement stuff here. He tried so hard."

"Tries."

"Tries. Listen to this: 'Goals: B-plus average. Get a girl-friend. Note: must like hiking. Be cool with Mom, be patient. Show Paul' "—Nina faltered and her voice thickened—" 'show Paul I am the best.' "

There was a long silence.

"You know he idealizes you," Nina said finally. "He jumped at the chance to come down here and learn from you."

Paul's jaw clenched. "Give me your cell phone." He pulled out the note he'd made with Danny's phone number.

Danny didn't answer, and Paul didn't want to leave a phony message. "We'll try again," he said. "Let's go over to my office. Wish might have called or stopped by."

"Good. I want to call Community Hospital."

"Davy's certainly already done that."

"Well, I'm going to do it again. Then I'll call the morgue and see if they're finished."

On the way back over the hill to Carmel, Nina said, "I hadn't been in Aunt Helen's house for a while. The cleaners are supposed to tell me if they notice any problems."

"Looked okay to me."

"I meant to check the Boyz' bedroom, see what they chucked in there when we called and said we were coming."

Paul pulled into the passing lane. "They rent the place. It's theirs. Leave them alone."

Nina had another moment of shock, the same shock she had felt when Paul told her to take the organizer. He was challenging her judgment, telling her what to do about her own business. Paul did it so naturally, assuming the role as if it were his. . . .Was it his? He seemed so strong sitting there beside her. He never questioned himself, while her whole life right now was a question.

She didn't even have a business card. Something gave way beneath her and she slid into doubt. "I don't like you telling me what to do," she said. It came out sounding whiny.

"Well, I like it," Paul said. He laughed and zoomed beyond the speed limit past Junipero toward Ocean Avenue, though the right lane was choked with tourists.

The irritation swept over her again. She was sick with worry about Wish, but this person beside her suddenly annoyed her so much! It is hopeless, she told herself, angry and pained.

Paul, oblivious, drove on, and after a while her anger turned back into confusion. Sitting next to him, she struggled again to understand what was between them.

He bent forward, looking hard ahead into the traffic like Ahab eyeballing the foamy brine for his whale, joyful in the midst of tension, his eyes bright and intent. She experienced the heavy shoulders next to her, the capable hands, the solidity of his body, and she caught his happiness at being fully engaged and out on a chase, even a chase that might lead to tragedy. If he had let his tongue hang out, panting joyfully like Hitchcock, she wouldn't have been surprised.

He's a big yellow Lab! she thought.

His aggressive energy, his lack of subtlety, his disdain for people who live in their heads—of course, since he lived in his legs!—she could live with that, she could love that, if she could only remember this moment, when she was finally in contact with his powerful, furry, canine essence.

Guess I just like big dogs, she thought to herself.

She leaned her head back on the seat, closed her eyes, and told herself that it could be worse. Paul, better than any man she had known, focused all this energy and wholeheartedness and bright-eyed intensity on her at night.

He had his way of loving her. He would click the dead bolt downstairs, turn off the light, and come noiselessly into the bedroom in the dim light of the seashell night-light. He would look a long time at her lying on the bed, and at those moments she knew for certain that she was the only one he wanted, knew it right down to the marrow. When he lowered himself onto her, arms supporting his weight, eyes looking into her eyes, he was fully involved, fully loving her. Simple and wholehearted, no question about how he felt.

No, it's not hopeless, not hopeless at all, she thought, her eyes still closed, a smile playing at the corners of her mouth.

With this comprehension, some worries about their incompatibilities fell away. Amused now, she turned her head to the left to see him and he looked back, winked, and got back to driving. As she let her hand move to his thigh and rub it, feeling the long muscle contract as he accelerated, she thought, he's an experience I can't imagine ever denying myself again.

"What?" he said, catching her smile.

"I was thinking about your song. About the love monster. May I add a verse?"

"Sure."

"It goes like this":

I am King Kong—you're a skyscraper
I am King Kong—you're a skyscraper
I'll climb up your angles, and up at the top
I'll swing and I'll holler, till you beg me to stop—

"I like it. You have talent. We'll see just how much tonight."

They entered the quaint tourist town of Carmel-by-the-Sea. Taking a right on Ocean, Paul had to slow down for traffic. The sidewalks were choked with early-season tourists from Germany and France, meandering along among the flowers and antique stores. They took another right onto Dolores Street and pulled into a secret parking area behind the Hog's Breath Inn and the Eastwood Building, where Paul had established his office. Clint Eastwood owned this brown rustic building with the jewelry store and Indian art emporium on the first floor, and once Paul knew that, he had told Nina, he knew this was the place for him.

Paul had met Clint once, while the actor was still mayor of Carmel. They had shaken hands and Clint had moved on, but Paul always said it zinged like God making contact with a mortal on the ceiling of the Sistine Chapel. Was it the soft-spoken, menacing persona Paul liked? The disregard of authority? The Lone Ranger roles he always played? After a recent night curled up with popcorn in front of one of the DVDs, observing Paul's grinning admiration as Eastwood got back at the bad guys, she thought she understood.

Clint wasn't afraid. He'd gone through a long career in movies and television without once showing fear. When the situation called for fear, Clint's eyes would squint and his lips would get snarly and he would get royally pissed off instead. Paul wanted to take on the world like that.

So renting the office in the Eastwood Building had pleased Paul deeply. They walked up the wooden stairway to Paul's office, and he pressed the remote to unlock the door.

Inside, Tibetan rugs, Paul's big desk with both a PC and an Apple sitting under a window that looked down at the outside bar area of the Hog's Breath Inn, photos of the Himalaya by Galen Rowell and Paul himself on the walls— Paul had been in the Peace Corps in Nepal, not that it made him peaceful—a black leather couch, the small conference table where Wish worked, file cabinets, and a bar fridge in the corner where Paul kept beer and sundries.

In a pinch, he could spend the weekend there.

The soul of the office, of course, was invisible—the client files, his source lists, the search programs purchased from collection companies and process servers, all behind firewalls and passwords in the computers.

Nina went to the desk and looked out the window. Morning had segued into afternoon. Down below on the flowery patio of the Hog's Breath, the vacation deity had granted permission to stop awhile, forget earthly cares, and sit holding a glass, talking about nothing much. Chatter and clinking drifted up to them.

"The permanent party," she said.

"Right. The people come and go, but the party never ends."

"He hasn't been here."

"No."

Nina pulled out the Monterey County phone book and Wish's organizer and began making calls. She called Community Hospital, the highway patrol, Danny again—no answer again—and Wish's friends up at Lake Tahoe, where he usually lived. She didn't like raising the alarm so loudly, but she had no choice. Paul worked the other line.

After a while, when they had run out of numbers, they paused. Paul looked at his watch. "You know what we have to do, don't you? It's three-thirty, and they'll close by five."

"Yes. We should go. It better not be him. What could have happened up there in the woods?"

"One step at a time. Lunch downstairs, then back to Salinas."

In the heat of midday, they could identify some crops strictly by smell.

"Brussels sprouts," Paul said. "I can't stand 'em."

"Mmm. Garlic. Fabulous."

South Main Street still housed struggling secondhand stores, the shopping center that had never taken off, the Arby's and Foster's Freeze and the air of being lost in time that Nina remembered from childhood.

"I used to come here as a kid when the Northridge Shopping Center had the only good department stores in the whole county," she said. "Then when I was clerking for Klaus, I would bring papers over to the courthouse for the lawyers. It looks just the same."

"You still think of it as a sleepy agricultural town?" Paul said. "It's changed. Silicon Valley is pressing down from the north. Executive homes are crammed together on small lots with high walls. A tired techie just snugs down in his concrete snail shell, never forced to meet a single neighbor."

"We're at least an hour to San Jose. They commute all that way?"

"Meanwhile, as the technical class hauls fifty miles between home in Salinas and work in San Jose, Mexico rolls up from the south and settles in the Alisal District. The population is eighty percent Latino these days. Did you know that?"

"Salinas has always been a tense place," Nina said. "High crime rate for the population density. Part Okie, part Latino. Good fuel for writers like Steinbeck."

"It does look sleepy, when you're not here on Saturday night on the east side of town, when the bars get lively and the guns go off," Paul said.

But no guns were in evidence on this sun-baked afternoon, just a few kids on bikes and moms pushing strollers past the thrift shops. Nina said, "Let's stop at Foster's Freeze for a dipped chocolate cone."

"Right before the morgue?"

"Then again, maybe not," Nina said. They drove through town in silence, each corner bringing Nina a fresh vista of memories. "You know, in front of the community center near the rodeo stands, there's a giant sculpture by Claes Oldenburg. Did you ever see that, Paul?"

"Really? That's a surprise. No, I don't go to the rodeo. I guess it's un-American of me."

"I'll take you this summer."

"No, thanks, I know how you and Bob love these spectacles like monster-car races and motocross and calf roping, but I don't like the seats."

"What's wrong with the seats?"

"They're concrete and usually beer spattered."

"Does that mean you don't like football games either?" Nina asked.

"I like tennis matches. Whap, headjerk, whap, headjerk. Tennis whites and women fanning themselves in the stands. That's what I like."

"But you like modern art, don't you?"

Paul told her, "Look, if Oldenburg put up a giant sculpture in Salinas, of all places, let's drive by it right now."

"You can't see it from the street."

"Too bad. What's it look like?"

"Three massive red metal cowboy hats. Each one about twenty feet across." They turned onto Alisal Street.

Speaking of modern art, the concrete fiends of justice perched on each cornice of the Monterey County Courthouse hadn't changed. These gargoyles, along with the white pillars casting sharp shadows and the deserted concrete courtyard within, still gave rise within Nina to a certain anticipatory dread straight out of an early de Chirico painting.

The dark-suited figures flapping like vultures up the hot street to make their cases inside added to the general air of malevolence, and the Honeybee restaurant, where many a sleazy legal deal had been cut over the decades, extruded more lawyers as they passed by. This courthouse had always felt foreign to Nina, so different from the courthouse on Aguajito in Monterey, which had been built in friendly hippie days in a vaguely Big Sur style.

"I always wondered why you didn't take Klaus's offer and join his firm after you passed the bar," Paul said as they searched for a parking spot in back.

Nina said, "Compressed version. My mother died, that was the main thing. Dad got married again very quickly. I wanted to leave. San Francisco was a good distance, and then I married Jack and he was ready to leave Klaus's firm too. Don't we all grow up and leave town?" She took out her cream and rubbed a flare-up on her arm.

"Not at all," Paul said. "In fact, I sometimes think the

world is divided into those who go and those who stay. So off to the big city, then a few years in Tahoe. And here you are again."

"I really, really hope it's not Wish in there."

They entered the dim courthouse hall and submitted to the metal detector. As they walked down the stairs toward the coroner's office she firmed her jaw. It better not be him, she thought fiercely, and prepared herself.

Inside, they waited almost half an hour in an anteroom before they were allowed in. Some telephoning went on in the office as they were checked out one more time. Although a man in a lab coat was swabbing down the tables with Lysol, the morgue had that familiar smell of decay.

"Is the autopsy report completed?" Nina said to the female lab assistant accompanying them. She was realizing that, if this was Wish, Sandy would need help to call a mortuary and—surely she would want Wish sent back home?

Better not think about that now.

"This morning, but the report hasn't been approved." This small young woman had a Spanish accent, a large mole on her chin, and a businesslike attitude.

"Findings?" Paul said.

"I don't know much. You'll have to go through the channels for finals." They came to the drawer. She unlocked it and Paul helped her pull it out in a blast of frigid air.

A long, blackened, naked body lay supine in the drawer like a specimen in some hideous experiment. Cracked-looking flaps of skin hung off the charred and blackened arms and legs. The arms were pulled up as if to protect the chest. The abdomen was concave, as though emptied of its contents. An acrid, wet-charcoal smell wafted up.

"Oh, God." Nina looked away, then back at the body. She forced herself to look for some sign of Wish. Long bones, some burned black hair hanging lankly over the skull—the skull, oh, boy, the skull—

Nina walked off a few steps. Paul continued to look. "What else did they find?"

"The remains of a concho belt," the lab assistant said, observing without emotion. "You know, leather with those silver things. We have partial black leather boots, Doc Martens. Laces burned off. Tatters of white T-shirt and jeans on the backside of the body."

"A concho belt?" Paul said. "Nina, go outside and call the Boyz. Ask them." Nina was staring at the skull, which still held on to the patch of long dark hair. DNA, she thought. They'll find out eventually.

"I can't tell if it's him, Paul," she blurted.

"Go on. I'll talk to this lady for a minute."

Nina went. In the bathroom outside, she rinsed her mouth and threw water on her face. She took a brush to her hair, sloughing off the black mask of death she had just seen. Outside, she breathed the blessed air, got into the hot car, and called the Boyz.

"This is Tustin."

"Hi. It's Nina. Tustin, will you please try to remember, and ask your brother—was Wish wearing one of those leather belts with silver conchos on it? You know what I mean?"

"Huh?"

"Silver decorative disks, engraved with designs. They attach to the leather of the belt. Was he?"

"Got me. Just a minute." He was gone more than a minute. Paul came toward the car, worry lines etching his usually smooth forehead.

"Hey," Tustin said into the phone. Nina held her breath. "Sorry, I don't remember. Wish had on that denim jacket."

"What about Danny?"

"He had that long-sleeved cammy jacket buttoned up pretty well."

She punched off. "I need to call Sandy," she told Paul. "It could be Danny."

"Don't tell her that. Just tell her we're on it."

"You're not convinced?"

"We ought to wait until a final identification is made before we give Sandy hope that it isn't Wish."

"Where to now?" Nina said as she dialed Sandy's number.

"Home. Regroup. We're only human."

"And we try to reach Danny again?"

"Right."

4

THEY STOPPED AT the Nob Hill in South Salinas on the way home. While they picked out artichokes and fish to grill, pushing their cart among tired women farmworkers in bandannas covered with baseball caps, Nina thought back to the Raley's in South Lake Tahoe, the buzzing expectancy of the fun-loving tourists trolling its aisles for frozen daiquiri mixes, cigarettes, lowbrow magazines, all manner of things they forbade themselves back home in the lands of political and dietary correctness.

Tahoe, lake of the free and the damned. She felt a pang of homesickness, and wished fervently that she had never dragged Wish down here. He had come because she had come.

Back at Paul's, where the air smelled of eucalyptus, Paul poured wine for her and Tecate for himself, then put the charcoal on to heat. Changing swiftly into shabby brown shorts, he disappeared into the bedroom, where Nina heard keys clicking.

Hitchcock nudged her. "Sorry, boy," she said. "Let's do it." She placed her wineglass in the refrigerator. Attaching Hitchcock to his leash, she followed the bounding black dog outside and up Paul's street, permeated with ocean scents.

At the end of a long block she stopped and unhooked him, pulling his favorite grimy ball out of her pocket. She tossed it toward the tall golden grass of an empty lot into the abalone sky. Hitchcock flew to the ball, slapped it around in his mouth, then hustled back to her, dropping the ball at her feet. He repeated this operation dozens of times, untiring, ever thrilled.

Tonight his joy couldn't lift her spirits. Guileless Wish was gone, maybe forever. All he'd ever wanted was to follow Paul around and get his degree and help people. She bent down to scratch the back of her knee.

A black thing about four inches across moved on the asphalt beside them. A tarantula! Fascinated, woman and dog stared. The tarantula lifted a hairy black leg and seemed to scratch itself too, in an arachnoid salute.

The spider didn't seem inclined to scurry off, and it was blocking their path. Hitchcock kept his nose out of reach, wary.

Nina stamped her foot.

No reaction. The tarantula's glossy eyes didn't blink. It stared them down.

"It's time to go back anyway, boy," Nina told Hitchcock. They turned around and hastened back to the line of condos below.

Hitchcock circled and plopped on his favorite spot in the living room, while Nina hid the slimeball and then washed her hands in hot water.

Nina made dinner while Paul worked in the bedroom. Fish and rice, the food of lovers, guaranteed not to cause gas.

She hurried outside to flip the ahi, located a blue bowl, which she filled with rice and carried to the table, pulled asparagus out of the steamer, squeezing lemon over Paul's portion and dolloping her own with butter, then set the fish on a dish on the table.

Fish. Dish. Wish. All the time, thinking about Wish. She was beginning to mourn.

She called Paul, picked up her napkin, and wiped under her eyes.

Paul practically leapt to his place, as if he were the one who had just spent half an hour playing with the dog. He rubbed his hands together, and took a big whiff of the meal.

"Phone rang while you were out," he said.

"Sandy again?" Their earlier phone call had been brief and unsatisfying. Sandy seemed not to understand the full picture, or, more likely, she was intentionally and stubbornly obtuse about what might have happened to Wish, and Nina didn't really want to trash her illusions.

"No. Your dad. He wants to see you."

"Oh. He called last week too. Somehow, because I'm only a few miles from him, there's a shorter leash, or something. He expects a lot of contact."

"And why not?" Paul asked. "He's getting on. You're close by for once."

Nina ran her hand through her hair. "I can't worry about him right now. I'm too worried about Wish. Dad's fine. He's got his thirty-year-old wife and his four-year-old son. Ten years younger than Bob, his grandson. All this generation-skipping stuff gets me down."

"All so modern," Paul said, taking seconds on the fish and the rice. "Want to know what I've been doing while you, who swear you cannot cook, were casually whipping up this superb meal?"

"What?"

"Computer chicanery, pirated software, reverse directory."

"Uh huh."

"That phone number in Wish's book for Danny Cervantes? Well, we now have an address. It's gotten so simple to find addresses from phone numbers these days. Google does it in ten seconds."

"Good work. Where does he live?"

"On Siesta Court in Carmel Valley Village."

"The Village? Close to—"

"Right, the fires. And there's another name listed at the same address: Ben Cervantes. Must be that uncle the Boyz mentioned."

"We'll go see him."

"Good plan," Paul said, smug, as if he hadn't already laid it out.

"Finished?" Nina asked.

"Ah, very full. Very happy," he said.

"The dishes are yours."

He stood, picked up his plate, and said, "Now I remember why I like to cook."

While Paul loaded dishes into the dishwasher, Nina surfed the channels, trying to find the news among the two hundred stations that flitted seductively by. Finally, she located a local channel that mentioned the most recent fire.

"At least one person is dead," said the blond anchorwoman. She wore a silk scarf over a tight low-cut "business" suit jacket. A map behind her pinpointed the locations of the various fires.

"Authorities believe that there's a method behind this madness. Apparently, the antidevelopment people are resorting to domestic terrorism. Their weapon of choice? Arson." She then identified herself and her station.

A commercial showing elderly zombies wandering in an eroded esophagus came on, touting a prescription antacid.

She flipped the television off.

"Let's go talk to *Tío* Ben. Unless you're too tired. It's been a long day," Paul called from the kitchen.

"I'll get my bag." She heard the phone from the bedroom and picked up the bedside extension.

"Mom?" said the voice on the phone.

"Bob! I'm so glad to hear your voice! I was thinking of you this morning."

"Why?"

She didn't mention Wish. Bob was Wish's friend, but he

had his own problems. "Just . . . I hope you're being careful."

His sigh sank into depths so low only a fourteen-year-old could find them. "Just in case these Swedes go berserk and come after me with hatchets. Right."

"Driving. Being out at night. With Nikki. You know." Stop, she told herself, you're lecturing him already. With an effort, she went on cheerfully, "How's the weather in old Stockholm?"

"It's raining."

"What time is it?"

"Nine o'clock. In the morning."

"Amazing. You're on the other side of the world."

"You don't have to remind me."

"Your dad okay?"

"Fine."

"So how are you?" she said.

"Not so good. See, Mom," he said, as if they were continuing a shared line of thought, "what I don't understand is, how come they like you one minute and the next minute they don't? What kind of B.S. is that?"

"Do you mean . . . Nikki?"

"No, I mean Genghis Khan."

How could one so young sound so dour? "You sound upset."

"She told me she really really liked me!" he burst out. "I operated on the basis of that!"

"I'm sorry, Bob."

"Yeah, sorry," he said. "It's just . . . see, we went to practice yesterday. All the guys in the band were there. Nikki fronts on a couple of songs, and sometimes she plays her guitar. I was doing digital recording that we might upload to the Web site she designed for them . . . anyway, Lars, he thinks he's so cool. He's like so much older than she is!"

"How old?"

"Twenty!"

Three years older than Nikki then, six years older than Bob. Oceans of time between them all.

"Well, I think *you're* cool, Bob."

"Being cool only matters if the people who think you're cool are cool. No offense, Mom. Anyway, Lars is the drummer. He was sitting on a couch smoking a cigarette and talking about how he's part Spanish, and somehow . . ."

She heard the pain in his voice and felt a little piece of her own heart chipping.

"Somehow she ended up next to him. Next thing you know, they're kissing. I was disgusted, Mom. I mean, she went to the practice with me, you know? We were a couple. Everybody knew it even though she didn't act like it half the time."

Nikki must favor sofas. The image of Bob and Nikki on her sofa back in Tahoe several months before was permanently burned into Nina's brain. Nikki, three years older, much too wise, and her fledgling son, entwined . . . Nina had poured herself a glass of wine, collected herself, and more or less kicked Nikki out. Which had only caused more hormones to hit the fan.

Unwisely, she went back to lecturing. "You haven't started smoking, have you?"

"I didn't call for this, Mom! I'm tryin' to talk to you about something important!"

"Okay, okay, honey. All right. So. Nikki and Lars."

"I can't stand to go to rehearsals anymore, Mom. She's made her choice. But I miss her. I don't like Sweden, Mom. Nobody smiles and they all wear black and smoke all the time."

And they're all way too old for you, Nina thought with huge relief. "You could take some music lessons. Your dad'll get you into a summer school. He's the one you went to visit, Bob, and now maybe you can spend more time with him." Bob's father, Kurt, a classical pianist, had not known Nikki was coming to Stockholm either.

"You don't get it. You just don't get it."

"Honey, what are you going to do?"

"I want her back."

"I know you do."

"But when I told her that, you know what she said? You won't believe this."

"What did she say?"

"She told me I was too young for her."

"Well, those three years . . . they are big ones, Bob."

"Anyway." She visualized his shrug. "Screw it. I have to come home and figure things out."

The shock waves this announcement generated made her sit back, gulping.

"Question, Mom. Where exactly is home? Am I going to Carmel or Tahoe? I need to know."

She put him off. It wasn't hard.

They talked for a few minutes more. Bob told her how he spent his time when he wasn't getting into trouble with Nikki, and about Kurt's latest performance. By the time they hung up, he sounded less miserable.

She had done her job. Bob felt better. She felt worse, so much worse. She went out to the deck and slumped across from Paul.

"Well? How's the boy?"

"His heart's broken."

"Nikki dumped him?"

"Yep."

Paul shook his head sadly. "It's the first time, but it won't be the last," he said. "I hope Kurt's up to the challenge."

Nina thought but didn't say, I don't know if Kurt will get a chance.

"Women have this problem with constancy," Paul added.

"Men have this problem with thinking women are their property," Nina shot back.

They looked at each other. Paul's silence rang like the end of the fifteenth round at Madison Square Garden. She hung her purse off her shoulder. "Let's go, then," she said.

Wait a second, it was the doorbell making that racket. No dulcet chimes for Paul's door.

Nina smoothed down her hair and went to answer it.

She peeked through the peephole Paul had installed in his door.

"Who is it?" she said, but flung open the door when she saw who was standing outside.

"Yo, Nina," Wish said. "I'm so glad you're home."

5

HE WORE BATTERED black Doc Martens boots, Nina noted, still laced in some complicated fashion. He also wore the denim jacket and jeans the Boyz had described, but the T-shirt seemed to be missing and the pants were tattered and black. His eyes were almost swollen shut and what Nina could see of his hands, wrapped with white bandages, were red and blistered, glistening with petroleum jelly. His singed, wild hair hadn't been combed that day. All in all, he looked like a sadhu who had tripped on the coals.

Nina embraced him. He was so skinny!

Even with this distressing getup, Nina saw that someone had washed him up and bandaged him. He was walking and talking and medicated. She drew him in and helped him take the boots off.

"I'm thirsty," he said hoarsely. In the kitchen, Paul offered him a beer, which he refused, and a couple of Cokes, which he sucked down fast. "Sorry to cause all this trouble," he told Paul. "I got in a situation and had to go undercover."

Nina said, "I'm going to make you a sandwich. Peanut butter okay? Your parents have been so worried. Paul and I have been looking for you."

"I've been in the hospital."

"What? I called the hospital."

"I went to the clinic in San Juan Bautista." He'd driven himself thirty miles to another county.

"Why?"

"I better call my mom. Could I borrow the phone?"

The call lasted a long time, and if it was possible, when he finished the call and walked back into the living room he looked more disheveled after talking to her than before. He sat down heavily on the couch, fingers embedded in Hitchcock's fur. Nina sat close beside him.

"Now," Paul said, "what happened to you?"

"We've all been so worried," Nina said. "I guess your mother told you the whole county is looking for you."

"I got hurt," Wish said, holding his hand to his throat. "The clinic put me on an IV and I slept all yesterday."

"Your mother . . ." Nina started, but Wish interrupted.

"She's pretty . . . worked up," he said, wiggling a finger in his phone ear. "But I told her everything's dandy now that I've hooked up with you guys. She said to tell you she'll talk to you later," he added, unaware of how ominous this sounded.

"Does it hurt to talk?"

"No. I know I sound funny, though. Uh, sorry, I need to make one more call. My friend, Danny . . . have to make sure he's okay."

So Sandy hadn't told Wish about the body. "We heard about Danny from Dustin and Tustin," Nina said. "We've been calling him, but we can't get through."

"I need to call him right now." He got up.

"Does he live with Ben Cervantes?"

Wish said, "Yeah, his uncle. Ben's not there either?"

"I just called again a few minutes ago. They don't have an answering machine and there's no answer."

Wish sat down again and hung his head. "I'm very worried," he said. "Paul, I was attacked and I think Danny may have been too. I have to get ahold of him. You're gonna be mad at me about this situation, but I thought it was under control, I really did, when I told Danny I'd go along."

"You were attacked?"

"Could I have a glass of milk and another sandwich?"

Nina went into the kitchen, but she could still hear them talking.

"I guess I thought I'd be a hero," Wish was saying, heaving a sigh. "I had a narrow escape instead. Maybe I'm not cut out to be in law enforcement after all. I think I showed bad judgment, Paul. Danny may be in trouble. I should have stopped him, not gone with him, but he pushed my buttons. He's always known how to do that. Now what? I don't know."

"I think there are some huge misunderstandings all around," Paul said. "Now tell me. Danny Cervantes came to your house Tuesday night."

"Yeah, we hooked up again after I came down a few weeks ago. Danny left Markleeville in sixth grade, and we had his uncle's number in Carmel Valley, so I called him and we got together a few times and hung around together. He'd just lost his job and I had a few extra bucks and I was glad to buy the drinks, but, I have to say, Paul, I had decided not to see him anymore. I told him a couple of weeks ago that I was too busy to see him anymore because of working with you and all, and Danny lost it. I didn't want to hurt his feelings but I did anyway. I think he'd been lonely and—I don't know, he brought up some old problems we had years ago. This was at the El Nido bar in Monterey."

"Danny's twenty-one too?"

"Yeah, and he drinks. He was my best friend when we were kids, Paul. I thought I really hurt his feelings and I was feeling guilty, you know? And sad because our friendship was over."

Nina came out and sat next to him again, setting a tray of food in front of him. She patted his hand and said, "Thanks for coming here. We're your friends too."

Wish drank some milk. He pulled his legs up and put his feet on the coffee table, wincing. "I was sitting in the living room with my roommates on Tuesday night," he said. "We were watching the Giants–St. Louis game. Danny knocked.

He was in a great mood, better than I've seen. It's like we hadn't had an argument, like I never said anything. And I have to say I was relieved about that.

"He was all fired up. He said he needed me to go up to Robles Ridge with him. Grab some stuff and just go now, now, now. I was in for the night, but Danny—he made me feel like I'd be letting him down, or that I was a coward. You know how you always say, you got to have courage in this world, Paul? Well, this was my moment for courage. But when the time came, I didn't show much courage at all."

Nina licked her lips and said, "What did Danny want you to do up there?"

Wish stared at her. "You know. The arson fires."

"Right," Paul said. "The arson fires. And you went up there . . . why?"

"For the money."

"The money?" Paul wore a stunned expression. Nina thought, it can't be true.

"One hundred thousand dollars split two ways," Wish said reverently. "You know how much that is?"

"That would buy a lot," said Paul.

"Sure would," said Wish. "Instead, what a fiasco. And you can't even see the worst of it!" he said darkly. "My throat is completely swollen up with poison oak! That's why I belong back in Tahoe! I am never hiking these woods again."

"You know, Wish, I'm trying, but help me out, will you? You went up there with Danny on Tuesday . . . why?"

Wish looked at Paul as if revising a previously positive opinion. "I told you. For the reward."

Paul relaxed back into his chair. "Ah. A reward."

"Some people who got burned out put their money together with some money from the county, that's why it's such a large amount," Wish said. "Arson causes a lot of expensive damage."

"You followed Danny up there to catch the arsonist?" Nina asked. "In spite of the fact that you could get caught in a fire or killed?"

"No way," said Wish. "We were just gonna get a picture of the arsonist or his car, some evidence to show who was doing it. We planned to shoot and run."

He told them what had happened after they went up the ridge, the waiting, the heat and flames, Danny insisting on staying until they could get the shot, then the fear and confusion and getting lost. Nina held Wish's hand as he haltingly told them about Danny finding him, then losing him again. Wish buried his face in his hands.

"Then the firebug—he ambushed me. He came after me, knocked me down with a rock. I remembered my mom's advice to my sisters when they went away to school, because she has a double standard, you know? With girls."

"And that advice was . . ." Paul prompted.

"Grab and twist. But I was on the ground and he was too close for me to kick. Thing is, he got behind me. He thought the rock knocked me out. Even though the fire was right there licking at me, I decided to lay low. There were plenty of other rocks around.

"He stood over me for a few seconds watching to see if . . . I don't know. Maybe to see if I moved—I don't know. I felt his eyes on me. Maybe the wind shifted right then. Something went right and the fire didn't get me while I was playing dead.

"All's I know is, he hit me on the head with a big rock, and I fell. At the clinic they said"—his hand went to the left side of his head—"that I didn't get a skull fracture, because he hit me from a bad angle.

"When I thought he was gone, I dragged myself up somehow and ran straight through the fire, down the mountain through burning poison oak. But he was after me again! It felt supernatural, the way he was after me, like he was some kind of animal that could smell me through the smoke!

"I have never been so scared in my whole life," Wish went on, his voice trembling. "The firebug, he just wouldn't give up. I had long since dropped the camera somewhere but it wasn't the camera he cared about, it was getting me. He wanted to kill me. He almost did with that rock. Then when he found me the second time, he was relentless, crashing after me right out to the street like he didn't even care if he got caught, just so he could kill me.

"Next thing I knew, I came out on Southbank Road and there were fire trucks everywhere, pumping water straight from the stream along the road. My car was still parked a long way down the road. I couldn't wait to find out what had happened to Danny. I got in the car and drove out to Carmel Valley Road. I kept looking back, thinking the firebug might be following me.

"I drove to Salinas and got on 101. I drove as far as I could, until I realized I was going to pass out again. Then I saw the turnoff for San Juan Bautista and drove there."

"Did you see his face at any time?" Paul asked.

"Too much white smoke when I was trying to focus the camera," Wish said. "My eyes were watering and stinging. I could barely see anything. The rest of the time I was running or had my eyes closed. But he must think I saw him. It's the only thing that explains why he tried so hard to get me."

"What was he wearing?"

"No idea."

"Nothing that could identify him? Think, Wish!"

"I'm thinking. I'm thinking."

"Well?"

Wish shrugged helplessly. "Something sharp pressing against my back when he was behind me, but he had just hit me and I wasn't thinking too straight." An agonized expression appeared on his face. "I have to go out to Ben's house if Danny doesn't answer the phone. I mean, Danny disappeared. He went down up there. I think the firebug may have—I can't stand to think—"

"Let's call again," Nina said. She had the number memorized by now.

No answer. Wish stared at the phone. "It's late," he said. "They oughtta be answering."

"All right, we'll drive out to the Valley in a minute, buddy," Paul said. "But I have to ask, how did Danny know in advance there was going to be a fire up there?"

"Danny had a tip."

"What kind of a tip?"

"From a confidential source. He was pretty sure there would be a fire that night on the ridge."

"He'd have to know the arsonist."

"No, no, nothing like that. He said he had the license number of the suspect's car. He wouldn't tell me any more, just that he'd staked out various construction sites around Carmel Valley Village for the whole week and saw the car parked for a couple of hours at Robles Ridge earlier that day. Some big new houses are under construction up there. It all made sense to me then."

"So you saw the car again that night before you went up the ridge?"

"Danny saw it. Ahead of us on Southbank Road. He said that was it, but he didn't want to get close because, heck, the firebug might be in the car. I couldn't even see the color, but I saw a parked car. A sedan."

"Oh, Wish," Nina said. "You should have left and called the police."

"The police wouldn't do anything. A guy sitting in a car, that's all, and we'd lose our chance. What would it prove? You know how hard they make it to get those big rewards. All we wanted to do was get one shot, but it had to be a shot of the guy, not the car, and he had to be doing a criminal act. So we parked my car. Danny sneaked up the road until he could see the guy wasn't in the car. I got a funny feeling in the pit of my stomach. You know how you say you can feel it, when something big is about to happen, Paul? We started up the hill. In the dark, I had to trust

Danny to lead. I knew the construction sites were at the top and there was a road on the other side."

"You were asking for trouble," Nina said, angry now. How could he? Paul shook his head slightly.

Nina gave up. She sat back on the couch. Paul was right, recriminations could come later.

Paul said, "He must have gotten the license number from the police."

Wish shook his head. "He wouldn't say. But he's lived here for years. He knows all the locals. Somebody knew something, that's all."

Nina said, "Wish, as soon as the police know you're alive, you will become a prime suspect in these fires."

"Me? A suspect? I almost got my ass burned off! Sorry."

"We know that. Now to convince the world," Paul said. "The police are going to be looking for you. We'll have to contact them."

"Tomorrow morning. When you've rested a little and we have talked more," Nina said. She was wondering whether to tell him about the corpse in the locker in Salinas, who might be his friend.

"After I find Danny," Wish said.

"I still don't understand why you were there at all. Why did Danny invite you along? Wouldn't he rather have all the reward money for himself?"

"Danny knew the trails, I had the good camera. And I think he was scared to go alone. All we needed was some proof."

"I can see what you guys had in mind, but I wish you'd run it by me first," said Paul. Nina thought that showed superhuman forbearance.

"Is this guy gonna come after me?"

"I don't know," Paul said. "You lost your camera and didn't really see him. He has nothing to fear from you. Unfortunately, he doesn't know that."

"Maybe I should take out a classified ad, huh?" Wish

said in a glum voice. " 'I know jack, pal, so don't kill me, okay?' "

Paul looked at his watch. Looked at Nina.

"We should go if we're going."

"He has to put on some other clothes. Take a shower."

"A quick shower would be nice. But then I have to go to the Valley."

Paul had gone into the kitchen. He came out with a disposable camera with a flash. "I'm going in there with you, buddy," he told Wish. "Take pictures of your injuries."

"To prove I was there?"

"I don't know what we're gonna need them for. I just don't think this is over, and I want to document your burns and the injury on your head. I'll rebandage you. I have a first-aid kit you wouldn't believe in there."

"Good, Paul," Nina said. She thought, *for the jury*. What jury? She wouldn't let her mind follow that thought any further.

By the time Nina heard the shower stop in the bathroom, it was nearly midnight. Paul put some fresh clothes Wish could wear in the bathroom and called Danny's number one more time. Nina tossed Wish's filthy clothes into the hamper.

She heard someone pounding on the door. She looked through the door of the bedroom to see why Paul had not answered. Head cocked to one side, supported only by air, Paul was napping in a chair. She tiptoed past and peered through the peephole in the front door.

It looked like a police ID. It was in fact a police ID.

She opened the door to two deputy sheriffs, hands hovering over their weapons. Behind them she saw a sheriff's car, red light turning, and a Carmel Valley Police car with two other men in it.

"I'm Deputy Grace. Monterey County Sheriff. This Paul van Wagoner's residence?" asked the bigger one, a young man with a face pocked like an olive loaf. "May we come in?"

"I'll go get him," she said, ignoring the last question. She left them on the porch, closed and locked the front door behind herself, and woke Paul. They returned to the door together.

"We're looking for Willis Whitefeather. Like to ask you some questions."

"It's late," Nina said. "How about your office, tomorrow morning?"

"Sorry. We need to talk to you right now."

"That won't be possible."

"We just received information from the Las Flores Clinic in San Juan Bautista that Mr. Whitefeather has been hiding there. Mr. Whitefeather gave Mr. van Wagoner's phone number as an emergency contact. Now please listen carefully. If you have any information as to Mr. Whitefeather's current whereabouts and don't tell us what you may know, *right now*, Detective Crockett is going to consider that an obstruction of justice. I just want to make that very clear to you tonight."

Paul and Nina stood there. Paul said softly to her, "Your call, Counsel."

"Am I very clear?" the officer repeated.

Nina held the door open. "As a matter of fact, Mr. Whitefeather is here."

Wish was not under arrest, Deputy Grace assured them. But the arson investigator sure did want to talk to him. Now. Down at the station. Alone.

Wish, who appeared in wet hair and a towel, freshly covered in gauze and surgical tape, bleary-eyed and confused, went back into the bathroom and came out in Paul's clothes. The pant legs rode high on his dirty boots. "Sure," he said. "I'll be glad to cooperate. I've got nothing to hide."

"We'll come along if you don't mind," Paul said.

"We mind," said Deputy Grace.

"I'm coming," Nina said.

"Look," said the second deputy sheriff. The thin bristle on his upper lip in the watery glow of the porch light made him seem to have two upper lips. "He doesn't need company. We just want to talk to him."

"I'm his attorney," she said. She grabbed her briefcase, more to put on the expected official show than because she needed it in this case, since she didn't have anything inside it except a pad of paper and a pen.

"Take this," Paul said, sticking her mobile phone into her pocket. "Call me."

In her rush out the door, she forgot to kiss him good-bye.

The ride through the dark streets to the central police station in Salinas took only minutes in the dead of night. Inside, Crockett waited in his desolate office.

"So, you're representing Mr. Whitefeather, here," Crockett said to Nina, turning on his tape recorder without a by-your-leave. Nina noticed for the first time the mirror on the wall, dark on one side only, perhaps. And the video camera mounted in a ceiling corner. "He's obviously been through some sort of traumatic event. What happened to your eyes, son?"

"Yes, I represent him."

"You know he hasn't been charged with a crime? We just want to know what went on up there in the hills above Carmel Valley on Tuesday. That's where it happened, isn't it? Where you were injured."

"I've advised my client . . ." Nina began.

"Yeah. I went up there that day," Wish said.

Nina punched his arm. "I've advised my client not to speak. I know you consider him a suspect for the arson fires. He was Mirandized on the way here."

"Your client went to a clinic to get treated for burns," Crockett said. "That's how we tracked him down. We know he went up there to set fires."

"Not true!" Wish said. "I went up to the ridge that night because . . ."

"I told you in the car," Nina said. "Now are you listening, Wish? Exercise your right to remain silent. Don't say anything."

Crockett said, "We have the autopsy report. We know what happened." He said the words provocatively.

"Autopsy report? Did someone die? Danny? What happened?" Wish cried.

"For the love of . . . keep quiet, Willis!" Nina said. She couldn't remember ever saying his formal name out loud before, but circumstances demanded serious measures.

He closed his mouth, but he was stunned by Crockett's news, already drawing conclusions.

"Massive skull fracture," David Crockett announced, directing his comments to Nina. Since she had warned Wish to remain silent, Crockett could not, by law, ask him any more direct questions. "The victim, maybe Danny Cervantes, was hit over the head before he was left to sizzle like a piece of shrimp over hot charcoal."

"What!" Wish said. "Is it Danny?"

"Well," Crockett backpedaled. Still looking at Nina, he said, "He was up on the ridge with your client setting a fire, wasn't he?"

Wish jumped up. His metal folding chair clattered to the ground. "No!" he said, and Nina realized he was beyond control.

"Danny wasn't setting fires!" Wish said. "He was trying to stop the guy!"

"We have a witness," Crockett said.

"A witness to what?" asked Nina, to keep Wish from opening his mouth again.

"To the arsons. Our witness has ID'd Danny at one of the previous fires."

Wish stood up. "He would never . . ."

"We have a witness," Crockett said. "Oh, and . . ." he

said, directing his comments to Nina, "your client is under arrest."

"For what?" Nina asked.

"Trespassing." Crockett smiled. "He was up there running around on private property. He just admitted it."

And so he had.

6

"SANDY'S ON A plane to San Francisco," Paul announced on Friday morning as he spread cream cheese on a bagel. They were out on the deck in the crackling morning cold, both wearing heavy white terry-cloth robes that said CAESARS in looping red embroidery.

Hitchcock ate noisily from his bowl. They had just taken him for a good walk. "She lays over two hours and then flies to the Monterey airport. She'll get in about six."

"I heard the phone. Thanks for getting up—I just couldn't."

"She became somewhat exercised when she heard her son was spending the night in the clink after coming to us for help. Must have been difficult. First he calls and he's alive and safe. She calls Joseph and everybody sighs with relief. Then she hears that he's been arrested."

"Nothing else we could have done. Is she staying with us?"

"She harrumphed and said no way. She said she'd be fine. But I said I'd meet her and cook her dinner. Her and Wish, if you get him out."

"Great," Nina said. "I'll polish up the silver. Queen Victoria is coming."

"She won't care about the place. She just wants to see Wish. What time is the bail hearing?"

"Two o'clock."

"You going to get him out?"

"If they haven't added the felony charges."

"How's the rash?"

"The rash? Oh, the rash! Well, what d'you know. I didn't itch all last night."

"Miracle of modern drugs," Paul said.

"I'm going to be very careful of poison oak in the future, Paul. I don't want the rash, and I definitely don't want the prednisone."

"You did have your ups and downs. Is all that going to change to tranquility now?"

"Absolutely," Nina said. Paul laughed.

By nine-thirty they were both dressed and the living room looked acceptable for the formidable company they expected later. They went out on the deck and sat down in the metal chairs. Nina said, "Call the meeting to order."

"I vote we drive out to Carmel Valley Village and talk to Danny's uncle."

"The police may be there."

"So? That ever stop you before?"

"Why don't we try calling him one more time?"

This time Nina got a message. It said, "This is Ben. Call me on my cell phone."

She recited the number to Paul, then called it.

"*Sí?*"

"Mr. Cervantes?" She heard voices and clattering sounds.

"Who is this?" A soft voice, with a Spanish accent.

"My name is Nina Reilly. I'm a friend of Wish Whitefeather's. Danny's friend Wish."

"Yes?"

"I need to talk to you. It's important. Could we meet somewhere?"

"Why do you want to talk to me?"

"It's about Danny."

"Right now is not a good time. Friday the thirteenth is turning out to be as unlucky as the superstition says."

"Anytime today."

"I'm sorry. I have to go. You can give me your number—"

"Have the police been in touch with you?" Nina said. "About Danny?"

She heard a sigh. "I am with an officer right now. I am at the county morgue in Salinas and they are about to have me look at—I have to go."

"Mr. Cervantes, please stay right there and I will meet you in an hour. I'll wait for you outside."

"You are not a polite person."

"You will want to hear what I say."

"*Bien.* You can wait for me." She heard a click.

For more than an hour, they waited, watching the people walk in and out of the buildings, talking little, leaving the car windows open to the sun and the breeze. Finally they saw a handsome Mexican-American man in a cowboy hat, white shirt, and jeans coming down the steps toward them. Paul and Nina got out and they shook hands.

His face betrayed nothing and he displayed no interest in Paul's unannounced presence. "Where do you want to go?"

"We could get in my Mustang," Paul said. "Good air-conditioning."

He shook his head. His expression said, I don't know you.

"The law library inside?"

"I'm not going back in there. Come on." He led them down the street and Nina noticed his narrow waist and good build. It was her curse to react as a woman to every man she met close to her age.

He ducked inside a short doorway on Main Street near the old Cominos Hotel. A dive, she thought, dark, with red-pepper lights decorating fake cacti along the wall and a long bar holding up two guys playing some kind of dice game. The owners hadn't felt any need for tables, so she took a bar stool beside Paul.

"Corona," Cervantes said on the other side of Paul, his voice still soft. Nina ordered a ginger ale and Paul asked for water.

"You probably think I'm a boozer," Cervantes said. "I need a drink right now, that's for sure."

"What happened inside?" Paul asked.

"I saw my nephew all burned up, that's what happened." He tipped back the beer glass and set it down and heaved a sigh.

So it was official. The body was Danny. Wish would be crushed. They had all hoped the arsonist had burned himself up.

"Danny's your nephew?"

"My brother's son. He was only ten years younger than me."

"I'm awfully sorry," Nina said.

"That's tough," Paul said.

Cervantes turned on his stool to look at them, finally, and Nina saw that his eyes were red-rimmed. He loved him, she thought. She felt torn between sympathy and a dawning suspicion. He had lived with Danny. What did he know?

"I gave him that concho belt. Last Christmas. The one they showed me. Twelve conchos, black leather. Some of them were gone. Otherwise I don't know if I could have recognized him, he was so burned up. Poor Danito. God have pity on him."

"We went there yesterday, to see if it was Wish," Paul said.

"Wish got lucky. Danny, he never had luck."

"Wish isn't so lucky," Nina said. "He's in custody. The police think he and Danny were the arsonists."

"You think they weren't?"

"We think they went up the mountain to find out who was committing these arsons."

"Wish told you that?"

"He told us that and we believe it."

"Huh." Cervantes digested this. He thought things over before he said anything in that sexy voice of his, but Nina didn't think he was stupid. "I hope that's true. The way the police talked, I thought they had some proof—"

"We think the police are blowing smoke," Paul said, "if you can pardon the expression."

"Why are you telling me this? What do you want from me?"

"Wish has a bail hearing this afternoon," Nina said. "Maybe you know something that can help us."

"I would help you if I could. All I know is, Danny was talking about some big money coming in sometime. I didn't know what from. I never asked. I told Detective Crockett all this." He looked even sadder.

"There was a significant reward offered for information leading to an arrest and conviction of the arsonist. A hundred thousand dollars. Wish told us they went up the ridge to try to get a photo of the arsonist. It was Danny's idea. And he never mentioned this?"

Cervantes was brightening by the second. "Is this true? I never wanted to believe that Danny was setting fires. I understand this much better. A big reward, yes, that would pull Danny in. But how did they know to go up there that night?"

"Wish says that Danny had some sort of advance information," Nina said.

"So you think he must have talked to me? The answer is no, I didn't know anything. Danny—he'd been gone a lot, camping, I don't know. He was only twenty-one, but he'd been on his own for four years."

"Family problems?"

"His family lives at Tahoe these days, on the North Shore, King's Beach. Danny was an only child. His parents both work and moved around a lot, and I think—he just didn't have much going on up there. What Danny wanted more than anything was to belong, to have friends, to settle down.

"He came down to the Village to stay with me last summer, and I got him a job doing car repair at a shop I worked for until recently. Danny was pretty good, he could sniff out rust, leaks, broken belts. He liked it. He worked hard, but when the shop closed—they got bought out—he couldn't find anything else. No education, no connections, and like I told you—no luck."

Paul raised his eyebrows, and Nina asked, "A repair shop? Any chance this was the shop by Rosie's Bridge? The one that got replaced by a coffee shop?"

The lids narrowed over Cervantes's warm brown eyes. "Yes. Why?"

"The coffee shop that burned down?"

"Right." He gave them a challenging look. "And?"

"How did Danny react to losing his job?"

"Now you're accusing him? You now have decided he set the fires after all? Which is it? Ah, you people." He turned back to the bar. His moment of trust had passed.

"I'm not saying anything. I was just surprised. Maybe—maybe it's how Danny found out about the arsonist. Wish said Danny had a license-plate number," Nina said.

"I don't know. Danny didn't hang out with cops. I don't know where he would hear something like that."

"How did he get along lately?"

"You mean, money-wise?"

"Right."

"I paid the rent. Our neighbors on Siesta Court hired him for odd jobs. It wasn't so bad, he earned a little money and the work made him feel like he was part of the neighborhood, you know? He was a lonely boy. I didn't help him enough." Cervantes stood up. "Excuse me. I have to call some people, make some arrangements."

"Just one more minute. Forgive us, we know you have just had a shock—"

"Like I said, you are not polite."

"I'm a real jerk when it comes to my friends," Nina said.

Cervantes considered this, then, expressionless, said, "Okay. What else?"

Paul said, "The police say they have a witness. A woman named Ruth."

"The Cat Lady? Everybody in the Village knows her. What's she say?"

"She says she saw two people in a car leaving the scene of the second fire, the coffee shop. She got suspicious and followed them. They drove to Siesta Court along the Carmel River—"

"My street!"

"She saw somebody get out of the car and go into one of the houses, she doesn't know which one, then the car took off, and she lost it."

Paul had just learned this detail from Crockett. They let it sink in.

"So that must be how Danny found out. It was somebody on our street? One of them?"

"You got me," Paul said. "What do you think?"

"One of my neighbors?" Cervantes said, smiling. "What a thought. I know every single person on that street. These are regular people with jobs and mortgages and kids."

"Then we get stuck with the police theory," Paul said. "That it was Danny being dropped off by Wish."

"Ah. Poor Danny. You know, I know Wish. He's an honest person. You tell him I believe him, okay? As for the Cat Lady . . . she's not all there. I don't know what to tell you."

"Maybe she was seeing things," Paul said agreeably.

"You want to get ahold of her? She feeds the cats at the old Rosie's parking lot right by the bridge every afternoon at about three o'clock. I've seen her other places too. She drives around in an old white Olds Cutlass."

"Do you know her last name?"

"Sure don't." Cervantes shook his head. "One of the neighbors," he repeated with that incredulous smile.

"Nobody comes to mind?" Nina said.

"No. You believe Danny had nothing to do with setting the fires, he was just trying to catch the arsonist? Is that right?"

"That's what Wish tells us, and we believe him," Nina said.

"You're not just playing with my head?"

"Why would I do that?"

"How should I know?" He gave her a challenging look, and she thought, he's not naive either.

"Mr. Cervantes, I just want to help Wish." He was still thinking, observing her, eyes narrow.

"You want to add something?" she said.

"I have an idea. You want to find out for yourself about the neighbors? Come to the Siesta Court Bunch barbecue tomorrow night. We all get together once a month on Saturday night and have a potluck. We go way back, most of us. I'll take you."

Nina jumped on it. She said, "That's a very good idea. Thank you."

Paul looked dubious. He said, "They won't feel free and easy if they know why we're there."

"We could go anonymously," Nina said. "Mr. Cervantes won't tell anybody."

"You can go as my date," Cervantes said. Nina gave a start.

"What about me?" Paul said.

"I don't know how to explain you," Cervantes said. "I've seen you in the papers. Somebody else probably has too." He looked at Nina. "You want to come as my guest, or not?"

"Yes," Nina said. Paul gave her a small kick under the counter, which she returned.

Cervantes gave her the number on Siesta Court. "Six o'clock tomorrow," he said. "Don't dress up or you'll stand out too much. Shorts and flip-flops."

"I look forward to it," Nina said. Since Paul had already let her know that he didn't like the plan, she avoided his eyes.

"The drinks are on her," Paul said, and Cervantes put his wallet back into his pocket.

Paul had to get back to Carmel and the office, so he dropped Nina a block from the Salinas courthouse at a bail-bonds place. He let her know that he didn't like her going to the party without him as soon as they got into the Mustang.

"What's your problem with it?"

"You're not an investigator, you're a lawyer. You're a lousy liar and they'll see through you and get suspicious and if the bad guy is there, he'll know we're looking for him."

"You just don't want me to go without you. I'm not an idiot, Paul. It's just a neighborhood barbecue."

"Cervantes is a good bet to be the bad guy himself. I don't trust him."

"I'll be careful. I'll stay around other people. Besides, I have a different take on him. Why would he offer to take me if he didn't want to find out what happened? If he already knows, he's not going to get involved with us like this."

"He's attracted to you. He's using the situation to get you alone."

"Come on, Paul, give me a break. You sound like a preacher talking to a thirteen-year-old."

"This isn't about jealousy, Nina."

"No. It's about power. It's about you controlling me," Nina said.

Paul pulled into the curb in front of the fire hydrant, leaving the car in drive. He didn't say anything.

"I should be finished by four." She twisted around and retrieved her briefcase from the back seat, feeling regret at what she had said. But not enough regret to unsay it.

She talked to the bondsman while he ate his sub sandwich and set an account for fast action that afternoon, leaving her own credit-card number. Then she walked rapidly
back to the big white concrete building with its concrete
courtyard, found the right wing, and climbed the stairs to
the courtroom, arriving with fifteen minutes to spare.

Wish had already been brought in and sat in the jury
box with the other prisoners. Seeing him, hair lank, eyes
downturned, hurt her. At least his eyes were almost back to
normal. He must have gotten treatment for the poison oak
while in jail. It added to her feeling of kinship with him.

When he noticed her, he gave her a thumbs-up. She
passed through the gate to the attorney seating and had
barely sat down when a face from the past came over and
said, "It's been a few years."

Jaime Sandoval had aged prematurely in the eight years
since they had graduated from the Monterey College of
Law together. Law does that to you, if you're any good.
The thick hair she remembered was streaked with white
above his forehead. The narrow black specs were new too.
On the other hand, the shy Mexican-American boy who
never raised a hand in class looked a lot more self-confident
these days. As a deputy D.A., he had the state of California
behind him, always a confidence builder.

Nina smiled. "Good to see you, Jaime."

He sat down beside her, holding his briefcase. He wore
a wedding ring now and she smelled his spicy aftershave.

"You look good."

"So do you. I'm surprised you went into the D.A.'s office."

"Oh yeah, when I knew you I was going to be a corpo-
rate lawyer. I tried that for a year at a small firm in Monterey. Got so bored with the paper pushing I decided to try
this out. They told me I was stepping down but I decided
downward mobility beats terminal ennui. So here I am.
What about you? I thought you headed for the city lights."

"Long story," Nina said. "San Francisco, Tahoe. Solo
practice the last few years. I'm down here for the summer."

"A lot has happened since you left. We actually got a Latino judge. Of course, they're still trying to trump up some way to kick him out."

"How long did it take? A hundred fifty-five years, right?"

"Counting from when the U.S. took the place from us, yes."

"I'm glad to hear it."

"So you came back home. What are you doing for an office?"

"Well, uh, I'm borrowing some space right now." That didn't sound too impressive, but a fancy office wouldn't impress Jaime either. "You covering the Whitefeather bail hearing?" she went on.

"I'm covering all the bail hearings, in about three minutes. So you're here for the arson-homicide case?"

Nina's heart sank. "Last time I looked, it was a trespassing case. And I'm thinking he ought to be let out on his own recognizance this afternoon."

"Sorry I can't help you," Jaime said. "It's not just trespassing, it never was. We just got the complaint amended. Here you go." He handed her a document with several counts listed. Nina scanned it, staying cool, searching for a quick way out for Wish.

The charges were worse, far worse, than she had expected.

At this stage, she had anticipated a couple of arson counts, but as she read she saw in Count Four that Wish was being charged with second-degree murder under the felony-accessory rule. He and his accomplice, Daniel Cervantes, according to the amended complaint, had committed felony arsons, and during the commission of one of the felonies Daniel Cervantes had died. That made Wish as responsible as if he had killed Danny himself.

Still reeling from Count Four, Nina came to Count Five. According to this one, Wish had with malice aforethought killed Daniel Cervantes and attempted to cover up the murder with a fire.

"I don't believe it! Talk about trumping things up!" she said. "Premeditated murder? Are you nuts?"

"We had to rush it some, because we couldn't let him out," Jaime said.

"You don't have the evidence. You're making a mistake, Jaime."

"It's a murder. The coroner found kerosene traces all over the body. Somebody wanted to make sure it burned."

"But—"

"And your guy's camera was the murder weapon, according to a forensics report I received approximately ninety minutes ago," Jaime said. "Like I said, it's been a rush."

"You—you have fingerprints?"

"Not with the heat and flames. The camera's enough."

"But the arsonist was up there too! Listen, Jaime, I'm going to tell you in a nutshell what happened up there." She told him about the reward and the arsonist, leaning her head close to his. He listened carefully and nodded.

"That's what happened," she finished.

"Very interesting. You have any proof? Any hard evidence? Since you're not letting your client talk?"

"We're working on it."

"Good. Anything you come up with, we'll talk." Another lawyer had caught his eye. He started to get up.

"Wait," Nina said. She practically grabbed his coattail. She would have kissed his ring if he had held it out. She really wanted Wish out, today.

"This doesn't change anything," Jaime said. "Words are cheap." He looked down at her and she thought she saw a trace of triumph in his eyes. She had given something for nothing.

"I can't talk like this to you again, Jaime," she said. "I see that I made a mistake."

"I have to go. See you later."

"I want a copy of that forensics report."

"As provided by law."

"Don't do this. Let him out on the trespassing charge and let's talk. You'll be glad you did."

"It's outta my hands. He stays in jail, those are my instructions."

"Wait. Just one more thing—"

"What?" He balanced on his toes, ready to go, his face impassive.

"Did you find film in the camera?"

"Yeah. It's a Canon digital SLR, hefty for such a high-tech item. Has a memory card, not film."

He watched Nina's body tense, watched her bite her lip, trying to decide if she really wanted to know the answer to her last question.

"No shots had been taken," he said. He went off on his next errand of whatever the opposite of mercy was. She sagged against the table. So he had no bomb to explode, no photo that somehow implicated Wish in any of it.

But hadn't Wish told her that he took many shots?

The bailiff had come in. "All rise," he said. Nina got up. Judge Salas stepped up to the dais and sat down in his black robes. "Good afternoon," he said, not looking at anybody.

"You may be seated." A rustle. Nina looked at Wish, who smiled at her with total confidence that she would deliver him from his travails.

His case came last and when it was called she was waging a final battle with a flare-up of the poison-oak rash on her hip, trying not to scratch. Wish must be feeling far worse. She stood up and moved to the counsel table.

"We have an amended complaint just filed, Judge," Jaime said.

"You have given a copy to Counsel?" Judge Salas said. He was young for the job, high-voiced, in contrast with the thick brows that come with a high testosterone level.

"I have it, Your Honor," Nina said. Salas thumbed through the charges, reading Count Five thoroughly.

"Well?" he said.

Jaime said, "He's dangerous, Judge. Mr. Whitefeather is a transient. He has no family here. He's only been in the area a few weeks. After the fire he evaded questioning for several days. He's a flight risk. The murder charge is gonna stick, Judge. We just got the news that the murder weapon was a camera owned by Mr. Whitefeather. No question he was on the ridge on Tuesday night. He admitted that with his counsel present."

"Whitefeather. What kind of name is that?"

"Mr. Whitefeather is a member of the Washoe tribe from the Lake Tahoe area, Your Honor," Nina said, stepping in quickly. "His mother is working with the B.I.A. on a federal project out of Washington and she's on her way here right now. Mr. Whitefeather is working as an intern at a security firm in Carmel this summer, Your Honor. He's a good student going into his second year in the Criminal Justice Program at Lake Tahoe Community College."

Salas didn't react. He looked at Jaime. "Any record?" he asked. "I don't seem to have a sheet on him."

"We're still checking on that," Jaime said.

"I can personally represent to the court that Mr. White-feather has never been arrested for any crime from a misdemeanor on up, let alone been convicted of anything," Nina said, a true statement legally, since any juvenile record was officially expunged from history. "He worked in my law office at Tahoe for the past two years part-time and his behavior has been exemplary. Let me respond to a couple of points Counsel made earlier—"

The judge held up his hand, silencing her. He said to Jaime, "You charged him with trespassing and today you're charging him with murder?"

"We don't want him out," Jaime said. "We ask that this be made a no-bail case. This is the third fire in a month. This defendant can't control himself."

"Mr. Whitefeather didn't do anything, Your Honor," Nina said rapidly. "It's a mistake that comes from moving too fast. Mr. Whitefeather and Mr. Cervantes were present at the last fire because they were trying to catch the arsonist. He had never been on the mountain before—"

"That's not what we hear from a witness who chased Mr. Cervantes home during a previous fire," Jaime said, jumping on her words.

"I don't want to hear any evidence," Salas said in a complaining voice. "Am I supposed to try the case today? It's a bail hearing. He won't even be entering a plea for a couple of days."

"Okay, then," Jaime said. "First-degree murder charge. No bail is the appropriate response. Further, this guy is not a local. He stayed out of sight until the Monterey County Sheriff's Office, acting on a tip, found him at—sorry, Nina—his lawyer's condo in Carmel."

"Is that right." Salas turned baleful eyes on Nina. "I don't know you, Counselor," he said.

"As I mentioned, Your Honor, my offices are—were—in Tahoe."

"Were?"

"I have closed them and am spending the summer here."

"And where are you practicing law?"

"I share space in the Eastwood Building in Carmel."

"Hmm."

"The same office the defendant is allegedly working out of," Jaime said.

"I am appearing for purposes of the bail hearing and arraignment, if it comes to that," Nina said. "Naturally, Mr. Whitefeather might prefer local counsel in the event this goes much further."

Jaime said, "We have a nonlocal vouching for a nonlocal. These fires—a lot more people could die. We owe it to the public to hold on to Mr. Whitefeather."

"We are asking for reasonable bail to be set, Your Honor. Any reasonable bail. Mr. Whitefeather makes two thousand dollars a month. Something that will make it possible for him to get out."

"I'm going to allow bail," Salas said abruptly.

"But, Judge . . ." Jaime started.

Salas flung down the file. "One million five," he said.

Angels must have flown over, because the courtroom got reverent for a moment. Even the regulars in back stopped shifting from buttock to buttock along the benches. A small smile cracked Jaime's young-old face.

She wasn't a local like Jaime anymore. Salas was letting her know he didn't like out-of-towners.

"That would require that Mr. Whitefeather put up a hundred fifty thousand dollars for a cash bond," Nina said steadily. "His family can't raise that amount of money, and they certainly don't have collateral for the remainder either. I request that the court reconsider."

"One million five," the judge said again, addressing Nina directly. "You want bail, you got bail."

"That kind of bail I can do without."

"Then do without. You want no bail? You smart-mouthing me?"

"No, Your Honor." Geez, Nina thought, the first in 155 years and he's gonna make up for it all this month. She suppressed that unworthy thought.

The judge glanced at the clock on the wall and the roll of his eyes said, Judge to defense counsel: You are wasting your time.

"Anything else?" Salas said. Nina and Jaime stood silent.

"So ordered." The judge picked up his shiny gavel and gave it a rap. Only new judges did that.

She had a moment with Wish before the bailiff took him back to jail. "I wouldn't even let me out," Wish said. "Not the way it sounds. My camera! The firebug—he must've picked it up and hit Danny with it. Why did I give in? Danny and his dumb ideas!"

"Keep your spirits up, Wish. You'll be arraigned soon."

She explained the purposes of arraignment. "I'll see you then."

"Nina, you and Paul have to find out who set those fires. That's all I can think about. Who did it. Who . . ."— he choked on his words—"who killed Danny. Who put me in jail."

Huge questions. "Your mom is flying in tonight. She'll come to see you after supper."

"Yikes! That's all I need."

"I'll try to explain it all to her at dinner."

"Well, at least I finally have a topic for my term paper next semester," Wish said. " 'Life in the Joint.' Like the title? I'm keeping a journal."

Nina tried to smile. "So something good will come of this."

"It's an experience few law-enforcement officers get to have. That is, if I ever get to be a law-enforcement officer."

"I'm very sorry I couldn't get you out—" Nina said.

"If you couldn't, nobody could—"

"But you won't be in there long, Wish. I promise you that."

7

PAUL WORKED ON dinner while Nina left to pick up Sandy at the airport, borrowing the Mustang. They spoke in monosyllables to each other. They had quarreled, and neither of them seemed to want to clear the air yet.

Sandy waited outside the small terminal in the fog, wearing her familiar square purple coat, bag at her side. Nina loaded the bag into the trunk while Sandy maneuvered herself into the front seat, grumbling. She was a sizable lady and the Mustang rode low to the ground.

"You aren't driving with the top down," Sandy said, and it wasn't a question.

"Of course not." Nina raised the Mustang's roof and clamped it into place. "Good flight?" she asked.

"What do you think?"

Uh-oh. Sandy was not going to be conventionally polite. She was, perhaps, in a mood of towering fury. Nina braced herself. "You'll like Paul's condo," she said. "View of the ocean, up high on a hill. Private." She was trying for conventional politeness just in case.

Sandy swatted this small talk away. "Have you seen Wish?"

"Yes. This afternoon. He's okay, Sandy. Says it'll be a learning experience, being in jail."

"In jail," she repeated. "You call that okay." She folded her arms and looked out at the scenery for the rest of the ride without further comment.

Although they had invited her to stay at the condo, Sandy had decided to spend the night at a motel in Seaside. She had lined up a rental car and would be doing a blitz trip to Tahoe to see Joseph Whitefeather, Wish's father, before returning east, so she needed to leave early.

Sitting at the dinner table, she eyed the meal Paul had made especially for her, turned her obsidian gaze on Paul and Nina, and said, "I knew nothing good would come of this."

"I thought you liked meat loaf," Paul said.

The glare intensified. "Closing the office. Running away. Bringing Willis down here." She had a sip of ice water.

"I thought you were glad to go to Washington," Nina said, feeling defensive. "How's your work going?"

"Ever been there?" Sandy asked.

"No," Nina said.

"You never saw so many pink-cheeked little old men in one place at one time before in your life."

"I've heard," Nina said, "you're doing good work up there, Sandy. The people in Tahoe are really proud of you. I saved an article from the *Mirror* about how much you've already improved the visibility of the Washoe tribe. 'An effective and vigorous presence in Washington,' they called you."

"What do they know?" Sandy said, although Nina thought she detected a minuscule relaxation of the stern crease between her eyebrows.

"How long will you be working there?" Paul asked. "Must be hard on Joseph, you working on the East Coast."

"Maybe a couple of months, if these people working with me are ready to take over then. Then I'm back at the ranch with Joseph at Tahoe. And visiting my son, the convict, the way things look."

"Is Joseph coming down?"

"He's laid up for a month. He had a little accident and can't get around."

"Don't worry," Nina said. "We'll find a way out of this."

"At least he came to you as soon as he could."

"He's feeling very bad about his poor judgment in following Danny. And he's lost a friend. Don't be too hard on him."

"I won't be hard on him. Joseph's the one who's gonna be hard on him. Joseph was so proud of Willis. He was going to be the first one in our family with a college degree."

Shocked, Nina said, "Wait a minute, Sandy. Wish isn't going to be convicted of anything. Maybe you have the wrong impression. He didn't do anything."

Sandy picked up her fork. "Well, *bon appétit,*" she said. "He did something, all right. Got himself in legal trouble."

Nina couldn't deny that. After a moment she went on, "There's something I need to ask you about. This arson investigator, David Crockett . . ."

Her mouth opened slightly, an expression tantamount to astonishment in her. "Who? Are you kidding me?"

"Not at all."

"Davy Crockett? That's not a good sign. Oh, boy. You know who he was?" Sandy asked.

"The historic Davy? Sure. He was the king of the wild frontier, the buckskin buccaneer. Kilt him a bear when he was only three," Paul said.

"His grandparents were killed by the Creek and Cherokees when the grandparents tried to steal tribal land in eastern Tennessee," Sandy said.

"I didn't know that," Nina said.

"No friend to the Indians. Killed as many as he could. Commanded a battalion in the war to bring down the Creek Indians in 1813."

"This guy's name is just a fluke," Nina said. "I'm sure his politics aren't affected by anything so remote."

"Did you ask him?"

"No."

"Then how do you know? It's too much of a coincidence. It must mean something."

"Anyway," Nina said. "If I may return to my point, Detective Crockett told us that Wish was arrested as a juvenile for some kind of arson."

"Now, how would he know that?"

"Was he?"

"You know how many boys take fireworks out into a field and try to blow things up?" Sandy asked.

"Yeah, we had some fun," Paul said.

"They sure made a big deal of a pile of kids blasting out a dead stump," Sandy said. "Too bad they don't put as much energy into saving the live ones. And aren't those records supposed to be sealed?"

"Yes," Nina said, "but you can't always depend on the rules working properly. People . . ."

"Bend them," Sandy said. "Davy Crockett. Oh, boy." She took a bite of meat loaf, chewed slowly, tried some more, and then ate down to the bare plate.

"Now then," she said. "Let's get the money straight." She opened her purse and took out her checkbook. "I'm retaining you both."

"I knew it. You do love my meat loaf," Paul said. "Consider that my payment."

"It was good. Lots of ketchup, and the crumbs were toasted right."

"There you have it," Paul told Nina. "Now for some strawberry shortcake."

"But I want to hire you. Now, don't turn this into something mushy. Joseph and I are giving you this check." She tried to hand Nina a check for a thousand dollars. Nina wouldn't take it.

"We insist," Sandy said. "And there's more available when you need it."

"I can't take your money, Sandy," Nina said.

"Why not? My money's not good enough for you? My boy's a charity case?"

"Of course not—"

"I'll write out the receipt for myself. And watch out for that Crockett man."

Nina let the check lie on the table. For now.

They finished the meal quickly, then Nina and Paul dropped Sandy off at the jail to talk with Wish. Before she got out of the car, Sandy said to Nina, "When you coming home?"

"You mean to Tahoe? I just got here."

"Seen your dad?"

"Not yet."

"You should do that."

"What is bothering you about me being here?"

"Look around you." Sandy waved her arm with its silver bracelets. "See any mountains here? And what about this gray cloud you live in?"

"I'm glad she's here," Paul told her, squeezing Nina's hand, "and I'm glad Wish came down. In spite of everything." He seemed to remember something and withdrew his hand hastily. Nina knew it was their argument he had remembered. She let him move away.

Stepping away from the car, Sandy smoothed her coat, working up to something. Finally, she said, "Find out who's behind this, Paul. I'm trusting you."

"Wish is in good hands," Paul said. "Hard, craggy, experienced hands."

"Hmph." She went into the jail building.

"Have a good flight back," Paul called to her. Nina got into the front passenger seat and threw her arms around him before he could turn the key in the ignition.

"Paul, I'm exhausted. I forgot how she is."

His body felt stiff, but she held on anyway and pressed her face into his collar, because she needed him and didn't care about the stupid argument anymore.

"Ah, Nina," he said finally, and kissed her.

"Let's get home," she said. "That Sandy."

"She's stressed out. She'll get her sense of humor back. I'll send her a coonskin cap to wear in Washington."

"I wouldn't do that. I sure wouldn't."

"Tomorrow's Saturday. Let's go have a look at the Robles Ridge fire site."

"Not early."

"Not early."

8

"I'm just getting over poison oak. I'm not bush-whacking. Promise we'll stay strictly on a trail. And we can't take Hitchcock."

"You won't have to touch him. We'll take the Bronco and keep him in back on the way home, and I'll give him the bath of his life."

"We ought to see it," Nina said. "I agree."

"Notice how well we work together this morning."

"Two peas in a pod," Nina said. She changed the shorts to long pants, pulled on knee-high cotton socks and her hiking boots, and stuffed cotton gloves in her pocket. How to protect her hair and face from brushing against the evil leaves? A scarf.

"You make a charming babushka," Paul said.

Outside in the mist, she tossed the day pack with the water bottles into the back seat with Hitchcock, who stood on the bench seat, tongue hanging out the window, ready for anything. The oak trees were dripping and they might as well be underwater. She looked from Hitchcock to Paul, already strapped in, studying a map, leaning forward eagerly. "Two peas in a pod," she said.

They drove out of the fog bank in five minutes and blinked into brilliant sunshine. Carmel Valley Road followed the river, although you never saw it, just the fields and oak forests and houses and golf courses it irrigated. The river was actually only a trickle now that summer had arrived.

"Did you know that Sebastian Vizcaíno discovered this river in 1602?" Nina asked Paul. "Four hundred years ago. I mean, Plymouth was still a gleam in English eyes back then. When I studied American history they never mentioned how old the European presence really is in California."

"And why do you think that is?" Paul asked.

"American historians are Anglophiles?"

"They do all have those Waspy surnames."

"And they all come from the East Coast."

"Although we did study the California missions," Paul reminded her.

"Hmm. We did. I think you just blew my theory. But this happened before Junípero Serra. It was the winter of 1602, and Vizcaíno came limping into Carmel Bay in his little wooden ship. And he found a torrent. A white-water torrent. The Carmel River gets very high during wet winters, Paul."

"So?" Hitchcock saw a black Scottie in the next car as they sat at a traffic light, and barked and hung his paws over the edge of the window. Paul pressed on the electric window switch and it started up, causing Hitchcock to give a yelp of consternation and fall back into the car.

"You didn't have to scare him like that," Nina said.

"It worked, didn't it?"

"Grr. He's my dog. He is not your dog to correct."

"Okay, I'm sorry. He's your dog. So. About Vizcaíno."

"So Vizcaíno reported to his superiors about this glorious bay he had found with all the fresh water anyone could ever want. He said to look for a cataract pouring into the ocean on a white-sand beach. So the next expedition looked for it and couldn't find it, and the next, and the next. Because the ships came in the summer and there wasn't any river. As a result, the Carmel River wasn't discovered again for a hundred more years, by which time San

Francisco had already become the main commercial center in California."

"And your point is?"

"Well, this road would be wall-to-wall skyscrapers. The equivalent of the Financial District in downtown S.F."

"So we lucked out? That's your point?"

"Or maybe the river just delayed the inevitable with that little disappearing act," Nina said. "There sure is a lot of new development along here, Paul."

About fifteen miles inland the hills around them came closer and closer as the valley narrowed. They came to Carmel Valley Village, entryway to the enormous Los Padres National Forest. Stopping for coffee at the River Deli, they sat outside at a rickety plastic table to take in the rays, Hitchcock at Nina's feet. Across the empty street, a woman in a wheelchair, a tissue clutched between her teeth, led by a stalwart dog, rolled peacefully down the sidewalk toward the Village Market.

"I remember her," Nina said. "I'm glad to see she's still shopping on her own. I wonder if she still lives at Robles Vista."

"I thought Crockett said it was being torn down for the subdivision that got torched in the first fire. Green River, that was the name of it."

"But, remember, he said that some of the Robles Vista tenants refused to be relocated. I don't think they have torn Robles Vista down yet. It'll be a shame when they do. The Village won't be the same without them. They were always part of the scene, the blind guy with the beard tapping his way across the road to the deli, the people in wheelchairs checking out books at the library."

"Maybe one of them agreed with you enough to pour out some kerosene farther down the hill toward the river and take out the model home," Paul said.

"I suppose we should check Robles Vista out. Where in the world will they go? Salinas?"

Paul shook his head and said, "Salinas is cheaper than

here, but it is getting expensive. Look around the Village and you'll find some spiffy new restaurants. Older businesses can't pay the big rents. Lots of wealthy retirees have been moving out here instead of Carmel or Pebble Beach. It's gotten as upscale as Carmel."

"Ben Cervantes is no rich retiree, and he lives in the Village."

"No, and he's struggling too, I bet," Paul said. "Off we go. A dirt road turns into a trail above Hitchcock Canyon"—the dog's ears perked up—"which was the jumping-off place for the third fire."

Nina picked up Paul's camera. "Wish told me exactly where he and Danny parked. Let's do it."

"Good thing they caught it fast," Paul said as they drove down a hill, over a bridge, and up winding roads through neighborhoods of homes with wood-shingle roofs sheltered in the oaks. The road narrowed to a shady lane and they crept along over a series of small bridges across a meandering creek. The oaks shaded them but the day felt even hotter because the air was so still.

Each house had a unique character. The flowers and rocky cliffs behind were as beautiful as Nina remembered, but she could see that gentrification had changed Hitchcock Canyon. The expensive new glassy geometrical homes perched here and there just didn't fit the weathered older, more modest places.

A couple of miles in, Southbank Road forked. They followed the right fork and continued uphill in the dirt. Paul adjusted the gears of the Bronco into four-wheel drive and they powered on, raising a plume of dust behind. Soon they came to a last group of new and expensive homes with glorious views, the end of the road. A trail continued up toward the crest of the hill, and they saw what the fire had wrought.

A black, still-smoky swath of forest stretched above

them. They got out, not bothering to leash Hitchcock, and Nina swung the pack on her back, tied on the scarf, and pulled on her gloves. As hot as she was, she'd probably die of heat prostration, but she preferred that to dying of itching from poison oak.

"C'mon, mutt," Paul said. Nina, gratified, saw that Hitchcock looked her way for a nod, then waited for her to attach the leash to his collar.

They hiked up the trail where Wish and Danny had gone, Hitchcock pulling hard on the leash. Black tree trunks and fallen charred limbs littered the ground. Hollows and habitats lay exposed. No birds, no squirrels. No green anymore, not even the dry olive-green of central California.

"A lot of acreage burned," Paul said, walking along with his eyes on the trail. "There might have been footprints, but the firefighters had to come through here to fight the fire. It's all scuffed up. Stinks, doesn't it?"

"Guess it even burned up my favorite plant," Nina said. But she kept the scarf on.

Paul took photos of the trail, the skyline, the devastation. "Wish asked me what kind of camera to get, so I told him about my Canon," he said, stopping just ahead to look at a tree branch that held a torn piece of yellow cloth. "He was doing so well at the office. I had him working a special detail with the security staff at the La Playa Hotel. They liked him and asked me if he might want full-time work. He was helping me with the paperwork on a divorce case I'm handling too."

"I remember when he first came into my office in South Lake Tahoe," Nina said. "He came to pick Sandy up, and he looked around the office like it was the most glamorous thing on earth."

"What I always liked about Wish is, he's enthusiastic."

"We'll get him out," Nina said.

"Maybe Sandy can scare up the bail money from one of her pink-cheeked fellows. She's in Washington, after all."

"It's a ridiculous amount. But if I go in again and ask for a reduction, this judge might make it a no-bail instead."

"Salas? I've heard he's erratic."

"Well, you'll hear a lot of rumors," Nina said. "Just because he happens to be a Latino."

"You're standing up for him? I thought you said he called you a smart-mouth in open court."

"It's kind of refreshing. I was being slightly, uh—"

"Mouthy?"

"Forthright. Perhaps unduly forthright. Anyway, he's got to be under a lot of pressure. So what have you got there?"

"A piece of cloth."

"I know that. I've got eyes."

Paul whipped out a Ziploc bag and put the cloth in it. Then he wrote a note in his black notebook. "I wonder why the arson investigator didn't take it."

"It's probably his." They continued up, Hitchcock close behind. He didn't seem to want to get out in these woods.

Nina went on, "It's getting damn steep. Imagine how frightening it must have been, late at night. I wonder how Wish could see to run down."

Paul tapped his noggin and said, "That's why you're a lawyer and not an arson investigator."

"Huh?"

"The forest was on fire. He had more light than we do."

"Oh, right. Look, there's a hawk." It flew high above them, riding the currents, circling like a news helicopter over the story of devastation.

They walked the entire extent of the fire, all the way to the top of the hill. Nina saw no sign of the spot where Danny's body had been found. She wouldn't even have the police reports to look at until after the arraignment. She tried to imagine it, Wish lost in that crackling hell, Danny disappearing, and then the hand with the rock.

What kind of person had done this?

Looking around them from the top of the ridge, they

could see several hundred feet below. This fire had been set with no regard for human life, as there were homes directly below—or maybe the homes had been the targets? "We should find out who lives in all the homes that were threatened," she said.

"We have to prioritize," Paul told her. "I'll get on that soon, but right now, I think we better concentrate on the sure thing we do know—that one of the arsonists seems to live on Siesta Court. Look down. See the river we crossed to get onto Southbank? The riverbed, anyway. It's almost dry. Siesta Court's hidden in the oaks down there. Let's go down and take a look at it."

"I don't want to blow my cover for tonight," Nina said. "What if some of the neighbors are out?"

"Well, I'd like to see, since I wasn't invited to the party. You keep wearing that scarf and the sunglasses. They'll think you're Winona Ryder on a shopping spree."

They walked back down and Hitchcock drank some water, and then wound down Hitchcock Canyon in the Bronco. At the bottom of the Robles hill they came back to the substantial steel bridge over the river, which Nina remembered was called Rosie's Bridge. Across the bridge, Esquiline Road and the hill sloped up again toward the Village, and halfway up they could see the remains of the model home that had burned down in the first fire. Tractors and forklifts and stacks of materials were parked along Esquiline, indicating that a cleanup had commenced. At the top of the slope, where Carmel Valley Road ran, they could just see the handicapped facility of Robles Vista through what remained of the grasses and trees.

They stopped the car on Esquiline along a fence just before they came to Rosie's Bridge. Pointing to the narrow lane that ran along the river to their right, a dirty street sign read SIESTA COURT.

"We'll just put ol' Hitchcock back on his leash and take him for a sedate walk," Paul said. "Don't worry, you are unrecognizable."

"Oh, why not." They turned the corner and began walking down Siesta Court, trying not to look conspicuous as they passed the houses.

Nina thought more about the Spanish and Mexican history of the area as they strolled up to the road sign and turned right. Don José Manuel Boronda, Doña Catalina Manzanelli de Munras, and many other figures from the past had lived, loved, and died along the banks of the Carmel River. They built adobe houses, they nurtured pears, grapes, apricots, nectarines, cherries, they raised racehorses . . . they fought off the wildcats and coyotes, and even, until 1900, the grizzly bears that hunted through these wild lands. Though the grizzlies had gone, the occasional mountain lion still prowled along the riverbanks.

On the river side of Siesta Court a wall of riprap bordered the street, softened by buttercups and shooting stars that managed to root in and beautify the ugly concrete. A path made by owners and their dogs ran along the top, and they walked along it. The riverbed below on their left was at least eighty feet wide, only a streamlet hinting at its winter might. On the far side, a bank overgrown with laurel bushes lay below the scars of the first arson fire.

They reached the shadow of a mighty oak that had been allowed to remain when the riprap was laid down, one of the ubiquitous *robles* that lent their name to everything around here.

Across the lane, snug under the leaves, a few houses slept in a straggling row. On this hot, still afternoon, the lane was quiet. A couple of golden retrievers came sniffing out from their naps under the trees.

"Imagine what the Green River development will do to this street," Nina said, looking across the river to the hillside. "These folks will be staring at a hillside of identical roofs instead of greenery. Actually, the people in the condos will be looking down at them. It'll be like moving from the country to the city without even having to pack."

Paul pulled a piece of paper out of his pocket and studied it. "Let's start at this corner. That first house, with the chain-link fence around it—that's owned by a couple named George and Jolene Hill."

"How do you know that?"

"Went on the Web while you were getting dressed and accessed the county real-estate records. Since we were coming out here."

"You're good. I'm impressed."

"Especially in bed." He drew a finger down her sleeve. "Ah. I can still make you blush. A hard-nosed legal eagle like you."

The yard was lush with hollyhocks and roses. A tire swing hung off the tree beside the old white cottage. BEWARE OF DOG, said a metal sign affixed to the fence. Nina saw a dog bowl on the porch. "Gardeners?" she said.

"Let's see now. George and Jolene have lived here since 1970," Paul said. "That's when they bought it, anyway. Paid forty thousand for the property. The house is probably worthless, but they do have a half-acre. The land alone must be worth more than half a million now."

"That much?"

They were now across from the second house. A bigger contrast could not be imagined. The Hill house on the corner was set modestly back from the road, but this house with its two stories and portico sat right on the street and seemed to fill the whole lot.

"Theodore and Megan Ballard," Paul said. "Bought six years ago, just before the river flooded. Razed the old house and built this postmodern thing." A blue BMW convertible sat in the driveway. "Somebody's a telecommuter," Paul said. "I can smell the vanilla soy latte from a mile away."

"No sign of kids," Nina said. "Big incomes and they collect retro fifties furniture, is my guess."

"Living the good life. I'm gonna say, a pair of computer analysts."

"Techies. And the house is all made of ticky-techie." At a tall laurel that overhung the riprap, they caught up with Hitchcock, who was involved in an investigation of his own.

"Okay. Grass and neat flower beds on Number Three, middle of the block, old house but big and comfortable," Nina said. "A home-loving woman lives here."

"You're such a sexist. Men make better gardeners."

"Men are good with grass, I agree. But not with these delicate flowers, not with these pretty patterns," Nina said.

"Well, all I can say is that Sam and Debbie Puglia own this place," Paul said, consulting his notes.

"Looks like a big new deck out back. I wonder if that is where the party will be." As Nina spoke, a middle-aged woman in shorts and a halter lumbered out the back door, which they could see at an angle, and disappeared onto a corner of the deck. Paul and Nina turned toward the river and stood together.

"Debbie?"

"The age is right. Sam and Debbie bought the house twenty years ago, and she's in her mid-forties, I'd guess."

"Sam's at work," Nina guessed. "Debbie doesn't have a car. She likes Sam to drive anyway and she has plenty to do at home during the day."

"See how easy it is, this investigating?" Paul said. "You just generalize and stereotype and it all comes together."

"We could be dead wrong."

"We probably are. But we can learn something from houses, from the way they're kept, that sort of thing."

"My picture of that lady over there doesn't include sneaking up the hill at night to set fires." Nina knelt down to give Hitchcock a pat. "Doesn't it have to be a man, from Wish's description?"

"No. Recall that he didn't get that opportunity to 'grab

and twist.' He just thought about it, right after he went down."

"It must be a man. He killed Danny with a rock. He attacked Wish. He sets fires."

"There you go again. I ever tell you about the woman weight lifter from Los Angeles who strangled her boyfriend? It took four cops to subdue her."

"Come on, Paul. There's the witness who saw two men in a car—"

"We shall keep our minds open. Now, moving right along. House Number Four."

A small, well-kept house behind a white picket fence. An old Ford pickup and a beat-up minivan in the driveway, and an open screen door, from which issued the wail of a small child. "Meet Darryl and Tory Eubanks," Paul said. "Inherited their home from Charles L. Eubanks twelve years ago."

"A young couple with kids."

"Couldn't have afforded to buy it," Paul went on, keeping up the guessing game.

"No time for the yard." They looked the place over. A rusty swing set painted blue during some optimistic past was just visible in back.

"Salt of the earth," Paul said, and they passed by. "Now we come to a place owned by somebody named Rafferty, but that's got to be Ben Cervantes's place." It was the smallest house on the block, set well back on a gravel driveway amid mature trees, a tiny cottage on a narrow lot.

Number Five. So Danny Cervantes had lived there. Wish had sat on that slapdash front porch with the kitchen chairs. Nina would be back there in a few hours, knocking on the door.

"Ben must be renting," Nina said, starting the ball rolling.

"Saving up his money to get married and buy his own house."

"There's no car in the driveway."

"Ben's at work. He repairs cars, right? He must have a new job." Paul flipped to another part of his notebook and read, "Valley European Motors. I guess he must consider that a step up from the place that closed down, where Danny also worked."

"Here we are. Last house on the street. Number Six. What a contrast." Another enormous two-story house, with a balcony that looked unused, Mediterranean style, the brick driveway lined with urns full of geraniums.

"That's a big house," Nina said. "Bigger than the techie house."

"Our hosts, David and Britta Cowan," Paul said. "Paid three-fifty four years ago, and, like the techies, tore down the old place and raised up this monstrosity that's probably worth a million now."

"Oh, it's not that bad. It's just pretentious. Very pretentious."

"It's pink."

"Terra-cotta."

"It has colonnades."

"You mean those pillars by the front door?"

"I hope David is a colonel. To match his colonnades. But this doesn't look like the home of a military man."

"Or a man on a military pension," Nina agreed. "Look at the yellow car. Someone is home."

"A Porsche 944 convertible," Paul said. "It's a safe guess that they don't have kids."

"I hate Porsches," Nina said. "They look like roaches to me, scuttling down the road."

"I love Porsches. I think they're hot. But I think we have the Cowans pegged," Paul said. "Hmm. David Cowan. I've heard that name. He's an astronomer, I believe. Connected with MIRA, the Monterey Institute for Research in Astronomy. The institute was just a fabulous dream for about twenty years. They finally got their funds and built a telescope up on Chews Ridge."

"Sounds interesting," Nina said. "But it doesn't sound like the right résumé or look like the car of an arsonist."

"We shall see," Paul said.

They had completed their tour of the street. "Can we go back to the car?" Nina asked. They walked back along the riprap trail.

And lo and behold, an old white Cutlass, dented and dirty, had just parked across Esquiline Street. Cats were running toward it from everywhere.

"She's here!" Nina said. "The Cat Lady!"

PART TWO

We saw with our eyes the vermin sink
And what's dead can't come to life I think.

9

UNDER A SPREADING oak tree in the parking lot across the street, in deep shade, a woman got out and crouched. But she was not alone. Out of the woods the cats came tumbling.

Cats! Not quiet kitties, but yowlers, crowders, squeakers, meowers, pushing at each other, expressing their wild joy in fifty different sharps and flats, which ecstatic yet contentious sounds were accompanied by the scrape of many small cans being set down and pushed around on asphalt.

The woman didn't notice Paul and Nina, watching openmouthed. All they could see of her was straight gray hair and a baggy black sweatshirt.

The Cat Lady! Nina could hardly believe their luck. Pulling Paul behind a tree, she said, "How do we approach her? Make something up? I could be looking for my lost tabby and—"

"Relax," Paul said. "Let's just be honest. It's more efficient."

"Then how come I'm going to the party undercover tonight?"

"Because an arsonist will probably be there, who doesn't want to be discovered. The Cat Lady, well, she's a cat lady, a special breed. Stop it, Hitchcock! Let's get that mutt in the Bronco before he rips your arm off."

"Anything like the sound of a cat makes his heart go pit-a-pat," Nina said, misquoting the great Robert Browning.

Paul opened the back and patted the floor. Hitchcock gave a last yearning look and then jumped neatly in. Nina saw him press his nose against the back window and heard him sob like a puppy when he realized they were going over there without him.

"You know, I'm starting to get attached to your mutt," Paul said as they crossed the carless street. "Hmm. How come everything I say to you sounds obscene?"

"He's not a mutt."

"He is a mutt. Malamutes don't bark much, and Hitchcock does. He's got the hair of a black Lab, the slobber of a golden retriever, and the courage of a Chihuahua."

"Stop maligning my dog. He loves me and he brings me my paper," Nina said. "Which is more than I can say about most—"

The cats were taking notice of them. Several fled into the woods. More stayed right at the food cans. The woman stood up. She was tall and thin, like the Pied Piper, but she had forgotten her red-and-yellow scarf. The sweatshirt said IRON MAIDEN WORLD PIECE TOUR 1983 and featured some menacing grimacing from the band's notorious rotting mascot, Eddie.

"Did you have to do that?" she demanded. "They were trying to eat."

"Sorry. My name is van Wagoner. I'm investigating the arson fires in this area." Paul opened his wallet and flashed what looked like a badge, and Nina thought, Uh huh, let's just be honest. "This is Nina," Paul went on offhandedly. Nina shrank into the obscurity of Just the Girlfriend.

Saying nothing, the Cat Lady folded her arms. She would have been nondescript, pale, no makeup, a plain, early-wizening face, specs, stringy hair with long straight bangs, but for the fact that she was almost as tall as Paul. She bent, though, as though all her life she had been trying to hide it.

"I'm sorry, your name was smudged in the report I was

given about the car you witnessed driving from the second arson scene," Paul said in an official tone.

She peered at him and said, "Ruth Frost." Her voice was quite certain of itself.

"Of course."

"You could have made an appointment, and not disturbed the little ones. Some of them won't want to come back. You scared them."

"Can't they catch mice or crayfish around here?" Nina said.

"Not if they grew up in a nice warm house with cat food in the kitchen."

"It's nice of you," Nina said.

"They're starving. I have to do something." They all watched the cats as they polished off the tins of cat food. These cats were thin, unkempt, and suspicious. Nina tried not to generalize as she looked back at Ruth Frost.

"It must get expensive," Paul said.

"I would be happy to accept a contribution." This lady was smarter than she looked. Paul raised his eyebrows, said "It's a good cause," got his wallet, and gave her a twenty. She tucked it in her pocket.

"May I have five minutes of your time?" he went on.

"We can sit right here at the boathouse." They sat on a concrete step in the sunshine. Across the street to the east the Siesta Court sign hung disreputably from its pole, and Nina could just see the riprap. Rosie's Bridge crossed the river just in front of them.

"Your address?" Paul said.

"I live with various friends around here. I sleep in my car sometimes." Nina glanced at the Cutlass and thought she saw a mattress in the back seat.

"Do you have a phone number where I could reach you?"

"No. I'm usually here in the middle of the afternoon. If you need to talk to me again." She kept her eye on the cats, who were beginning to melt into the surrounding trees. "Bye, dearies," she said.

"Where are you from, Ms. Frost?"

"Ruthie. I've been here forever. When I was young we lived in Milwaukee."

"You and your parents?"

"Yes. They're dead."

"How do you get along?" Nina asked.

"Just fine. I'm not just a homeless person, you know. I am not a welfare case or some anonymous person to be pitied. I am a writer."

"How interesting. What kind of—"

"I'm writing a book on political philosophy. How do you vote?"

"What?"

"Republican, Democrat, you know. How do you vote?"

"Um," Nina said. She looked at Paul.

"How do *you* vote?" he asked Ruth Frost.

"I don't. Voting is futile since both political parties are interchangeable. Here. These are my Twelve Points. The *Monterey Herald* published them in the Letters to the Editor last year." She handed Paul a folded piece of paper from her pocket. "I am going to revolutionize American society when the Twelve Points are fully explained in my book," she said. "But it's hard to get an agent. Ayn Rand had the same problem at first."

"I will study them," Paul said.

"Somebody has to cut through it and tell the truth," she said.

"Now, Ms. Frost—"

"Ruthie. I don't like the patronymic."

"I understand that you saw a building burn down two weeks ago here in the Village."

"Yes. The Newbie Café. That's what the locals called it. It used to be Village Auto Repair. The owner used to let me feed cats in the parking area behind the shop. But he lost his lease to a couple from San Jose and they opened a restaurant for rich people this spring. All on behalf of almighty Moloch. A useful business was replaced by fatty Atlantic salmon sandwiches. Which are farmed and live out their lives in unhealthy conditions. Only buy wild Alaskan salmon. That is my advice."

She paused for a breath, then went on, "Sometimes twenty cats came. It was the middle of the night on a Thursday and I was asleep in the lot in my car. The new owners told me I couldn't park there overnight anymore, as if they had some use for the lot in the middle of the night. What do you think of the notion of private property? Ayn Rand was brilliant, but what a rightist capitalist apologist she was. What do you think of Ayn Rand?"

"So you were awakened from your sleep?"

"My sleep in the car? Or the great sleep we all pass our lives in? What do you think of Buddhism?" She paused and smiled a little, obviously not expecting an answer. Her attitude was one of benevolent condescension, as though they were a few more benighted strays who had come from the forest to receive her help.

"Oh, you want to limit yourself to your small incident. Yes. I was awakened from my sleep. I smelled smoke and the fire exploded out the windows. Glass everywhere. I started my car and drove on Carmel Valley Road toward the fire station. A van passed me and took a hard left onto Esquiline. The windshield was covered with ash and they were running the wipers—"

"They?"

"As I reported, there were two of them. Two heads, but I couldn't see them well, and the license plate was covered with smoky black stuff. It was an old van, beige, I think." Paul wrote this down, his forehead a map of concentration. "I'm not much good about cars. I knew they had set the fire—"

"How did you know that?"

Ruthie rolled her eyes. "Because they threw an empty

can of kerosene out the window as they turned the corner. I have reported this several times."

"No kidding," Paul said. "I didn't know about that."

"I suppose your bureaucracy doesn't communicate with the other bureaucracies. So. They were ecoterrorists, I suppose. I am against this sort of ecoterrorism because living things perish. The issue is quite simple if you look straight at it."

"Did you stop for the can?"

"No. I followed the bastards. I didn't stop for anything. I was way behind them at first and I don't think they saw me. I followed them down the hill and watched them turn left after Rosie's Bridge. Onto Siesta Court, right across the street there. I was going after them but just then a sheriff's car and two fire trucks came roaring down the hill and over the bridge and I had to wait. Then I turned. And I heard a door slam shut. And I saw the van or whatever it was start up and go careening around the far corner."

"Which house was the van in front of?"

"I couldn't tell. The other investigator asked me that. I know Danny Cervantes lives in one of those houses on that street, and I know he was killed in the latest fire, so it must have been his house. But I can't say I saw which house at the time. Some people came out of their houses to see what the commotion was about. They stood in the middle of the street and blocked it."

Paul chewed on the tip of his pen. "Did you know Danny Cervantes, Ruthie?" Nina said.

"He used to hang out at Kasey's in the Village in the morning with the other laborers, looking for work. He never hassled me like some of the others."

"Did you ever talk to him?"

"No. I can't believe how many innocent animals have been killed in these fires. Massacres. They didn't have a chance. Cats, squirrels, moles, snakes, bobcats, owls, wild turkeys—how many insects? The heavens shrieked." She started gathering up the empty cans and putting them in a trash bag.

"Well. Thanks for talking with us," Paul said.

"I hope you catch the other one. I hope he rots in hell. Hell being, of course, an absurd concept."

"So long." Nina and Paul walked back across the street. Nina's jaunty mood had evaporated.

They got back into the car. Hitchcock stuck his head between the seats.

Once they were back on Carmel Valley Road, she said, "I keep thinking that if she'd been born rich, she'd be considered an eccentric grande dame. She'd be a philanthropist and receive humanitarian awards at fancy receptions. But—"

"She gave up on humanity and cast her fate to the cats," Paul said. "I always liked oddballs."

"I think she'll make a credible witness anyway."

"Then it's someone on that block. But consider this. She's a big woman. She makes her own rules. She could have set the fires."

"But she loves all the animals!"

"Who knows how her mind actually works?" Paul reached into his pocket with one hand and gave Nina the folded paper. "Here's a clue. Let's hear the Twelve Points she gave me."

Expelling a sigh, Nina said, "Okay. It's handwritten. Up at the top there's no information. It just says POINTS in caps.

" 'ONE. Obscenely wealthy people should have their wealth taken.'

" 'TWO. We're all so hypnotized you can't tell what the reality out there is, if any.'

" 'THREE. Men like to be passive in bed.' " Paul gave an incredulous half-laugh.

"Don't get all defensive, now," Nina said.

"She's off her rocker."

" 'FOUR. Women resent being violated and make sure men get punished for it.' "

"That does explain a lot about modern society," Paul said.

"Listen. 'FIVE. Cold sensationalists is what we are. At least the feudal system allowed people comforting illusions to compensate for their misery, like religion and romantic ideals.'

" 'SIX. We are miserable because we are creatures in conflict between our bodily instincts and our half-evolved minds. The truth is, we don't think very well.'

" 'SEVEN. Abortion is terrible. It only exists because our society does not support motherhood.' "

"I knew it would come down to abortion," Paul said.

"She's right," Nina said.

"You're not serious."

"Hey, abortion is terrible. That doesn't mean we don't need it. Let me continue. 'EIGHT. There is a class system in America. Two classes: the exploited and the exploitees.' "

"Hmm. Sometimes it certainly feels that way."

" 'NINE. They pay us as little as they can and make sure to take any extra by turning us into insatiable consumers of unnecessary things.'

"This is a long one, Paul. She goes on, 'The income-tax deduction for homeowners benefits banks and lenders, not homeowners. The purpose is to encourage enormous loans, not ownership. Who owns their property outright? We are carefully distracted from noticing that we are actually paupers.' "

"I'm starting to like this lady philosopher. Keep going."

" 'TEN. The stock market panics when the unemployment rate goes down. The system relies on workers' misery.'

" 'ELEVEN. Divorce is encouraged because it leads to small households, which benefits consumerism. The ideal is for each person to buy a house, furnish it, duplicate everything. Extended families are discouraged because they share resources.'

" 'TWELVE. New products are mostly old products we already have. Unnecessary refinements are added so we'll throw away the old and bring in the new.' There's one more. It says, in caps again, 'CONCLUSION:'—" Nina stopped.

"Well, what's the conclusion? I'm dying to hear it," Paul said, eyes on the road as he took a sharp curve.

"That's it. She stops right there. Actually, she wrote something, but it's crossed out."

"Can you make it out?"

"No, she put x's through it and then squiggles."

"I'm going to have to ask her," Paul said. "I can't stand the suspense."

"Are you making fun of her?"

"She could use a good editor."

"She's half pathetic and half brilliant," Nina said. "A seeker. I notice she doesn't mention love anywhere."

"She's a political philosopher. Like Tina Turner. 'What's love got to do with it—' "

Paul changed lanes. He looked dashing in his sunglasses. Nina leaned over and kissed his cheek. She said in his ear, "What did you think of her theory that men like to be passive in bed?"

"I would debate that with her anytime, anyplace," Paul said. "Anyway. She's a crackpot."

"Can I keep the Twelve Points? Someday they might be worth something, like Ayn Rand's manuscripts."

"Be my guest." They came to the turning lane for the Mid-Valley Safeway. Paul went on, "An overwhelming urge has come over me. To insatiably consume some unnecessary things."

"What things?"

"Paper towels. Rug cleaner. Some blueberries for my breakfast and some steak for my dinner, since you will be partying and I have to eat alone."

"Go for it," Nina said. "I'll stay in the car with Hitchcock." While she waited, she read over the Twelve Points again. "What do you think, Hitchcock?"

But Hitchcock, uninterested in these all-too-human epiphanies, was asleep.

10

"BEN?" NINA KNOCKED again on the door of the old bungalow on Siesta Court.

It was quarter to six on this long summery Saturday afternoon. She could hear the stream flowing behind the riprap wall and smell the inimitable pungency of charcoal lighter fluid mixed with animal fat. The party must already be starting two doors down at the Puglias'.

She felt like a narc. Paul did it all the time, but she wasn't sure she could carry this off. Again, she mentally counted the houses on the street: David and Britta Cowan in the big house on her left on the corner, Ben's door right in front of her, Darryl and Tory Eubanks's roof past a fine fir tree on the right, and past that, the Puglias, then Ted and Megan Ballard, and finally the Hills. She could hear kids screaming somewhere and the thought came, maybe one of them was a kid, arsonists are often young.

Ben opened the screen. "You're early."

"I love a good party." She went into the dim low-ceilinged living room with its tweed couch and shook hands with Ben, who wore a black T-shirt and jeans. Condolence cards lay on the coffee table where they had been tossed. Someone had brought a huge flower arrangement, which still sat by the door.

He didn't smile, and his eyes still had the puzzled, hurt look that comes with the shock of sudden death. Though he couldn't be older than his early thirties, Ben's face was lined and the tops of his ears were red as if from a permanent sunburn. She imagined he worked outside at least some of his day at Valley European Motors. None of this made him any less attractive. "Thanks for letting me tag along," she said.

Ben sat down and said, "Anything, if it helps you find the killer of my nephew. I can't sleep at night. He died so young, and while he was in my care. He played the flute. See it there, on the table?" The black flute case lay half-buried by the flowers like a miniature casket. "Danny's flute," he repeated, shaking his head.

"We have the same goal in mind," Nina said, sitting down beside him. "I know my friend Wish didn't set any fires, so I don't see how Danny could be involved."

"What is Wish to you?" Ben asked. She apologized mentally to Paul, because she couldn't help enjoying sitting next to him. He had warm brown eyes in a smooth face in which she glimpsed the sun-drenched walls of a Yucatán pyramid.

"He worked for me. He helped with my law-office work at Tahoe. His mother is—was—my legal secretary."

"Why are you here instead of at Tahoe? Is that why Wish was down here, too?"

"That's a long, irrelevant story, Ben."

He accepted this. In his soft voice he said, "We buried Danny this morning at the Catholic cemetery in Monterey. He was sort of Catholic. I said some things."

"Who came to the cemetery?"

"My brother and his wife—Danny's parents—came down from Tahoe, but they had to get back to work and they left right after. A couple of his cousins came too, and my sister and her husband. We decided to keep it small, even though some of the neighbor ladies wanted to come and have a meal after."

"I'm sure Wish would have come if he could."

"I guess. I don't know what went on between them, but Danny—he gets so irritable, maybe Wish just had enough.

Danny had a hard time making friends. He used to go out to Cachagua and spend the evening at Alma's with his buddy Coyote. I didn't even know how to call his buddy to tell him Danny's dead."

"Cachagua? I haven't been there in a long time. I don't remember a place called Alma's."

"There's only one bar in the place. It used to be the Dew Drop Inn."

"Oh, sure."

"You know it? You don't look like the kind of person who would go there."

"Well, I haven't always been thirty-five," Nina said. "Ben?" Ben had immersed himself in a sad reverie. "Do you have a picture of Danny? I'm trying to get to know him, understand him."

"Sure." Ben went into the bedroom and came out with some snapshots.

A long, lanky, long-haired Native American boy, she thought. She could not see his face, hidden by a baseball cap. In one photo, Danny stood by a fence post, some scrubland behind him; in another, Danny sat at Ben's kitchen table, a beer in hand, his head down, still wearing the cap.

"That's the concho belt?" Nina said, showing him the outdoor shot.

"That's it. Other than that belt, he didn't care about clothes."

"He doesn't look happy in this picture in your kitchen."

"That was the day after he was laid off," Ben said. "He was low. I told him he could get another job, but he said he didn't want to look yet. I'd come home from work and he'd be laying on the couch watching sports, anything that was on in the afternoon."

"Do you think he was depressed?"

"You start depressed," Ben said. "You feel hopeless, like you just can't make it. You don't have money to take a girl out, get parts for your car, nothing. Finally one day, if you're lucky, you put your head down like a bull and you get out there and try to find work, whatever it takes."

Nina nodded. "I've been there," she said, and it was true.

"I didn't know if Danny was going to make it that far until a couple months ago he told me he was doing some yard work for George Hill. Then Mr. Cowan hired him for some odd jobs. You know, he always wanted to be part of the neighborhood. Be one of the guys. But we were the outsiders on the street."

"Outsiders?" Nina said.

"*Sí.*" He's subtle, Nina thought. That one Spanish word had explained pretty well why he and Danny had been considered outsiders. "Danny is half Washoe, half Mexican-American. His mom is a full-blood Washoe. I'm not related to her or the Washoes."

"He wanted to belong, you said before."

"Maybe because he never had any roots. He didn't even have a brother or sister to fight with. Anyway, everybody in the neighborhood suddenly figured out how good Danny was with his hands. He was working thirty or forty hours a week, gardening, repairing stuff, building a shed for George, doing errands for Debbie—it was like he had a family here. He had some money in his pocket and he started living again, making plans."

"What kind of plans?"

"Same old thing. The other thing Danny needed besides a family was to make it big. When he was feeling good, it was always about getting the money fast. One night I said, 'For what?' And he told me, 'Maybe start a business you and me can run ourselves.' "

Nina nodded.

"I didn't blame him. Our parents came into this world poor and they're gonna leave poor. Danny didn't want to do the same, but look what happened. He was murdered. He died at twenty-one. And now people think he was a bad person."

Ben shook his head. "Is it bad to want the same thing we all want, a better life for us and our families? Enough money to live"—he looked around the cottage—"better than this? The system . . . it relies on workers' misery."

He got up. "Well, let's do it. The party goes on no matter what. People come and go, but the party stays right here on this street, once a month, Saturday night."

He stretched out a hand and Nina let him help her up. She watched him tuck in his shirt in back. He didn't really notice her; the life had been kicked out of him for now. "Ben, I understand you're not in a party mood."

"I have other reasons for going. Reasons you don't need to worry about. So, let's get our story straight, okay? You're my old high-school girlfriend, around for the summer. Right?"

"Right. What high school did we go to?"

"Douglas High, up at Tahoe."

They walked down his gravel driveway to the street, turned left, and, passing the Eubanks house with its brightly lit windows, turned into Sam and Debbie Puglia's concrete drive. Balmy evening air carried the charcoal and wood smoke drifting through the forest. The laughter of children and the clinking of glasses emanated from the backyard.

"This house has been around awhile," Nina said.

"They keep it up. Debbie is the street housemother. She's always around, doing her projects. She and Sam like having the block parties. They like to know their neighbors, get close. Let's go around back."

They climbed the stairs to a wooden gate festooned with miniature white lights, which seemed to wrap all around the big deck the Puglias had built for entertaining. Nina felt panicky, and Ben wasn't going to help much. She reminded herself that this wasn't her social debut. Nobody should care about her if she kept a low profile. She was there to observe and keep quiet.

She didn't expect much. Nobody would inadvertently let fall that he was an arsonist. She couldn't ask many questions.

But if the Cat Lady was right, tonight she might meet an arsonist.

Would she know him when she met him? Keep an open mind, she reminded herself.

"Oh, my poor Ben. Poor, poor Danny. We are so sorry." A middle-aged woman in a Hawaiian sundress rushed over to greet them, her arms held out. Nina, with Paul, had seen her that afternoon on the deck. The woman pulled Ben to her and held him as tight as a lug nut on a tire, patting his back. When she released him her eyes were wet with tears. "Such a loss," she said. "I can't imagine."

"Thank you," Ben replied.

He had some dignity, some presence. Nina had already realized that she liked him. Hope it's not him, she thought to herself, but he was young and strong. He could commit arson. His kindness could be a pose, and his cooperation with her could be a way of defusing the opposition.

"And you brought a date! Introduce us, Ben."

"Uh, here's a good friend of mine from high school. Visiting in Monterey this summer. Nina."

"Hi there, Nina. I'm Debbie Puglia." Debbie took a small step forward and Nina took a small step back, not wanting to suffer Ben's fate. Debbie wore a lot of makeup and had one of those faces that exaggerate emotion. Nina thought guiltily of Tammy Faye Bakker. Debbie went on, "You know, Nina, in all these years, Ben has never brought a guest before."

"Thanks for letting me join you."

"I'm glad you have company tonight, Ben. Oh, it's so awful. We stopped by but you weren't home. Is there anything we can do? We don't know what to think. Danny—"

"Let 'em in, Debbie. Yo, Ben. Cerveza for you. Let me guess. White wine for your friend." A short beer-bellied man came up and slipped his arm around Debbie's waist.

"This is Ben's friend Nina. Nina, my husband, Sam."

"Hello, pretty lady. What can I get you?"

"White wine sounds great."

Sam turned to Ben. "I don't know what to say about Danny, man. Let's get drunk first, okay?"

"Sure, I'll have a beer." They followed Sam onto the deck. A hundred silver lights twinkled festively along the railing. A cluster of fluttering candles and a red vinyl table-cloth decorated the big table in the center of the deck. Some dishes had already been laid out: a big bowl of tortilla chips, salsa, and guacamole.

Branches hung over the deck and about ten adults stood around in small groups. Off the deck, in the darkening backyard, Nina watched small children flitting in and out of the trees and a pair of older kids jumping on a huge tram-poline, yelling as they flipped and bounced.

Sam went over to a blue cooler and Nina saw a bulky young man who looked like a football player standing at the charcoal grill, wearing a garish green-and-red apron. He noticed her looking at him, smiled, and waved.

"That's Darryl. He's cooking tonight. The men trade off," Debbie said beside her.

Ben was shaking hands with a lean young man in shorts and expensive running shoes, his ginger hair cut short. Next to him stood a tall athletic woman, her face all angles, also with short hair brushed back, also glowing with health.

"Meet Ted and Megan. The Ballards."

"Hi."

Ted and Megan wore the determined, agreeable look of those who come out of duty. They shook hands with Nina. "Wow," Megan said to Ben. "We're just floored. We're sorry, Ben, we really are. No matter what Danny did, we are really sorry." She and Ted stood so close they might have been one body. Both had the overdeveloped calves of fanatical bikers, both held diet sodas. They had identical earnest, sympathetic expressions.

"He didn't do anything," Ben said. "He was up there

with his friend, trying to catch the firebug. The real arsonist murdered him."

Megan nodded politely, but Nina didn't think Ben's words had made any impact on her. "I can't believe he's gone," Ted Ballard said. "Did you know him, Nina?"

"No."

"I'm not going to say he was perfect," Ben said.

"You don't think it was him? I mean, don't the police have his friend in custody? It said in the paper—" Ted said.

Sam returned, holding an icy bottle for Ben and a tumbler full of wine for Nina. She sipped. Cheap plonk. It tasted like it came out of one of those gallon boxes of wine you could buy at the supermarket, but she didn't really mind. White wine was like chewing gum for her, a guilty pleasure, and she was glad tonight to feel it building a numbing buffer between her and her tingling nerve ends.

She felt like the target of an eyeball inquisition all around her. Was it so astounding that Ben would bring a date? With her body language, she tried to tell them all, I'm not here. Pay no attention to the woman knocking back the cheap white wine.

Debbie was back. "Let me introduce you to the rest of the Siesta Court Bunch," she said, leading Nina from her haven at Ben's side. "It's a sad occasion tonight, what with Danny and all. But we try to get together whatever the weather. We're kind of cut off here on the river by ourselves, so we try to be good neighbors. Is Ben really all right?"

"He's managing. Uh, your house is so nice, and your flowers are sensational," Nina said, setting her glass down for the moment. A tumbler this size ought to last the evening, if she wanted to last the evening. She noticed that Sam, talking to Darryl at the barbecue, was waving a bottle of Jack Daniel's. He poured himself a healthy dose on ice.

"Oh, I just love puttering around our place," Debbie said. "Sam goes to his office and now that our kids are at college I have the whole day to myself."

Hey, thought Nina, maybe Paul and I do have ESP. Debbie had just confirmed exactly the fiction they had invented for the Puglias. Somewhat encouraged by this, she allowed Debbie to shepherd her over to the couple standing at the railing.

"Ben finally brought somebody to the party," Debbie told the couple. "This is Nina. Nina, this is David Cowan and his wife, Britta. They live on the corner."

Nina flashed to the big concrete house with "colonnades" next to Ben's place. The Cowans. Yellow Porsche. Hmm. Pretentious sprang to mind.

"Pleased to meet you," Britta Cowan said. Her husband held back, smiling slightly. They hadn't been talking to each other. Like Sam's glass, Britta's glass held a cascade of ice cubes, but she was already due for a refill on the whiskey. She shook her empty glass, turning full-face to Nina.

Whoa!

Nina looked back, and found herself staring straight into green eyes shining with suppressed rage. Britta was a knockout, a blond with a lush body straining against the stretch in her black minidress, curving expanses of freckled, fine skin on full display. She kept shaking the ice, swaying slightly, while the others seemed to circle around her.

Her husband was the afterthought. He adjusted his glasses. Nina got an academic impression. He wasn't wearing a corduroy jacket with leather patches on the elbows, but he should have been.

What he wore was baggy shorts and a baggy shirt. And, if she was not mistaken, a gold Piaget Emperador watch on his wrist.

Debbie shifted her weight from one foot to another, clearly not comfortable, while Britta gave Nina the twice-over.

"I didn't think Ben had it in him," she said finally. "You're not bad."

"Excuse me?" Nina said.

"Britta, behave," David said.

"Don't you people recognize a compliment when you hear one?" Britta said. She sidled up so close to Nina, she could practically rub against her, and her moves suggested she intended exactly that level of invasion. "Where you from?"

"Tahoe. But I'm spending the summer down here."

"Doing what?"

"Just hanging around for a while."

"How nice for you. So many of us work for a living."

"What do you do?"

"I arrange expensive, exotic trips for lazy rich people at Carmel Valley Travel in the Village."

"Interesting?"

"No, but it gets me out of the house. Once in a while, if the boss isn't looking and a promotion is heavily discounted, I get to do a preview. Adventure travel. Now, that's fun." She paused and licked lasciviously at her glass, then looked at Nina appraisingly again, and said, "You cruise?"

Nina tried to smile, but failed. "No. No," she said. "I get seasick. And what do you do?" she said to David Cowan. Before he could speak, his wife broke in.

"Oh, he rests on his laurels. You'll find them down there on his butt."

Debbie let out a nervous laugh.

David Cowan's expression didn't change. Nina picked up her wine and took a slug. He did the same. "Actually, I'm an astronomer," he said mildly.

"Really."

"With the Monterey Institute for Research in Astronomy."

Paul had mentioned that. Smart and detached, Nina thought. "Oh," she said. "I've heard of it."

"His head's in the clouds," Britta said, laughing gaily. She put her arm around Nina's shoulder. "Tell me, how is Ben?"

"He's all right. He's had trouble sleeping. He misses—"

Britta frowned. "No, no. Forget Danny. I mean, how is Ben? How is he in bed, you know? Do you and he actually do it? Because he's so good-looking and he lives like a eunuch." She leaned over and whispered into Nina's ear. "I wondered if maybe he was a—"

"God, Britta," David Cowan said, no inflection in his voice except maybe fatigue.

Britta's arm dropped from Nina. Her eyes swept the yard. "Wonder what Sam's up to over there with Darryl? Ooh. I see he's got the bottle." She whirled around and left them.

The three left behind each took another sip.

11

"So," Debbie said, wiping her mouth with her hand. "Look, it's Tory! Honey, you're late." She gave the other woman a hug. "Oh, goody, deviled eggs! Don't they look scrumptious!"

"Poor Ben, I'm so glad he came," Tory Eubanks said over Debbie's shoulder.

Nina looked past them, eyes drawn back to Britta, who continued her campaign to raid the personal space of every man and woman at the party. She snuggled up, whispered, got a rise out of them, and moved on, abrupt and capricious. She had already nipped at Sam and was trying now to get Darryl's glass from him.

Tory Eubanks looked in the same direction.

"Darryl's Tory's husband," Debbie told Nina brightly, waving toward the young man in the chef's apron.

"That bitch," Tory said, watching Britta fawn, feint, and paw. "The kids were at the movies and got home late, so I sent Darryl over to get started." She noticed Nina. "Hi."

"Hi. I'm Nina. Ben's friend."

"He told me you were coming. Nice to meet an old friend of Ben's. Did you go to the funeral?"

"No, I got here too late."

"We weren't invited either," Debbie said. "I would have been more than happy to have a get-together at Ben's house for his family. But they came and went so fast."

"Hello, David. How are you?"

"Tory," Cowan said.

There was no heat between these two, but did David Cowan actually have any heat at all? He seemed to be one of those acutely self-conscious people who make everybody feel awkward. Maybe living with Britta had done it to him. Nina couldn't think of anything else to say to him.

"Elizabeth here yet?" Tory asked Debbie. These two seemed to be good friends. Tory Eubanks was a lot younger, maybe thirty, a natural blond with blond eyebrows, no makeup, and lashless Sissy Spacek eyes. She wore a denim jumper and Birkenstocks.

"No," Debbie said. "But she said she's coming. Elizabeth's my sister," she explained, turning to Nina. "She lives way up on the hill in a house she designed herself, the lucky duck. She's so isolated up there. I try to get her down here to join our get-togethers."

"Well, I guess I'll go see what my husband is charring tonight." Tory looked over the railing. "Hey! Justin! Don't jump so hard with your little sister on that thing! Careful, now!" She wandered over to the table with her big plate of plastic-wrapped eggs, pushed a few things out of the way, and set them down.

Another couple appeared at the gate. More people! How would she ever remember them all! Debbie took Nina's arm and led her toward them and away from David Cowan. Just in time, Nina thought. She had almost gotten sucked into Cowan's vacuum back there, where you existed only as a personality-free blob of nonmatter.

"Oh, Jolene, what in the world?" Debbie asked. Jolene carried at least four dishes on a huge pewter tray. Debbie sniffed at the wrapped platters. "Yummy!" she said. To Nina she said, "Jolene's such a magnificent cook. She makes the party."

"It's nothing," Jolene said. Okay, Nina told herself, George and Jolene . . . Hill. Yes. The old cottage on the corner nearest Rosie's Bridge with the great garden and the chain-link fence.

"Tell," Debbie said, trying to peek under the foil. "What did you bring this time?"

"I tried a few new things, a spinach pie with a fancy Greek name I forget, a shrimp dish from Thailand, that mac and cheese George likes so much, and goulash," Jolene said. She was a sprightly woman in her sixties, wearing bright earrings and a well-cut pair of slacks.

Debbie and Nina helped her unload the food on the table. They removed the foil and found serving spoons for each dish. From the smell and look of these dishes, Jolene was more than a good cook.

"Well, just look at you," the elderly man named George said, coming up to them. "Miss Aloha 1982." Debbie blushed like a girl.

George Hill had gone straight over to greet a couple of the men. He was carrying a black musical-instrument case. About sixty-five, he was still puffing from climbing the short stairway up to the deck. His florid face told Nina that he wasn't well.

Sitting down on the redwood bench that ran along the railing with the case on his lap, he clicked it open and extracted a gleaming Spanish guitar. He swung it around his neck on its leather strap and let it rest on his paunch, then ran long, surprisingly graceful fingers across the strings.

He played a few chords, warming up, grinning at Debbie.

"George, this is Ben's guest, Nina—what was your last name, honey?"

"Balzac," Nina said, then bit her lip.

"Balzac? What kind of name is that? Hungarian or something?" George said.

"Yes, as a matter of fact."

"Maybe you could play us a Gypsy tune," George said. "I only play country myself."

"I can't wait to hear you," Nina said, smiling. She heard a crash behind her and they all turned around to see that at the other end of the deck near the grill, Britta had dropped her glass on the deck. She was barefoot, laughing, standing in the middle of the glass.

"Sam! Rescue me!" she cried. Sam Puglia stepped over the glass in his moccasins. Lifting her into his arms, he carried her a few steps, and set her down in safety.

Debbie ran into the house. She emerged moments later with a broom and began the cleanup. Darryl stooped down to pick up glass shards, putting them delicately into a plastic bag.

"Britta's lit," George told his wife. He looked at his watch. "Seven o'clock. Not even dark yet. This could be a record."

"The kids are having a great time in the yard, though, aren't they?" the woman said. "Hi there," she said to Nina. "I'm Jolene. I'm glad you're here. Ben needs a good friend right now. George and I have two granddaughters out there running wild in the woods tonight, Callie and April."

"Ah," Nina said.

"So how do you come to know Ben?" George asked. "You bein' a Hungarian and all."

"We went to high school together," Nina said.

"Where? In Tijuana?" He started laughing. "They have Hungarians down there?" He started to strum. "I know a Mex song. Marty Robbins. The best country song ever written. I dedicate this to Danny, rest in peace. He used to bring his flute over and play this with me sometimes. Good old Danny. Right, everybody? Let that boy rest now." He played a few chords, started fingerpicking surely and nimbly, then opened his mouth and started to sing in a startlingly beautiful baritone,

One little kiss and Felina, good-bye. . . .

" 'El Paso.' Gave away the best part," he said. "It's a tragic ending. Felina, sounds like a cat."

"I never thought of that," Jolene said. "Shall I get us something to drink?"

"And a couple of those deviled eggs Tory always brings. Save me some of your mac and cheese, don't forget. And don't even think about bringing me any of that crazy yuppie guacamole Megan makes, with all that spicy shit she puts in there."

"Well, I'm sure gonna have some," Jolene said. She winked at Nina. George started singing about how he shot a man in Reno just to watch him die. To Nina's surprise and delight, he was a terrific singer, gravelly and expressive.

Hearing the music, the liveliest thing happening in the yard, Britta came over to give him a kiss and flash her green eyes at him. He squeezed her waist. "Why does a blond wear her pants around her ankles?" he asked her.

"Tell me why."

"To keep her ankles warm."

Ted and Megan, who had also been drawn by the music, cringed.

"Why are men like linoleum?" Britta retaliated. "Because all you have to do is lay 'em, then you get to walk all over them for life."

"Come on, Nina," Jolene said. "I see you need a refill."

An actual wine bottle bobbed in melted ice in a tin pail on the table. Nina helped herself.

Ben came over to join them. Jolene said, "Ah, sweetie," and hugged him. Ben murmured something to her and she said, "We enjoyed him. He worked hard. It wasn't for charity, honey. Now then, you takin' care of yourself? You get that supper I put on your porch?"

"Sure did," Ben said. "Thanks." They started talking about the burial.

Nina wandered off, looking for Debbie. She found her in the kitchen on the phone. Hanging up, Debbie said, "That was Elizabeth. She wanted to stay home but I talked her into getting over here."

"Is Elizabeth your older sister?"

"No, younger by a lot of years, only thirty. I try to look out for her. She's shy, kind of like Ben. Intelligent, but she doesn't understand people. She's a conservationist. She's going to get her Ph.D. next year."

"That's something to be proud of."

"Is it ever. I never made it past high school. Married Sam, had our babies. We've been married twenty years. Our kids both went down to L.A. for college."

Smiling, Nina said, "That's also something to be proud of."

"Elizabeth is special. You might like each other. She'll be here in five minutes."

"Food's on the table!" they heard from the deck.

Jolene came in saying, "Where's that mac dish?"

"Well, in the oven. I forgot all about it."

"George gets grumpy when he doesn't get his mac and cheese." She put on two orange oven mitts and pulled a magnificent casserole with spicy peppers, tricolor chunks of melting cheese, and a crunchy paprika topping, out of the oven.

"Ow!"

"Oh, honey, you okay?"

"I'm going to get you some thicker mitts, Deb. Don't worry about it, I'm just clumsy tonight. We're all off-key because of Danny. I mean, we just got over the fire across the river, and now this. George's blood sugar has been all over the place."

"He's happy tonight."

"Yes, I think he's feeling better the last couple days."

"Britta's a sight tonight."

"I think Tory's pregnant. She's not telling yet."

The two women went out, Nina trailing behind.

The children had crowded onto the deck, bringing noise and chaos along. A separate table had been set up for them. Jolene, at Nina's side, said, "There's my dolls. Callie's got the red hair and April's the smaller one." The girls ran past them toward the food set up on the big table.

"Those over there are the Cowan boys. They run wild. Britta neglects 'em." Two small towheaded boys filled up their plates. One wore nothing but a sagging diaper and tiny red rubber boots.

"Darryl and Tory have four. There's Mikey, he's the oldest." Nina gave Mikey a sharp inspection. The handsome Eubanks kid with sunburned skin and light eyes was shaved to the skull like his dad in the current sports-figure style and couldn't have been older than thirteen. He couldn't have killed Danny or threatened Wish. Scratch the Eubanks kids, she thought.

"What about Ted and Megan? Do they have kids?"

"No. They want to have all their time for their biking and sailing and whatnot." Nina could see that Jolene couldn't countenance this. Jolene's lips pursed. She shook her head. She went on, "We better get our plates before it's all gone. I'm gonna go see what else George wants." George was entertaining them all with his guitar.

"He's talented, isn't he?" Nina said. She looked all the kids over one more time. They were all too young.

"Used to play in a country-western band. He didn't get anywhere. Then we started the nursery. Sold out and retired five years ago and we thought what with the money from that and the social security we were set. Just goes to show."

"How so?"

"Oh, you know, investments went down the tubes. Then our daughter ran into trouble. Drugs, I don't mind telling you. She almost lost the girls. We took 'em, George and me, and my daughter moved to Oklahoma City with her boyfriend. And now we have the girls to raise. Oh, it's fun. I love 'em to death. But George can't work anymore, he's got diabetes, and he worries about how to keep us." While she kept up this nonstop narrative, Jolene had drawn Nina to the railing.

"And then I had a stroke, nothing much, really, but it added to George's burdens, and he finally got a bright idea, that he'd subdivide our lot. It's deep, you know, goes back from the river two hundred feet. So we'd keep the house in front and sell the area in back. Nice lot like that would go for three, four hundred thousand. We'd be set."

"Sounds like a good plan."

"Well, just goes to show."

George stopped playing and beckoned to his wife. All the other men except for Ben surrounded him, plates piled high with food. In between bites, they were engaged in intense conversation, their voices low.

"Be right there, hon," she called, and went on, "You're gonna have a hard time believing this, but see that little old stream down there? Looks like nothing much, right? Well, this is a drought year, remember. A few years ago we had two winters in a row where it rained three months straight. The first winter, I just watched that water get muddier and faster and higher and didn't worry at all. There had never been a flood here or close to one in the thirty-six years we've lived here.

"So when it happened, the fire department, the neighbors, we were all took by surprise. About 4:00 A.M. in pouring rain in February, it came over the top, where the riprap is now, and rolled down the street and wiped it out. Rolled through our lot and flooded our house, took out the garden and the fences, and rolled like the Mississippi down the next street. Took out that street, houses and all. Believe it? We had to evacuate for two days. The Red Cross set up a tent by the bridge and made free dinners and we all got tetanus shots. Took us six months to fix up the house, and the other street? Took them the whole year."

"Amazing," Nina said.

"Kind of thing supposed to happen once in maybe a hundred years. But the next year it happened again. Believe it? It did. This time it took out the bridge. We were all ready to evacuate, we had our stuff out of the house, so it wasn't quite so bad as the first nasty surprise. Since then, that river has been sleepy as a baby. Probably never will get loco like that again."

"Jolene! You get me some food!" George hollered over the din. The singing over, and whatever conversation they had going interrupted by their frequent trips to the buffet for food, the other men dissolved into the crowd.

"Comin'! So anyways, we thought we were back to normal except for that puke-producing riprap the county put in and the new bridge. So George started getting ready to sell the Back Acre, that's what he calls it. Guess what happened. The county told us we couldn't do it."

"No."

"Yes, ma'am." Jolene folded her arms. "Right after the Green River development got approved. Some new commission passed an ordinance after the floods. George and I heard nothing about it until it happened. We sure didn't see it coming. The new law says you can't build, you can't remodel, you can't do anything within two hundred feet of the river. We can't subdivide."

Nina said, "Were you home when the model home across the river burned down?"

"It happened in the middle of the night. I heard the fire trucks and looked out and saw the smoke, so I woke George up and we went out to see what was the matter. Just about the whole block got up to watch it. I hate to say it, but I was glad to see it burn. And I'll tell you something else. I hope they decide not to rebuild. For thirty-six years I've come out my front door and seen a green hill and willows. I don't want to see fancy houses that somebody else got to build when we couldn't." Her mouth was set. "I'd be full of hate and bitterness, watching George and the girls struggling because we couldn't do the same."

"What are you going to do?"

"Trust in the Lord. What else can we do? Well, I know you'd like to talk to me some more, honey, but maybe later, okay?"

Jolene gave Nina a pat on the arm and wended her way

toward her husband, and Nina headed toward the food, thinking that she wouldn't want to come up against Jolene in court. That woman would be a huge hit with juries.

The adult neighbors sat down at their table, and Nina noticed they fell naturally into groups.

On the left end of the table, the Hills, the Eubankses, and Ben Cervantes.

On the right end, Ted and Megan Ballard, David and Britta Cowan.

In the middle, Sam and Debbie talked to both sides.

Even the food had been set on the table with some invisible demarcations. On one side, Jolene's "mac" dish along with Tory's deviled eggs and a big bowl of potato salad; in the middle, platters of ribs and chicken; on the right, in front of Ted and Megan, the Thai and Greek dishes, green salad, fruit salad, and soy milk in cartons. The liquor was similarly split into beer on the left and wine on the right, except for the whiskey glasses in front of Sam and Britta.

Sitting down next to Ben, Nina filled up her plate with starchy food. She pushed her wineglass back and Ben opened a bottle of Dos Equis for her.

Surprise, surprise, Jolene was holding forth at this end of the table, while George shoveled mac and cheese into his mouth and Darryl, Tory, and Ben listened with consternation.

"*And* she said she saw one of the arsonists pull into Siesta Court and drop the other one off!"

"The Cat Lady's nuts, though. You can't take somebody like her seriously," Darryl said. "Remember when Debbie invited her to one of the parties and we all had to listen to her Twelve Points?"

Ben said, "I didn't know she was that definite about what she saw."

"Yessir, she was buying cat food at the market—they

must give her a discount—and that's exactly what she told me. She said she doesn't know who it was but she thought it was men in the car."

"But it wasn't Danny," Ben said uncertainly. "The kid, Danny's friend Wish, says he and Danny were just trying to catch the guy."

Tory pushed her hair back and scratched her head. "But if Ruthie saw that, and it wasn't Danny, it'd have to be somebody else on this block."

"That's a good one," George said. "Like who?"

"Like you," Jolene said, and kissed him. "Maybe we should do a lineup," she went on. "The Cat Lady might be able to pick out the bad guy."

Tory looked around the table. Nina followed her eyes on each man: Tory's husband first, big Darryl; George Hill, already tired out from playing a few songs, drooping a bit over his plate; broad-shouldered, compact Ben; Sam, ignoring his food and pouring himself another shot of Jack Daniel's; Ted, talking animatedly to Britta and Megan about a hiking trip to New Zealand; and David Cowan, silent and birdlike at the far end of the table.

Hill broke the silence with a laugh. "It was probably Elizabeth," he said.

"Please don't hate me 'cuz I'm beautiful," Tory said in a high voice, laughing too. She took her husband's hand, and Nina saw Darryl wince.

Debbie said, "Hey. Watch what you say about my sister," but in a joking voice.

Jolene said, "Aw, Debbie, it's no reflection on you. It's not your fault she's got a burr up her ass."

"She's beautiful and smart and you're just jealous."

"She's Miss Priss," Jolene said, "but if she wants to come down the hill and slum with us regular folks, why, she's welcome. As long as I don't have to hear any more about keeping Robles untouched, now that she's built her glass house."

"Speak of the devil," Tory said, and nudged Debbie. "Your sister's here."

At the gate, Nina saw a young woman in a soft gray sweater and black leggings, toting a leather purse. She waved to Debbie, who jumped up and opened the gate and hugged her, then led her, holding her hand, toward the table.

Elizabeth seemed unsure of her reception, and from what Nina had been hearing, she could understand why. But Darryl jumped up too, and went to her and Debbie with a bottle of beer in his hand. "Hey, there," he said. "Glad you could make it."

An awkward silence ensued. Tory was glaring after Darryl. Nina happened to glance at Ben and saw that he was glaring at Darryl too.

12

SOMETHING HAD CHANGED for Nina as she ate dinner with the neighbors. Before, she had been an observer, but now she had become part of the party. It was like going to the theater and finding yourself on stage. She was involved in some sort of drama, and she didn't know the story line yet.

Or maybe she shouldn't have drunk that Dos Equis on top of the wine.

Elizabeth accepted the bottle. "Thanks," she said in a low voice. "Hi, all. Sorry I'm late." She had luminous skin and high cheekbones. She wore her shining black hair simply, in an old-fashioned straight bob with a fringe. On her the effect was ravishing.

"It takes a while to climb down from one o' them big redwoods," George Hill said. Jolene giggled at this.

Elizabeth went straight to Ben, sitting at the table, and put her arm around him. "I am so sorry," she said. "Are you all right?"

"I'm all right. Thanks for the flowers," Ben told her.

"Come sit with us—" Darryl started, but Megan called from the other side, "We saved a spot for you."

Smiling, Elizabeth said, "I need to say hi to Megan." She went to the group at the far side, and Ted and Megan made room for her between them. The loud conversations resumed, but Darryl seemed to have lost interest. He couldn't keep his eyes off the beautiful woman at the other end of the table. Tory, beside him, was seething.

Why, he's madly in love with her, Nina thought with dismay. Four kids under the age of thirteen, a devoted wife—how could he? No question, Tory must know, because Darryl was about as subtle about it as a chain saw biting into a chunk of hardwood.

Nina hoped he and Elizabeth weren't having an affair. She had liked Darryl, before.

Ben, too, seemed distracted by Elizabeth's presence, although he was not as obvious. Elizabeth didn't glance down the table again. She set her bottle of beer aside and poured herself some soy milk.

"You know what?" Tory said suddenly. "I'm going home."

"I'm not ready," Darryl said.

"Then stay here, damn you." Tory got up and went into the house, followed by Jolene and Debbie. Darryl started to rise, then sat back down again.

"She gets into these moods," he said.

Nina ate some more of Jolene's tasty pasta. The night was young, and she had a feeling that she'd better keep her strength up.

Jolene and Debbie returned from the kitchen without Tory and the party moved into a new phase as they all started moving around again. Nina helped carry endless paper plates and dump them into trash sacks while Sam and Darryl went out into the backyard, working on something. The kids ran back into the woods.

George took up his seat on the bench, picked up his guitar, and started playing, looking now and then at Britta, who hung on the deck railing.

Green eyes and white lies
Like a fool I fell in love
An' I'm haunted by the memory of her
Soft skin . . . so lost in

Dreams of those few nights together
I can't seem to forget her
Green eyes . . . and white lies

"That's your song, Sweet Lips," he said.

Megan and Ted gathered with Elizabeth and began talking intently, and Nina, reminding herself of her mission, drifted over to listen.

"He worked on David's Porsche a few weeks ago," Ted was saying.

"He did all kinds of odd jobs for David and Britta," Megan said. "Jolene got George to pay him a few bucks to clean up the Back Acre. He was immune to poison oak. I saw him back there a month or so ago, tearing up the brush, working hard. He did a good job, but he was troubled. He always looked so unhappy."

"But he'd lost his job," Elizabeth said. "Of course he was unhappy." She had moved aside slightly to let Nina join the group. Standing next to her, Nina smelled the strong soap she used, something expensive and fresh.

Megan said, "No, he always had a problem. But, listen, I'm being nice about this, here's what happened that same night. Danny was out front wrapping twine around the stuff he had pulled up, and Jolene invited him to dinner. Which would be okay, except they sat on the porch and George kept feeding him alcohol. You know some Native Americans have a big problem with that. Not to perpetuate a stereotype or anything."

"Alcohol should be banned," Ted said, and Elizabeth and Megan nodded. "Marijuana, there's nothing wrong with that. It doesn't make people go out and commit crimes."

"Wine is good for you in moderation," Elizabeth said. "That's not alcohol in the sense you're using it."

"We tasted the most incredible merlot at Galante Vineyards last weekend," Megan said. They talked about wine for a while, and Nina was about to leave when Megan suddenly returned to her earlier topic.

"Anyway, I heard Danny tell George that George was like a father to him. Danny was maudlin. And you know what that doofus George said?"

"What?"

"He said, 'You were my kid, you wouldn't be such a useless little loser.' He actually said that. Danny didn't say a word. He went up the street past our house toward home and he was crying. I saw him."

"That's the saddest thing I ever heard," Elizabeth said.

"Let's talk about something else," Ted said.

"How's the new place coming?" Elizabeth said.

"Oh, the permit process was terrible." Megan turned to Nina and said, "We're going to move up the hill from Siesta Court soon. Green River's going to ruin this street, so we're building up on the mountain, about a quarter mile from Elizabeth. And it's getting too . . . too . . . oh, you know, all the locals down here. God, the jokes tonight. I mean, get some wit." Ted and Elizabeth laughed.

"We had such a scare," Megan went on. "The fire on the ridge came within a hundred feet of our construction site, and we had just got the framing completed. Ted has spent every spare second up there for months. When we found out the next morning—Ted had a fit."

"Oh, look, they're building a bonfire," Nina said. Just below the deck, in a clearing circled by stones, Darryl and Sam had just finished constructing a huge pile of dead wood. While the others watched, they set fire to it in several places.

"They always have a bonfire," Elizabeth said. "It's illegal, I think, but they don't care. They grew up with the local cops."

"Oh, my God, Nina," Megan said. "Look over there. You better go protect Ben."

"Britta keeps trying," Ted said. "Ben's never been interested."

Megan lowered her voice. "I don't know how David puts up with it. I mean, Britta and Sam last year. Debbie was so upset when she found out. Sam promised her, never again, and she stayed with him."

Nina saw that Ben had picked up a couple of plastic chairs to bring down to the fire, but Britta had moved in on him.

As the evening progressed and Britta got drunker her eyes had taken on the wet insatiable look of a dog in heat. Ben kept his head down in defense mode. Britta worried him like one of Ruthie's cats worrying a rat. She eyed him across the deck. She oozed close to him. His face reddened as she whispered in his ear. Then she turned, but just as he began to relax she would go at him again.

Finally she landed right in his face, saying something again, tongue flicking, plump lips moist and open. Ben must have had enough. He raised his hand and put it on her chin and gently but definitely pushed her away. She swayed in one place for a few seconds, shrugged, gave him the finger, staggered off, pulled out a pack of cigarettes, and lit one to steady herself.

The other neighborhood women watched her faltering progress along the deck without comment, her eyes speckled yellow from the porch light.

The men had not noticed what had just happened. Except for Ben, who had gone into the house, they were lounging together across from the fire, hidden in moon shadows. Bursts of talk and exclamations flew into the air like hails of bullets.

"A toast!" David Cowan said from down there. The men punched their cans into the air. Britta approached the men. "What're you guys talking about, hmm?" she asked.

"Danny," Sam said. "We're toasting Danny." Britta's hips swiveled his way, drawn like a magnet to a Frigidaire. She sailed down the stairs toward the fire.

Nina picked up her chair and started down the stairs behind her. She passed Debbie, who looked worried.

A rough circle of chairs grew up around the fire, as most of the neighbors drifted down from the deck and sat near the warmth. Nina sat down beside Ben, who had reappeared.

"Figuring anything out?" he said.

"Having a great time," she answered.

George and Jolene sat down beside her, saying to the others, "Debbie's all tired out. She's gone inside and said good night to y'all."

Across the fire, David Cowan, Sam, and Darryl had set up their chairs. Ted joined Megan and they pulled up chairs on Nina's other side.

Illegal or not, Nina loved the big fire blazing up. It reminded her of the old days on the beach at Carmel when they still allowed fires at the foot of Ocean Avenue. But Darryl and Sam had settled back and she was wondering who was going to tend it in the liquor-soaked post-dinner hour.

Darryl's eyes followed Elizabeth as she moved around the circle. Suddenly he got up and followed her and said something to her.

She shook her head and he took her arm. Nina heard him say "Please." The woman shook him off and came over to sit by Megan. Nina noticed she no longer wore the soft purse over her shoulder.

"Here," Ted said, "I brought something for the good guys." He passed a silver flask to Elizabeth, who tipped it back sharply, like she needed a shot. Her face flushed and she said, "I understand Courvoisier is good for the heart also."

"Absolutely," Ted said. "Was Darryl bothering you?"

"He's harmless."

"He thinks he's in love with you," Megan said with a laugh.

"I like Tory," Elizabeth said. "She's dedicated to him

and their family. I honor that." They all were silent for a few minutes, and then Ted and Megan started talking with each other about their construction contractor.

Elizabeth turned to Nina and said, her head close to Nina's so no one else could hear, "So you and Ben went to high school together?"

"Uh huh."

"Nina Balzac, huh?"

"That's right," Nina said. Elizabeth's gray eyes had a steady insistence.

"The French writer," she said.

"I heard there was one."

"Oh, yes. There certainly is. I did a paper on him at Stanford. Honoré de Balzac. Alas. He was not at all Hungarian." She crossed her legs. "His family came from the South of France. His name came from the Latin *Balteanus*."

"You're making that part up for sure," Nina said.

"I remember because of the anus part. I thought it was funny. When you're eighteen stuff like that is funny."

"Well, my grandfather's family came from Budapest."

Elizabeth looked down. "Your shoes betray you," she said with a blinding smile. Nina looked down at her new shoes, which had seemed quite innocuous when she put them on.

"Børn shoes," Elizabeth went on. "Hand-sewn in European style. You don't belong in this crowd any more than I do. And you seriously don't belong with Ben."

"Because I wear expensive shoes?"

Elizabeth laughed slightly. "Well, let's just say, it tells me a lot more about you than you intended to tell. Are you a Fed? Is this about the fires?"

"Whatever." It was all Nina could manage.

"I'd like to get your phone number and talk to you some more."

"Sure," she said. She dredged a scrap of paper from her purse and wrote it down.

Just then Britta came down the stairs, holding tightly to the railing.

"She's got my purse," Elizabeth said in a voice that was stricken with sudden anxiety.

Britta picked her way around the fire. When she came to Elizabeth, Elizabeth stood up and said, "Give me that."

Britta smiled and whispered at the woman, putting her arm around her so Elizabeth had to stoop. Elizabeth listened and laughed desperately, as if trying to ingratiate her way free.

Looking around with a wicked grin, Britta said loudly, getting everyone's attention, "I was looking for a match and your purse was handy. But looky what I found." She held up a square black object.

"A tape recorder!" Britta crowed. "And it was rolling! She's been taping us!"

"That's not mine!"

"Oh, then I'll just keep it and listen to it and tell everybody what's on it tomorrow."

"Look, Britta, just give it to me," Elizabeth said. She seemed about to cry.

"Give it to her," Ben said. Moving to Britta fast, he snatched the tape recorder out of her hand and gave it to Elizabeth. "And the purse." He gave that back too.

"What's that thing for?" George boomed.

Elizabeth didn't answer. The fire seemed to answer in her place, surging up.

"Why are you spying on us?" George said. His voice held a new note of menace.

"I forgot about it. It wasn't on," Elizabeth said. "Anyway, I should go."

"Don't go," Ben said, standing close by.

She looked at him and looked at Nina. "I guess I could stay for a bit." She took his hand and walked away from the group staring at her and sat down on the steps leading back up to the deck.

"What's going on?" Darryl asked them all. "Is she spying on us?"

Megan said, amused, "Outrageous. Who knew she cared."

The dispassionate David Cowan looked rattled. "What exactly do you think she was trying to find out?"

Sam said, "She's a little sneak."

"Don't you dare talk about her like that!" Debbie said.

"It was on," Britta said. "Swear it was. Red light blinking."

"I'm gonna find out why," George said.

"George, leave it," Jolene said. "We didn't say a thing she shouldn't hear a hundred times, if that's what she wants." Her husband leaned back. In the firelight he looked old and frightened.

The party went on. Inertia, brought on by heat and drink, captured them all. The pace of movement slowed, the talk sputtered. Only the children continued, exhausted but relentless, running and screaming.

Britta's youngest, a three-year-old, had been crying intermittently for hours. He'd had an accident and his diapers were hanging over his little rubber boots. His parents didn't seem to notice.

He and the other children gathered dead grass and twigs and leaned forward to toss them into the fire, while the grown-ups looked on with glazed, indulgent eyes. For one terrible moment, Nina thought the toddler would topple into the fire, but then he emerged like a dwarfish Vulcan from the smoke, black-faced but unscathed, and rushed back into the forest.

Ben and Elizabeth emerged from the house, fresh glasses in hand, and took seats by the fire near Nina. Darryl had tipped his chair back too far and now, amid general laughter, he fell backward to the soft ground.

The kids stripped sticks and some of them roasted marshmallows. Others just caught their sticks on fire and waved them around. A few feet behind the bonfire, a small group of children hunkered down. A moment later they sprang back. They had been making their own fire, outside the fire stones.

Preoccupied with their own affairs in the circle of chairs around the fire, the adults didn't seem to notice. Nina saw Debbie at her kitchen window, rinsing dishes in a pool of light, but all around her was black sooty forest and the circle of flames.

Full dark had fallen around them. The birds no longer twittered and the stars shone indifferently through the oaks onto the pagan fire and its devotees. Nina had begun to feel hypnotized in these dark, smoky woods.

Britta, still conscious, although barely, had begun goading Sam, who had also drunk himself into mild stupefaction, with sexually pointed comments. She threw out this thunderbolt: "So do you still want me, Sammy?"

"Yes, Britta," Sam replied, sounding weary and sardonic. He seemed to feel that further resistance would lead to gnashing of teeth, general bloodthirstiness, frightful consequences.

Britta had been gathering herself for something all evening. That time had arrived. They all knew it. She would not be denied. Nina imagined her naked, dancing on a corpse, her jeweled belt hung with skulls. What was going to happen?

Sitting a few feet from Sam, David Cowan slumped, seeming to have the strength only to lift his drink to his mouth one more time. The fire burned brighter, shooting up sparks that made George get up and move farther away, cursing. The added heat felt vivid, sharp, oppressive.

As the shower of sparks died down Nina saw through a veil of smoke that Britta, maddened by drink and boredom, had made her move; somehow she had slithered onto Sam Puglia's lap.

She faced him, legs wide apart, dress hiked up. Slowly, she began grinding her groin against his lap. All that could be seen of her was her round gelatinous rear revolving obscenely, her freckled arms firmly hugging Sam around his chest, and the pale skullcap of her hair. Her face was buried on his chest.

Sam's arms were raised on both sides, his right hand still holding his drink. Above her nestled head, he smiled hideously, seeming to salute them with his drink and to beg them not to notice, distancing himself from the unseemly plowing taking place below.

In the woods, the children screamed and played. Britta moved implacably, rhythmically, upon Sam. Nina couldn't turn her gaze away, but a veil had fallen over her eyes and the movement in the chair right over there turned blurry.

Anything could have happened in those moments. Cowan could have stood up and shot his wife. The devil could have appeared in a shower of sparks. The maintenance of the universe seemed to depend on not noticing.

They all held their breaths and pretended not to notice. George Hill held on to the arms of his chair to keep them attached.

Sam kept his arms held high like a catatonic, his smile a rictus. Britta made no sound, but worked away with a will.

A few moments later, using her strange magic, Britta rematerialized through the flickering fire onto her husband's knee, her arms around him, whispering, wheedling, and jiving. Cowan's pallid face yielded no clue to his reactions.

After what she probably considered a respectable period, Britta resumed talking to the others.

Relief filled the air. The rest of them, Nina included, looked at one another like tattered survivors of a terrifying natural event.

They had held it together in the face of chaos. The social fabric had not been torn, all was sort of as it was.

But Britta did not play her encore for long. She slipped away, alone. She was gone for good. Soon Jolene asked, "Where's Britta?"

"Putting her kids to bed?" someone said. But, no, Nina saw that her boys were still making mischief out there in the shadows, their faces streaked with tears and carbon.

The adults rose clumsily together, moving toward the street, calling to their kids. David Cowan disappeared too and Megan rounded up the young Cowans. Ben offered to walk Elizabeth to her car. After a querying look at Nina, and a nod back, Elizabeth accepted his offer.

Sam continued to sit in his chair, drink in hand. He hadn't moved since Britta had screwed him into it. He might have been unconscious, but no one wanted to look closely enough to find out.

The fire still blazed, but the party appeared to be over.

"So long, great party," Nina heard a few voices call out to whoever might hear, and she and Ben joined the crowd stumbling along the road.

13

TOP DOWN ON Paul's Mustang, they whipped past the wineries and dry hillsides on Carmel Valley Road, which had just turned into G-16, on Sunday morning. Paul took the curves too fast, and Nina held on tight. This time they had decided to leave Hitchcock at home.

They were following Danny's routines in order to find out who had tipped him off about the fires. Ben had told Nina he hardly went anywhere, except to a bar called Alma's in the hamlet of Cachagua, deep in the Los Padres National Forest.

"So," Paul said, negotiating a particularly harrowing bend in the road, "you ever been up this way before?"

"I used to come here to swim sometimes when I was a teenager," she said. "There's a place called the Bucket along the river here. Kids used to go naked in a deep pool in the Carmel River."

"Where exactly is it?"

"Why exactly would you care?"

"Hot day," Paul said. "Nice way to cool off on the way back."

"Uh huh."

"Who did you come with?"

"To the Bucket? That's private," she said. Paul's sudden interest ballooned like a semi coming at her.

"I can just see it."

"No, you can't," she said. "Banish whatever pictures you're conjuring up."

Paul wore his khakis and a polo shirt. Nina, in deference to where they were headed, had dressed in jeans and a tank top, her hair tucked under a baseball cap. A flock of wild turkeys burst out and skittered across a field, staying very low in the air. They had already passed Carmel Valley Village and lost the houses. The one-lane road, striped with light and shade, wound around the rock banks like a narrow asphalt river.

"Well, you promised to tell me about the Siesta Court Bunch party once we hit the road. When I mention it you get this expression—what is it, disbelief? Amusement? Disgust?"

"That was some party." Nina shook her head. "Was it ever."

"So? What do you think?"

Nina said slowly, "I say we take off, nuke the site from orbit. It's the only way to be sure."

Paul laughed. "That bad?"

"*Lord of the Flies* bad. *Deliverance* bad."

"Did you learn anything?"

"Well, I learned how to lap dance," Nina said. She wet her lips and began describing the party, from Darryl's mooning over Elizabeth to Tory walking out; the black-faced kids screeching through the woods; George's tasteless jokes; Ted and Megan grinning beatifically from the sidelines; Elizabeth's tape recorder. Paul burst into laughter here and there as she talked.

"Trust me, it wasn't funny while it was happening," Nina said. She finished with Britta and Sam on the plastic chair. Paul laughed long and hard at that one.

"Sam's probably still sitting there in his plastic chair, holding his drink up with that look of horror," Nina said.

"I can't believe I let you two talk me out of going," Paul said. "I wondered if there were any good parties left, and here I had the chance to go to the best one in ages."

"But I'm not sure I learned anything about the arson. I didn't look at one of the men and say, it's him, like I thought I would. One of them, Darryl Eubanks, is a volunteer fire-fighter, which I suppose gives him an automatic place on the list."

"What did you think of him?"

"A lunk."

"I was looking for something more precise. More pro-found."

"He's dissatisfied, though he has everything—health, youth, a family, work, a home—he was hitting on one of the other women. He's likable, though, and I kept watching him and reminding myself that a lot of my guilty criminal clients are likable."

"Anybody else?"

"David Cowan is alienated. He has money. I suspect he's obsessive, and these fires may be the product of an obsessive mind. He's secretive, that's what it is."

"That's interesting," Paul said, "in an academic sort of way."

"Well, George Hill is used to getting his own way, and he has a concrete grievance." She told Paul how the Hills had lost their right to subdivide. "Danny worked for him a lot. If I had to pick, I'd say George, but then again, he's got health problems and I can't see him climbing a steep trail. I don't know."

"We'll just keep gathering information, and you'll be able to link up those impressions," Paul said. "I think you learned a lot."

"I think you better slow down."

"Anything you know about this place we're going? Cachagua?"

"Ca-sha-wa," she corrected.

"But a hard g for agua?"

She shrugged. "It's how we pronounce it here. Hmm, Cachagua. I always thought of it as this magical valley in the middle of the forest, timeless, quiet, the sun always shining. It's sensationally beautiful and remote."

"Can't wait to see it, then."

"But it's probably not so quiet at the moment. Remember Ben mentioning the old dam up there? The San Clemente? The locals fish and hike there. The village, what there is of a village, is built right next to the dam. Well, there's talk of putting in a bigger dam.

"Ah, you think the idea of a new dam has the locals worked up," Paul said.

"Sure it does. The Salinas Valley growers are running out of water. The locals feel like the water's being stolen from them."

"We're gonna wring the earth dry before we're done," Paul said. "The truth is we don't think very well."

"Hey, Paul. That last line is one of Ruthie's Twelve Points."

"So it is. They're contagious."

"Water is *the* big issue in the West. The South steals from the North. Las Vegas steals from the whole state and neighboring states too. Mono Lake is suffering. Salmon die in Oregon because the Feds divert water to the farms. There just isn't enough fresh water to go around."

"But it's so hot and still here. I feel," Paul said, giving the wheel a spin, "like someone heading into the waving fields of Iowa, one of those outposts where there should be miles of untouched neat rows of corn, American frontier, peace, and no issues."

"Visit Iowa. I'm sure you'll find they've got fights about pesticides, the end of small farming, whatever," Nina said. "Meanwhile, California's got its water fights."

Stiff and impatient with the long drive, they arrived in Cachagua before noon. Even the spectacular views of forest, wineries, and horses along the way hadn't diminished the feeling that they were riding into the Wild West, visitors to a place they did not belong. The village, a clearing in the woods with a couple of mom-and-pops and a dusty county park with a tot lot, had only one gathering place of note, the bar.

"Alma's. I could use a drink," Paul said.

She knew he meant a real drink, the kind that actually hydrated. They parked in full sun in the dirt lot, and Nina followed him through the door of the long, low brown shack.

After the blazing summer sun, the dimness and cool inside provided a haven. Four men already sat at stools along the bar, three grizzled from years in the outdoors, and one down at the end, gray-bearded but wearing a couple of gold rings in his right earlobe. All eyes turned toward the tourists who had driven up in a fancy red Mustang convertible. Paul gave the men a nod.

"Ice water," he said.

"Ice water," Nina echoed. She checked the menu chalked on a board behind the bar. "And nachos."

Paul said, "And add a couple of turkey sandwiches on wheat."

"White's what we serve," said the woman behind the bar, not unfriendly, but not smiling either.

"White'll be fine."

When the water arrived in drizzling, cold glasses, they drank thirstily. Down the bar, the three cowboys resumed what seemed to be a comfortable, ongoing discussion, with an occasional sideways glance toward them. They griped about the lack of jobs, the drought, the divorces, and the child support, and no fact went uncontested. While heated, the conversation was peppered with peevish humor.

After a suitable time, Paul asked the bartender what was going on with the dam. She answered, "Nothing bad has happened yet," and retired to a stool by the curtain that led to the back, but the question set off the others at the bar. Nina quickly dubbed them Cowboys One, Two, and Three, since the three sitting together wore identically battered denims and work shirts, and from the smell of them, seemed to be taking a break from a morning of arduous outdoor labor.

"Smoke, dust, traffic, blasting, medical problems, strangers in the park . . . that's what's gonna be goin' on if that damn dam gets built." Cowboy One wore jeans that rode too low over scrawny hips. His drooping eyes looked permanently unhappy.

"It's a Godzilla," said Cowboy Two, a beat-up young man wearing a hard-used tan cowboy hat. All Nina could see of him was his mouth and chin. "And we're Tokyo. It'll lay waste to this town."

"You know what they want to build?" asked Three, a short, plump man who squinted as if needing to protect sensitive eyes from even this murky light. His baseball cap and sunglasses sat on the bar. "A concrete wall two hundred eighty-two feet high, quarter of a mile long. That's four hundred feet wider than Hoover Dam. You ever seen that?"

One and Two shook their heads.

"You get to Vegas, you're not thinking about dams," said One.

"Well, this thing is gonna drown one of the prettiest valleys in the Ventana wilderness. The Los Padres Dam already forces the steelhead salmon that run the river here to climb the highest ladder in the country to spawn. Destroy over a hundred acres of habitat, some of it wilderness. Spotted salamander. Steeleye. We can forget about fishing."

"Bastards," said One and Two, drinking deeply of their drafts.

"Bastards," agreed Three, keeping up.

They drank again. So did Paul and Nina.

"They say it's gonna cost us a hundred twenty-five million dollars," Three went on. "Hell, it could cost three times that."

"Shit," said Two. "You kidding me?"

"That's what the Sierra Club says," Three said, nodding.

"Bastards!" Two said.

"The Sierra Club?" Three asked.

"All of them. Outsiders. Why can't they leave it alone? The old dam's done the job all these years. We don't want any more water. It's all for people who live miles from here."

"Somebody's getting rich off this."

"And there's no tellin' who."

"So the damn developers can keep building until we all live up each other's asses," said Three. "Let 'em get their own damn water."

"I didn't move out here to listen to noise and deal with hammering, hollering, and hauling all day long," Two said.

"Damn right," One agreed.

"Somebody'll blow it up, we get lucky," said Two.

"I'll do it if you'll do it," said Three.

This statement resulted in a long period of silence, as if the boys needed time to adjust to the change in dynamic before continuing. Down at the end of the bar, the fourth customer, the one with a gray beard, nursed a glass of ale.

He wore paint-spattered shorts and sandals, and on the floor beside his stool rested a folded easel, confirming Nina's impression that he was an artist rather than a house-painter. She knew many of the people in the area formed a loose-knit community of artists and craftspeople.

"Let me know how to join the posse when the time comes," the artist contributed now.

"Oh, good idea, Donnelly," said the lady bartender from her perch in the corner.

"That's right. Run 'em out of town," said One.

"A hundred and eighty trucks a day rollin' in!" Two said. "Think of it! We only got eight hundred people in Cachagua. That's one truck per four people!"

"Not like they're gonna hire locals either."

"Place'll be crawling with Mexicans," Two went on.

"Shut up, Randy. I'm Mexican, in case you forgot," said Three.

"Yeah, but you're my friend," Two said.

"And how about the Esselen Indians? Here for at least a thousand years. There are ancient relics all over the place, grinding stones, all that. The Esselens have been fighting this idea for years. Shouldn't somebody listen to them?" Three asked.

"My sister's husband is part Esselen. He's all right," said One. "I agree with you, they ought to be considered."

"Ditto," Two added.

Nina and Paul ate their sandwiches, paying close attention.

"You folks from around here?" asked Three of Nina and Paul. Having finished his current beer, he moved his mug back and forth along the bar, agitating for service.

"I grew up nearby," Nina lied. She had grown up in Pacific Grove, fifty miles away in a whole different culture, but she certainly felt she knew these guys intimately. Any one of them might have been her first boyfriend, the skinny-dipper and bad boy, refocusing all his lawless youthful energy into a hard job and bar talk.

"You do look familiar," Cowboy One said, examining her. "I think I used to see you at the Bucket."

"I doubt it," she answered, feeling the red creep up her cheeks and down her neck.

"No." He showed his teeth. "I'd remember you."

The others at the bar cast sidelong glances at her, then looked innocently back into their beers.

She could feel Paul bristling beside her, so she hurried to erase the naked frolicker who seemed to have taken up residence there beside them. "We're looking for . . . a friend of a friend. Danny Cervantes?"

"Dead," said One, his eyes gloomier than ever. "Don't you read the paper?"

"Danny spent many a evening here, drinkin' Coronas," said Two.

"Seems obvious this is just plain what it looks like, a case of Danny being Danny," said Three. On this sobering thought, the rest of the guys drank again.

"You really think he set those fires?" Paul asked.

"I don't think he had a thing to do with those fires," said Cowboy Three. "I ain't gonna speak ill of the dead."

"Last time he was in here, you sure had a different version. Started with *F* and ended with *loudmouth asshole*," said Cowboy Two.

Cowboy Three sucked in his cheeks. "That's because he was with Coyote that night."

"Now, Coyote, he was Danny's good buddy."

"Uh huh," said Nina.

"So what's your interest in Danny?" said the artist.

"Actually, it's Coyote I'd like to talk to," Nina said.

"Why?"

How easily the lie flowed. "Danny's uncle, Ben, found something in Danny's room that belonged to Danny's friend—I guess that's Coyote, and my friend and I were coming out here anyhow to walk around the dam, so we said we'd ask around."

This was rewarded with nods and pursed lips. Paul nodded too.

"Couldn't be money," Cowboy Two finally said. "Coyote sure ain't got any of that, and Danny wouldn't have saved it for him if he did."

"Could you tell us where Coyote's camp is?" Paul said.

"He's got a camp out Arroyo Seco way."

"Way out there," Nina said.

"But you could just leave him a message at the one place we all go to when it all comes down."

Nina nodded and smiled.

"Where's that?" Paul said, and the whole bar, including Nina, said, "The Mid-Valley Safeway."

"Ah. Right. We all have to buy groceries," Paul said.

"Right," Two said. "Even if he lives mainly on grilled squirrel."

"What else can you tell us about Coyote?" Paul asked.

Two laughed. "He only talks when he's drunk, but then you can't shut him up. He collars you. The bar empties out when Coyote gets to talking about how he caught that big steelhead and gutted it and how good it tasted fried in a pan over a campfire."

"How about the rest of you?" Paul asked. "You know the man?"

"He's just . . . prickly. Yeah, that's it. That's why he yells at you if you say hey," said Three, setting the roll of his stomach into movement as he chuckled. "Or even try to use the head, if he's in there. He lives so deep in the boonies, he probably thinks the running water here is really special."

"I remember he said once he grew up around Lake Tahoe," said One. "But that's right. Mostly he talks about hunting and fishing."

Nina and Paul looked at each other.

"Hey, Donnelly, you were drinkin' with him last week!" Three said suddenly.

Donnelly, the artist, had been watching them. He seemed to be working up some steam. "Boys, I don't trust these people," he said. "They come in here and they want to know where a man who likes his privacy lives. Who are you people?"

Surprised, Nina gave him her full attention. He had a twitchy, drumming presence that made Nina think about the dangers of crack cocaine. He seemed old to be abusing stimulants. In her experience older addicts preferred to mellow out.

"Just what we said," Paul said with his innocent look.

"Lies. You're the System."

"The System?"

"The fucking exploiters and spies."

"Oh, them. No, we're just friends of Danny's uncle."

"IRS," the artist said, counting on his fingers. "County sheriff. Welfare. Repo man. Child support. Which is it?"

"Look, I'm not after your friend at all. Danny left two

hundred bucks in an envelope marked Coyote and his uncle wanted him to have it. Nobody cares what it's for—drugs, loan, work, whatever. Screw.it. We tried. We'll buy dinner at the Sardine Factory instead. Let's get out of here," Paul said, turning to Nina and nudging her off the bar stool.

"Wait." Two's strong hand grasped Paul's arm. "So it was money after all? Let's see this envelope."

"She has it." Paul nodded casually toward Nina.

She opened her mouth and closed it. Opened it again. "I tossed the envelope," she said. She opened her purse and pulled out ten twenties she had just received from the ATM and flipped the edges like a deck of cards.

"Lies," said Donnelly. "Don't tell them anything."

"Oh, be quiet, Donnelly. You oughtta ease up on the controlled substances," said Two, which brought on a hearty laugh from his *compadres*.

"But—"

"I said shut up. You hear? These nice folks come here to do a good deed. So shut the hell up." He glowered at the artist, who stroked the gray soul-patch on his chin rapidly a few times and then got off the bar stool and walked out without a backward glance.

Two said, "He oughtta get some sleep. Now. About getting Coyote his money."

"Coyote come in here regularly?" Paul asked.

Two shook his head. "Could be weeks before he stops by again. He has a younger brother he takes care of and I don't think he likes leaving him alone."

"How old?"

"Twelve, maybe thirteen? Less said about that kid, the better."

"Big-time screwed up," One stated.

"Screwed up how?" Paul asked. "Drugs?" Drugs were on both their minds at the moment.

Cowboy Three squeezed his little eyes littler, and snorted. "Drugs might have helped that kid. I'm afraid it's probably too late to get him anywhere near normal."

"You should meet Nate. Then you'll have the full picture," said One.

"Does he come in here?"

"Not hardly. You'd have to go out there to the tent to see them both, probably. But if you do that, watch it. Coyote keeps a pit bull."

"Yeah, a real friendly animal," said Cowboy Three, adjusting his hat back on his head. "Just like us." That made all three of the men at the bar laugh. Hopping off his stool, Cowboy Two doodled a map on a napkin for Paul and Nina. "Go back to G-16 where it goes left around Sycamore Flat back to town. You want to take a right there instead, onto Arroyo Seco. He lives up a dirt road in Wood Tick Canyon. It's a long way."

This time Nina drove. She kept the air conditioner blasting on her arms while Paul dozed on the seat beside her. He slid back and forth, first against her, then against the side door as the road zigzagged around the canyons and hills of the Paloma Ridge. When they came to the main turn, she woke him up. "I need you to navigate. Pull out that map the guy gave us, okay?"

"Hey, I'm still alive," he said, opening his eyes.

"You don't trust my driving?"

"Of course I do or I wouldn't let you drive." He found the map in his pocket and studied it. "It's irrational, this need I feel to scream when you take a blind curve fast, so I close my eyes to keep the peace."

"So you're letting me drive? I'm not taking a turn at the wheel as an equal?"

"It's just a figure of speech. Lighten up, babe. I had a brainstorm when we were talking to the cowboys. Remember the one who was talking about Godzilla?"

"No. You thought of something about Coyote?"

"No, this is another verse for our monster song." He sang in a deep growl:

I am Godzilla—and you are Tokyo
I am Godzilla—and you are Tokyo
I just can't help it—I'll try not to bite
I'm gonna lay waste—to you tonight

"They'll love it at the Grand Ole Opry. Speaking of turns," she said, "is there a turn coming up?"

It should have been right there, although almost an hour of searching nearly convinced them otherwise. The snarl of dirt roads ended in gullies, fences, boulders, and debris. They finally located the right turn, exactly where the map showed it.

"How did we miss it?" Nina said, taking the pitted road too fast, irritated and tired, feeling as dusty as the road. As the afternoon progressed it had only grown hotter. They finally spotted a distant gray tent in a clearing up ahead. Nina parked. Paul jumped out of the car, closing his door silently while Nina pulled socks out of her bag and put them on along with her hiking boots. She also pulled out a long-sleeved shirt, unsnagged her rolled-up sleeves, and buttoned them tightly at the wrists.

"Why are you doing that?" Paul asked her. He had forgotten already.

How infuriating, that he had no such cares. "You can't see it? Paul, this forest is crawling with it." Poison oak swarmed up the trunks alongside the road, crossing on the Spanish moss from tree to tree. Clumps of it framed the road and flourished all the way up the hills around them.

They walked up the road toward the clearing, cautious, both wary of the pit bull. Paul held a thick branch. Nina stopped.

"What's the matter? You see something?"

Long black shadows of the late afternoon made the road ahead look like something out of a fairy tale, where threatening beings wavered, waiting for them, and trees creaked and whispered as they walked by. The silence, aside from the hysterical buzzing of insects, seemed total.

"Know something? I have no idea where we are," said Nina.

"I'm looking forward to getting the hell back to the river. You can shake your stuff at the Bucket for me alone."

"I don't like it here," Nina said, slapping a mosquito that had crept up underneath her sleeve.

The heat rose up from the road, suffocating in the stillness.

"You want to wait for me in the car?"

She visualized herself in the Mustang, alone with her imagination in this atmosphere. "No."

"Well, then. Ready?" He waited until she started up again.

An old Chevy van blocked the entrance to the clearing. They walked around it, peering inside. Nina's heart jumped. It looked like she imagined a kidnapper's van might look, filthy tan, paneled, full of ratty bits of rug and trash. "Ugh," she whispered. "Paul, the Cat Lady thought she saw a beige van."

"I'm looking, I'm looking. Hold my stick." He brought out his penknife and, glancing at the motionless flaps of the tent, quickly scraped something behind the front fenders into a baggie.

A boy in a plaid lumberjack shirt walked across the muddy meadow toward them, cap pulled low, head down, limp animal hanging by its ears loosely from his left hand, stick in his right, a day pack on his back. A dark stain made a blot over the pattern on the front of his shirt. As he got closer, Nina could see the animal was a skinny gray jackrabbit.

"Who are you?" he asked. Shaking hands didn't seem like a good plan, so Nina smiled and said, "I'm Nina Reilly and this is Paul. I'm a lawyer. And you?"

"Nate. A lawyer helped my mother once. Look what I have."

"You shoot it?" Paul said. He was looking for a weapon.

"Trapped it. Trapped it and wrapped it."

"Make a good dinner," Paul observed, as if he and Nina routinely ate dead animals for dinner, which they did, but Nina didn't want to think about that right now.

"My brother makes stew." He looked confused. "Used to. Not anymore."

"Let's all sit down and talk for a minute," Paul said. "Aren't you Coyote's brother? Nate?"

"When I was." Nate perched on a rock not far from them and plunged the stick into the ground. What he might be thinking, with the eyes she couldn't see and the shaggy hair and the general air of being off-kilter, Nina couldn't imagine.

"Have you lived here long?"

"Why do you want to know?"

"Uh, just wondering."

"It snows up on the mountains here, sometimes. Bet you didn't know that. When it snows I stay in the tent. Bent in the tent. But I don't know what to do now. He doesn't like me." He dropped the rabbit, which plopped to the ground without complaint. Nate pulled on his eyebrow and commenced an alarming series of loud moans.

"I vote we go get Coyote," Paul said hastily.

"Nate? Nate? We want to see your brother," Nina said.

More groans. Nate rocked back and forth.

"Where's your brother?" Paul asked.

"Gone." Another groan.

"Where?"

He stared at them. "That's the mystery. My mother told me a story. About a train. Trains are a strain."

"Let's go look anyway, okay?" Paul said.

Nate followed with his rabbit and stick, docile enough, as they moved cautiously up the track to the sprawling tent, still emitting the occasional moan.

"Nate's not well," Nina said to Paul in a low voice.

"No shit."

"Someone ought to be helping him. A doctor."

As if hearing this, and deciding against it, Nate suddenly disappeared.

"Nate?" Nina called.

A tall, tan young man with an ugly pink-nosed white dog built like a tank stepped out of the tent about fifty feet away. He wore the kind of T-shirt her son, Bob, called a wifebeater, white and sleeveless, jeans, and a brown cowboy hat low over his eyes. When he saw them, he seemed to jump back a step, but the dog jumped forward, growling. Thank God, Nina thought, that thing's on a tight leash. Actually it was a chain, but Coyote was holding it looped several times around his knuckles.

Nina swallowed. Paul liked her to take the lead in these encounters, saying, heck, let the sexists feel safe because you're a woman. Why not use it to our own advantage, this sexism stuff?

"Your brother trapped a rabbit," she said.

"So we eat tonight. That's good." Next to him, the pit bull at the end of the chain made no sound, waiting. "Meanwhile, I politely say, just the one time, get the hell off our property. Now."

"Are you Coyote? We'd like to talk to you about Danny."

"Beat it. Or I let the dog go."

"We're leaving," Paul said. He swung around back toward the road, but did not completely turn his back on the man or his dog.

Nina stumbled behind. As she followed Paul back to the car, she reminded herself, "Stay away from the poison oak," but really, all she could think about was the muzzle of the pit bull and that poor boy standing by the tent, eyes searching the distance for answers.

"Did you see?" Paul said, as they reached the Mustang, started it up, turned on the AC, and sank gratefully into its leather seats.

"See what?"

"Up in the tree."

"See what?"

"Nate built a nest up there."

"No. I was too busy watching Coyote's fingers on the dog chain. He's perfect, Paul. He's got the van. I see him setting the fires and driving away. It's no stretch of the imagination."

"So who's the second dude, then?" Paul said. "The second guy in the van? We're operating on the assumption that the second guy isn't Danny."

"Doesn't have to be," Nina said. "Simple. Danny found out from Coyote, and decided to get the reward. He'd know to look for the van up on the ridge."

"He was going to finger his buddy?"

"His buddy was an arsonist."

"To tell the truth, no one could be this dude's buddy," Paul said. "Drinking partner, yes. But—"

"But what?"

"But who did he drop off on Siesta Court that night? Who's his partner?"

"Someone Danny hooked him up with," Nina said, excited. "Another reason to kill Danny."

Paul patted the baggie in his pocket and said, "Hope this is ash."

They drove back to the turnoff for the Bucket. The sun was low and the shadows had lengthened, but the temperature was still in the nineties.

"Look for a hole in the fence just before you see the iron gate with a Stone Pine sign."

They got out of the car, sloppy and tired. "This it?" Paul asked.

"I think so."

They clambered down a steep path. Following the trail, they wended their way through a fifty-foot grassy field to a fork in the path. "We go right," Nina said. They crossed one creek, and minutes later, arrived at the rocky shore of the swimming hole Nina remembered so well. No one else had lingered so late in the day. "Oh. It doesn't look the same." Floods had devastated the scene, tearing at the protective foliage. "My gosh. It was all hidden! Oh, well. I'm too hot to care."

She peeled off her jeans, shirt, and underwear.

Paul took off his boxers. He kissed her hungrily. She ran her hands down him, admiring him. High above, on the highway, those who knew to look could see the tiny embracing figures in the twilight next to the pond. Nina felt the heat rising from the stones and a late-afternoon breeze stirring on her bare skin. Birds called to each other in the laurel trees.

They slid gratefully into the Bucket's gold-and-silver water, and the light split and shattered across its surface, then gathered itself and followed behind as they swam.

14

ELIZABETH GOLD'S SUNDAY turned out to be eventful too. After packing her new Subaru with water and sunscreen, she left before dawn that morning, heading east into Los Padres National Forest, to Tassajara Hot Springs. She wanted to get the most out of her visit, and knew she had a two-and-a-half-hour trip on G-16 to get there.

She had a bad taste to expunge after her foray to Siesta Court the night before.

For the first thirty miles, she enjoyed the expanses of yellow and olive-green hillsides, the dry grasses rolling like ocean waves in the hot wind, the occasional ranchito with its grazing horses, then the forest closing in. At the tiny community of Jamesburg the asphalt ended and the warning signs began: TASSAJARA ROAD IS IMPASSABLE DURING WET WEATHER. THE MONASTERY IS CLOSED FROM SEPTEMBER TO MAY, PLEASE DO NOT DISTURB THE MONKS.

As the road climbed steeply and ruts and stones took over, she switched to four-wheel drive, slowed down, and bumped and ground her way the last fourteen miles up Chews Ridge and down into the Tassajara Creek Basin, reminding herself with each teeth-clattering lurch how much she needed this retreat.

Morning's overcast broke and the sun began to burn hot. After checking in with a friendly student, she strolled around the monastery grounds, starting at the footbridge. She walked the length and breadth of the property, over the footbridge, up the path to the yurt, breathing in the smells of the forest around, enjoying the security of the hills that framed the central clearing.

Since the sixties, Tassajara had undergone a slow metamorphosis and now included, in addition to the redwood cabin complex built in the mid-seventies, bathhouses, plunges and hot springs, stone meditation rooms, and a large dining room and dormitory. Too remote for tourists, this serene paradise was visited only by those seeking peace.

Holding her towel and water bottle and stepping carefully in her sandals, Elizabeth picked her way to her favorite boulder next to the river, where random rocks made art of the landscape. A branch hung down and sheltered a flat spot on this river rock.

She looked up the mountain at the broad scar running all the way down its flank, from the wildfire a few years before that had forced the monks to evacuate. No fire now, just heat, the hillsides shimmering with it.

Today the temperature might top a hundred degrees. She would go inside by 10:00 A.M. During the winter and fall months, the monastery closed to all visitors, while its residents engaged in intensive, ninety-day practice periods called *ango*. Elizabeth had done that in September. She had mourned a lot and slept a lot. One day she had enough, and went home. Simple, like Zen.

Today, she would return home before sunset. Finding a spot in shade on her boulder, crossing her legs, she sat for a long time amid the disheveled business of her Self, not trying for anything or expecting anything, just sitting. Like a monk of old on a rock above the river, she heard rushing water, allowed patterns of light to drift through her downcast eyes.

Old thought-patterns arose and she let them in.

They had died in a head-on collision in San Francisco. She had been at home, taking a nap. Five years it has been, she thought in wonderment.

She breathed in and out on her rock.

What she couldn't get over was that at the moment of impact she hadn't even woken up, hadn't had enough of a connection with them even to feel them cry out as they left the earth. A certain moment occurred and all she loved was gone. She had nowhere to go and nothing to do and several million dollars from her dead husband. From her dead daughter, May, she had only memories.

For a while she drifted around like a wraith. She went to Kyoto and Dharamsala and Mount Kailash and other holy places, avoiding people. She ended up back in the high-rise in San Francisco, seeing a shrink three times a week. May's last moments came to her frequently in her dreams.

After a long time, Elizabeth gathered herself together again. She still didn't think she deserved to be alive, but she made a contract with life—to spend it helping others.

And so she went to Africa for two years and gave most of the money to various groups and worked for Médecins Sans Frontières until she came down with dengue fever and had to be airlifted out. She despised herself for her lack of stamina even more, but she stayed in the U.S. this time. She joined an environmental group in Humboldt County protesting logging of first-growth forest there, and for two weeks she even sat in a tree.

During a visit to her sister and a subsequent retreat at Tassajara, she saw Carmel Valley and thought, I'll build a home there, close to the monastery, close to a place to run to.

Then, when the home was finished nearly two years later, she again looked around for something to save.

Moving into traditional political activism and Valley conservation issues, she worked furiously and gave more money, and soon she was a member of several local boards and commissions that were trying to stop further degradation of the viewsheds and water sources into the Valley.

And finally she decided to get back on the Ph.D. track. Why? Because there were still so many nights when she sat alone in her living room, drinking brandy, thinking too much. She got a Ph.D. committee together and chose a subject, and found it gave her a reason to wake up in the morning.

Stop running the pictures, she thought. She came back to the rock, the river, and the breathing.

And fell back into her blackest place.

And let the waves of pain wash away, then return in their eternal cycle.

She didn't know how long she sat, legs cramping, sunshine burning down through the leaves, but when she came out of the moment and back to the setting, she noticed the shadows around the oaks and chaparral had shrunken. Her arms had turned red. Her stomach growled and her back ached. The stream ran below. She reached into her bag and had a meditative smoke, then stood up, making her way to the dining room for food.

Although several others were eating their plates of rice on wooden picnic tables outside and were involved in small discussions, she avoided them as always, moving away to sit on some wooden steps, eating under the lines and shadows of a cooling trellis. She didn't want to waste her time in group chitchat. She had had enough of that at the party on Siesta Court the night before.

After she finished eating, she soaked in the outdoor pool lined in round stones outside the bathhouse, then moved inside to the tile tub, all the time staying out of conversations. One thing about people here, they left you alone.

Lying in the hot tub, she began thinking about how the events at the party the night before might fit into her thesis.

Too bad about Britta outing the recordings. She had continued to tape anyway. Nobody expected that, so she did it. Nevertheless, last night's Siesta Court party would be her final information-gathering session. The newbies and locals could interact without her interference from now on.

Getting out, she dried off and changed. She had the tape to transcribe and scholarly thoughts to express, objective thoughts that never got out of hand. Lapsang souchong to drink. Another day to get through.

The long drive back went quickly. She felt renewed by her mini-retreat, and the trees and hills flashed by like benevolent green presences in a beautiful world. She even thought to herself at one point, am I getting better?

Dark had come. Elizabeth turned on the light in her kitchen and found some cold brown rice in the fridge. She added some plain yogurt and that took care of dinner.

Bath time. She drew it out, shaving her legs carefully, letting all the hot water run out. She found a blue silk kimono in a bamboo pattern to wear, fitting for the day and her mood. With a towel, she ruffled her wet hair.

The silence of the house surrounded her. She descended the stairway, moving various things out of her mind, the sound of the floors creaking, the emptiness of the bedrooms. She checked her watch with a kind of despair. Nine, too early to go to bed yet. Do some work.

The biggest room downstairs was octagonal and painted forest green. There, she kept her desk and her work. And there, she stared out the window at the hillsides and the moon. Adjusting herself in her chair, she picked up the standard cassette, labeled it, and set it into the compartment of the transcribing machine she used.

The doorbell made her jerk.

She peered through the side windows that showed her who might come calling, though no one except FedEx and Debbie ever did.

She reached for the handle of the door and opened it.

"But why have you come?" she asked.

Darryl Eubanks sat on the wicker settee across from her desk. She leaned over in the Queen Anne chair, attending to the pot on the brass tray on the wooden chest. He sipped the sweet smoky tea she had handed him and grimaced.

"You don't like it."

"I hafta say, I'm an orange pekoe man, myself."

"Someone I know bought this at Ten-Lin in San Francisco. It's the best."

"I believe you. I'm no connoisseur. Nice photos. Wow."

"They're from Tanzania."

"It's a very impressive house," Darryl said. He wore a sport jacket and jeans and was sober, or she wouldn't have let him in.

"Bigger than I need. I know," she said.

"I didn't mean that. It's just . . . teachers live in reduced circumstances these days. It makes Tory so mad, the way we're underrated."

"I can understand that."

"Because she believes we deserve more."

"She's right. What do you teach?"

"Phys ed. Eighth grade."

"I thought you were a firefighter."

"Oh. I am, but it's volunteer work."

"Right. Do you like it?"

Darryl laughed. "It's a duty. I dread being called out to a fire. But we have to work together or the whole forest would burn down some summer. I got called up to your neighborhood on the ridge fire. It came within a quarter mile of you. You were lucky."

"You fought the fire? I owe you for that, Darryl. All that smoke, the sirens—"

"We almost had to evacuate you."

"I didn't know it came so close."

"Ted and Megan's new place almost burned down. Don't know how we saved it, really. I was worried about you. I watched out for you."

"Well, thank you, Darryl. Thanks for doing that." They were keeping up the convention that he had dropped by after dark just because he was in the neighborhood. Elizabeth wondered what form the pass would take—would he sweep her into his arms? Get down on his knees? She felt curious and a little cruel. He had no right to be here. He had children, a wife. He was acting outside the mores, hers as well as his.

Then she thought sadly, I'm too lonely, tonight, to turn even this away.

What would she do when he made the pass?

His eyes ate her up.

Darryl was saying, "Actually, I came over to apologize. For my behavior at the block party last night. I made a fool out of myself."

"Do you remember what you said, when you grabbed my arm and pulled me over toward the deck?"

His face went red. "To be honest, I don't know exactly what I blurted out."

"I'll forget about it too, then."

"Thanks. I'm not so good at talking even when I haven't had a couple of beers."

"Uh huh."

"So," Darryl said. He had run out of conversational gambits, so he just sat there.

"So." Elizabeth nodded. She felt like slapping his big slow face, giving him the back of her hand a few times, to see if he could wake up. If only he would cut to the chase, because she was losing even her curiosity now.

Finally he resumed, "Britta got pretty wild there at the end."

"It's not the first time."

"What was that all about? The recordings you were making? What were they?" He sounded abrupt.

"I'm . . . curious about people."

"You sure had us freaked."

"I gather information," she said. "For my work. Just general things. I'm sorry it made everyone so self-conscious. That was never my intention."

"You expected something to happen there? Have you always taped the parties?"

"No." A lie. He really wanted to know, she could see that in his face, and she wasn't about to tell him.

"I always hoped you were having fun. I always thought you seemed lonely. What kind of work do you mean?"

"Forget about it, Darryl. It was stupid of me."

"It doesn't have anything to do with Danny or the fires, does it?"

"Of course not."

"What are you going to do with the tape?"

"Oh, give it a rest, will you? Do you want some more tea? Otherwise, let's call it a night."

"Because we're good people on Siesta Court. Family people. Maybe you should give me the tape." A warning, as if he felt she must be inimical to them? She wasn't inimical, she was merely objective. Darryl was a local. He would never understand her work.

"Of course I won't give you the tape," she said. He shook his head in disappointment and stared at her body under the robe. He was young, strong, and not bad-looking, and she thought about him again.

"You're widowed, aren't you," Darryl said. She almost breathed a sigh of relief as he finally got into it.

"Yes." She noted clinically that she had been able to answer without a stab of pain for the first time.

"Tory and I met when we were thirteen."

"Very young."

"Right. And we were together for five years before either of us mentioned marriage. I left college and came back here to finish up."

"Do you think you married too young?"

"Now I do. We weren't really ready. Tory didn't want to leave her family here in the Valley. I . . ."

"You?"

"I could live anywhere. I could live in Tanzania, teach

school. I'm different from Tory." He put his hands on his knees and his body tensed slightly.

You think you're better than Tory? Elizabeth thought. You're so wrong. I've got you all figured out, right down to clumsy adultery, if you can manage it. She felt contempt, and realized she had made her decision.

"To be honest, Tory and I have grown apart. She's content leaving things as they are. We talk about the kids, visit family—I keep thinking I've missed out on some important things in life."

"Must be hard, having a wife who doesn't understand you."

"Yeah."

Moisture formed on his upper lip. She couldn't stand it any longer. "Darryl?" she said. "Why did you come here tonight?"

"I always wanted to. You're all alone," he said, "and so nice-looking. I love your black hair. I love those blue eyes of yours. I don't think I've seen such a shade before, ever. I love the way you live, so free."

Elizabeth finished her tea. She poured herself another, then topped off Darryl's cup. "You thought I seemed lonely?"

"Aren't you?"

"Because I'm not married and live alone in this big house?"

"Because of . . . aw, shit. I'm not so good at this."

"True."

"I'm tryin' to say . . . you and I could . . ."

"Could what?"

He pushed his foot out until it touched hers. Raising his eyes, he looked for a response in hers. "You're so beautiful." He leaned close enough to touch her cheek. "All my life I've done the things that were expected of me. Just once I want—I want—"

"You don't know me."

"I know a lot. I know you lost your family. . . ." He

seemed to realize that he had said something wrong. He stopped.

Elizabeth stood up. "I suppose you all talk about me behind my back."

"Of course I know about you. I've had my bad times. Everybody has."

"You with your four beautiful children. You say you envy my freedom. Maybe you also envy my money. Well, I envy you your babies. Go back to Tory," Elizabeth said.

"Doesn't a man have a right to pursue love in his life? I could help you. You're so sad. We could be good for each other. I could surprise you."

"Go home, Darryl."

He stood up to full height. "You need a man, Elizabeth. You're young and beautiful. You couldn't save them, but you could still save yourself."

"Get out!" she cried, thinking, You pompous asshole! You predatory married man! He was tall and close and burning to grab her. She stepped backward behind the study door and held it, ready to slam it in his face.

"Don't come back!" she said.

"I'm sorry," Darryl said. "I'll go. I don't know how to talk to you. But I'm pretty sure I'm in love with you, and I can't fight it. I can't."

15

JOLENE'S SUNDAY MORNING had started out peacefully. While George slept in and sun filtered through the windows, she had whisked up blueberry pancakes for the girls. April loved the ones with a face in them, Callie preferred fewer bits of fruit.

Jolene mixed them in a big green glass bowl, waiting for the griddle to get hot enough. Scooping huge spoonfuls on the iron skillet, she watched the bubbles form and pop before flipping them, spreading them lightly with butter, then calling the girls, who, like their mother before them, didn't get up until forced.

She called. Nobody came. She climbed up the long flight of stairs, her ankles complaining. Knocking on the door to the tiny attic room with her spatula, she called again. Finally, she heard stirring. "Wha . . . Grandma?" said Callie.

They needed to get up for church anyway. She didn't cater to this idea that Tory had once told her, that kids were worked so hard during the week they needed to relax on the weekend. They should get up early for chores. Children needed responsibility and a sense of purpose in this nutty world. Maybe if she had been stricter with the girls' mother . . .

She stuck her head through the door. Two sleepy, curly heads emerged from the flowered sheets.

"Rise and shine," she said. Her mother used to say that, and she said it too, hoping for good moods.

"I'm awake," April announced. "We'll be right there."

"Where's Grandpa?" Callie asked a few minutes later, sliding onto a stool at the counter, at eight years old, the older and more aware of Jolene's two granddaughters.

"He works all week. He's catching up on his sleep."

"I thought you said he retired," Callie said.

"Nobody retires from worrying. He needs a break."

"Doesn't he have to go to church with us?" asked April, only four years old, but already looking for angles. April's red hair made you want to worry about her temperament, but she was nothing like Cathy, her mother, at the same age. She tended to think more in advance of any misbehavior.

"He usually does," Jolene answered, a lie, but a forgivable one. George used to attend church in the days when he felt better, when the world helped him be his best self.

"I never saw him go. Not once," Callie said, pouring syrup on her final, gigantic pancake. "You make the best pancakes in the world, Grandma."

"Callie, your Grandpa's been sick for a long time."

"Where's Mama?" April asked. Her face, shiny with hope, glowed, poreless, young, innocent. "Can she come with us? Why doesn't she come see us?"

"She'll come when she can," said Jolene, reverting to her standard answer.

"Sometimes I have dreams about her not coming," Callie said.

"Don't you concern yourself like that, child," Jolene said firmly. "Why, she's coming in a couple of weeks." She decided to call her daughter and insist on a visit. Cathy didn't mean to be so mean. She didn't intend to abandon her two darling children. But her life was so hard, she couldn't always do the right thing.

Wouldn't it be nice if the girls' father were involved. Where was he, anyway? Sailing ships around the world? In prison? Whenever she asked, Cathy got canny. "He's in the merchant marines, Mama, out at sea. Unreachable." Or, "He's trying to provide for us, for God's sake. He's just had a lot of bad luck." Like he was really just a traditional husband, slaving away for a living wage.

George had always provided. He might be stingy, but he hadn't ever asked her to work outside the home. His legs were really bothering him these days, and he had to stay in bed a lot. Thank goodness he could play his guitar even in bed. He got more pleasure out of that old hollow-body than most men get from their wives. He was playing it in the bedroom right now, working on a new song.

"Grandpa's up!"

"You stay right here, Callie."

George sang from the bedroom,

> *I'm at the Humble Pie Motel in Room two-thirty-three*
> *And if you ever loved me, honey, ask the manager for the key . . .*

Her heart filled up with love for him. But I'm going to have to do something, she thought to herself, not for the first time. Yessirree.

Then they heard something else, a yowling Jolene knew well. George's muffled voice trailed off. He was listening too, but he wouldn't do anything about it. "Hey!" April said, now having fun arranging the mangled food on her plate with the contentment of a well-fed child. "I hear the kitties."

"That woman's a nuisance," said Jolene. "Poor Ruthie. Spending all her money on those animals. We don't need a bunch of wild cats roaming around this neighborhood. I wish she would just smell the roses and quit."

"Such pretty kitties," said Callie. "She's my hero."

"You know," Jolene said, "people who feed abandoned animals aren't doing anyone any favors. In a place like this, those animals can't get by without being fed. They're domesticated but they don't have homes anymore. Cruel people have abandoned them. In nature, they would . . . move on."

"But if they're hungry?" Callie asked. "Why can't they get food if they need it? I think the Cat Lady is right. Otherwise, they just wander around crying, they're so sad and hungry."

Well, naturally, she would feel that way. Maybe she remembered those days with Cathy, when none of them had enough to eat. She and George had not known about the deprivation until the court stepped in that day Cathy left the babies strapped into car seats in the car for four hours while she played house with a new boyfriend in Seaside.

Luckily, shade had come to protect the car and preserve the girls' lives after an hour or two. A few days in the hospital and the girls were fit as red ants in August again. "Why don't you two get yourselves upstairs now and find something cute to wear today?" Jolene suggested, not wanting to think anymore about that ordeal, which she hoped the girls didn't remember.

Her grandchildren cleared the table quickly, well-trained by Jolene, rinsing the dishes and stacking them neatly in the dishwasher.

Jolene couldn't ignore it anymore. Cats, making that ear-shredding yowling right outside the kitchen door. After church she planned a game of Monopoly with George and the girls. But first she needed to do something to shut up those dang cats.

"You wear the blue," she called up the stairs to Callie. "April, how about that white dress trimmed in pink?"

"It's too small," April said.

"Just for today."

"Well, okay. But something new next week, Grandma, if we can afford it. This one's above my knees."

The two girls trooped around upstairs quietly, whispering so that they wouldn't disturb Grandpa's songwriting. While they ran floods of water in the bathroom, Jolene wiped the table, still trying to ignore the keening whimpers of the cats outside.

George had said only yesterday when she remarked on the daily bedlam outside, leave Ruthie alone. Ruthie had the title of town character and what you do with town characters is you don't molest them or stare at them, you let them sing to themselves and mutter or in Ruthie's case feed cats and hand out leaflets.

Her Twelve Points were all over town. Jolene saw those leaflets spreading all up and down the valley, moving down to Big Sur in the pack of some Danish tourist, riding up to San Fran in some migrant worker's beat-up truck, moving east into the forest like a flea on a squirrel . . . if only Ruthie had something to say. The problem was, she didn't think very well, like most human beings.

But the cats . . . Jolene knew George didn't like them any more than she did. She had heard about what contamination they might cause in a sandbox, and they had one out back, mostly for April, because at four, she still liked to dig around and dream her baby dreams.

Jolene rubbed a spot into the window with the edge of her apron so that she could see across the street, past the bridge. Ruthie's heap of junk dominated. Obviously, Ruthie had slept in the lot over there. Someone ought to get her into an assisted-living situation. Maybe Ruthie wasn't so old, but she was incompetent. The money she spent on those wild cats must absorb any income she had coming in.

Slamming the dishwasher door shut, Jolene pulled at her apron, locating a peg to hang it on. She would have to go out there, speak to her. Make Ruthie see sense.

She had her hair up in rollers, big ones, because she liked a softer look, but it was still early, nobody else would be out. Full of resolve, she marched across the street to the dilapidated white car.

"Hello in there," she said. Ruthie sometimes slept in

this car under a quilt made of old wool suit fabric. She checked the back, but couldn't see inside.

"Ruthie?"

The front seat remained invisible. The car seemed covered with a fine, oily wet layer of skin, as thick as a seal's. A gust of warm wind lifted her housecoat.

Why did she bother, she groused inwardly. Still, a horde of caterwauling cats of all shapes and sizes clustered around the car. Some moved toward her, sidling up to her ankles, purred, and began to nudge her.

Enough! she thought. She pounded on the driver's-side door. When there was no response, she tried the handle.

The door, unlocked, fell open, and Ruthie, who never did anyone any harm, fell down out of her seat onto the hot asphalt.

Oh, Jolene thought. Oh, you poor thing. Ruthie looked so little and helpless. Her skin was bright red and her mouth hung open and she wasn't moving at all.

Was this what death looked like?

Because Ruthie, eyes closed, otherwise looked peaceful. As if she had just fallen asleep.

Nina and Paul had been home from Cachagua and the Bucket for half an hour, and Nina was still in the shower, when Ben Cervantes called with the news. "I thought you'd want to know," he said. "I heard it from Tory, who just got the call from Jolene. She found Ruthie's body this morning."

By the time Paul and Nina arrived, the police had photographed, dusted, and examined for hours. Ruthie still lay on the asphalt after all this time, cordoned off and harshly lit, while the ambulance stood by, waiting for the body to be released.

Gawkers continued to come and stare, to act as witnesses to the ritual of death. Nina recognized Darryl and Tory Eubanks. Tory was carrying her youngest. Some of the neighborhood kids ran back and forth across the street, yelling with excitement as though they were at the circus.

"Find anything?" Paul asked the detective in charge. With a weary look, the detective told Paul to back off, and in the interests of good relations, Paul did that. They waited in the Mustang while the ambulance drove off and the detectives called it a day.

Then they went back over to the parking lot. Ruth Frost's battered Cutlass was surrounded by yellow caution tape. A deputy had been posted, but, distracted by a pile of questions from Nina, he was rendered innocuous long enough for Paul to take one good look at the car.

"Crab and langoustine ravioli," Nina said to the waiter at the Terrace Grill. The Terrace Grill was an adjunct to the La Playa Hotel, a lovely old place that had been a fixture for many years in Carmel. They had chosen a table outside. It was nine-thirty at night and Nina's stomach was as empty as a crater on the moon. She had already started on the bread and butter.

Tonight the fog spared them. The warm air settled over them as softly as a veil. Birds shook the trees and flower garden nearby, settling in for the night, and the few streaks of cloud above the waterline were stained cherry.

"We'd like to start with crab cakes," Paul said, "then I'll have the prawns." He studied the wine list for another moment, then ordered a Gewürztraminer, very cold.

Nina reached across the table and took his large hand in hers. Hard, craggy, experienced, she thought, and smiled. "I feel guilty."

"Here we sit, playing violins, figuratively speaking," Paul said, "while Carmel Valley burns. People are dying. But we have to eat."

"The party goes on," Nina said.

"So it does. What's bothering you? I mean aside from Wish's problems, Ruthie's death, your hangover today from the party, and being tired and hungry from this whole long day."

"Isn't that enough?"

"Is it about Bob's call?"

"No . . . it's nothing."

"Not true."

"He's okay."

"So you're not ready to talk about it?"

"I'm thinking it'll blow over, Paul. I don't want to talk about it, as a matter of fact."

"Why not?" Paul demanded, as peremptorily as if she were a prisoner at Guantánamo Bay withholding vital information.

"It's none of your cotton-picking business," Nina said, her back up. Again.

"You won't tell me?"

"I will soon." When I have a solution, she thought.

Paul tolerated Bob, but children, in the generic, he did not like. He would not want Bob in the second bedroom he used as an office. Of course not. Fair enough.

One bathroom. Bob's forty-minute showers. Paul's lips would get as tight as an abalone shell at low tide.

Why couldn't Bob follow the plan? It had been so tidy. He had insisted on going to Sweden. Let him stay and build character.

But.

He was overwhelmed. He needed to come home. Home in quotation marks. Home in the abstract. Alas, in truth, there existed no home for Bob to come home to at the moment.

"It's Nikki, isn't it? Nikki's older," Paul said. "She does things she shouldn't and that makes her attractive to Bob. What else is new?"

Oh, not much, Bob wants to come home, Nina thought. "Nikki's cooling off toward Bob."

"Ah. And what's his response?"

She decided she would go no further in this direction,

especially given the interest she saw rising in his greeny-yellow eyes. Which, in spite of the glass of wine he had just downed, remained sharp. "So, Paul," she said, licking the tip of her already-shiny spoon, "what did you think happened to Ruthie?"

He cocked his head, but let it go. "I have a few ideas," he said. "Ruth Frost's car was old, so I can't be sure."

"But . . ." she offered.

"Right. But . . ."

"Something struck you?"

"You know how when you have a hunch?"

"You never buy my hunches."

"But I buy my own."

"What hunch?"

"The police think because it was a cold night, she left her motor and heat running."

"You don't think so?"

"I think she'd run it for a while, then turn it off."

"Because?"

"Because she was slightly cockeyed, yes; stupid, no. Have you ever noticed that if you're an outsider, people will believe you're capable of all sorts of unreasonableness?"

"Maybe she felt running the motor outside would be harmless. She didn't know she would die. Probably thought the outside air would dissipate any carbon monoxide. Maybe she passed out before she could turn off the car."

Paul said, "Witnesses say she hasn't had a back seat in years. That she often left the motor running to get heat, when she needed it. Not smart, with leaks in the exhaust system, but she knew that and didn't do it for long."

"Does anyone say she threatened to kill herself?"

"No."

"So what do you suspect? The police seem satisfied our Cat Lady died a natural death, out feeding her beloved animals in the night, trying to stay warm in her ruin of a car."

"I guess if I was looking at the situation from the point of view that she was living a risky existence and had a bad accident, I'd be satisfied too. But there were those marks on the exhaust pipe," Paul said.

Nina stopped eating. "Marks?"

"Maybe natural aging, maybe not. I took a few photographs and looked at them before we came here, but they don't really prove anything. Those marks could have happened a lot of ways. And it doesn't look like the forensics people are planning to figure this one out for us. The authorities seem pretty set on natural death."

"You pointed out what you saw?"

"They saw what I saw. They took photographs too, but, you know, strange way to kill someone."

"Are you sure what's been happening around here isn't inspiring your imagination?"

"Maybe. But maybe somebody rigged a hose into the car to help out the fumes in the back. She went out there to take care of the animals. She ran the motor and fell asleep. Someone ran a hose from the pipe into the car."

"Without her noticing?"

"She was sleeping. And she slept on. After a while, he removed the hose."

"Oh, Paul. That poor woman." Nina pictured her long hair, the heap her body made on the pavement.

"Someone got to her before she died."

"Was she hit? Did you see a bruise?"

"Nothing so definite. But there was something off about the whole thing. Maybe a hot drink put her to sleep first. Maybe a knock upside the head, then the hose inserted into a window, was the final scenario."

Nina rubbed her forehead. "You believe she was murdered."

"She was the only witness to the arsons. You realize that? Remember what you said happened at that party just a few hours before?"

"I've been thinking about that. There was jokey talk," she said, "about doing a lineup for Ruthie, making her pick out who she saw fleeing the arson. I guess if our Siesta

Court arsonist happened to be within earshot, he heard that. Maybe he took it seriously."

"Maybe that got her killed."

"I'm thinking, how does this help Wish? I hate to be so cold, but his arraignment's in the morning. And it does help Wish, but we have to prove it was a murder. The theory currently is that Danny was the Siesta Court arsonist and Wish was the outside man. But Danny's dead and Wish was sleeping on a state-issue mattress."

"Right. So—" She let Paul say it.

"Who killed the Cat Lady?"

16

"HEY, WISH," NINA said. "What's with your hair?"

"Nobody wears long hair anymore. It's a symbol of the Res." Wish looked scalped, there was no other way to put it, and Nina's heart went out to him. He was giving way to the peer pressure of the other inmates herded together into their seats in the jury box of the courtroom.

These tough guys wore the haircuts of male Marines and indifferent expressions, but they didn't look tough to Nina. To her these kids, minority kids mostly, looked like inmates of any gulag or concentration camp, right down to being tattooed.

"How are you?"

"Tired of this, since I didn't do anything to deserve it."

"I made an appointment to talk to Jaime Sandoval—the D.A."

"So I don't get out today?" Her expression answered him and his face twisted. Nina checked her watch. Monday-morning arraignments started in five minutes.

"Soon, Wish, I promise you. Something important has happened. The main witness linking Danny to the previous fires is dead. The lady who fed cats, Ruth Frost. Carbon-monoxide poisoning when she ran the heat in her car night before last. An accident, they say."

Wish's back straightened. He took hold of his lip with his fingers and started worrying it, a habit he shared with his mother, and she saw with joy that the law-enforcement student had come to the foreground.

"That's suspicious," he said. "Paul doesn't believe it, does he?"

"He's getting the autopsy report right now," Nina told him. "He believes someone may have incapacitated her before turning on the heat."

"Somebody killed a woman who fed hungry cats," Wish said. "I don't know what to think."

"I went to a block party on Danny's street. The neighbors talked about her report."

"One of the neighbors. Who, Nina? Someone strong who smelled burnt. That doesn't help. Something sharp digging into my back."

"Like what?" Nina said, latching on to a new thought. "Where on your back?"

Wish rubbed his hand on the small of his back. "I don't know what. How many people on that street with strong arms?"

"Four. Danny's uncle, Ben—"

"He's got no reason. He's cool."

"David Cowan."

"Danny's neighbor on the left. He paid Danny to do odd jobs for him, but he didn't treat Danny very well."

"I doubt anyone likes Mr. Cowan much," Nina said. "What motive would he have?"

"He's odd. I don't understand him."

"Danny had a thing with his wife. Mr. Cowan knew about it, but he never said a word."

"I'm not surprised."

"Who else?"

"Ted Ballard. The Ballards live three doors down on the Rosie's Bridge side. They ride bikes, hike, go kayaking. They both make a lot of money, I think. Right now, they're building a new house on Robles Ridge, not far from the fire locations."

"Burn it down for insurance?" Wish said.

"The construction is still at the framing stage. But Paul is looking into their finances."

"I can't see why he'd set fires."

"Another possibility is Darryl Eubanks, Danny's neighbor on the Rosie's Bridge side." The clerk came in and Nina realized they were running out of time. "He's a volunteer firefighter. Did Danny ever talk about him?"

Wish shook his head.

"Wish, there's another possibility. Remember the driver of the car the Cat Lady saw? The one who dropped off somebody on Siesta Court?"

"You got a line on him?" Wish said, hope in every bone.

"Ever heard Danny talk about a man named Coyote?"

"Sure!"

"I met him. He drives a minivan like the one Ruth Frost described. Danny had to get his tip from somewhere. Who else did he see regularly?"

"That's a very good line of thought, Nina. Coyote—they were drinking buddies."

"All rise," the bailiff said. Wish got up with some difficulty. Nina saw with anger that he was shackled.

He whispered amid the general shuffle, "I almost forgot. Tell Paul I left his bank statements in the file marked 'Dough,' like he said."

"Dough?"

Wish nodded. "Tell him to eat the cottage cheese I left in the office fridge before the expiration date."

Nina walked swiftly to the attorney's section and sat down with her briefcase in her lap. Wish didn't seem to think anyone on Siesta Court had done it. And she hadn't even had time to ask him about Sam Puglia.

This time she had to sit through an hour of other cases. Jaime and Judge Salas processed them efficiently, but there were thirty or forty of them. Resigning herself to a long wait, she observed the process. Just like old times, the first break came up at 10:15. Maintenance had left the heaters on and the courtroom felt like the Sahara on this June morning, the first record-breaking day of another California summer. If they were lucky, later the usual foggy breeze would snake its way up the river from the Pacific, but right now the lawyers sweated in their jackets and the clerk whispered urgently into the phone trying to get them some relief.

Outside Courtroom Number Three of the old Salinas Courthouse, the town had come to life after the weekend. A few blocks away at the Steinbeck Center, the staff would be holding a meeting to figure out a way to dredge up more money. Closer by, red beans would be frying in steaming metal skillets at Rosita's. Young mothers pushed their strollers toward the thrift stores on Main. The Hartnell College students hurried to class. All around the town the early-summer lettuce and strawberry pickers would be bending over in the fertile fields, faces covered to keep out the pesticides.

Fifteen miles west of Salinas, on the coast, weekday life would be picking up. Nina imagined the denizens of Carmel: rugged retiree ladies throwing sticks into the water for their purebred retrievers at Carmel Beach, athletic graybeards chatting with each other at the post office, the chic tourists unloading their hard-earned money. In Monterey, there would be lawyers and insurance types clicking their pens in preparation for another week of rooking people out of this and that; and in Pebble Beach, Japanese golfers already finishing their eighteen holes, looking forward to sipping mimosas at Club XIX.

Funny, Nina thought, two societies so close and so separate. She didn't agree with the Cat Lady that there were only two classes, the exploiters and the exploitees, but the enormous difference in wealth did seem at the heart of the social schism.

Her mind returned to the Twelve Points. Who can say

what is a successful life? Ruth Frost had expressed her opinions in the newspaper, no doubt influencing some people. She had saved the lives of some animals. She had been free and she had done some good. Nina wondered what would happen to the cats.

The bailiff called Number Thirty-Five on the docket, *People* v. *Whitefeather,* the big case for today, the homicide. As Wish was brought to the counsel table shuffling in his leg shackles, lurid with his shaved head and the orange jumpsuit that made the defendants resemble Halloween janitors, the reporters in the second row woke up.

Wish would not be going home today, not with bail set at a million five. Nina pulled out the chair for him and helped him sit down.

Judge Salas, like everybody else, observed them; he stared at Wish, the star today, if not the hero. Wish wasn't a head-hanger; he paid attention, his eyes jumping back and forth.

Nina glanced down at the official charges Jaime had just handed her, conscious of the mundane sounds and sights of the courtroom around her, the bailiff lounging against the wall by the defendants in the jury box, the clerk shuffling her papers, somebody reading a newspaper in his lap in the back, the yellow light, the clock on the wall.

Salas read the charges out loud. Daniel Cervantes had died on or about June 9, a Tuesday.

"In the county of Monterey, California . . . How do you plead?"

How *do* you plead? Do you get down on your knees and beg?

They were standing. In the moment before Wish had his first chance to say a word, Nina and Wish looked at each other. Nina felt flustered, as if something had jerked in her reality, as if her mother had reached down from heaven to tap her on the shoulder. Wish, standing next to her with his forehead furrowed and his hands clenched together in front of him, gave Nina the same look her mother used to give her, the one that said, Nina-pinta, they won't get us down. We can survive anything.

Not just his expression, but the way his eyebrows drew together, the way he put his chin up and firmed up his mouth, moved her. Nina thought with a pang, He trusts me completely. He thinks there's no danger.

Passing her fingers lightly over her forehead, she pulled herself together.

"How do you plead?" Salas repeated.

Nina nudged Wish. "Not guilty." His voice didn't waver.

Nina couldn't say a word about Ruth Frost. Now was not a time to raise a defense, unfortunately. The rest of the arraignment ritual commenced.

Jaime asked her again for a waiver of time, this time in front of Salas. He had been flabbergasted when Nina had explained several days before that she would not waive the ten-day rule. Wish had a right under the Penal Code to have a judge examine the charges in a court hearing, even in a murder case, within ten court days.

But no defense counsel in a murder case ever refused to waive time. The information passed on to the defense was usually overwhelming, and the defense attorney wouldn't want to miss anything. Even in the Robert Blake Hollywood murder case, the defense was still complaining bitterly about the volume of information and asking for more time before the prelim, eight months after the arraignment.

Nina had her own ideas about the conventional defense-counsel wisdom, however. She had noticed that if she worked very hard during those ten court days, she could master everything the prosecution had and still mount a defense of sorts. California district-attorney's offices had gotten lazy about prelims, which they liked to process like widgets on the factory line. The deputy D.A. couldn't put the time in that she could. The evidence was much more fluid, the witness statements more subject to attack, than at a later trial.

So she would refuse to waive time, attack at the prelim, be well prepared, and cut no slack. This caused unpleasantness with the D.A.'s along the lines of, don't come asking us for any favors. Like a good deal for the client.

So it was usually a trade-off. Jaime would give her a hard time if she needed a plea bargain. But a plea bargain would never happen in this case, because Wish was as innocent of evil as Jimmy Carter.

They set the prelim for June 30, a Monday, Salas shaking his head, giving her a hard look, and asking her how long she had been practicing law. The clerk wrote the date down and gave the lawyers their copies.

The bailiff grabbed Wish by the elbow. Hauled up like a dolphin in a tuna net, Wish lost whatever dignity he had left. Nina decided to complain to Jaime about showing more respect handling the defendants.

The next defendant stood up, ready to get started, and Nina looked over at Wish once more, saying with her eyes, just a few more days, hang on.

With recess finally announced, Nina went out into the hall.

"Ms. Reilly!" Salas's clerk called to her. She had followed her out. "Judge received a phone call."

"Yes?"

"For you. Apparently this person didn't know how to reach you and called the court instead." She handed Nina a note.

"Thanks." Nina walked outside, reading.

The almost-incoherent message had apparently been transcribed verbatim from an after-hours tape.

For Miss Nina Reilly. He makes me eat bad things. Maybe you could come get me. Liar liar pants on fire and choir singing in tire. His hands are bloody but you can't see it he hides them in the forest and silver things aren't his. Thieves do that. And he said one more the big one it will be done. So please set me free, yours truly, my mother said always to say that at the end.

She knew immediately who it was. She called Paul on her cell phone. "Busy?"

"I have the autopsy report and some news. Are you finished at court?"

"Yes. Nate called."

"Coyote's little brother?"

"I think he needs help."

"I'll meet you at the condo. We'll talk there. How did it go with Wish?"

"As expected. I'm going to call a psychiatrist about Nate and read him this note the minute I get back."

17

Nina hung up the phone in the living room and reported, "Dr. Cervenka says it's typical schizophrenic speech, but he can't tell whether there is actually an external problem. Nate may be unhappy, he may be in danger, or he might just be expressing some inner reality."

Paul pushed back in his chair, crossed his legs, and put his hands behind his head. "I don't think we should interfere," he said.

"You think that boy is adequately cared for in that tent he lives in? By that hostile man he lives with?"

"Coyote's his brother," Paul reminded her. "Kept him alive this long. You could call the county and ask for a Child Welfare check."

"That might take weeks. They're so far out in the country. I've been thinking about Nate, about what you called his nest."

"And he hadn't seen a kind woman for a long time, I bet," Paul said. "So he's been thinking about you ever since too."

"Think how hard it must have been for Nate to find a phone number that might reach me—he has to be desperate! He obviously has no one else. We have to do something," she said. "I don't want to read in the paper that something happened to him." She pulled her jeans out of the suitcase.

"He's not your problem or responsibility. Wish is. And,

Nina, I don't know if you've noticed, but things are falling apart around here. We need a couple of hours to do chores and get things in shape. And I have the autopsy report on Ruth Frost. We need to talk about it."

"On the way. I want to go back to Arroyo Seco."

"Since when do you have to take every sad case in the world under your wing? He's not your problem, Nina. You're like the Cat Lady, picking up strays. You need to focus on this case. We owe it to Sandy to get Wish out of jail, and fast."

Nina finished lacing the boots and hung her purse on her shoulder. "I'm going," she said. "He has come to my attention. That makes him my problem."

"Suit yourself." Paul stretched and went back to his computer.

Nina clumped down the steps and onto the street, where her truck was parked. Climbing into the Bronco, she strapped in and opened the glove compartment to look for the Monterey County map. Paul's face appeared at the passenger's window and she rolled it down. Hitchcock leapt at the door.

"I was thinking, we ought to go check on the kid," he said.

Nina smiled. "I've got bottled water and cold drinks in a cooler, and the tank's full."

"We can talk about the autopsy report along the way." He climbed in beside her. "Hitchcock too. He needs the exercise."

"Same rules? You expunge all evidence of poison oak from his fur?" Nina said, opening the back door and scratching the dog between the ears.

"He's the first dog I ever met that loves the hose, a real sport," Paul said, clipping on the seat belt. "I wonder what he is."

Nina started up and lowered the back window a couple of inches so Hitchcock could stick his nose out. "How many times do I have to say it? He's a malamute!"

"There's no such thing as a pure black malamute. Plus they don't bark, they howl, and Hitchcock barks. He's part Lab or something."

"Will you stop? He's got that curling furry tail. And he smiles like a malamute," Nina said. Hitchcock showed no interest in their ongoing argument over his origins. He only gave a brief whine, which meant, let's get going, shall we?

They drove out the Valley Road, each curve of which was becoming familiar to Nina, Hitchcock no doubt getting carsick in the back. Paul had brought the autopsy report. As they careened around the turns he said, "Now may I take up a few minutes of your time to discuss this latest homicide?"

"Let's hear it."

"Ruth Frost had a hematoma on the side of her head the size of a plum. It wasn't visible when we saw her, because she had so much hair. Now, even law enforcement agrees. Somebody hit her hard, turned on the ignition and the heat, closed the windows tight, and left her to die. The coroner says so. Is that going to be enough to convince the D.A. to let Wish out?"

"I don't know. But who else would want to harm her but the arsonist? Who is heading up the investigation?"

"The Monterey County Sheriff's Office."

"Does Crockett know about all this?"

"I faxed him the report while you were in court, to be sure he's staying in the loop," Paul said.

Nina's hands clenched the wheel. "It has to be somebody from Siesta Court, afraid she could identify him."

"Let's talk about a few thoughts running around in my head," Paul said as they rolled through Carmel Valley Village. The school bus flashed its red lights, and Nina stopped. A group of children with the name of a day-care center on their T-shirts jostled one another into a beautiful afternoon, bumping across the street in front of them to meet waiting parents. They called laughing good-byes to one another as they ran shouting toward TVs and backyards.

The sun burned a yellow hole in the cloudless blue sky. They passed a Smokey the Bear sign telling them that the fire danger today was Very High. "I'm listening," Nina said.

"Okay. First, ask yourself about the MO used to kill Ruth. Ruth had a defective tailpipe that billowed exhaust fumes into the trunk area, and no back seat to prevent it from drifting into the passenger compartment. She had to drive with all the windows open, and I just don't believe she'd go to sleep with the windows closed and the motor running."

"You said something about a hose."

"There's no evidence of a hose at this point. The marks I saw turned out to be natural."

"Somebody knew about the exhaust problem, then."

"Ben Cervantes repairs cars."

"So do a hundred other people around here."

"He works at Valley European Motors in the Village," Paul said. "I went up there and talked to his boss before the cops got there. He was upset about Ruth. He's known her for years. He said Ruth would bring her car in there and they tried to keep it going without charging her."

Nina said, eyes on the road, "I like Ben. But I'm willing to look at him."

"This isn't just about Ben. Turns out Ben replaced another guy, a part-timer who drank on the job and was fired. This guy's name is Robert Johnson. He's half Washoe, like Danny."

"So?"

Paul squeezed her thigh. "So Coyote's real name is Robert Johnson. Watch it, there's a truck coming."

Nina pulled to the side and let the truck go by. "So Coyote probably worked on Ruth's car at some point."

"There you have it."

"Then she probably knew him, Paul. If he had been in the car she saw, wouldn't she have recognized him?"

"She told us she didn't see well enough," Paul said. He drank some water out of a plastic bottle. "But if—let's follow it through—if Coyote was in the car, he might have been worrying about Ruthie. Maybe so worried he thought about that broken exhaust pipe and the lack of a back seat, which would let the fumes in and kill her."

"He had the means and maybe the motive," Nina said. "The minute I saw that van at his camp I was sure he was involved in the fires."

"So let's take it further. Let's say Robert Johnson—Coyote—was the driver that night in his van, and he dropped someone off on Siesta Court. Like the Cat Lady said."

"Okay."

"Who did he drop off? Assuming it wasn't Danny?"

"Danny had a tip," Nina remembered.

"Right. Smart girl."

"Ben Cervantes and Coyote?"

"My thinking exactly. Danny knew who they were climbing up the hill to photograph."

"He would turn in his uncle? His uncle was doing this with Coyote?"

"Maybe. Or maybe just Coyote."

Nina said slowly, "But instead Coyote saw Danny and Wish first and Coyote killed Danny on the mountain. And tried to kill Wish."

"You're leaving Ben out, but I can understand your squeamishness. You liked him, I could tell. I'd also prefer to think Ben didn't help kill his own nephew. But . . ."

They had hit the hairpin turns in the road. To one side, a fenced golden meadow waved, and on the other, a glorious old oak forest rustled, maybe some of those same trees surviving from Steinbeck's time, when he loved this same land. In the midst of all this beauty, someone out there was burning trees and killing people. She felt sick thinking that Ben Cervantes might be part of it.

"I don't think it's Ben."

"Because?"

"I just don't. I don't think he could lie that well to me."

"Ah, Nina."

"Anyway, Coyote is probably a very dangerous man," Nina said. "We have to check on that boy."

"That's why I came along, even though I think it's premature. Because my woman insisted on coming."

Nina glanced quickly at him and saw that he had unconsciously patted his shoulder holster. "I'm glad you came. Maybe we'll get lucky and Coyote and that saw-toothed dog of his will be busy somewhere else hunting deer together."

They drove on through the buzzing forest, immersed in their separate thoughts.

Eventually, tired and hot again, but this time more sure of the way, they found the tent in the clearing in Wood Tick Canyon. Once again, Nina avoided the malevolent poison oak, mature vines thick as her wrist, coming hungrily at her from the branches and bushes she passed. She took some satisfaction when it crackled underfoot, but then realized she would have to ask Paul to detoxify her boots along with the dog.

Outside the tent were few signs of activity—a stump with an ax stuck in it alongside a fresh stack of kindling, and a dead geranium in a black plastic container. The canvas door was lashed down. A tin bowl half full of water sat under the nearest tree, with a long chain wrapped around it once, the other end lying on the ground.

No sign of a car. No pit bull, no sign of Coyote. Nina expelled a breath she hadn't realized she had been holding. Paul put Hitchcock on a leash. They picked their way to the tree where Paul had noticed the boy and Nina saw, where three stout branches intersected, Nate, huddling on a pile of branches and rags. He had been watching them for some time.

"Hello."

"Hello, Nate."

"Did you come to get me? I made a call. Mother taught me to call."

"Would you like to come down and talk to us?" Paul said.

"I'm not allowed. Loud and louder until you want to scream like I scream. Ice cream. Never get any anymore. More."

"I brought you a Coke," Nina said, holding up one of the cans they had brought along. "It's cold too. But I can't get up there."

"But I can't come down. So, so, I need to sew my pants, they're ripped." But he made some movements, as though he were trying.

Paul bent down, examining the tree. "Shit," he said. "Look here." In the back, screwed into the tree, was a ring with a chain welded to it. The chain led upward.

Nina looked, following the chain up into the tree, where it ended at Nate's nest. Down in the ground at the foot of the tree, she spotted signs of disturbance, signs of a struggle. "That's it," she said. "He's coming with us."

Paul drew her aside. "Listen," he said in a low voice. "I'm not too up on schizophrenics, or whatever the current parlance is, but I have a feeling nobody is making sure this kid takes his meds. He's going to be unpredictable. We should call the sheriff."

"We'll take him to the sheriff. This is child abuse. I won't stand for it another minute! Look, let's get him out of here before Coyote gets back. Let's avoid an incident. Anything could happen. Please, Paul."

Paul said, "Just stick him in the back seat? I don't want him behind me."

"In the front seat."

"Where he could grab the wheel?"

"Okay," Nina said. "I'll drive and you two sit in back where you can keep an eye on him."

"That ought to be a pleasant journey." But he took hold of the ring and tried to pull it out. "I get the feeling Coyote did not want Nate to be able to take this thing on and off easily. Can you talk him down so I can look at the other end?"

Nina moved out so she could see Nate better, and said, "Can we take you for an ice cream, Nate? Will you come down so my friend can take off the chain?"

"He'll be mad, mad, mad. Oh, he'll be mad."

"We'll keep you safe."

"Can I tell him you made me?"

"Sure you can." The boy seemed to shake his nest and then a skinny leg appeared and positioned itself on a branch. He hauled himself out of the pile. His leg bore a heavy shackle that looked a lot like the one Wish had been wearing in court that morning. The rest of the chain swung down suddenly, clanking, and pulled him off-balance, but he managed to hang on. He slid down and his feet came close enough to Paul for Paul to grab him. In a moment he was on the ground.

"Here I am. How do you do."

Nina held out a hand to steady him while Paul knelt down to examine the shackle.

Nate was skinny and short, but the beginnings of adolescent stubble and the Adam's apple confirmed to Nina that he was just past puberty, about thirteen, as the cowboys at Alma's had said. He looked Native American. He still wore the dirty flannel shirt with his narrow chest exposed in front, his jeans were in shreds, and his feet were bare. He smelled bad. The chain gave him about ten feet to wander around the base of the tree.

Paul hurried back to the Bronco for Nina's tool kit, while Nate and Nina waited. Nate seemed nonchalant, as though he had placed his fate totally in their hands. He looked around, surveying everything, without anxiety, with an expression of wonder and pleasure and something else, a light in his eyes that made Nina uncomfortable. He drank down the soft drink thirstily and Nina noticed that he was missing some teeth. Hitchcock sniffed him and Nate backed away. "Go lie down," Nina told Hitchcock.

Paul came back and knelt with his toolbox by the shackles. Pulling on leather gloves, he took a small hacksaw and began sawing.

Hitchcock's ears pricked up and his head swiveled toward the Bronco. Nina thought she heard something and looked anxiously down the dirt road that came off Arroyo Seco.

A car.

"Uh-oh," Nate said.

"Hurry!" Nina said.

"I hear it."

Nate said, "Ow!" Just as Coyote's tan van pulled into the clearing, the shackle fell away. The pit bull in the front seat of the van was already growling, its bullet head extended out the car window.

The van's motor died. Coyote sat inside, about a hundred feet away, not moving. Afternoon light behind him made his face indistinct. Paul straightened up. He picked up Hitchcock's leash and handed it to Nina, saying, "Hold on to him. Nate, you stay with Nina."

He walked slowly toward the van, his boots kicking up miniature dust storms behind. The sun beat down hard in the clearing, making a minidesert out of the setting.

Nina, leash wrapped around her hand, stood beside the boy, fighting off her fear for Paul.

The pit bull leapt out of the half-open window and came at Paul. At the same time, Hitchcock leapt forward, teeth bared. She could have held him—could have stopped him—but she let him go, to fight.

The pit bull, seeing Hitchcock, veered behind Paul and the two dogs met in a snarling, snapping fury, rolling over and over in the dirt. Paul backed away and pulled out his gun, but he couldn't do anything with it. The two dogs made one whirling blur. Nate pressed against Nina, whimpering. She pulled him behind the tree.

Coyote sat in his van, unmoving. Paul picked up a piece of cut firewood from the woodpile and ran up to the dogs, who snapped and bit, completely beyond command. Looking for his chance, Paul held the piece of wood up and hit the pit bull on its back. It let out a shrieking sound, but it had its jaws embedded in Hitchcock's neck now and would not let go. Paul hit it again.

Out of the van's window a rifle barrel appeared, growing longer as it extended out. "Paul!" she screamed. Concentrating on the maddened dogs, he didn't hear her. She kept her eyes on the rifle, now pointed directly at Paul—what could she do? "Paul!"

Paul hit the pit bull on the skull. Its jaws opened slowly. It let go of Hitchcock, rolled over, and lay still. The rifle swiveled, following Paul's movements. Again, she screamed. This time he heard her. With a movement so fast she barely registered it, he threw himself facedown to the ground, then began crawling rapidly into the brush.

But Coyote didn't shoot. Suddenly, the ruckus quieted, the bugs and animals seemed subdued, the air was still. Paul, lying in some manzanita, had his gun aimed toward the van. The rifle barrel caught a glint of sun. The wind died. Hitchcock crouched, whining, near the body of the pit bull. The picture froze. She would never forget it—the rank smell of the boy clutching her, Paul's expression, hard and terrible, the blinding sun—

Small sounds started up. Hitchcock, still whining, hurt. Her own harsh breathing. Meanwhile, the rifle never moved, frozen in space. She couldn't see the man behind it, just the outline of his head in a cowboy hat.

The roar of the engine caught her by surprise as the van started up. The rifle disappeared and the van bucked backward and turned. Wrapped in a robe of dust, it accelerated out of the clearing.

He was gone. Nina ran to Hitchcock, who crouched like a sphinx. Wounds on his neck and ear actively bled. Paul had gone to the other dog, stick at the ready, but it didn't move. He poked at it. Nina saw its muzzle, flecked with saliva and blood.

"Dead," Paul said.

Nate stayed back. "Dead dog," he said in a high, anxious tone. "Hedgehog, there are wild boars around here. They rush out of the bushes with tusks. Or mothers with babies all in a row behind them."

Paul came over to stand beside Hitchcock. He knelt down. "I'll get the picnic blanket out of the back," Nina said. They wrapped Hitchcock up and put him in the cargo area of the Bronco.

"I'd like to search the tent while Coyote's gone," Paul said.

"No, Paul. Please." She didn't say, it's illegal. All bets were off, but they had to get Nate out of there safely and get Hitchcock to a vet. "Hop in back," she told Nate, and he did.

Paul studied the tent.

"He almost shot you," she said. "I don't know why he didn't pull the trigger."

"I killed his dog."

"You had to. Paul, if—if you want to go in there, I'll wait out here with Nate and Hitchcock."

"Stay here." He jogged to the tent and entered. In about three minutes, which amounted to three years of nail-biting fear in Nina's life, he came out.

Nina got in front and Paul climbed in back. Reversing, she drove them all out of there.

18

THEY SWERVED THROUGH the curves, Nate curled up in a corner of the back seat. He did not warm to Paul, who after a few minutes decided that Nate wouldn't do anything rash and leaned over the front passenger-seat headrest to watch the road.

"Where should we take him?" he said eventually. "You got this figured out?"

"The sheriff's substation," Nina said. "Carmel Valley Village is the closest."

"He might have relatives."

"The authorities can notify them. And screen them. I'm not taking any chances. Nate? Nate?" Nina rolled up the windows and turned on the AC, so the Bronco was quieter. "Is he asleep, Paul?"

"No, he's looking out the window. Hey, kid, Nina wants to ask you a question, okay?" In the rearview mirror, Nina saw Paul tap Nate's knee. The boy turned that wondering, anxious, otherworldly face to them.

"Nate? You talked about your mother. Where is your mother?"

"Are you my mother?" His head cocked.

"No, where is your mother?"

"Home."

"And where is home?"

"Markleeville."

"Markleeville!"

"Did I say something wrong? Ring, rang, wrong. The mission has a big bell."

"Nate, are you Washoe? From the Washoe tribe?"

"My mother says Washoe all the time. Washoe my shoe. It must be dirty."

"Paul," Nina said, "it would make sense. Danny was half Washoe. He would have hooked up with other Washoes who lived down here." She was excited. Sandy was a Washoe elder. The tribe could help Nate. He would be identified, claimed, and protected by the tribe.

She asked questions, trying to find out how Nate had come to that godforsaken clearing in the woods to live with his brother, but Nate didn't seem to know the answers. He would try to explain, but got sidetracked so quickly she couldn't get the sense.

"We'll call Sandy tonight and find out about him," Paul said.

"Yes. Nate, Paul and I—we won't let anyone hurt you. We are going to see that you have a bath and food and . . ."

"Ice cream!"

"Ice cream. And nice people to stay with while we call your mother."

"But you're the one that I love," Nate said, sounding frightened.

"I'll see you again soon."

"He's going to take some children."

"What?" Paul said.

"He is. Take them in the van someplace. I heard. Who are they?"

Nina almost ran off the road. When she could, she slowed, pulled off, and stopped the car, then twisted so that she could see Nate. On his face was an expression of innocent inquiry.

Paul showed many emotions. He held up his hand, keeping Nina quiet, saying, "Nate, listen to me. Okay? Are you listening?"

Nate nodded.

"Coyote is going to take some children?"

"That doesn't sound right. Did I say that?"

"How did you find out? About taking children?"

He appeared more confident. "He talked on the phone. Then he saw me and put me in the tree. Nailed me to the tree."

"What did he say on the phone?" Nate looked out the window, and Paul tapped his knee again and repeated the question.

"He said nobody stiffs him and you better have the money ready next day."

"What else did he say?"

"He said, you goddamn little weasel, you were listening to me. And put me in the tree. At night there are sounds."

"Is that all you heard? All he said?"

"Birds. Squirrels. The sounds acorns make when they fall. Wee-zull. Weasel. Please freeze. Ice cream."

That was all they could get from him. After ten minutes during which Nate degenerated into complete nonsense, Nina started up again, driving them to the sheriff's department in the Village. Inside, Paul let her handle it. She quickly put on her invisible lawyer togs, insisting on talking to the station captain, insisting on filling out statements, insisting on having Child Welfare contacted while she and Paul waited.

They left Nate in the care of a sympathetic female deputy. He hadn't had his ice cream yet, but they made a solemn promise he would get his wish soon. The sheriff's office would talk to the D.A.'s office about getting a search warrant for the campsite and an arrest warrant for Robert Johnson, aka Coyote, for child endangerment.

"Don't worry," Nina said one last time, as Nate was led away.

"Mother told me, say yours truly. Yours truly," the boy told her calmly. The police officer opened a door to a room where he could rest and Nina gave him a wave. He didn't wave back, just observed her until the door closed.

Nina looked at her watch. Seven-thirty in the evening,

darkness outside. "I think it's safe to fall apart now, Paul," she said. She opened the back door. Hitchcock woke up and wagged his tail, but his head was crusty with blood. "Good boy," she said. "Brave boy."

"I'll drive home. Here. Climb in. Put your head against the window. You're tired. Here's my jacket. Use it for a pillow."

"Should we have taken Nate back to the condo? I hate to think of him in that sterile—"

"He needs a shrink. He needs medication. He'll get what he needs. You can check on him."

"I'm so tired and so concerned about Nate."

"We'll check on him."

"Coyote's going to take some children. We have to do something."

"We did what we could. We told the deputy. I'll call Crockett's office tonight and leave a message there too. Meanwhile, let's get you home and get Hitchcock to the vet, honey."

The next morning, Nina woke up without a memory of getting out of her clothes and into bed. She had fallen asleep in the car and had only a vague memory of Paul reassuring her about Hitchcock's condition. Clouds hovered in the skies outside the windows and a brisk breeze ruffled the trees outside the bedroom window. She was alone.

Remembering Nate and Hitchcock, she sprang out of bed.

In the kitchen, Paul talked on the cell phone, stirring eggs. He wore the black silk boxers she had given him. The laundry must be getting dire. "That's it," he said. He hung up, said "Crockett," and leaned over so she could hug him. The condo felt warm and safe.

"I got hold of the vet who saw Hitchcock last night," Paul said. "The mutt needed seven stitches on his ear, and six on that nasty neck tear. They put him under, but we can pick him up later."

"He's all right?"

"His ear will be permanently cocked."

"Poor fellow." Nina sat down at the table. "I'm so relieved that he's going to be all right. What time is it?"

"Ten-thirty."

"No! I haven't slept that late in years. I'd better get dressed."

"Relax. Have your coffee. A lot of people are working on this."

"Nate?"

"May soon be in a foster home. His mother's name is Susie Johnson. She lives in Markleeville. She's a Washoe tribe member. Sandy knows her."

"You've been busy."

"Yes. Sandy says Susie's husband died recently in a farm accident. Coyote is her oldest kid. He told her he was doing fine in Monterey County and held a big job with the Forest Service. Susie has two younger daughters besides Nate. So she sent Nate to live with him."

"She should have known better!"

"It's puzzling. She says Coyote always treats Nate gently and loves him a lot. Also, Nate was on meds when he went down there and has gotten into this state since then."

"Coyote gentle? That's a good one. The mother needed to persuade herself that Nate would be taken care of."

"And he sure isn't an employee of the Forest Service. After he lost the part-time work at Valley European, he did day labor on ranches and vineyards out there."

Nina ate, leaving Paul the cleanup. He was efficient in his tidy kitchen. They didn't talk, like old married folks, but one issue they should be talking about weighed heavily on her heart.

What was she going to do about Bob? The moment was quickly arriving when she needed to discuss this issue with

Paul. She should buy Bob's airplane ticket. She should call him, tell him where they would be living.

She had no idea.

She needed more time.

She shelved it and was relieved when Paul kicked shut the pots-and-pans drawer and said, "I have to go talk to Crockett. We have to find Coyote before he hijacks a school bus."

"You're going to report on what you found in Coyote's tent? But we haven't discussed it yet. I told you, you have some exposure there. You could possibly be charged with obstructing justice or—"

"Don't worry, honey. I've got it covered."

"It's a legal matter and I'm a—"

"Yeah, you're a lawyer, I noticed. But I know Crockett. If I'm fair with him, he'll be fair with me. The sooner I tell him about the conchos I found, the better."

"I agree." Nina spoke coldly. He wasn't consulting her, and this insulted her self-pride.

"That's good," he said shortly. She interpreted this to mean lay off.

"You didn't mention telling him about the deposit slip you stole from the bankbook in the tent," Nina said, because she was unable to let him go in peace.

"I decided not to mention that. I'm leaving the deposit slip here."

"Want the benefit of my legal advice?"

"No."

"Good decision."

He went into the study and came out with his envelope. "See you later."

"Call me if you're wrong about Crockett and need to have bail arranged."

"No worries." But he lingered. They both felt that they had just spoken to each other from a distance, and it pained them. Nina went to him and laid her head on his shoulder. After a moment she felt his hand stroking her hair, and breathed a sigh of relief as the moment of conflict passed.

"I'll hold the fort," she said.

"Just rest today."

"I'll be fine. Paul, uh, I just wanted to say, you're a prince. Yesterday, with the dog—you saved Hitchcock. I couldn't have helped Nate on my own."

"No problem."

"For so long I've done everything by myself . . ."

They had separated and Paul was examining his gun by the front door. He replaced it carefully in the shoulder holster before responding. "Me too," he said. "Eat my eggs alone, face the dishes alone, pass out in front of the tube at night. You've made this place feel like home."

"Okay, then," Nina said. She offered him her biggest smile.

"Eat up the pineapple in the refrigerator."

"Go save the world."

"Back asap, world all saved."

She blew him a kiss. "I love you," she said.

"Love you too."

The day passed. Afflicted by a strange paralysis of the will, she slept, read, worried about Bob. Night came on. Sometimes she heard creaks from the wind, chittering, distant voices. Nina got up and sat at the kitchen table.

Who was Coyote's partner on Siesta Court?

Had they understood Nate? Was there really a threat to some children?

Frustrated, she got up to sort laundry. She threw in a load of whites that tested the limits of the washing machine. She emptied pockets of pens and miscellanea, marveling at the things Paul stuffed into his pockets, reading each crumpled business card and receipt for clues to his inner self.

Wish's half-burned jeans and jacket and socks were lying on the floor of the laundry room in the corner. She didn't have time to deal with them now, so she rolled them up and left them there.

Paul didn't return. Rain began falling on the roof. Sometime past eleven, Nina finally fell into troubled sleep.

PART THREE

Silver and gold to his heart's content
If he'd only return the way he went.

19

As Nina fell into restless dreams at Paul's place on Tuesday night, Elizabeth started and stopped the tape recorder with the foot pedal in her house on Robles Ridge, her fingers moving rapidly over the keys as she turned the party tape into written data.

She paused and moved to the word-processing file containing the draft of her article, and the title page came up:

Locals v. Newbies:
INTERACTIONS, AFFILIATIONS, AND CONFLICTS IN A SIX-HOUSEHOLD ESTABLISHED NEIGHBORHOOD UNDERGOING GENTRIFICATION

The title was too long and the word *gentrification* wasn't technical-sounding. Still, it would do for the draft.

She sat at her desk, wearing her robe, curtains closed tightly against the rain, her notebook bulging with her transcripts and observations of the Siesta Court Bunch over the past two years, her tape of the over-the-top party on Saturday night at the side.

For the next hour, she rapidly processed the tape into word-processing files. Then she began organizing the local v. newbie interactions.

Locals: old-timers. They had grown up in the community and adapted very slowly to new conditions. They

experienced jealousy and outrage as the more affluent newbies moved in and initiated rapid, sometimes devastating,
change.

Newbies: newcomers. They moved in from San Francisco, L.A., or Silicon Valley. As soon as possible, they built
their dream homes or developed their property to the max,
and now did not approve of any further change in the
neighborhood. They had what they wanted, and shifted
over into conservationist mode.

She referred back to her Basic Population Description:
eleven adults, eight children. Six households. Of the adult
population, not counting Danny Cervantes, who had once
been on the list:

Seven Locals:
Darryl and Tory Eubanks; four children
Sam and Debbie Puglia; no children at home
George and Jolene Hill; two grandchildren
Ben Cervantes

Four Newbies:
David and Britta Cowan; two children
Ted and Megan Ballard

She looked the names over, classifying them more
closely in her mind: the Eubankses, young traditionalists,
low in ambition, family-centered. They wanted to live as
their parents had and deeply disliked change. They were
perfect examples of young parents making do on working-
class salaries. Tory would probably never work outside the
home. Darryl would never make any more money than he
did now. And they would never move, barring some catastrophe. They got along, went to church, adopted conventional opinions.

A stray thought went through Elizabeth's mind: But
Darryl doesn't love his wife anymore. She would have to
leave this out of the thesis: It didn't fit at all. It was an aber-

ration caused in part by her own presence, which she had intended to be invisible.

Yes, leave that out.

The Puglias. Also conservative, also low in ambition, also family-centered. Debbie was pivotal in the group because her gregariousness and lack of other outlets were the glue that had brought the neighbors into such close proximity. She wouldn't allow them to isolate from one another. She had close ongoing relations with each household, greased by her social skills. Sam was an adjunct to his wife, less involved because he had the outlet of his work.

The Hills, examples of the older generation who had started disadvantaged and stayed that way, hooked into history because their Okie parents had come here as part of an important American geographical shift in the thirties. Also conventional and conservative. Financial problems had caused them to attempt change—to subdivide their property—but they hadn't been sophisticated enough to get around the maze of land regulations.

And Ben Cervantes, saving for his house and his bride, which his parents, who had returned to Mexico, no doubt would pick out for him. A conservative from a minority group, grateful to have any job at all. His nephew, Danny, had fallen into the underclass due to his lack of education.

Ben had such fine eyes. He spoke well. Elizabeth wondered if he already had a fiancée.

Again she had to suppress a thought that didn't fit into the descriptive paradigm: Ben was ambitious. He might move out and away from his origins.

Elizabeth had observed a subset among the locals: One group wanted no change, period, but the other group looked at the change going on all around them and said, get me some of that. Ben, who worked for anyone that would hire him, and George Hill, with his attempt to subdivide his property, adopting a newbie stratagem, belonged in this interesting subset.

The newbie population on Siesta Court was small but

powerful. It hadn't felt so small because she herself had been a part of the ongoing interactions over the years, but of course she could not insert herself into the thesis.

So: Take the Cowans and the Ballards.

David Cowan, inherited wealth, graduate education, rootless, moved every couple of years, unconventional outlooks. He had no interest in conservation per se but wanted to preserve the status quo now that he had built his palace on Siesta Court. His money made it happen, without consideration for the environmental impact or the impact on the neighborhood.

Britta Cowan, another flouter of the mores, only her area of impact was societal. Her dysfunctional relationship with her husband, her seductive attitudes, her negative attitudes toward her occupation, and her wild acting out made her a kind of relief valve.

The Ballards had to be considered en bloc. Ted and Megan shared the Cowans' rootlessness and lack of interest in conventional societal mores. They also welcomed change and had disrupted the local environment with their building projects, but wanted no more change to the environment now that they had their own homes. However, Ted and Megan were different from the Cowans in that . . .

. . . in that they smile and flex all the time, Elizabeth thought to herself, tired. Quarter past eleven, and she had nowhere to go and nobody and nothing to do but think about these stupid people. . . . She opened the curtains. Down the hill she could see through the mist a thin thread of river. Down there on Siesta Court, the Bunch carried on their pathetic . . . yes, she was losing it. She ought to knock off for the night.

She took off her headphones and turned the tape on again, loud, letting the noise of the party fill the room. The material wasn't very useful. The newbies and locals alike had been so disturbed by Britta's outrageous behavior that . . .

Elizabeth remembered how Ben had lightly, but with

emphasis, pushed that slut Britta away from him. She liked that.

She heard loud talking on the tape. Right here, Britta had gone up to the group of men and now Elizabeth heard her say again:

"What're you guys talking about, hmm?"

And that was Sam's voice, boisterous from whiskey, answering:

"Danny. We're toasting Danny."

Then she heard some confused, alcohol-fueled laughter from the group of men, and one of them said:

"Good riddance."

She hadn't heard that line before. How could he speak so coldly about Danny? Who was that? She pressed rewind and went back and heard again: "Good riddance."

Then she heard faintly, in the background, "Yeah." It sounded like a chorus. Perplexed, she shrugged and turned the tape off.

Her mood changed. She sat for a moment staring at the screensaver. Then she opened the file that had her journal in it. She wondered if there would ever be hope for her, and wrote:

> *Our children are our happiness*
> *But they are gone tomorrow*
> *Like meteors they fly*
> *Brilliant in our sky*

She was losing it. The rain no longer pleased her. At the stove, she lit a long brown Sherman's cigarette on the burner, the heat of the gas fire hot on her lips. Crazy, she could set her hair on fire. Midnight. She should go to the gym in the morning. She could call Debbie in the morning to see if she wanted to have lunch.

Debbie never had any doubts about anything. She was immersed, local to the bone. Once Elizabeth had been a local. Now she was just—outside. Outside all of it. Outside life.

Turning to leave the kitchen, Elizabeth saw the snapshot on the refrigerator freshly, as if it hadn't been there for a year. One moment May had been with her, a small warm companion who would share her time on the planet, then she had . . . been removed from the study. Yes. The mother-daughter study had been terminated for unknown reasons. And Jake. No time to work out their problems, just a disappearance, abrupt, irrevocable.

Viciously, she yanked open the door of the cabinet above the refrigerator, searching for the Courvoisier.

20

MIDNIGHT ON THIS same magnificent Tuesday night on Chews Ridge, ambient light low, skies crystalline. David Cowan saw the Trifid Nebula materialize on his screen as the thirty-six-inch reflector followed its computerized instructions. The light in the control room had been set as dimly as possible to see the detail. "Ray, you have to see this," he said.

Ray, at the next table full of computer equipment, grunted and came over. A small astrophysicist with a beard, he worked at MIRA full-time.

"Beautiful," he said.

"More than beautiful." Rose, it was, shading from pale to brilliant pink and deepening to red on its three petals, shedding light below it, a rose. One new star seemed to shine from its center, though David knew that was a trick of the galaxy, the star was actually much closer.

He was peering forty-five hundred light years into space, and the grandness of it, the spectacularness of it, the knowledge of the vast energies roiling and twisting all around this pitiful planet where he existed, were so good for forgetting. He typed in the commands that would photograph the nebula but continued to stare at it.

"Sometimes, looking into it, always bright, always superb, I feel like I'm falling forward, leaving forever. There's vertigo, movement as I leave my body," he told Ray.

Ray didn't answer. Beauty wasn't visual to him, it was

mathematical. His screen, showing window piled upon window of moving graphs, gave him the same kind of pleasure.

"Rain's coming in from the coast," David said. "I'd say an hour or so."

"You ought to get back to work," Ray said. "We have to get this mapping done by next Thursday or we lose the grant."

"So what?" David said.

"We can't keep volunteers who don't care."

"I'm thinking about building my own observatory." But even Ray knew he wouldn't. That would take an independent, motivated person, unlike David, who didn't like doing things on his own.

David also knew that Ray didn't like telling him what to do, because David had given MIRA over a hundred thousand dollars. All David asked for was access to the scopes.

For two years now he had watched the stars, bolstered by his connection to the universe, pretending to participate in the work. David didn't care about the work. He just liked watching through the scope, falling into that endless blackness. They wouldn't kick him out. He knew it and so did Ray.

David's money had bought him salvation here, as it had brought him Britta at home.

The affairs she heaped on him didn't matter. He understood and accepted her as you should accept a force of nature. Audacious, untamable, reckless, she burst into his life, a hot star-forming nursery at the center of his desolate universe. She threw her colorful clothes on the floor, onto the living-room chairs; she smelled of B.O. and perfume. She kept the air ionized with her angry chatter. She was very angry that he had made her move to Carmel Valley, land of hicks, but she did what he told her. He had the money, it was that simple.

He viewed her behavior with dispassion, because he viewed all natural things that way. That didn't mean he didn't have feelings. It didn't mean he didn't have passion for her and didn't get jealous. He just recognized his emotions for what they were, impulses of the organism, and rejected them because he chose to tap into detachment.

After Sam had come Danny; perhaps Sam would come again—so what?

What mattered, the one thing he demanded of her, was that Britta had to sleep with him every night. Sleep, lay her head next to his and breathe next to him and dream. She had to allow him to grasp her hot body in the night, allow him to hold her by her solid hips, let him press his face against her backbone. Because without her, all that would be left would be the void.

His eye caressed the nebula. Pink, pulsing, living light came to him. Closing his eyes, he opened his mouth slightly and relaxed his face, as if the computer screen could allow him to bask in the heat he saw.

"Phone," Ray said, yanking him back. He handed it to David.

"Britta?"

But it wasn't Britta on the phone.

Ted came in from putting away the bicycles in the garage as Megan finished spritzing the salad with balsamic vinegar. They both still wore the black spandex shorts and tight shirts from the long bicycle tour they had taken that day—fifty miles along the foggy coast, dodging cars, pouring it on on the uphills, letting it all go on the downhills. They had had a long leg-stiffening trip home and she couldn't believe the clock—after midnight! Oh, well, tomorrow was Wednesday. They could sleep and sleep. Neither of them was a rat-racer anymore.

"Pont Neuf," she said, pointing to the glass of wine awaiting him. "For our fashionably late supper."

"Good choice." He took off his shoes and socks. Even his veins were carved; his legs looked like they had wires wound around them. Massaging his calf with one hand, Ted went on, "We were so fast at the Point Sur curve I thought we'd fly off the road."

"Incredibly cool," Megan agreed. She set cold shrimp on ice and shrimp sauce in front of him and sat down at the table, lit by candlelight. They both dug in and in five minutes the meal was over. Following the habit they had built up over their six years together, they went out in back to the hot tub, stripped, and stretched out in the hot water for a few minutes.

Then they went back inside. Megan lay down on the massage table in the bedroom. Ted dribbled warm oil on her, all down her back and the glutes and the thighs, and began stroking her with his long strokes, his strong arms smoothing her muscles. She relaxed fully, knowing he appreciated the tight muscles along the back of her thighs, where his hands moved now. He moved down to her ankles and feet, rubbing her big toes with his fingers, while she gave out low appreciative noises, started getting drowsy.

"Now you," she said.

"Such a good day." He lay down on his stomach on a fresh towel and she leaned over him, slick with oil, and rubbed him into as close as Ted could ever get to relaxation.

"Ted?"

"Mmm-hmm?" he said sleepily.

"Did you set those fires?"

His eyes didn't open.

"I wouldn't tell," Megan said. "Remember a long time ago when we were talking in bed and you told me about—"

"I was a kid. It was hormones. Nobody died."

"But you said you got off on the fires."

"So?"

"I've been wondering. How come you're not interested in me lately." His back went stiff again.

He said, "I don't want to talk about this. I was enjoying

myself. You think I would be part of anything that caused someone to die?"

"Ted, that's such an interesting way not to answer me. You know, I saw you looking at Danny one time, and I thought maybe . . . I thought maybe you might be bi. It's perfectly fine to be bi, you know? I'm an accepting person."

"So I'm bi and set fires and I killed Danny?" Ted's muscles had hardened even more under her hand. He sat up and put his hand around her slippery neck. "What is this crap?"

She was suffocating. His hand was a vise.

"S-sorry," she said.

"Get this, Megan. I am not bi."

"Okay. I was wrong." He took his hand away.

"What crap," he said. "Ruining such a nice day. Hey. Listen. It's my cell phone in the kitchen."

He ran for it. When he came back into the bedroom, he got dressed again.

"I have to go out, one of the neighbors thinks she saw a prowler." He hesitated, then said, "I'm sorry. I don't know why I did that to you."

"Sorry doesn't cut it," Megan said from the bed, but he was already gone.

On the corner of Siesta Court nearest Rosie's Bridge, George and Jolene had been in bed for hours, but George couldn't get to sleep. His feet didn't hurt.

That was the problem. His feet didn't hurt because he couldn't feel them anymore.

He had knocked his left foot against the bathtub that morning and in spite of Jolene taking him to the doctor, it was going to ulcerate, he knew it. He opened one eye and looked at the clock on the bedstand. Midnight.

Not everybody gets to know what their death will be before it happens. His death was going to blind him and kill him off piece by piece. His dad had died of diabetes at forty-eight. They could keep you alive pretty near to a normal life span now. How old am I, sixty-three or sixty-four, he thought, and didn't want to remember.

The main thing was how to leave Jolene enough money to raise the little girls properly, like ladies. Jolene never had asked for anything else but she wanted this, did she ever. They had some money in a bank account George had never told Jolene about, but it wasn't enough. It wouldn't keep them for a year. It wasn't nothing the way prices of gas and clothes and food kept going up and up. Might as well just throw that money out the window.

Throw it out the window and let it catch on fire in the night and burn something that needed burning.

Out back, all that useless land covered with live oak, and he couldn't even sell it because these damn yuppies came in and got theirs and then fought to keep him from getting his. It stung like fury. Here they were developing across the river, wanting to rip down the trees, stealing his views along with his peace of mind.

Had the fire stopped them? Maybe it was too early to tell. He had walked up there, in the meadowy area between the river and the handicapped place, before supper. They didn't seem to be rebuilding the model home that burnt, not yet, and the land sure looked ugly where it burned.

And after that walk, he couldn't feel his goddamn feet. He'd have to see the doc again in the morning.

Jolene might go twenty years with the four hundred thousand, which the realtor said he could have gotten on the Back Acre, had he been able to do what he wanted with his own damn property.

Too late now, he'd never get that ordinance changed. He'd done everything he could for the family, right up to things he couldn't ever tell Jolene about. All he could do now was try to live a little while longer.

He heard the phone ring at the bedstand. Jolene beat him to it. "Oh, hi, Sam," she said. "Everything all right?"

She handed it to him and he listened. Then he reached down for his slippers. "What is it?" she said.

"Sam thought he saw a prowler. I'm gonna meet him outside."

She sat straight up in bed, her nightie slipping down her shoulder, pretty as a postcard. "I'll go too."

"You stay put. I mean it. It's probably nothing. I'll be right back."

Tory was vomiting in the bathroom again. Darryl heard her wash her mouth out. She crawled back into bed, pulling the covers off him.

One thing after another.

"You'll forget all about this in a couple of months," he said. "Remember, you had all that trouble the first trimester with Mikey."

Tory just rolled over to her side of the bed and gave him her back. She was mad at him for trying to talk to Elizabeth at the party, and he could make no explanation. He didn't know what had possessed him. He'd only had a couple of Coronas.

Lately, he'd done several things he'd never dreamed he'd do. He'd been lucky, and here he was now, ready to push his luck again.

Tory had no idea that he'd gone to see Elizabeth. Fine, let her sleep, he just wanted to go to sleep too. Darryl rolled over in the opposite direction.

A song was running through his head, a song George sang, a cowboy ballad, and Darryl kept thinking about some of the words:

> I've got a good life, and a good wife,
> Too much to throw away . . .

They had an appointment with Pastor Sobczek next Thursday, and Darryl was afraid all his fantasizing was going to have to end at that point, because God would be involved, and God would come down, when it came to Tory and his soon-to-be-five kids and his commitment to love and honor forever, on the side of his marriage. That his love for Tory had turned to a mild, fond kind of feeling didn't matter to God. That he wanted Elizabeth so bad he was breathing harder just thinking about it now didn't matter.

God's God. He doesn't indulge these crazy emotions.

Elizabeth was beautiful and tragic. Debbie had whispered the whole story to Tory and Tory had told him, all about the car crash and the husband and daughter who died.

He couldn't believe he'd actually gone to Elizabeth's house. He'd talked with her, had the chance to drink her in. That's what he had done, drunk her into his soul and made her part of him.

But he hadn't expressed himself right. Words didn't come easy to him. She'd thrown him out.

I could make her smile, he thought. I'd go to France with her if she wanted. She'd probably do something like that, go live in Paris. She had money and freedom. Wouldn't life be fabulous with Elizabeth in Paris, free and rich?

A man had a right to do one thing before God intervened. He had a right to make his feelings fully known to the woman he loved, privately and without humiliating his wife. If he didn't have that, well, he'd explode. And he'd hate his wife, because he'd blame her for not letting him at least say it once to the woman.

> All my life I've done the things that were expected
> of me
> And if I wasn't happy, at least I wasn't hurtin'
> anybody
> But I want her, I need her, she stole my soul away
> And whatever choice I make, I'll be sorry . . .

He slaved for Tory and the kids. Tory must know that. Sometimes he hated what he had to do, meeting the demands of his family and neighbors, working too hard and too much, day in and day out, the parties, the yard work, the troubles, but he did what he had to do, didn't he? He took care of business just like he was supposed to, so if he wanted more out of life . . . well, didn't he deserve it?

Bringing the blankets up to his nose, Darryl put his hands together under the covers. Silently, he said, Lord, am I allowed to speak to her one more time? Am I allowed this one thing? Should I?

The Lord may have answered him. But Darryl didn't really want to hear what He said. Besides, the phone was ringing in the living room. Tory had finally gotten to sleep.

Confused, guilty, and scared all at once, Darryl rolled out of bed to find out who needed him now.

Out behind the Cowan house on this late night, Debbie thought she could see two silhouettes making their way behind the garage.

Sam wouldn't! What if David came home! Of course not! She looked harder out the kitchen window, across Ben's grassy yard, but now saw only shadows. Sam was at the office working late just like he had said. Sam would never do it to her again. He really did love her.

He tried so hard to take care of them, always making plans that came to nothing, through no fault of his own. He didn't have the magic touch with money, which was too bad, but he was a good man. She knew he was hurting, with this awful development going up across the way and his job always at risk.

He was a person who needed to exercise power, and he had few enough opportunities. All the railing and noise he made about Green River, going to meetings, trying to get the neighbors up in arms, and he was like a parking ticket in a shredder. They shredded him and barely knew they had done it. No wonder he got so wild now and then . . . he had to prove to himself he was a man. She never doubted it, and she was sorry he did, that was for sure.

She would ask him again tomorrow if they could adopt a child from China. He didn't like babies so much, so maybe a little one a couple of years old. House-trained, he would call it.

Now that the kids were grown the house was so empty. The dogs—they were just dogs, they weren't like a human child who learns to talk to you and laughs and learns to be like you and who you can do something for. . . .

The house was so quiet she would have enjoyed hearing mice in the walls. Debbie unloaded the dishwasher, then got her fuzzy old robe on, and flipped on the TV to see if Letterman had a funny monologue going, or something. The digital display told her it was past midnight.

When the ads came on, Debbie started worrying the way she did. This time she was worrying about the disabled people about to be evicted at Robles Vista. She could almost hear the noise of the bulldozer engines idling behind the trees, ready to tear up the ground and ruin their lives. We're at war, she thought, but she couldn't quite figure out who the enemy was. She only knew what everybody knew—that the fires in the Village were battles in the war.

At least she could bring those people in their wheelchairs some human comfort. She would buy doughnuts in the morning. She'd give a sackful to the cook at Robles Vista so that people could have them for brunch in the common room there.

Finally hearing Sam's key in the door, she felt greatly relieved. Fires and Ruthie and Danny . . . all so sad . . . and frightening . . . so hard to understand. I love him, she thought with gratitude, getting up, and he loves me. We are so lucky and blessed. . . .

21

"I WAS CONCERNED that there might be some danger leaving the tent unattended," Paul said. Crockett had told him to meet him at the D.A.'s office at the Salinas courthouse this morning. Apparently his office was a movable feast. He hadn't been available the morning before and Paul had spent the day looking into other matters.

"Explosives, guns, something kids might find. I wasn't sure Coyote would come back, once Child Welfare and the D.A. got together and went after him. The remote location, his use of a rifle—these were factors in my decision."

Crockett's metal desk shook. About six feet from them, electricians were installing a ceiling fan in the hot office. The phone on the desk rang but Crockett didn't answer.

He had a honker like a ship's prow that you only noticed when he turned his head, thin lips, and a brow ridge that hung like a balcony over the etched face. The brown eyes never wavered. The bony casing of his head must house a lively brain.

Ticklish situation, Paul thought again. Crockett needed enough information to get an immediate search warrant, information Paul could provide. But Paul had made an unauthorized entry into the tent. Some unsympathetic joker might call it a burglary. For that reason, they had already discussed what he would say on the tape.

"So you went in. To secure the tent until the police could arrive," Crockett said for the benefit of the tape. He continued to treat Paul with the wary respect of a former ally, but Paul still had to be careful. Deputy D.A.s, defense lawyers, and at least one judge might decide to review the record of this interrogation.

"Correct." The recorder clicked, reminding Paul to stay succinct. He had already decided not to mention scraping something off Coyote's van on an earlier visit. It had turned out to be nothing but mud, anyway.

"And what did you observe?"

"Two rooms. The outer room contained a cot with bedding and a camp-stove setup. Kitchen gear on a folding table. I observed a .22 rifle and a large buck knife in a leather sheath on the table."

"Did you pick up the rifle?"

"I checked it, yes. Held it with my shirtsleeve. It contained three shells. I ejected them and put them in a baggie and put them in my pocket."

"You carry baggies?"

"They make good pooper-scoopers."

"Out in the woods you need that?"

"My friend, Ms. Reilly—it's her dog. She's one of those Sierra Club types. Find half-digested blueberries from a bear sitting in a pile on the road and she might even be moved to take a photo of it. Her own dog who never ate anything but dry kibble does it in the road, it's gotta be picked up."

"Sierra Club," Crockett said, shaking his head. "So. This baggie. What condition was it in?"

"Unused," Paul said. "I might add that the baggie has not been out of my possession since that time, nor have I touched the shells since that time."

"And you've just handed over the three shells." The baggie with the shells sat on the desk next to Crockett's coffee cup.

"Yes."

"What else did you see in that first room?"

"Three gallon cans of kerosene lined up against the far

wall. I lifted each of them, again using my shirtsleeve. They were almost empty."

"Any uses for kerosene you could see there?"

"He did have kerosene lamps, but three gallons constituted overkill for that purpose, in my opinion."

"Okay. What else?"

"I pushed aside a blanket that separated the two rooms. Looked like the kid lived in front, usually, and Coyote—Robert Johnson—had the back room. Bigger cot, tools and hats and clothes lying around, big trunk at the foot of it."

"And you felt a compelling need to check the trunk. For explosives or whatever."

"I felt there was a definite possibility I might find more weapons or hazardous materials."

"And that was your sole reason in opening the trunk?"

"Yes. I found a suede leather jacket on top. Underneath that I found a brown paper bag containing a quart bottle of whiskey and another smaller paper bag, which I opened. It contained conchos."

"Conchos?"

"Small silver medallions used in Southwestern jewelry, especially attached to leather belts."

"Describe them."

"Tarnished silver, two of them, holes in the center for attaching them to something, chased with fancy filigree designs, about an inch and a half across, round but with an indented pattern around the outside edge."

"You saw these conchos before?"

"Yes. I recalled that the body found after the most recent arson fire in Carmel Valley wore a belt decorated with conchos. I decided to report this to you as soon as possible as I felt there might be a relationship."

"Like what? Like he took them off the body?"

"You tell me."

"What did you do then?"

"I left the tent. There were reinforced holes on the main door flap and holes on the side. A bicycle cable looped through the flap holes and a combination lock was lying on the floor just inside the tent. I attached the cable and lock and pushed the lock shut and spun the dial. I tested the flap. It seemed reasonably secure and there were no openings where a human could get in without cutting through the lock or the tent."

"And then what did you do?"

"We brought Nate to the sheriff's field office in Carmel Valley. I took Nina home. Our dog needed veterinary attention. I drove back out to the animal hospital in the Valley."

Crockett's eyes closed and a small silence settled around the men. Having said what he needed to say, Paul waited.

"You left those conchos in the tent? You took nothing from the tent but the rifle shells?"

"Correct."

Crockett repeated the date and time of the interview and turned off the tape. "You are one lucky son of a gun. Because if those conchos match the burned conchos on the belt of the victim, the Cervantes kid—"

Paul smiled.

"If you'd messed with that evidence—"

"Never touched 'em. Used the baggies."

"They're gonna match," Crockett said. "So it was Cervantes and this Coyote fella, this Robert Johnson."

"I'm with you on the Coyote part," Paul agreed.

"Come on. Who else is this loner Coyote gonna know on that short street? What's the name of it?" He shuffled through the reports in front of him. "Siesta Court? We know he was close to Danny Cervantes. We know Cervantes went up the mountain that night with Willis Whitefeather."

"Yeah, I don't quite understand the sequence, but I told you before and I'm telling you again, Whitefeather was an innocent bystander."

Crockett said, "I already told you I'm not gonna talk about those charges with the D.A.'s office. Have your girlfriend talk to Jaime Sandoval about it. I can't support letting Whitefeather out at all, where we are now."

"I understand. So go through the tent yourself, pick up Coyote, and see what he says."

"Come back in a couple of hours after we have your statement typed up. You sure you told me everything the kid brother told you? About kids getting taken?"

"Yes. But don't forget the other thing," Paul said, "the other thing that really surprised me, during this phone call that Nate overheard. Coyote was talking to somebody about getting paid for this hit. Now. He couldn't have been talking to Danny Cervantes, because Danny Cervantes is dead. He couldn't have been talking to Wish Whitefeather, because I know and you know you monitor those jail calls, and so does Wish. So what that says to me is, there's another party paying for the party."

Crockett got up and offered Paul his hand. "Who the hell knows?" he said. "It's the ramblings of a sick kid, maybe, about something that has nothing to do with the arson fires. Maybe the conchos don't match."

"The kerosene cans ought to help. Maybe you'll find some bank records or something."

"What with one thing and another, I think we have plenty for the search warrant. Then we'll see. Maybe lots of charges to file."

"Davy?"

"What?"

"Are you related to the famous Davy Crockett?"

Crockett said, "Do you have any idea how often I hear that?"

"I'd really like to know."

"Why?"

"I'm interested in heroes."

Mollified, Crockett answered, "He was my great-great-great-grandfather. I'm a direct descendant; in fact, my family lived in Tennessee until after World War Two."

"How about that," Paul said. "He was an Indian fighter, wasn't he?"

"He kicked Cherokee ass," Crockett said. "The Cherokee killed his grandparents. Now, I have to get back to work."

Paul went out back to the parking lot, musing about Davy Crockett's ancestry and what cosmic impact it might have on Wish's case. He would talk it over with Sandy.

The interview had gone well. He had a personal strong conviction that Coyote was the outside arsonist. It just couldn't go any other way. He liked feeling sure about this one thing at last. They were making progress.

Mexican food, definitely. He got into the hot Mustang and entered the Main Street Salinas traffic, thinking about how many times he and Wish had driven around looking for lunch on one of Nina's Tahoe cases. Wish got such a charge out of their gigs that Paul would find himself appreciating his life all over again.

Wish's Ray-Bans . . . he had found some old Ray-Bans somewhere and he had a way of carefully drawing them on and nodding and saying, "Let's cruise," that Paul liked a lot. The kid was so uncool he was cool.

Paul found a *taquería* on a side street and went in. A swamp cooler blew noisily in the corner and the place was almost empty. While he waited for his chile colorado he looked through the classifieds in the Salinas *Californian* for a pre-amp for his stereo system. *Nada.*

What happens next, he thought to himself as he ate his lunch. He wondered again about that phone call Nate talked about. Somebody new comes out of the shadows, he thought, the Moneyman. He tried to put it together, Coyote and Danny and Wish on the mountain, three fires, the Cat Lady murdered right after the Siesta Court party with all the talk about her.

The Cat Lady. Paul looked at his diver's watch, good to

three hundred meters or fathoms, whatever, he never dove more than six feet down in the pool.

Unnecessary refinements, he thought, and mentally saluted her. The waiter brought his bill and he put the credit card on top without bothering to look.

Coyote dropped somebody off on Siesta Court after the second fire. Danny knew him and went up the mountain just in time for the third fire. So—was it Danny after all who was the inside arsonist?

If so, Coyote must have killed his partner, Danny, for unknown reasons on the mountain, a falling out between thieves. Wish just happened to be there, so Coyote had to go after him too—but why would Danny get Wish involved?

Didn't make sense. Did not make sense.

He muttered a succinct word to himself and decided to go see how Nina was doing.

The condo fan ran quietly. Nina sat under it at the new iBook, brown hair pulled up in a ponytail, wearing cutoffs and a tank top. She looked about sixteen. She turned those square little shoulders and that kestrel profile he loved so much a little to the side, cocking her head.

"All squared away?" she said as he walked up behind her and put his hands on her shoulders.

"We did our duty," Paul said. "I made another pitch that it couldn't be Wish, but Crockett couldn't seem to put two squared and three point one four together. He said you're welcome to talk to Jaime."

"You gave him enough for the warrant?" The screen she watched showed endless columns of figures.

"He's going to have that tent vacuumed out by five is my guess."

"Good. You didn't mention the checkbook you looked at?"

"That wasn't my duty. I didn't take it and there won't be

any prints on it. Crockett will find it and do the same thing we're doing."

"Except he won't have to hack into the bank records," Nina said, scrolling down rapidly. "Where did you get this software anyway? It's scary."

"A Big Brother company on the Net."

"It went right into the bank's computers. This is legal?" Paul didn't answer.

"Then I hope it's as good as it seems and nobody ever finds out we've been creeping around in one of the accounts. Ugh. I hate sneaks on the Internet. I hate doing this."

"Even to save a life?"

"I spend all my time worrying with the subtle refinements of morality, but today I'm going for a crude goal, get Wish Whitefeather out of jail."

"Your money back if you're convicted of a felony."

"That's not reassuring."

Paul had started massaging her shoulders. He leaned down now to look at the numbers scrolling down the screen. "Coyote's checks?"

"For the past year. What I expected. A Social Security disability check for Nate comes in each month. He cashes it and mostly lives on the cash. He writes a check to Susie Johnson for fifty bucks each month. He's late this month."

"Susie Johnson. His mother in Markleeville."

"He also receives money from odd jobs. The total income from the two sources is around fourteen hundred a month."

"They weren't starving, then. Did you get some lunch?"

"A tuna sandwich." She pulled on his sleeve. "Bend down." She put her arm around his neck and gave him a long, deep, thrilling kiss. "I found something else," she whispered.

"What?" His hands were under her shirt.

"Six thousand two hundred and fifty dollars in cash, deposited a month ago into Coyote's checking account. Don't stop."

"You are such a sexy woman. I think you need a nap."

"A half-hour nap would be nice. Oh. Look at you. You want a nap too."

By three o'clock they had gotten back to business.

"Cash deposit," Paul said. "Crockett will send somebody to the bank to see if the teller remembers the depositor."

"Except the depositor is probably Coyote. The Moneyman gave him the cash and he deposited it."

"Thus ending the money trail," said Paul.

Nina thought about it. "We could work this from the other end," she said. "The Moneyman probably took that money out of his bank account a day or two before Coyote made his deposit. Cashed out on some stocks, maybe."

"Yeah, but we can't check every transaction like that in the U.S."

"Think about it, Paul," Nina said. "I keep coming back to the Cat Lady's report. Coyote, I assume it was Coyote, dropped someone off on Siesta Court."

"Right."

"We seem to be down to a couple of scenarios. First, maybe Danny was the second arsonist and Coyote dropped him off. Danny couldn't be the Moneyman, he was broke, but he clearly knew the Moneyman. So the question is, who did Danny know? He was new to Monterey County and a loner like Coyote. He knew Wish, and he knew the people in his neighborhood. So we could hack into the bank accounts of the neighbors on Siesta Court."

"We could."

Nina said, "I shudder to think what we might find out about these people."

"Ordinary citizens," Paul said. "Right?"

"We would be committing multiple felonies and with

different banks your hacking program might not work so well."

"What's the second scenario?"

"Okay. Danny was *not* the second arsonist, but the second arsonist met Coyote through Danny. I say that because Coyote lived a long way away and was a loner."

"Which explains how Danny had inside information, and which makes what Danny told Wish, about trying to take a photo and collect the reward, the plain truth."

"Right. And again, who did Danny know? Same group of people."

"It's the same outcome," Paul said. "Except then the Moneyman and the second arsonist are one and the same."

"No matter what, somebody on Siesta Court is involved. Paul, I just realized something."

"What?"

"If it's Scenario One and Danny was the second arsonist and the Moneyman is a separate person, then—"

"Then?"

"The Moneyman could be anybody with access to money. A woman." Nina pushed aside the laptop and opened her notebook. "That means the whole Siesta Court Bunch," she said. "Eleven adults. And I think we need to include Elizabeth Gold, who is Debbie Puglia's sister and who knew Danny too. That makes an even dozen."

"Actually, didn't we already establish a woman could be the arsonist? Wish was hit on the head with a stone. Anyone could do that. In my mind, Ben Cervantes is still the obvious one, just because he was closest to Danny. But if someone hired the arsonist, that someone could easily be a woman. Or even the disabled guy, George whatshisname."

"George Hill. The guitar player at the party. So check the bank accounts on all of them," Nina muttered. "How are we going to find out where they bank?"

"Check their mailboxes for a month?" Paul said. "It's the time-honored way."

"We don't have a month. Not with Wish in custody and

the prelim coming up. And that's a felony too, Paul. And somebody's going to notice in that neighborhood."

"How about we ask them?"

"Just ask them? 'Hi, there, have you or a loved one recently withdrawn six thousand bucks for any purpose? Like, oh, say, murder and arson?' "

"It's another time-honored technique. It has the virtue of simplicity."

"Just asking might lead to some action," Nina said, biting her nail. "We're throwing a rock into a pond, making unexpected ripples."

"We'd have to come out from under cover."

"Okay. We become a couple of rocks disturbing the calm."

"You call that neighborhood calm?"

Nina said, "Okay. We're throwing matches into an explosives warehouse. Seeing what blows. That doesn't bother me anymore, Paul. I think there are some children out there in danger and my guess is that the children are the ones on Siesta Court. I know we have talked to Crockett, but if he hasn't warned the parents—I think we should."

"Shall we pay the neighbors a friendly visit?" Paul said. "Talk about money, tell them to guard their children? Spread chaos?"

"I don't know what to do about the threat to the children."

"I'll call Crockett and see what he plans to do about warning them. Let's pretend we're responsible citizens."

"Good idea."

"It's three-thirty already. We could go out there during the cocktail hour. Gossip Central will be the Puglias' deck, where they had the party." She picked up the phone. "I'll call Debbie and confess all, and see if she and Sam will have us over for a drink."

"It could be fun," Paul said. "Not as much fun as I just had with you, but drunken, dangerous fun."

"Welcome to Siesta Court," Nina said.

22

DEBBIE PUGLIA MET them at the deck gate. "How do you do," she said to Paul. "Hi, Nina. So. I can't believe what you told me. Come sit down."

In Nina's memory, the party flickered, orange fire and black night, voices howling in the forest, bodies writhing together. Now, in this same landscape, a warm California evening descended, the sun changing from yellow to gold where it flashed low through the trees, substituting a peaceful emptiness. A pair of squirrels ran along the branches of the big oak that overhung the deck.

From where she sat in one of the plastic chairs at a small glass-topped patio table with Debbie and Paul, Nina could see Darryl and Tory Eubankses' backyard on the left. A dog scratched on their back porch; the screen opened via an unseen hand and the dog went in. Clashing plates and children's voices drifted out through the window screens. Dinner must be in progress over there.

Crockett had told Paul, ordered Paul, to say nothing about the possible threat to the children. He wanted to confirm it first somehow. But hearing the Eubanks kids' laughter next door, Nina felt uneasy about that order.

Farther to the left, past the Eubankses', she could see the corner of Ben's house almost hidden in the brush and trees, and, past that, deeper in the woods, Britta and David Cowan's manicured back patio, all traces of nature meticulously removed.

On her right the deck faced a blank stucco wall that abutted a house with a roof higher than the Puglias'. That would be the home of Ted and Megan Ballard. Debbie and Sam enjoyed no views in that direction anymore.

"What shall we drink?" Debbie said. "Paul?"

"What have you got on hand?" Paul said.

"Well, Corona, Dos Equis, Coors. Red or white wine. Vodka gimlet or collins or straight up. Jack Daniel's. Rum and Coke. We have some good tequila. I make a mean margarita." She smiled uncertainly at Paul, playing the hostess, worried about what the hell they were up to.

Paul smiled back, and Nina noticed how warm and reassuring his smile was, how easily he sat in the chair. "I haven't had a margarita in a while. Nina?"

"Sounds terrific," Nina said.

"I'll be right out. Don't go 'way." Debbie disappeared through the kitchen door, and Paul leaned over and whispered, "Could this woman by any stretch of the imagination be our arsonist-murderer?"

Nina shushed him. She had heard steps coming up the stairs to the deck.

Britta's flushed face appeared at the gate. In her low-slung jeans and tight top she looked taut and tightly packed. Paul sat up in his chair.

"We-hell," she said. "So you were the spy, not Elizabeth. Debbie called Tory right away, and Tory told Darryl. I just passed Darryl in the street. I was curious. Thought I'd stop by. And who are you?"

Paul got up and introduced himself. Britta preened and smiled for him, before turning her furious green eyes on Nina. "I knew you couldn't be with Ben," she said. "Now, Paul I understand." She reached up to touch his shoulder. "What the hell happened to your arms? They're awfully red."

"Poison oak."

"Yuck." Britta moved a chair up close and sat down beside Paul, giving him a long glance from the corner of her eye. A small twinkling red jewel in her navel caught a ray of sun.

Debbie came out with a tray and stopped cold. "What are you doing here?"

"Sammy wanted to make a plane reservation or something," Britta said, winking at Paul and Nina. "He wants me to wait for him."

"He's not due home for half an hour."

"Ooh, margaritas! So Paul and Nina are trying to prove Danny didn't set the fires, right?"

"How'd you know that? Oh, never mind." Debbie seemed to accept that Britta wouldn't go away and set the tray down with its pitcher and enormous stemmed glasses. She poured them out the pale green slush and they all said no to a salty rim.

"Cheers," Debbie said glumly, and they all drank. The margaritas were phenomenally good, refreshing and strong.

"Mighty fine drink," Paul said.

"Deb's the hostess with the mostest," Britta said.

Nina hoped Britta was not referring to Sam, but the mean sparkle in her eyes said otherwise. She cleared her throat. "We appreciate your letting us talk with you, Debbie," Nina said. "I do apologize for coming to your home on Saturday under false pretenses."

"That's all right. But I'm awfully confused. What do you want from Sam and me?"

"You and Sam are the heart of the neighborhood, it seems to me."

"We try to be good neighbors."

"You might know something that would help our client, Wish Whitefeather."

"Danny's friend? I think I saw him with Danny once."

"If Danny's innocent, then Wish will be released," Nina said. "You liked Danny, didn't you?"

Nina sensed a certain amount of discomfort in Debbie's hesitation. "Pretty much. He was about the age of my younger son, Jared. Jared is at Chico State. I always felt sorry for Danny. I'd like to think he didn't do it."

Britta, for once listening intently, sucked fast on her icy margarita.

"Unfortunately, someone else from Siesta Court might be involved," Paul said. In the still air, Nina could hear the two women breathing, hanging on his words. "I can't go into details, but someone from the neighborhood may have paid a friend of Danny's over six thousand dollars to set the fires." Debbie set her glass down carefully while Britta drained hers.

"A friend of Danny's?" Britta said.

"Now, who would that be?" Debbie asked.

"I can't say right now."

"What did this friend tell you?" Debbie asked.

"Nothing. He has disappeared."

"Really," said Britta. She turned the empty glass in her hand. "So you don't really know anything."

"A young man has provided some information," Nina said. "A boy named Nate. His, uh, caretaker had shackled him to a tree to prevent him escaping and talking about some things he overheard."

Debbie said, "How awful. How old is this boy?"

"Thirteen. He's disabled."

"What's the matter?"

"I'm no expert," Nina said. "He has mental problems."

"So he can't tell you anything either," said Britta. "That must be frustrating." Nina had the distinct impression Britta was laughing, but her face was dead serious.

"You didn't leave him tied to a tree, I'm sure. What happened to him?" Debbie asked.

"He's at Juvenile Hall in Salinas while the county looks for temporary housing for him."

"That's terrible."

"There's nowhere else to put him."

"She can't stay on topic," Britta said, "but I'm curious. You say somebody on the block took out six thousand some odd dollars and paid it to this guy and he set a bunch of wildfires."

"Right," Paul said.

"Who? Any idea?"

"We'd like to narrow it down."

"You really believe it's one of us, one of the Siesta Court Bunch that hired an arsonist and got Danny killed?" Debbie said. "Why would one of our neighbors do that?"

"There's a lot of animosity about the Green River development. It's possible that's the real focus of these fires."

"Well, of course there is. That doesn't mean we killed people because of it!" Debbie said, her eyes welling. "It's just too much. Now you're accusing my friends—my family—of doing these things, when we're all scared to death ourselves. Just last night Sam thought he saw a prowler and the men went out back and looked for him. I was so frightened."

"No, now, Debbie, sweetie, let's stay with this. Look at us! The bunch of us. Who's got a chunk of money that big to burn?" Britta said, giggling at her joke, as if playing a game. "Count Ben out. I doubt he could put a down payment on a bicycle on what he makes. And it can't be George and Jolene. The Hills shop at the Wal-Mart and George's too cheap to spend that much money just to set a couple of fires and off some people."

"So, in your opinion, we should take them right off the list," Paul said.

Britta smirked. "I'm not sure you should take anyone off the list. What do I know, after all? Maybe George keeps a stash of big bills under potting soil in a locked barrel, like that gangster on TV. Maybe Ben won the lottery and didn't tell anyone. He's a dark horse. He has secrets."

"He's not the only one," Debbie said, glaring at Britta.

"What do you think, Debbie?" Nina said.

"About who might have six grand on this street? Don't ask me. I wouldn't know."

"Aw, come on, Deb," Britta said. "Every single person

on this block has cried on your shoulder. You know. Tell them, go ahead." What could have been a compliment from someone else had a sharp edge to it coming from Britta.

"Well, you and David come to mind," Debbie said. Nina thought, So there's some life in her yet.

Britta wasn't bothered by this sally. She said, "Absolutely. Except David has the money, not me. I get my allowance and I get my paycheck. But now David, he's got a trust fund from his parents that would knock your socks off, Paul. Yes, maybe it's him. Maybe he's gone political and decided to be the closet savior of the neighborhood. It's completely out of character, him being heroic or spending that kind of money on anything that doesn't have the syllables *optic* in it somewhere, I have to say."

"You say those things about your own husband?" Debbie broke in.

"Maybe I did it," Britta said. "Broke into the trust funds." She was busy pouring herself another margarita.

"Why would you?" Nina asked.

"Same reason as everyone else on this block. Because I don't want my view wrecked. To save the neighborhood, you could say. I'm a real nature lover." She had added salt to the rim of the glass this time. She licked it off.

"Who else might have money?" Paul said.

"Ted and Megan have some money socked away, I'd guess," Debbie said, clearly unhappy with the whole line of speculation. "I don't really know. I really don't see how Darryl and Tory could have that much money with four kids on the money Darryl takes home."

"How about you and Sam?" said Britta. "Sam makes good money, enough so you don't even have to work."

"You know, Britta, maybe you better watch yourself," Debbie said, "making those kinds of accusations while you're sitting on our deck drinking our booze." She had become increasingly uneasy. Nina couldn't understand why she didn't throw Britta, who had leapt upon her husband with the abandon of a wild animal a few nights before, out. Here she was letting Britta get homey on her deck, acting unreasonably civil. Evidently, Debbie worked to keep the social peace at all costs.

The kitchen door opened with a crash. Sam Puglia looked out at them, thick eyebrows drawing together like dark storm clouds. "You should have waited for me," he told Debbie.

"I'm sorry, Sam."

"Hi, Sammy," Britta said. "I just dropped by."

"You dropped by, now you go home," Sam said. "I mean it."

"Sure you do." Steadying herself with a hand on the back of the chair, Britta stood up. "See you later, everybody." She passed close by Sam, brushing him.

After Britta left, Sam said, "What've you been telling them, Debbie?"

"That we had nothing to do with it."

He relaxed slightly. " 'Course we didn't. What's in the pitcher?"

"You know."

Debbie poured him a margarita. Victims of a common marital curse, Sam and Debbie no longer looked the same age. After twenty years these partners now represented different generations. Debbie's hair, almost gray, blew in a frizz cloud around her head. She bore a worried air and tired look around the eyes when she wasn't acting the hearty hostess. Sam's hair remained black and plentiful. The cracks time had etched into his face gave him vigor and character. A deceptive look of character, Nina thought, correcting herself. She would never forgive Sam for letting Britta— letting Britta sit on him! All right, as awful as it was, it was funny too. The two participants might not even remember the event, but Nina would swear Debbie had heard all about it.

From the way Sam had just tossed Britta out like rotten meat, Sam must remember plenty too, come to think of it.

"You're a lawyer?" he said to Nina. "And you're a P.I.?" To Paul.

They nodded.

"What do you want from us?"

"We'd like to know how well you knew Danny."

"Why?"

"Oh, Sam, don't make a big deal out of this," Debbie told him. "Danny was our neighbor, and he helped Sam with the car, and he hung curtains for me."

"You would have adopted him if I let you," Sam said.

"Not really. He was already a man, but he was very lonely and I think it did him a world of good to be part of our little community."

"He was an outsider here and always would be," Sam said. "He could try to fit in until the cows came home, he never would."

"How did he feel about the development across the street?" Paul asked them both.

Sam just sucked on his margarita straw, so Debbie said, "He hated it as much as any of us, I guess."

"Did he ever talk about the café fire?"

"Not that I recall," Debbie said.

"He might have had a grudge going there, don't you think, Sam?" Paul said.

"I got nothing to say," Sam told him.

"You have a lot to say, I think," Nina said. "About all this. What's scaring you so much?"

"*Fuck* you," Sam said in response. His face had turned white and he was shaking. Paul set down his glass hard, scraping the glass table.

"Sam!" Debbie said. She put her hand on his arm.

"Come to my house, my neighborhood, accuse us all of whatever evilness. We're just trying to get along down here in the woods. Ruthie was as crazy as a rabid coon. She didn't see squat get out of a car on this street."

"Mr. Puglia, have you made a withdrawal in the last two months out of any account in the amount of sixty-two hundred fifty dollars?" Paul said. His voice had hardened.

Sam said, "No, I fucking haven't, and neither has my wife. My wife and I love each other. We pay our taxes and our kids' tuition. We support our president and we love our God. And we're not criminals. Now, get offa my property."

Paul stood up, chest sticking out, hands balled into fists. Nina got up too, hastily, to step in front of him. "Thanks for the margaritas," she said to Debbie.

"You're welcome."

"We'll be going."

Paul and Sam stood eyeball-to-eyeball.

"Right, Paul? We have to go now."

Paul moved back a step. "Yeah. Let's go."

Releasing his eyes from their deadlock, Sam turned his back on them and sucked on his drink. Nina led Paul to the gate.

"Good-bye," she said to Debbie.

"Have a nice day," Debbie said.

Nina and Paul walked across the street to the riprap and looked down at the trickle of river, aware of eyes on them. "Debbie's on the phone," Paul said. "Sam's at the back fence, jabbering at Darryl."

"You behaved well," Nina said.

"His turf," Paul said. "I wasn't going to start anything."

"Let's see what shard of human heart comes flying out of the explosion."

"Well said. I need food to balance the tequila."

"There's an Italian place in the Village not three blocks from here."

"Let's go."

They returned to the Mustang and left Siesta Court. At dinner Paul said, "Are we any closer to finding out who the children are? The children Nate talked about."

"It has to be one or more of the Siesta Court kids."

"We don't know that. Could be some other scam, some other kids."

"That's my feeling."

"You and your feelings."

Nina thought of Britta's little towheaded boys, Darryl's handsome boy Mikey. Callie and April, the apples of Jolene's eye.

"But if it's the neighbor kids, why?" she said. "Why?"

23

MEGAN CAME IN late from her martial-arts lesson about seven-thirty. Ted had already done his stretches and was lounging in the hot tub outside. Starving, she hunted around for whatever he had made for dinner, but all she could find was a dry chicken breast.

He hadn't left her any dinner. He was sulking.

In six years, they had built a home, biked from L.A. to San Francisco, run a marathon together, traveled to Acapulco and Hawaii, invested their money and gotten rich, gone through his father's death and her brother's divorce, and generally supported each other to the megamax. Ted was more than a husband, he was her boon companion, that was how she liked to think of him. They were a modern family of two, tight, permanent.

And now this. This choking incident. And Ted's lack of interest in sex.

They were extremely competent people with resources. These were just maintenance problems, like the sim card in the cell phone dying, or the sink stopping up.

Munching on the chicken, she went downstairs and onto their private deck. In the long last rays of the sun, Ted floated with his eyes closed, his arms hooked onto the tub wall out of the water to keep himself cooler. Next to him on the deck, the laptop showed the Yahoo finance screen.

"Hey," she said. "I see George is over there grubbing in his garden. I saw Jolene going up the driveway at Debbie's.

She's usually in for the night by now. Has something else happened?"

"There's a phone message for you from Debbie. She said she just called to chat."

"Oh. That's Siesta Court code for hot neighborhood gossip. I'll listen later."

"Maybe you better get to it," he said. "You never know."

"Okay. I wonder if it's about the prowler."

"Did you see the faxes?" Ted said.

"Yeah."

"B of A is doing lousy, but it's still paying out four percent dividends. Brenda thinks we should put fifty thousand in. Buy while it's down."

"I already took care of it. Brenda called me at two."

"The contractor broke a water main up the hill. It's fixed now."

"That's life," Megan said.

Ted opened his eyes. "Strip down and hop in."

"I'm going to ride the reclining bike for twenty minutes first."

"I won't last that long in here."

"Meet you at the massage table, then." Megan went back inside into the bedroom and locked the door. She had changed her mind. She didn't feel like riding the bike after all. She felt like reading the paper while lying on the bed.

Ted knocked twenty minutes later. She let him in. "What's wrong with you?" he said, naked and holding his damp towel. "Why'd you lock the door? There's some kind of crap going on with you."

"I felt like reading the paper."

"What about my massage?"

"I thought about it. I don't see why I should give you massages when you start choking me in the middle of them."

"Oh. So that's what this is all about."

"Yes. That's what this is about."

Ted sat down on the edge of the bed. He was so buff that Megan could see each individual ab muscle. He had a dick fit for a porn site. Too bad he never exercised that with her anymore.

"I'm sorry about what I did. But do you remember what you said, Megan? You called me a pervert, accused me of a few major crimes, and topped it off by saying I can't get it on anymore."

"Which part didn't you like?" She threw *The Wall Street Journal* on the floor.

"Since when did you think you could get away with talking to me like you did?"

"I never said you're a pervert," Megan said. "I don't believe in perversion. People have a right to express their sexuality however they please as long as it doesn't harm another person. But they have to be open about it with their partners. Trust their partners to understand and accept. Something in our relationship is turning you off, babe. I'm developing some frustrations as a result of your inattention."

Ted's mouth twisted, and he said, "You're right. You're absolutely right. About everything. As usual."

"Then just tell me how I turn you off, and we'll fix it."

"It's not that."

"Is it this other business? Danny dying? The fires?"

"Forget all that. You've got a sensational body and you're a great companion. I love you. I just don't—"

"Was it the same with Amy?"

"No."

"So it's me. Or—"

Ted said, "I am not gay, Megan."

"You could get a physical workup. Maybe you have an infection or something."

"I had a physical three months ago, remember? I'm as healthy as a twenty-year-old Argentine soccer player."

"Then maybe a shrink could help. Why don't you go to

a shrink? You can't choke me, babe, I don't play battered woman." Megan raised her long leg out straight and started rotating it at the ankle joint, admiring it. "You know I'm a brown belt. You're lucky I didn't rip your head off."

"I don't want to hurt anybody. I was shocked at myself. You could have hauled off and slugged me and I would have taken it." He paused. "Maybe I was even trying to provoke you into doing that." He looked surprised at what he had said.

"Do you feel guilty about something?" Megan had studied psych in college and felt comfortable with the role of amateur shrink. She was determined to diagnose Ted and get on with the cure. Whatever it was, they could cope. They did love each other.

"You think I'm gay?" Ted asked, his face anxious.

"I don't know. Are you attracted to men or not?"

"No!"

"Well, are you attracted to women?" Megan said logically.

"Of course I am!"

"Then what's the problem?"

Ted lay down on the bed in a fetal position, his back to Megan. "I don't know what's wrong with me," he said, his voice muffled. "I've been stressed out lately. Maybe that's it."

"Let me help."

"Megan, could you just leave me alone right now?"

"You must know what you want, deep down. I am totally accepting, babe. I love you. Every hard inch of you." She felt an uprush of desire. She ran her hands along his back. "Make love to me," she murmured. She lay back and waited, stretching luxuriously, letting the electricity move up and down her body.

Ted didn't move. He had nodded off, or he was pretending.

After a few minutes Megan got up and got going on the reclining bike, mega pissed off and sexually frustrated. She had to pedal forty-five minutes at top speed before she could even think about sleep.

When Jolene got back to the house from Debbie's, she ran to the back door and peeked out. Yes, George still knelt in the lettuce beds, rooting out weeds, even though the light had dimmed and the moon poked over the trees. As she watched, he sat up on his haunches and rubbed his sore back.

She locked the back door quietly. He'd have to pound and yell and she'd say it was an accident when she finally came and let him in. That way she'd have plenty of warning.

From the girls' room she could hear the TV and chatter. The dishwasher was still running and the clean clothes lay piled on the couch in the den.

Later for them. She had half an hour, maybe.

She went to George's old metal desk in the corner. He guarded this desk like a Doberman. On top he had his typewriter and stationery, his ivory-handled letter opener, and their wedding picture. A couple of envelopes were tucked into the blotter. These she took out and examined.

Water bill and cable bill. No.

In all these years, Jolene had never gone snooping in George's desk. George made the money and took care of the money as head of the household, and though she had been tempted many a time to see if he didn't have something stashed away for them, she felt that he'd tell her when he thought it right.

The truth was, George was a cheapskate. Scrimp didn't begin to describe it, the coupons, the penny-pinching, the flea markets and the secondhand shops. He loved to go out at 5:00 A.M. on Saturdays and come back at 10:00 with the back seat full of broken lamps and tools and dollies for the girls. Then he'd spend the rest of the weekend gluing and hammering out back. And play his guitar all night.

He did love his food too, thank goodness, because Jolene loved her cooking. She liked sewing the girls' clothes,
she enjoyed fixing her friends' hair and taking the girls to
Fisherman's Wharf in Monterey on Sundays, but most of all
she loved cooking. Not the drudge stuff, the daily dinners,
but real cooking, foreign recipes and New Age organic
dishes included. She could always bring over her latest dish
to the block parties if calling it by a familiar name didn't fool
George and the girls into trying it. Jolene was a natural-
born chef, daring and talented, and she knew it.

One time she really wanted to take an Asian cooking
class at the Sunset Center in Carmel. Two hundred fifty
dollars it cost. This was when Cathy still lived at home and
before the girls were born, and they were just as short of
money then. George couldn't stand that kind of cooking.
Bamboo shoots in his soup, not gonna happen, he would
say.

She showed George the ad and asked him for the
money. The idea put him in physical pain, she could see
that. She didn't say another word, just washed the dishes
and went to bed and got up the next morning and cooked
breakfast.

After breakfast, he handed her the check drawn on
Wells Fargo Bank. She'd always remember the wagon-and-
the-oxen picture on that check, like a wagonful of treasure
being brought to her. "Waste of money," he said, smiling, as
she hugged him.

She learned a lot in that class, but most of all, she never
doubted again that George loved her and would always love
her, and this sure knowledge had given them a good life together.

So now she didn't feel too happy about what she was
about to do. The two file drawers on the right-hand side of
the desk had always been kept locked, and in there George
kept the checkbook and bank statements.

She could just ask, but asking wasn't seeing. George
wasn't feeling good, his mind wasn't as clear as it used to be,

and she was going to have to find out for herself if he'd done anything foolish. And if he had, because he was so mad about not being able to build out back, she wanted to be able to take care of it quietly and soon.

She tried the letter opener, but that didn't work. She tried a bobby pin and tweezers and a safety pin. No luck.

She went into the bathroom and unzipped George's shaving kit, his secret hideout place, and wrapped in a baggie she found two silver keys. In a jiffy, she had those desk drawers wide open.

He kept folders for each utility and for the mortgage company, the doctors, taxes, the car insurance, and so on. A big thick folder had the title "Wells Fargo."

Jolene tiptoed back to the window and peeked out the curtains. George had finished with the weeding and was bagging up his pile. In a hurry now, she went back to the folder and opened it up.

They had two accounts, both in her name too. Why, she'd never known her name was on the accounts along with George's. One was a savings and one was a checking.

George would never do anything fancy with extra money, like put it in the stock market or something, so she knew any money they had would be in the savings account. She pulled out the latest statement and took a look.

"Well, I'll be," she muttered. They had forty-two thousand dollars!

She looked back a few months. No withdrawal of around six thousand. The most was twelve hundred fifty drawn a couple of months before. Thank goodness! She looked back further and further in time, at the same money sitting in the same dusty account gathering its paltry interest. George's nest egg had probably been sitting there for twenty years while they got along on the nursery money and lately the Social Security.

Her eyes went back to the most recent statement. With forty-two thousand dollars they could be doing so much to make their lives easier, for Cathy, for the girls . . . George could get a medical consultation at Stanford. They had a secret fortune!

She heard the back door rattle. Then she heard George saying "Now, what's this?" to himself, and the door rattling again. Meantime she was pulling out a blank withdrawal slip from the savings book, closing the file up, closing the file drawer, and locking it up just like before.

Rattle rattle. "Goddammit!" George roared. "Jo-lene!"

"I'm comin'!" she called. She whisked across the kitchen and opened up, the withdrawal slip crammed into her pants pocket.

"Somebody locked the goddamn door!"

"Those little rascals," Jolene said, "played a trick on you. Well, come on in."

At 3:00 A.M. Elizabeth woke up. She went out onto the deck to see the stars, wrapped in a blanket. Looking out into the quiet black, she lay down on the chaise lounge. The Milky Way was an old creviced lane of light. She followed the handle of the Big Dipper to Arcturus and on to the Corona Borealis and Vega. A satellite moved across the sky, a solid point of light, consistent, fast. Soon the night sky would fill with such man-made lights, glittering space stations would wheel around, rockets would leave trails of brilliant debris . . .

Darryl had called and left one of his urgent, inane messages around noon. It disturbed her deeply. She had a hard enough time keeping herself together without this insistent male interest intruding on her life.

He better leave me alone, she thought. And felt such a pang of loneliness that she had to clench her teeth and wrap herself tight in the blanket to make up for the arms that weren't there. Darryl, damn him, had reawakened some needs that she had tried hard to forget.

When she could think again, she told herself many things: about how connections are not worth it. About

how all is impermanent and transitory, most especially human relationships. It all led to nothing but acute suffering.
Loneliness was nothing compared to loss. She had made her
decision to remain alone, and it was so unfair for this foolish
married man to bring his warmth and wanting to her
home, to interfere with her and knock her off-balance.

But then, perversely, she thought, if only I had someone
just for a few minutes, I could open my arms and he would
fill them and I could press my cheek against his warm living
cheek. . . .

She went back inside and flipped up the computer
screen, brought up her journal, and wrote:

> Please don't say anything
> I know loneliness too
> Just cup your hand
> Behind my head
> Open my mouth gently
> With your lips
> And with your tongue
> Search, search for me

Then, finally, she could sleep.

That first moment, opening her eyes and seeing the red
line across the trees that meant the night had finally left her,
Elizabeth was content. Morning, hope, the dawn, old and
effective symbols, drew her from bed into the weary round
once again.

Today is a special day, she told herself, trying to hold on
to that evanescent hope.

Downstairs, she made herself breakfast, listening to the
sparrows and jays. She ate oatmeal, because that was the current health fad, which should keep her alive to suffer the in-
dignities of an undeservedly long life, and then she dressed

carefully. She needed to present an aspect of mental and physical health. She wanted to look important.

Today she would present a progress report to her thesis committee at the University of California, Santa Cruz. She repacked her burgundy briefcase, making sure she had everything, and went out to the Subaru. The mountains lay gentle under the morning sun, and in the quietness she began to feel a strong urge not to go out there to the land of freeways and people.

Get a grip, she told herself, you're getting phobic. She decided to get it over with efficiently and get out. There were some problems with the study right now that she didn't want to get into with the committee.

She went over Los Laureles Grade to Highway 68 and picked up Highway 1 in Monterey, entering the coastal fog bank. As she drove north up the coast toward Santa Cruz she thought again, I don't feel up to this, and admitted to herself that her thesis was in danger. Her little group of subjects faced so many conflicts from so many directions right now—Green River, Danny's death, the suspicions, Britta's increasing outrageousness—maybe she should put off the meeting.

Oh, well, I'm halfway there, might as well struggle through it, she thought, and then, just at the turnoff for Manresa Beach, she felt a thunk, then a thud. Flap—flap—flap. Left front tire, damn Michelins too. Even at sixty-five the Subaru steered straight and the brakes didn't let her down. Pulling over to the side of the road, Elizabeth read the number taped to the back of her mobile phone and punched it in.

The tow truck took some time. She gave up and called her committee chair and postponed her meeting for a week. She felt delivered, light. The sand came right up to the road on the side opposite her and she could smell the ocean. Leaning against the car, her back to the freeway, she let her hair fly in the breeze and watched the gulls.

A long yellow truck finally pulled up behind her. A man got out of the cab.

She squinted behind her sunglasses, recognizing him. Ben Cervantes. And felt huge relief and a little excitement. No new stranger to deal with, just Ben from the neighborhood. Who looked really good smiling at her.

"*Buenos días,* Elizabeth," Ben said. "Looks like you could use a change."

His words, following her thinking so closely, startled her, and she felt herself smiling back. "I have a spare in the trunk," she said. While he went to work with the spare and the tools, jacking up the Subaru, unscrewing the nuts on the tire, she folded her arms and watched.

She had always felt comfortable with Ben. He had clarity in his eyes that she took to be a high level of awareness, although she didn't really know. Most of the locals saw through a thick gray film of murk. Maybe he didn't, or maybe she was just much more sensitive to him for some reason.

For two years at the parties, Ben had come alone or with Danny, never with a woman. Then on Saturday night he had brought the attractive woman along, the pseudo-Hungarian who Elizabeth already knew was a lawyer. Were they close? She wouldn't have thought Ben would—

Or maybe Ben's type was different from what Elizabeth had thought.

He knelt at her feet, putting on the spare. His hands in the leather gloves moved the big tire around effortlessly. He leaned over and she watched his back in the T-shirt, strong and V-shaped. The breeze blew across the dunes. The cars roared by on the highway.

"I didn't know you worked for the emergency road crew."

"New job," he said.

"Are you a mechanic?"

"Used to do body work only, but I'm a quick study."

He didn't work for long. Minutes later, he slammed the flat into her trunk and pushed down the hood. "You'll want to get that to a station. Don't want to drive around without a spare."

"It does make me nervous."

"You'll be okay."

She stood there looking at him for a long moment. Time stretched out. He stuffed a rag in the pocket of his overalls then looked back at her, patient, with those clear brown eyes.

He added suddenly, "I'll follow you if you're worried. You can get it fixed later."

"You would do that?"

"Of course." Simple human kindness, she thought, he's kind, and it felt like rain on her soul. "I'll pay you for your time," she said, but he smiled and shook his head.

He jumped back into the yellow truck, pulling the door shut behind him with a thump. She saw him making a radio call.

Observing his face in her rearview mirror, she started up her car. They cut through the fog and back into summer as they turned inland, driving past fields of red snapdragons and orange poppies. All the way down Carmel Valley Road, she studied him. He had lost his job and his nephew, both recently, yet here he was, out on the road helping her and whoever else needed that big helping hand. How must he feel, really?

Back home, she took her purse out and searched for her checkbook.

"Please," Ben said. "My pleasure."

"Oh, no. I owe you. This is business."

"Not for me."

He wasn't joking. He meant, he had welcomed the opportunity. "Thank you," Elizabeth said.

"*De nada.*"

She hesitated, then said, "Today is my birthday."

"Really?"

"I'm thirty."

His smile widened. "Happy birthday, then. I hope thirty is a good year for you."

"Thanks again."

"I'll be going, then. Take care." Reluctantly, she thought, he turned and walked off. She fitted the key into the lock and opened the door to her empty house and looked back.

He had stopped and was watching her. She saw the desire in his eyes.

She stepped inside and held the door open. He bounded back up the steps and came inside with her, kicking the door shut. Then he had her tight in his arms, supporting her, his hands tangling in her hair, his mouth on her mouth. He was searching for someone, the someone behind the great gray fortress of words and money.

And he found a way in. He found her, exposed her, soothed her fright, caressed her. She began to moan and twist in his arms.

She took his hand in hers and led him into the bedroom. They hardly spoke.

24

DEBBIE TOLD NINA on the phone that Thursday afternoon, "You better not be making all this up. People on
Siesta Court are getting scared of each other. You really
think the Cat Lady was murdered?"

"That's what the medical examiner found." Nina
scratched her ankle, though the poison oak had faded away
at last and the scratch was just a leftover nervous tic, like biting her thumbnail. Paul had gone to town to talk to Crockett again.

"Well, I asked around about the money. Whoever set
the fires and killed Danny and Ruthie has to be found. But
you have to understand, these are my friends."

"Hear anything back yet?"

"I've heard plenty. But not about the sixty-two hundred
fifty dollars."

"Anything you have heard might help us."

"Do you really believe your client, that young man—"

"Wish Whitefeather—"

"Didn't kill Danny?"

"I know he didn't, Debbie."

"Of course, you'd have to say that. I don't know why, but
I believe you anyhow. Well, then. Darryl and Tory had a
loud discussion this morning before Darryl left for work. I
couldn't help but hear part of it. Darryl told Tory he's not
happy and Tory was crying and carrying on. She's pregnant."

"Is it about your sister? Elizabeth?"

"Mm-hmm. So I called Elizabeth and I wanted to know whether she and Darryl—I mean, it's none of my business in a way, but she *is* my sister—"

"Sure."

"And she said, no, she doesn't want to have anything to do with Darryl, *but* she has started seeing Ben Cervantes! I was thrilled to hear it, so I thought I better let Tory know she has nothing to worry about, so I gave her a buzz and left a message. And guess what. Talk about bad luck, I *never* thought something like this might happen—"

"What?"

"Darryl called home from school and picked up the message instead! And he called me and wanted to know everything. I told him that's all I knew. I was *very* embarrassed. But also, I'm worried. Because Darryl acted so upset. He sounded jealous. Of Ben."

"Not good," Nina said.

Debbie heaved a sigh. "I was just trying to help out. So I called Elizabeth. And she said she was sorry she ever told me about Ben and she must have been out of her mind. I'm afraid I've complicated things."

Nina thought about this, decided she couldn't link it to Danny, arson, or murder, and said, "Has anything else happened, Debbie?"

"Well, David—you know, the Cowans on the corner— he usually sleeps late, into the afternoon, because he goes to the observatory at night. But this morning I heard the Boxster start up early. One time last year Danny told me that David tried to hire him to spy on Britta. Danny laughed when he told me this and I was curious as to why he was laughing, and the whole sordid story came out that Danny couldn't spy on *himself*!"

"Oh. You mean, Danny and Britta."

"Right. None of us can understand why David stays with her. He actually made a joke about it once. He said he was getting the lay of the land."

"What else did Danny tell you, Debbie? About anything?"

Debbie needed a moment to change her focus. Then she said, "Lots of stuff. We talked quite a bit."

"Ever talk about this guy named Coyote?"

"Just that he knew this part-Washoe character who lived out in the woods. A drinker. How is Nate?"

"I don't know."

"I'd like to bring him something. I bet he doesn't have any clothes or anything."

"That would be nice." Nina gave Debbie a number to call. "By the way, I'm sorry Sam was rude to you when you and your friend came over. Sam hasn't been himself."

"No problem." Nina hung up.

What had she learned? Nothing, she thought, but she had enjoyed talking to Debbie, a talented gossip. She ought to have a talk show: She's another Oprah, she thought.

She called Jaime at the D.A.'s office and had the incredible luck of finding him in. "I'd like to come down and see you," she said.

"About?"

"Ruth Frost's murder."

"I've already consulted with my boss on that. She may have been murdered, but I don't know why or by who, so I can't link it to the arson case. So I'm not dismissing, you're wasting your breath."

"But why else would someone kill this poor woman? She had no money to steal. Come on, Jaime, you think someone did it to lash out at cat lovers?"

"We'll find out. This is my only free time today, Nina, what else do you have?"

"Is there any progress on finding Robert Johnson?"

"Coyote? I haven't heard a thing. State highway patrol has his license number, though, so we ought to grab him soon."

"Before he takes these children as he threatened to do on the phone?"

"You mean the schizophrenic kid's statement? Let me tell you, Nina, I'm using the word *statement* loosely. He didn't feel like talking when my investigator went out to the juvenile facility to interview him."

"You should warn the parents and grandparents on Siesta Court, Jaime. I don't like having this information—"

"What evidence do you have that this alleged threat has anything to do with them?"

"The conchos in his tent link him to the fire."

"They're similar to the ones on the dead man's belt, yeah."

"He had an infusion of cash. That fits Nate's story."

"But doesn't link him to the fires."

"He worked on Ruth Frost's car!"

"So we're back to that. It isn't a credible threat yet, Nina. I'm not going to throw those people into a panic."

Five more minutes with Jaime convinced her that Wish was facing a real live preliminary hearing in ten days and she'd better get ready for it. She called a temporary secretarial service and arranged to interview someone the next day at Paul's office. There would be motions, all kinds of paperwork.

Let the cramming begin. She had always been a crammer in school.

All right, let hell break loose, she could prepare for that with ten days' lead time!

"Hi, Nate." The boy looked at her slackly. He had been watching afternoon soap operas on TV. An orderly at the facility hung around close by, curious.

"Hi." A string of saliva ran from the corner of his mouth and he looked pale and wan. She thought, Maybe he was better off undermedicated.

"How are you doing?"

He watched the TV. Diamonique bracelets were on sale on QVC. "It's okay. But they never gave me any ice cream."

"I'm sorry. I'll see if I can help with that. Nate, you remember, when we came and got you"—he was nodding—"you told us why you had been chained to the tree?"

"Chained to the tree. I was."

"Could you tell me again about the phone call you overheard?"

"Wee-zull. The phone call I overheard. The phone made a song and he answered. His face got funny and he looked around for me, but I was outside listening inside. He said, Don't try to stiff me. It's that simple. Or else I'll take the children."

"Did he say anything else about the children? Which children, Nate?"

"No."

"Do you remember calling me at the court?"

"You weren't there. She wrote it down."

"Right. And you mentioned fire in your phone call. And you said something about 'the big one.' Remember?"

Nina waited, biting her nail. Nate hadn't turned his head from the TV. He sounded remarkably coherent compared with the last time she had talked to him. Nina had represented mental patients before and believed that antipsychotic medications, with their side effects, were often overused in the interests of the institutions, not the patients. But today Nate sounded almost normal: dulled out, drooling, but almost coherent. The medicine was helping him, she had to admit.

"Take the children. Take the children. Take the children. Take the—" Again, Nina felt the clutch of fear.

"Thanks, Nate. Thanks very much. A friend of mine will be coming to see you soon. Dr. Cervenka. You'll like him. He looks like Santa Claus."

"Okay."

"Do you know where your brother might have gone?"

"He must be dead."

"What makes you say that?"

"Or he'd come get me out of here."

"You—you want him to come get you?"

"He always took care of me. I don't like it here."

Nina walked swiftly down the concrete-floored hall to the front and was let out. At the counter, she asked the attendant where she could find the nearest ice-cream place. She dropped off a half-gallon of Neapolitan for Nate before she headed for Carmel Valley down 68.

Another hot, perfect summer day. Mount Toro loomed on her left.

The cell phone rang, and Paul came on. "I'm still waiting to talk to Crockett. What are you doing?"

She told him, then said, "I'm going to Britta Cowan's travel agency and see if I can catch her."

"What for?"

She heard that tone again, the one that told her he didn't like her coming up with ideas on her own. She bridled.

"Don't be overbearing, Paul," she said.

He seemed surprised. "All I asked was—"

"Debbie said that Britta had an affair with Danny last year. Maybe she met Coyote at some point."

After a short silence, Paul said, "That's a good thought."

"I have them sometimes. I asked Nate if he knew where Coyote might be and he said the strangest thing—that he wished he would come and get him out. After the maltreatment he suffered, I was surprised."

"I called the condo to pick up voice mail. Sandy wants an update. You or me?"

"I'll call. I'll call Joseph too."

"Great. What time will you be home?"

Home, Nina thought. "Late afternoon."

"What's for supper?"

"Whatever's around."

"I'll stop at the store," Paul said, hurt-sounding.

Carmel Valley Travel was located in a small strip mall on the main road just before the Village. Siesta Court was right down the hill. A school bus stopped just in front of Nina and disgorged its freight of children bowed like porters under their heavy backpacks. She saw George's granddaughter Callie grab her little sister's hand as they crossed the street, and it gave her a tight feeling in her chest. She didn't agree with Jaime. The parents should be warned about a possible threat to the children.

Inside the travel agency, frigid air-conditioning, the usual racks of cruise folders, maps on the walls, Britta Cowan and another woman on the phones. She saw Nina but gave no sign. Nina went back and sat down in the chair next to her.

Britta was saying, "The Bangkok leg has aisle seats but no window except over the wing. You want that? Okay. And vegetarian meal, right? Okay. I'll see what I can do. What?" Nina looked over the desk. All she saw was travel brochures, tickets, notes, and schedules. No plant, no photos, nothing personal. How odd, she thought. On the wall she saw a poster for Icelandic Airlines.

Britta hung up. "So where are we going today?" she said in her mocking voice.

"I wonder if we could talk for a few minutes."

"As you can see, I'm trying to make a living."

"It's important."

"To you, maybe." But curiosity got the better of her, and she said, "Irene, I'll be out back."

She led Nina outside to a small, sunny, flowery courtyard. They sat down on some ironwork patio chairs. Britta pulled out a pack of cigarettes, stuck one in her mouth, and lit it with her Zippo. She wore tight white pants and a polo shirt. Her arms were toned and tan and the gold bracelets she wore showed them off.

"Nice poster. By your desk. Are you originally from Iceland?"

"Yes. Home of hot springs and Bjork."

"You don't have an accent."

"I speak four languages without an accent. I was a flight

attendant for Icelandic when I met David. He was drunk and I was poor. A perfect match, I thought."

"How long have you been married?"

"Eight years." She inhaled the smoke with pleasure. Sun filtered through the trees and made a halo of her hair. "And here I am."

Nina was having trouble finding an opening. She decided to try to match Britta's bluntness.

"A happy marriage?" she said.

"Sure." Britta smiled slightly, enjoying Nina's discomfiture.

"But you had an affair with Danny Cervantes last year."

"Yes. And Sam Puglia too. But Sam was only good for a few nights. He ran home to Mama."

"And Danny?"

"A kid."

"Was he in love with you?"

"No. In fact, I think he despised me. But we got along in bed. Are we having fun yet?"

"How did your husband take these affairs?"

"David doesn't care."

"Then why do you stay married to him?"

"Faithfulness is overrated. We have things in common. Next question."

"All right. Danny. How did you leave it with him?"

"I told him to get lost. He was borrowing money from me. The thrill was gone."

"Did Danny talk to you recently about making some big money?"

For the first time Britta's eyes clouded. She smoked some more, then said, "Maybe. Maybe I don't want to be a witness in court about any of this, though."

"I can understand that." I'll take that as a yes, Nina thought to herself, and furthermore, I'll subpoena you if you know anything. She went on, "Did you ever meet Robert Johnson?"

"Coyote? Yes."

"Where?"

"At a bar."

"Alma's?"

"Very good!"

Nina chose her next words carefully. "What did you think of him?"

"A jerk."

"How so?"

"The type who gets belligerent and shoots his mouth off when he gets drunk. The type who dies in a bar fight."

"What were he and Danny talking about?"

"The score."

"The score?"

"That's what they called it."

"They were going to make some money?"

"Danny hired Coyote for some job. A big job."

"What else, Britta?"

"I don't want to say."

Nina apologized to Paul, Jaime, and all authority figures in her mind, then said, "You know, Britta, Coyote has disappeared. He may have killed the Cat Lady. And he has made some threats."

"Against who?"

"Some children. We don't know yet whose children."

"I'll be sure to take mine out of town." But her mouth trembled. "So he's the man you were talking about at Debbie's house."

"If you know anything about Coyote that might help, you shouldn't keep it a secret, no matter how much you don't want to go to court."

"You think he'd come after me?"

Nina shrugged. "What do you know?" she said.

Britta stubbed out her cigarette under her sandal. "You told me something," she said, "so I'll tell you something. Your client's guilty."

Nina closed her eyes and took that in. "Why do you say that?"

"Because Danny was in on the fires. With Coyote. They had this Tahoe connection, Washoe Indians or something. And your client, he's another Washoe, right? He went up the mountain, right?"

"How do you know?"

"Alma's. We're sitting at the bar and they're talking, and Coyote says something about laying in enough kerosene. And Danny says shut your mouth, and shoves him right off the bar stool. Coyote lies there for a while and then he gets up and shoves Danny back. Danny gives him this look and Coyote sits back down like a good boy. That's it."

"Was anyone else there who could have heard that statement?"

"I was drinking too. The room was turning into a carousel. But let me think. Yes. A cute guy with a gray beard. Paint all over his clothes. I think he knew both of them."

The paranoid artist spent a lot of time at Alma's. What had Cowboy Two said? Something about him doing drugs.

"I met him," Nina said.

"He didn't talk much, he just listened. And stared at me. I managed to slip him my phone number. He called and a couple of days later I went to his place."

"I don't need to know that—" Nina started, but Britta held up her hand.

"Danny and Coyote were just leaving when I got there, and I didn't want Danny to see me, so I left and came back later. Donnelly—Donnelly was a dud. Wait. I won't make your ears burn. But he told me that the two guys had been drinking with him, then he got a little scared of them. They were asking for a loan and he said no."

"Thank you, Britta." Stay calm, Nina told herself, and began analyzing this information, deciding how it impacted Wish's case.

"Maybe it's my ass on the line now. Or my kids. I think I better go home and deal with this."

"Just one more question. At any time—did Coyote or Danny ever use my client's name? Wish or Willis?"

Britta said, "I never heard of your client. He came out of the blue. Maybe Danny hired him later on."

"Okay," Nina said.

"But if you subpoena me, I'm gonna hurt you."

"I see that you might."

"Good." She smoked calmly. She was quite beautiful, shiny with her polished nails and lip gloss on her plump mouth.

"Britta? I still don't understand. About your marriage. About you."

"And I'm not going to enlighten you. I'll tell you just one thing. David and I will be together until the end of time."

"Just a suggestion," Nina said. "You might want to double-check your husband's bank accounts to see if he's the one who paid Coyote. Just to be sure. About that end-of-time thing." She left Britta on the sunny patio, looking thoughtful.

"Hello, Sandy," Nina said into the cell phone. "So you have a cell phone too now."

"I got right in there with the twenty-first century. It does come in handy. Have you got Willis out of jail yet?"

"Not yet." Nina updated Sandy, then said, "I'm afraid it's going to go into a prelim."

"Well, you're pretty good at those. You're gonna put up a defense, aren't you?"

The preliminary hearing in California had only two purposes—to determine if there was probable cause to believe that a crime had been committed, and that the defendant was the person who had committed the crime. If so, the defendant would be bound over for trial.

At this early stage, the defense usually assumed probable cause would be found to exist, and let the D.A. present its minimal evidence for that purpose. Though the defense might cross-examine, in general the defense did not put on its own witnesses.

Nina did not agree with this traditional strategy of defense attorneys. With current discovery rules, the defense often knew as much as the police at the time of the prelim, and with hard and fast work could put on a sort of minitrial. Since a defendant might be incarcerated for months before finally going to trial, it made sense to fight hard every step of the way.

So Nina said, "Yes, I'll call witnesses. Time is of the essence, though."

"What are you doing for an office?"

"Using Paul's. He's got a spare iBook for pounding out paperwork, and a fax and all that."

"What about a legal secretary?"

"I called a temp service. I'm interviewing a woman at two tomorrow at Paul's office."

"You won't get anybody who knows law."

"I'll choose carefully. Don't worry, Sandy. I'll do a good job for Wish. But—but if Wish is bound over for trial—I can't commit to handling a full-fledged murder trial, you know that."

Sandy said, "Then win the prelim."

"Right."

"I talked to Susie Johnson. Robert Johnson's mother. She's not close but I know her. She says Robert hasn't been in touch. She's telling the truth."

"Okay." So Coyote hadn't called home. Where would he go? Deeper into the forest?

"Social Services for Monterey County called Susie about Nate. They say he's almost ready to leave. She's not sure she can take care of him. Did Dr. Cervenka go see him yet?"

"No. I think he's making the trip down from San Francisco in a day or two. He'll help. Tell Susie he has to talk to Nate first."

"Okay. Robert Johnson and Danny Cervantes, they

both had Washoe mothers. I checked around. Those boys went to high school together in Minden."

"What's their connection to Wish?"

"He and Danny were friends when they were in elementary school, and they stayed in touch. Danny's family moved from Markleeville down to Minden for a while. His father worked construction down there. Then when Wish came to Monterey County this summer, he looked Danny up. Danny was the only soul he knew, other than you and Paul, when he came down here."

"Does Wish know Coyote? Robert Johnson?"

"Ask him. But I don't think he ever went to school with him. I don't think he knew him from Tahoe."

"Okay," Nina said.

Sandy said, "Willis's father is a tad worried."

"I'll call Joseph."

"That's all right. We talk every night."

"Do you miss Tahoe, Sandy?"

"This Washington trip'll be over whenever I say it's over. But good things are happening. The Washoe tribe is going to get twelve acres on Lake Tahoe at Skunk Harbor. That's one of the tribe's summer spots."

"Fantastic, Sandy!" The Washoe tribe had summered at Tahoe for ten thousand years, until the previous century, when logging and silver mining interests took it over. Ever since, the tribe had been trying to get recognized and get some land back. "That's historic," Nina went on.

"It's historic, all right," Sandy said. "Guess what the conditions are."

"What?"

"We can only do activities that are traditional. Hunt, fish, grind up pine nuts. Act like Indians in the westerns."

"Really?"

"Yeah, we get the land, but in a time warp. It's okay, we didn't want to build a casino. We're just glad to get our toes back in the water."

"A toe at Tahoe," Nina said.

"Hmph."

"Excellent work, Sandy."

"Did you talk to Crockett?"

"Paul did."

"What did he say?"

"Well, to Paul's surprise, he *is* a descendant. And he sounded boastful when he talked about what an Indian fighter his ancestor was."

"I knew it. I knew it."

"He's really not so bad, Sandy."

"It's deeper than that. We have to get Willis out of jail."

"We're working on it."

A silence. Then, "Paul treating you right?"

"Great."

"Good. Hmm."

"Something else on your mind, Sandy?"

"I just had a thought."

"Anything you want to tell me?"

"Not yet. You'll find out." And with that ominous statement, Sandy signed off.

Nina thought about Sandy in Washington, setting up a Tahoe land trust for the Washoe tribe. She felt quite proud, but not surprised. Sandy was smart and unbelievably sure of herself. Nina had seen that the first day she'd met her, when she showed up for a job interview with Nina with no qualifications to be a legal secretary besides total self-confidence, having been a file clerk at another law firm, and a will to learn.

Sandy was probably regretting that she'd ever met Nina at this point. Wish wouldn't be in jail if he hadn't come down here to work for Paul, who'd met Wish through Nina.

Nina closed up her cell phone and pulled the Bronco back out onto Carmel Valley Road. Her mind went back to Britta, to the astonishing thing Britta had told her: *Danny was in on the fires.*

25

AND SO IT came to pass that on Monday, June 23, Nina went back into law practice, in a half-assed sort of way.

She had a case and half an office, which, because it was shared with a nonlawyer, presented certain ethical problems. She wasn't supposed to split fees with nonlawyers or partner with them. They might have cooties, the state bar had decided.

She inspected Paul, who leaned back in his yellow leather chair talking on the phone and looking out his window, for those mythical insects. He could use a haircut but looked clean withal. Satisfied, she turned back to putting away the new secretarial supplies purchased that morning from Office Depot into Wish's old desk. She was a lawyer; she would draft up some paperwork defining her professional relationship with Paul that would leave the state bar puffing uselessly.

Outside, fog blanketed Carmel. Mark Twain once said that the coldest winter he ever spent was one summer in San Francisco. He obviously hadn't spent June in the microclimate of Carmel-by-the-Sea. A few miles inland, the radio said, the central coast was having a heat wave.

Problem: The new temp would have to sit at that desk. So where was Nina going to work? She looked longingly at Paul's fine desk with its client overhang, covered with Paul's computers and files. She surveyed the office. In the corner by the door, Paul had a padded leather client chair and a small table beside it with a lamp and some adventure trekking brochures, where his clients could sit.

So be it. She dragged her new cardboard file boxes over there and stacked them. Now she had a file cabinet. She removed the lamp and brochures and pulled the table around in front of the chair. Luckily, it was high and broad. The corner had one electrical plug into which she plugged a power strip with many outlets. She opened her laptop and it brought up its ocean desktop picture, popping up the icons like long-submerged buoys.

No one must ever come in here and see her like Little Jack Horner. But with Wish in jail, her client wouldn't be visiting, and her tenure here would be short: a few days of preparation for the prelim, the prelim itself, which probably would last about two to three days, and out.

She began filing the material she had on Wish's case. Paul stretched and said, "Guess it's about time for your job interview. I'll make myself scarce. If you need me, I'll be at the Hog's Breath having a late lunch."

"Thanks, Paul."

"Nice setup."

"It'll do."

Paul went out and Nina continued organizing. Two o'clock came and went, and nobody came from the agency. Nina had to go down the hall to the ladies' rest room. She left the door to the office unlocked.

When she came back into Paul's office, the applicant was there, already seated at Wish's desk, reading a file, her back to Nina. Nina saw black hair and a purple coat.

"Hey! What do you think you're doing?" she said, and rushed over to grab the file. The woman turned her head.

"Aughh!" Nina cried.

Sandy said nothing. She lifted an eyebrow and continued reading.

"What are you doing here! You almost gave me a heart attack!"

"What does it look like? I'm your new secretary."

"Where—where's the temp?"

"I caught her outside and told her the job was taken. You need envelopes and a Rolodex. What are we going to do for a law library?"

Nina sat down at her new desk. Sandy continued her reading. Finally, Nina nodded.

"I thought you had big business in Washington."

"My son's in jail."

"I should have known," she said. "When you said, 'Hmm,' on the phone yesterday."

"I've only got two weeks," Sandy said. "We could spend that time looking at each other, or we could get to work."

Paul came in. He saw Sandy in her purple coat and sneakers and broke into a big smile. "Welcome to Carmel," he said.

"That's more like it."

The phone rang, and Sandy picked it up.

"Law offices of Nina Reilly," she said.

Strange twist of fate: The phone call actually was official, and for Nina. "There has been a development," Jaime told her, over a wail of sirens. The D.A. sounded unusually calm, a bad sign.

"What?"

"An assault. On a woman who lives on Siesta Court. Her name is Britta Cowan. She's at Community Hospital."

Paul and Sandy had stopped moving around and seemed to be listening, too, though they couldn't possibly know what Jaime was saying. Nina's shock must have shown on her face.

"How serious is it?"

"Serious. She was hit in the head with a baseball bat. She's in surgery. Skull fracture. Her husband is with her."

"Is she going to make it?"

"Only God knows. I'm just a lawyer. She was found this morning by a janitor at the business where she works in

Carmel Valley." By now, Nina had put on the speakerphone and they were all listening.

Jaime went on, "Her associate says you visited her yesterday, and she went home right after your talk."

"I warned her, Jaime. About the children. Are her children all right?" She gripped the phone.

"You know, Nina, you and I have known each other for a long time. And I want to tell you something today. I always thought you were bad lawyer material. Because you never listen to anybody."

"Don't blame me for this."

"The timing is right. You talk to her, you set the alarm in motion, and this woman gets hurt. Yes, her children are all right."

Paul looked like he was going to seize the phone. She motioned him away, then said, "Who did it?"

"You might have some ideas on that."

"So you don't know?"

"Forensics is working the site right now. I'm standing here looking at travel brochures and blood, and I didn't call you for nothing. Now you better speak up. You know who did this?"

"No."

"You have a guess?"

"I think it was Robert Johnson. Danny Cervantes's buddy. The man called Coyote."

"Based on?"

"I did see Mrs. Cowan last Thursday. She told me something about Robert Johnson."

"What?"

Nina didn't have much time to decide what to tell Jaime. She ran the legal questions through her head: Was the information privileged? No, Britta wasn't her client, she was a victim, and this was a criminal investigation. But would it hurt Wish's case in any way to tell Jaime what Britta had said?

It might. If Danny and Coyote were coconspirators,

Wish's story about being on the mountain made little sense. Wish had gone up there with Danny. The judge would assume they were all together.

But she wanted Coyote found, she was hot with anger at what he might have done, and she knew he was the key to the story. Jaime needed to work harder to find him. She could make that happen.

The truth could only help Wish.

Or was she being naive? A D.A. should never be told anything. Too dangerous, and you never could tell how the information could rebound.

"Well, Nina?" Jaime said. "I called you, remember? Instead of bringing you in."

"She was seeing Danny last year."

"I knew that."

"She went to a bar with him. Coyote was there. He and Danny talked about laying in supplies of kerosene. Danny had hired Coyote. They were talking about making a score."

Jaime digested this. *Danny was in on it.* I shouldn't have said it, Nina thought. But Britta was lying on a gurney with a skull fracture. She had to say it.

"What else?"

"Only her speculations about what she overheard."

"Her speculations may have led her to the hospital." Jaime's cell phone was whistling. Wind, whistling through a parking lot.

"I hope not."

"Well?"

"That's all I can tell you."

"I can send a sheriff's car over and pick you up and hold you as a material witness."

"I won't have anything to add. I told you what she said. She heard Johnson practically confess to the arsons. Maybe you should use your police car to get some police work done, like finding him."

"You think a hard-ass attitude is gonna win you any

points when you come cryin' to me for a deal? Her speculations are important. Her state of mind, her motivations,
are important."

He was right. "I'll search my memory. I'll call you tomorrow," Nina said.

Jaime took some more time. She heard him whispering
to someone, probably an evidence tech.

"You do that. I have to go, Nina, but before I do, there's
one more thing. The victim wrote your name on an envelope."

Hearing that, Sandy moved her head on her neck,
toward Nina, slowly. With portent. She blinked. Meaningfully. It was an oh-shit moment. They had had so many together. It was really great to have her back.

"What was in this envelope?" Nina said with extreme
care.

"Nothing. But there was a sentence written under your
name. On the envelope. I'm going to read you this sentence
and I expect you to tell me what it means, fully and truth-
fully. Right now."

Sandy picked up a yellow pad and a pen. Nina said,
"Let's hear it."

"The sentence reads as follows. 'Nina, just in case, I
heard about a cute artist's studio for rent.' "

"That's it?" Nina said.

"Don't jive me," Jaime said. "Don't evade. Don't act
like a lawyer. Somebody is out of control and running
around cracking skulls. And maybe a whole lot more. Now.
What does it mean?"

"We were talking. About vacation places. To rent."

"I don't believe you. Shit." There was another whispered exchange. "I have to go now. But I am going to catch
up with you later. So think about it some more. Hard."

"I sure will. Jaime?"

"Yeah."

"Thanks. For letting me know about all this."

"I thought I might get some help from you in return.

Not that I should expect it. In fact, I have noticed that you turned into a maverick. I thought you said your ambition was to be a big shot in the legal profession way back when we were drinking vending-machine coffee between classes."

"Well, at least one of us turned out respectable," Nina said.

Jaime laughed. "You may still hit it big. You may be right about jamming us on prelims. I just hope it doesn't become a fashion among the defense lawyers." He paused for a moment and when he began talking again he was serious. "But I think you're lying about the note, Nina. That's obstruction of justice."

"I told you. Britta knew Robert Johnson was an arsonist. He lived out in Arroyo Seco. You know about the Child Welfare warrant. Go get him."

Jaime said, "Maybe it was her husband." The thought hadn't even crossed Nina's mind. She had experienced that feeling of absolute certainty about Coyote that drove all other thoughts away.

"That's not my bet," she said. She laid the phone in its cradle.

Sandy took off her coat. "It's always a barrel of laughs," she said.

"I'm hoping I didn't cause this," Nina said. "I told Britta that she and maybe her children might be under threat from this guy."

"Then she would run the other way, if she's sane. And she is sane," Paul said.

"She wouldn't contact him. She's not stupid. He was after her. Paul, listen. She did know something more."

"What do you mean? How do you know that Britta knew where Coyote went?"

Nina ran her hand through her hair. "The note," she said.

"I was going to ask you about that. About taking a vacation," Sandy said.

"Obviously I don't need a vacation rental."

"True. The vacation is obviously over," Paul said. "It's obvious to the D.A. too. What does it mean? About the cute artist's studio?"

"It means we go back to Alma's and find out where the artist lives. The one who accused you of being a repo man. Britta told me he was listening that night at Alma's."

Paul got it instantly. "Ohh, *that* cute artist. It wasn't the studio that was cute, it was the artist."

" 'Just in case,' she said, Paul. She must mean that she thought Coyote went to the artist's place when he ran off from the camp after we rescued Nate."

"Why would she think that?"

Nina thought back to her conversation with Britta. "He asked the artist for money one time. The cowboy at Alma's called him Donnellen or something."

"What I want to know is why you didn't explain all this about the artist to the D.A.," Paul said. "The deputies could be over there by now."

"I needed to think."

"You needed to think. Okay. That's a good idea. Let's all do some thinking." Paul went over to his fabulous leather office chair and looked out his window, hands behind his head. Nina scratched her arm. Sandy raised her eyebrows and they stuck up there.

The clock ticked over a minute, then two. Finally, Paul broke the silence. "We can't, honey," he said. "The man's too dangerous."

"I agree that he's dangerous. But—"

"We should tell the police about the vacation rental. I'm sorry."

"I don't know if he will implicate Wish, Paul. I don't know what he would say. I don't know if he did anything, or if Britta's husband finally lost his patience and attacked her. Maybe he won't be there at all, and we can talk to the artist. If Jaime gets there first, he'll arrest Coyote and then we won't get any information out of him."

"Whew. Sandy, she's talking rings around me again."

"She's very persuasive," Sandy said. "You have to watch out for her."

"Paul, you have a gun."

"This is cowboy stuff."

"We could be really careful. It's for Wish."

"You just can't resist. Because you know something the D.A. doesn't."

"You know you're going with her," Sandy said. "So let's get on with it. I'll stay here and get organized."

"I suppose we could visit Alma's and see what we see," Paul said. "You know, between the Cat Lady and Nate and the jabbering artist, I feel like we're having a nuttiness epidemic."

"Most people are nuts," Sandy said. "You just have to clue in to their points of nuttiness."

"Well, Britta Cowan was nuts if she drove back to Cachagua to find the artist."

"He's probably sitting at Alma's right now, coming down from whatever he takes," Nina said.

"It's a country-music song," Paul said. "I know that one." He launched into an off-key, twanging tune:

I'm drownin' my sorrows at Alma's
I'm drownin' my kittens at home
I'm drownin' my paycheck in cash for cocaine
But you're a good girl—you'll forgive me again

He gave them a crazy grin and reached his hand under his sport coat and felt around, and Nina realized he'd been wearing the Glock in a shoulder holster the whole time.

26

JOLENE, DEBBIE, AND Tory sat on Debbie's back deck on Monday afternoon. Tory's kids had just jumped up from the picnic table, leaving a mess of ketchupy hot-dog buns and potato chips strewn from here to kingdom come. They ran down in the woods and Tory screamed a couple of warnings to them, which Jolene sincerely hoped they would pay attention to.

Callie and April, now, they were safe in summer school, learning how to be good citizens in a drug-free America, how to get up when the alarm sounds, how to do their homework every night no matter how tired or distracted they felt. But Tory and Darryl had decided to home-school, which meant Tory was their teacher, which was not working out because Tory's pregnancy had knocked her for a loop.

The whole neighborhood was knocked for a loop. Jolene sipped her iced tea and considered how many years had gone by without much change. Maybe twenty-five years, before new people started adopting Carmel Valley. The new people weren't supposed to supplant the old. They were supposed to blend in. Instead they brought in their strange slanted ways of looking at things until you didn't know which way your head was screwed on anymore.

Today, another hot one, Tory wore a beige T-shirt with sea otters on it. Nobody sewed anymore except Jolene, clothes were so cheap to buy at the Ross Store in Seaside.

The huge T-shirt hung like a nightgown on Tory, almost covering the loose shorts that brushed her kneecaps. The girl was a fashion disaster.

And look at Debbie, puffing on a cigarette right close to Tory, who they all knew was pregnant. Debbie in her gardening jeans, busting out of that tight tank top and wearing those hip-hop sunglasses. My.

"I'm not sure I want to go," Debbie said. "Tell you the truth, I'm scared to death to go see her. What'm I supposed to say? She made a spectacle of herself with my husband a week ago. I don't want to be a hypocrite." She got up to bring the plates in and Jolene and Tory got up to help.

"No, you sit and rest," Debbie told Tory. "Watch the kiddies."

When the deck was all clean and swept, Jolene and Debbie sat down again.

"So? What about you?" Jolene asked Tory. "Our neighbor just about got killed, somebody has to go see her."

"I don't have anybody to watch the kids."

"I'll watch 'em," Debbie volunteered, because she felt guilty, even though Britta was definitely not her favorite person, Jolene could understand that.

"One o'clock, then," Jolene said to Tory, who nodded reluctantly.

"She must know who did it, but she's been unconscious," Tory said. "They've had to keep her knocked out so she wouldn't get brain swelling. Darryl knows one of the deputy sheriffs, that's how I know. She won't even know we're there. But I know we have to go."

"Maybe she'll clear all this up when she comes to," Debbie said, and they all pondered this, sipping her heavy-honeyed mint tea.

"I'm not even sure I want to get it all cleared up. You know how Danny was sort of the handyman around here? How he did all the odd jobs?" Jolene said, choosing her words.

"So?" Tory said.

"It looks like one of us neighbors sure as hell did hire him to set a couple fires. He was used to doing the dirty work. Now, don't give me that surprised look, Deb, you know it too."

"I knew as soon as I smelled the smoke from the development across the river," Debbie said. "Truth to tell."

"Me too," Tory said. "So like the lawyer says, all we need to know is who paid out over six thousand dollars a month ago. I'll go first. I checked our bank account. Darryl paid out some money for his sick dad in Arizona about then, but it was nothing like six thousand. I didn't want to do it, but it was pay for a nurse or have him come live with us."

"What about that account of his in the Bahamas?" Jolene said, pointing her finger at Tory.

"Yeah, I should check on that one, shouldn't I?" Tory said, and they all had a good laugh. "Okay, Debbie. Speak up, that's what you do best."

"I didn't hire Danny. And neither did Sam."

"And you know this—how?" inquired Jolene.

"Sam has the business account, and he keeps all that at the office. I waltzed in there and looked at his bank statement. As usual, too much money going out, but nothing like six thousand."

"Maybe he's been squirreling cash on the side," Jolene said.

"He's not a crook. Real people don't keep two sets of books. Sam is too lazy to do that, even if he wanted to. He's made some payments out too, but same as Darryl, just small amounts, a couple thousand at most."

Jolene nodded thoughtfully.

"Not that he wasn't royally pissed about the subdivision," Debbie added. "Elizabeth reads about all this stuff and she told me the company has now put the project on hold."

"Until they catch the arsonist," said Tory.

"Arsonists," Jolene reminded. "The one who hurt Britta, who I suppose is this man named Coyote. Danny, who's dead. And whoever paid them."

"What a mean man," Debbie said. "Coyote. To chain up his own brother. It's so sick. He's the sick one. You know, the boy is really sweet. I brought him some snacks and spent some time with him at the juvenile facility. His eyes are so sad." She hitched up the tank top. "So, Jolene. You and George do all this?"

Jolene couldn't resist. She told them about the forty-two-thousand-dollar stash. "Hadn't been touched for years, except a little over a thousand a few months ago," she said. "I wouldn't have known about it till George died."

"That's sweet," Debbie said. "He was going to leave you an inheritance." Seeing Jolene's expression, she said, "It wasn't sweet?"

"We need the money right now," Jolene said. "So I stole it. Every bit. Withdrew it out of that account and opened a new one at Security Pacific. I had to."

"Jolene!" Debbie breathed.

Tory said, "You go!"

"What are you going to do with it?" Debbie asked.

"I don't know yet. But it'll come to me. It sure will," said Jolene. "We better get going, Tory. The girls get home from school at two-thirty. Debbie, I'll leave a note for them to come over to your house if I'm late."

"I'll take care of them. But I thought we were going to figure this out. What about Ted and Megan? What about Britta's husband? And what about Ben?"

Tory said, "At least we narrowed it down."

"Did we?" said Jolene. "It's like an octopus, I swear, all wavy tentacles getting into everything."

Nina and Paul shot through the fog wall at Mid-Valley, where the organic stand sold expensive flowers and tomatoes to the tourists. Golden sun, benevolent, fertile land, bumpy road snaking through the narrow valley along the Carmel River. At Carmel Valley Village Nina got a good look down Esquiline Road toward Siesta Court, past the old buildings at Robles Vista and past the ashy land and black seared trees of the fire.

She was thinking about Coyote's right to remain silent under the Fifth Amendment, which stood in Wish's way right now. All the amendment said was that a person couldn't be compelled to bear witness against himself.

The reasoning of the Founding Fathers went something like this—confessions become "confessions," which become coerced confessions, a euphemistic phrase for confessions obtained by torture. So they decided to make it official—a defendant can't be made to testify against himself.

Defense lawyers ran all the way for a touchdown with that one. Not only did the defendant have the right not to be tortured into a confession, court decisions gradually extended that right to a right to say nothing at all, to refuse any questioning. And this refusal to speak, even to save a victim's life, could not be held against the accused in or out of court.

In her work as a criminal-defense attorney, Nina almost never let her clients take the stand or make any statement to the police. She used this powerful impediment to conviction whenever it would benefit her client. So it was ironic that she and Paul should be driving out to a hole in the woods, intent on catching Coyote before he could exercise the same right she exploited to the fullest extent in her work. Wish might sit in jail for months, or be convicted, because no one could make Coyote say anything, if he exercised that right. All anyone would know was that Danny was in on it.

And if Danny was in on it, and Wish was at the fire with him . . . what jury would believe that Wish wasn't in on it too?

Her only chance was to find Coyote first, and make him tell his story.

They rode on for an hour along the olive-green ridges with their open views, through the heat, until the road flattenced and rolled into the peaceful, sun-baked village of Cachagua. Nina jumped out and slammed the door, kicking up dust as she walked over to the screen door that led into the dark, air-conditioned cool of Alma's. Paul followed.

Nobody at the bar this time, just the lady bartender behind the counter, her eyes watchful, her cough straight out of a Marlboro carton.

"Two Dos Equis," Paul said, sliding onto the stool beside Nina. The beers appeared within seconds. "Four dollars," the woman said.

"Excuse me," Nina said. She put the cash on the counter. She looked, really looked, at the woman, trying to figure out how to approach her.

She was careworn, but chubby rather than haggard, her face soft, her eyes not stupid but not expecting trouble, her hair freshly styled and her jeans new. Nina liked her in the way that she liked the other mothers at Bob's school, and she said, "We need to find someone pretty fast. He hangs out here a lot."

"Oh, yeah? Who?"

"Coyote, Robert Johnson."

"Sorry. I haven't seen him in weeks."

"Then his friend. A guy with paint all over his clothes and a gray beard."

"Donnelly's not Coyote's friend. Who are you?"

"Good guys," Paul said. "We're the good guys."

She smiled. "Glad to hear it. And now, who are you? Because if you want information, you have to give it."

"We could ask someone else."

"In this neighborhood, we watch out for each other. Nobody's going to talk to you unless you explain your business." Nina waited for Paul to make something up, as they had when they talked to the cowboys, but Paul had sized this lady up as too smart to bullshit.

He explained their business. He passed over his P.I. license. She examined it. Then she said, "He may not welcome you. Donnelly's got some IRS problems."

"Oh?"

"He's famous. He's a famous sculptor. He'd rather be a painter and that's all he's doing this year. Anyhoo, he needs privacy, but I'm afraid it gets out of hand."

"Pit bulls?" Nina asked.

"No. Walls. The biggest walls and gate in the valley. But I could call him."

"You have his number?"

"I'm his sister. My name's Prem."

"Ah. Hi, Prem."

"Because from what you just told me, I don't want Coyote to be there. If I didn't have to mind the bar I'd go out with you. Yes, I'll call him." She picked up the phone and punched in some numbers, which Nina tried unsuccessfully to catch. Holding the receiver to her ear, she grimaced and shook her head.

"He's gone," she said.

"I hope that's it," Paul said.

"Listen, I'm coming with you. I know the code and I know him. Mr. van Wagoner?"

"Yeah?"

"You better be scaring me for nothing." She took a handwritten sign that said BACK SOON, taped it to the door, and waited for them to follow her dusty Explorer out of the parking lot.

They drove off the main road onto a gravel road that became narrower and narrower, until they came to a metal electric gate ten feet high, with spikes at the top. The adobe wall on both sides displayed the same wicked-looking metal spikes. Oak branches inside had been carefully trimmed back.

At the entry stood a call box. Prem punched a button and leaned her head out the window, ready to shout into the box, but the box stayed mute. She punched in a number sequence next, and the gates creaked heavily open.

Inside, the forest continued, thick branches of olive-leafed oaks, and on the ground, in clumps along the drive, twining along the stumps and trunks, the glistening poison oak. Here and there Nina glimpsed strange bronze figures, much too tall and skinny to be human, performing private rites, leaning over, fallen, jumping, sitting on a branch. One of these sculptures peeked out from behind a tree near the car. The body was elongated and bronze, but the head was the bleached skull of some horned animal, teeth intact. It wore a porkpie hat.

Nina thought, not for the first time, what has modern art come to?

The artist's home consisted of a series of adobe cubes piled haphazardly alongside each other, anchored by tall double Indonesian doors painted in garish gold leaf, reds, yellows, and greens. Brown shutters on all the windows, closed. Satellite dish, chimneys, tiled roof. Primitive stencils on the wall here and there. A million-dollar home, so altered that it would perhaps be unsellable.

"The garage door's open," Prem said. "The Jeep's gone. Shit!"

She ran to the door and fumbled a key out of her bag, though Nina called "Wait!" She pushed open the door and disappeared inside.

"You ready?" Paul said to Nina, taking her hand. "You could stay outside." She could see it in his face, the anxiety, the grim anticipation.

"I'm with you." So they went in together.

Polished echoing floors, an almost-empty foyer. A sideboard, all the drawers pulled out. Place mats and tablecloths lying on the floor where they had been tossed.

From somewhere to the right they heard a full-throated, anguished shriek. Nina's eyes met Paul's. He shook his head slightly. He held his gun in his right hand. Nina fell behind as they moved right, into a painting studio.

Canvases propped against the wall. A long scarred Gothic table down the center, covered with a tarp and tubes of oil paint, brushes, bottles, plates, cups, animal skulls, mirrors, dead flowers. And what were those vines in the watery glasses? Nina shrank back.

She looked at the pictures. He was painting poison oak, skulls, dead things, hyperrealistically. While her eyes raked the otherwise-empty room, a vision came to her of the interior of his mind, and she shrank from this too.

And yet. And yet, the brilliant light filtered through the shutters to stripe the concrete floor; the dead things lay passively, giving up their essence, at ease at last; the painting technique, so old-fashioned, brushless, jewel-colored, was so accomplished that the overall feeling she experienced was a sense of quiet and formality, the sense that only great painting can give. She thought of Hieronymus Bosch, Henri Rousseau, Vermeer.

No sound anywhere, now. Paul's hand around hers tightened and he pulled her toward an arched doorway. Nina felt no fear, because of Paul, but also because in this world of deathly harmony she already knew what they would see and she already knew it would be quiet, unmoving. The jittery energy of danger had left.

Prem knelt in the kitchen, behind a prosaic butcher-block kitchen island, copper pots reflecting the shining stripes of light, knelt over a large bloodied creature on the floor. Nina saw hanks of hair, a pool of blood of the most saturated, purest red, with its tributary stream meandering down a slight declivity in the floor. A face covered in this scarlet paint, arms and legs akimbo; he must have been beaten to death. Paul stretched out an arm and stopped her.

"No farther," he ordered. Then he moved gingerly in toward Prem, sobbing next to that bleeding head, and gently lifted her up and brought her back to Nina. Nina put her left arm around her and, with her right hand on the cell phone, punched 911.

27

THE NIGHT BEFORE in Cachagua had gone on too long. The police needed statements. Paul, evasive but tired, wasn't his usual suave self and practically got himself arrested. She had played the tight-ass attorney to get him out of trouble. What they learned at the scene was that the artist was wealthy, had many fans, many detractors, and many possible killers.

She started off Tuesday morning sitting in her visitor's chair in Paul's office, laptop on her knees, listing the things she felt might be important to remember in her preparations for Wish's preliminary hearing. On the wall she had pasted her hand-drawn map of Carmel Valley Village, showing the location of the fires and Siesta Court. Faint laughter filtered up from the Hog's Breath.

Sandy, at Wish's old desk, was reading the Monterey newspaper out loud, in between working on court papers they needed to file.

"Donnelly really was famous."

"He'll be more famous now," Nina said shortly.

"The motive seems to be robbery. His sister said he often kept cash in the house. He was a lumpy-mattress type. Plus Coyote stole his Jeep. You'd think the highway patrol could pick out every Jeep in five hundred miles with helicopters."

"I agree, fleeing in a Jeep is as desperate as dodging a taxi by running into a bus."

"Says here, he was a bit of a recluse. Kinda like Stephen King. People knocking at his door toting bombs, wanting money."

"He despised fame," Nina said. "Unusually private type, but if you ask me, some of that was drug-induced paranoia."

"So it might not be Coyote?"

"It's Coyote. Has to be. We talk about Coyote, and Britta leaves me a note telling me to head for Donnelly's if anything happens to her, and something happens to her. Then something happens to Donnelly. That's what I explained to the homicide detective last night. Not that he appeared to be fully convinced, but he was interested."

"How's she doing? Britta Cowan?"

"When I called David Cowan this morning, he said they'll bring her out of the coma in a couple more days. She's going to make it. What did she do when she left me that day? How did she know he might try to rob Donnelly? I really need to talk to her."

Unable to come to any useful conclusions, Nina and Sandy returned to their work. The clock on Paul's desk ticked. He was out at the handicapped facility in Carmel Valley Village, interviewing the people there, and the phones were blessedly silent.

Nina began doodling names. Britta. Elizabeth Gold. Coyote. Danny. George Hill.

How to prove that Coyote set the fires without implicating Danny, and by further implication, Wish? She got out the autopsy report on Danny and studied it again, reread Wish's story, thought again about the more than six thousand dollars in Coyote's account, wondered again how Danny got his "tip." *Tip* in quotes, because she wasn't at all sure there had been any tip.

Now she started drawing little sketches of the objects surrounding this case—little sketches for little objects. A piece of paper with Twelve Points. A margarita glass. A cat, a concho belt, fire, cowboys, a little kid with his diapers hanging down, a Jeep, Danny's flute . . .

She shook her head and tried again. Sandy had come over to get something and was looking at her paper.

"Why do you do that? I've seen you do that for every case. What does it do for you?"

"It's how I think."

"What about logic?"

"It's never about logic, Sandy. It's always about emotion."

They tapped on their keyboards for a while. The phones rang a few times. Sandy dispensed with calls with her usual mixture of tact and ironhandedness. At lunch, they called an order down to the restaurant. Nina went down to pick up the food and breathe some of the cleansing fog into her lungs. They ate at their desks, communicating, as they often did, in a shorthand that pricked the silence like static.

"Those papers," Nina would say.

"Done."

"Did you call . . . ?"

"Called at ten. Weren't you listening? They say they'll have the discovery papers couriered over this afternoon."

"Wish wanted us to bring . . ."

"I took that stuff over last night."

Nina asked a question that had been bothering her. "Sandy," she said, biting into a pepper, "do you need a place to stay, or are you staying with that friend of yours who lives near here?"

"Staying at your place."

"You are?" Nina struggled for neutrality. Had Paul invited her without saying? How in the world could they have any kind of a life with Sandy on the couch or in his precious den?

"Gotta say, those boys need me."

Boys? Dustin and Tustin sprang into her mind's eye.

"You're staying at the house Aunt Helen left me? In Wish's room?"

"Like I said," said Sandy. "Rent paid. Furnished. Except for a whole lot of dirty laundry, it's empty, thanks to you."

Was she teasing, or criticizing? With Sandy, Nina never knew. "Not for long, if we get our plans in order."

"I've looked over your plans," Sandy said, "and they remind me of the living room at your house in P.G."

"It looked pretty neat the day I visited."

"It would that day, yeah."

Nina tried to imagine the Boyz confronted by Sandy and her luggage, trotting into their domain and taking over Wish's private lair, but here was a situation where her imagination faltered. She was sorry to have missed the moment.

Back at the office, amid the group of phone messages was one from Elizabeth Gold. Nina called back immediately.

"I'd like to meet with you," Elizabeth said. "Maybe I can help. You weren't the only one at the party under false pretenses. I'm a trained sociologist. That's why I was taping the party. I've been studying the Siesta Court Bunch for two years."

"What can you tell me?" Nina said.

"I want to play the tape for you. I can come to your office."

"Not a good idea. I'm tied up."

"Then . . . how about tonight at my house? About eight? I'll make tea."

"I'll be there."

"You better take this one too," Sandy said, her finger on the hold button on the phone.

Nina picked up the extension she had rigged on her table. "Hello?"

"Hi. It's me."

Across an ocean, flying over a continent, only slightly

distorted by the thousands of miles between Stockholm, Sweden, and Carmel, California, the voice was almost instantly recognizable. "Hello, Kurt."

"Nina."

"It's good to hear your voice." Was it? She couldn't tell how she felt. Kurt, so much part of her past, father of her only child, lived too far from her to do more than dance along the edges of her consciousness now and then.

"Same," he said. "Listen, Nina. I'm sorry to spring this on you, but Bob . . . he's impulsive. Like his mother."

"Like his father," she said, kidding, as Kurt had been, but wondering what he meant. "He's okay?"

"Fine. I mean, he was fine last night when I saw him last."

"What's going on?"

"I told him to call you, but he said he just gets a recording. He wouldn't leave a message. He's on a kick."

"Kurt, I'm trying to follow here."

"Well, there's news," he said, an understatement, as it turned out.

When she hung up, Nina turned to Sandy and said, "Bob's getting into the Monterey airport at three. I'm going to pick him up."

"You want me to go?" She didn't seem surprised.

"No. You have to get our motions over to the court by five."

"How do you sign them, if you're not here?"

Nina grabbed several sheets of pleading paper and signed them about halfway down. "You're so good I'm going to assume you can transcribe the motions perfectly, proof them, and make them end right above the signatures on the papers." She was signing proof-of-service forms as she spoke. "If Paul calls . . . don't tell him about Bob, Sandy."

"You sure?"

"I'm . . . kind of behind with this," Nina said.

"Ooookay."

Sandy did not say, this is what you get for not dealing with what is really happening in your life, and, for that, Nina was grateful. Nina lingered at the door for a while, issuing instructions that Sandy took in good spirit, then finally went out to the street to locate the Bronco, which had a ticket, as usual. She stuffed it into the glove box with all the others. Another thing she could not tell Paul was that she couldn't stay in Carmel forever. The boot would get her for sure.

She drove through light afternoon traffic to Highway 68. She took the airport exit. A million questions rose in her throat. She tamped them down.

The sight of Bob waiting on the curb, as battered as his duffels, looking insecure and uncertain of his welcome, tore through all questions and doubts. Jumping from the Bronco, she grabbed him and hugged him tight. "Oh, honey!" she said.

He said nothing, just clung to her.

With no other option, she took him directly to Paul's condo. In the car, they didn't talk much. Bob was exhausted and incoherent. At his age, fourteen, incoherence was the norm. She had forgotten how difficult it was to pierce the haze of adolescence, but the trip reminded her immediately. Mom did not ask probing questions. Mom awaited moments of revelation. Since a fourteen-year-old boy did not understand himself, he had few such moments. Plus, he did not wish to subject himself to Mom's judgment.

She reached over and ran her hand through his spiky hair instead.

At the condo, she helped him unload his duffel and the case with his bass in it. He couldn't sleep on the couch in the living room; the television had its corner in that room, and the area opened up to the dining and kitchen areas.

They would all go crazy with a teenager installed on the couch there.

Bob would have to set up shop in Paul's high-tech study.

While she pushed books around on shelves to make room for a few of Bob's things, and pulled out the sofa bed, he showered.

She found extra bedding in the hall closet, and put it on the sofa in the study along with a few throws Paul had accumulated over the years, one saying 49ers, another saying R U Experienced?

Bob came in, rubbing his hair with a towel, trailed by Hitchcock. She was sitting cross-legged on the floor near the couch. "I'm glad you're here."

"Me too," he said. He tossed the wet towel onto a desk full of papers. Nina got up to remove it. Paul would not want his papers runny and moist. Seeing the sofa with its fresh sheets, Bob crawled inside, pulling the sheet up to his neck. "I'm so tired," he said.

"It's a long trip from Sweden to the West Coast," Nina said. "How long have you been traveling?"

"Forever. Honest, Mom, I lost track. I don't even know what day it is."

"Bob, we need to talk."

"Sure, Mom. Go ahead." His voice already sounded muffled.

"Because . . ." Because Paul doesn't know anything about this, she thought in despair. Because I'm afraid what his reaction will be, finding this kid ensconced in his private space without warning. Because he always said he didn't want kids at all.

"Because," she started again, more firmly, "we have to find a better situation."

"It isn't the most comfortable bed in the world," Bob said, "but it's fine for now."

"I didn't know you were coming! I would have gotten a room ready."

"I tried to call! You were never around!"

"What about my cell?"

"I always got your message center. I hate that. It's too complicated for a message."

"So what's going on."

"I wanted to come home."

"So you did." Home meaning . . . Mom?

"Right. They only charged me a hundred bucks to change my ticket, and I paid for it out of gifts I got from Uncle Matt, so that's okay, right?"

"But, Bob . . ."

"It's okay, Mom. I don't care that this bed is hard. I could sleep out on the deck until the weekend, and never wake up." His voice was drowsy. "There's more. Tell you later."

She couldn't get another word out of him. His eyes rolled up and closed and that was that.

The duffel was full of dirty, stinking, in some cases damp, clothes. She took them into the laundry area off the hallway and started to sort, whites, darks, permanent press, unable to think about Paul coming home, what he would say. After she sorted his things, she decided to add the growing pile in the laundry basket in the main bathroom.

In the corner she saw the rolled-up pile of clothes Wish had left the night he appeared at their door.

"Ugh," she said, pulling them out. They should have tossed these the day Wish got back. Holding the reeking ball at arm's length, she marched to the kitchen, to the main trash can. Before she dumped the contents, she forced herself to pick through the pockets, changing her mind in the process. Let Wish decide what to do with his motley assortment.

Wish was a pack rat, like Bob. Bottle caps, crumpled paper, an old lollipop melted into its paper wrapping . . . he had an accumulation of goodies, some of which she couldn't even recognize. Forcing herself to be diligent, she took it all, right down to the denim-colored lint, and stuffed it into a plastic bag. She set the contents on the kitchen counter to give to Wish later and, feeling productive, gathered up all the kitchen trash and carried a big load out to the Dumpster at the end of the buildings. She yawned. She was beat.

It was five o'clock, the adults' witching hour, when the work stops and, if you're lucky, the fun begins. Right on cue, she heard Paul's Mustang muscling into the driveway.

He swept in, kicked his shoes off, and gathered her up into his cold arms. "Ah," he said. "Alone at last." His grin, so soon to be brutally erased, was one she knew well, and signified that he was feeling playful.

"Paul," she said.

He put his finger over her lips. "Let's have ourselves a TGIF nap. We are not going to discuss work. We are going to take our clothes off and frolic. I need a quick shower. Dinner after. I'll take you out for barbecue."

"No, Paul, wait . . ."

He covered her mouth with kisses, nudging her toward the bedroom. "I want you in bed, naked and ready in two minutes. Can you do that? I think you can."

"Really, I need to tell you!"

He shut the door on her. "Shh. Save it."

She heard him slam the door to the bathroom, and the shower going on. Might as well do what I can to mitigate the shock, he'll find out soon enough, she thought. Hint to investigator: no hot water.

Meanwhile, she combed through her brown hair, sitting at the mirror. The woman in there was turning back into a mother right before her eyes.

He took a long time in the shower, cold water or no cold water. She crawled between the sheets to warm her cold feet. She pulled a fuzzy blue blanket up from the foot of the bed. She would just get warm . . . she could explain everything. . . .

Paul wrapped the towel loosely around his waist and peeked into the bedroom. In the light of early evening through the deck doors, Nina lay on her side, pillow spread with her long soft hair, hands in prayer position under her head, knees bent. She was asleep, and he took a long moment, admiring her. What a beauty she was, and she was his now.

• Humming, he decided to take a second to check his E-mail. He opened the door to his den. He stopped.

A form covered with blankets too heavy for summer lay on the sofabed. At its foot, Hitchcock lolled, eyes closed, lost in canine cogitation.

Who?

He moved in closer. Gingerly, he lifted the blanket from the face.

Bob.

Bob Reilly. Nina's son. Home to roost.

Stepping back into the living area, gently closing the door behind him, he thought about it. He considered Nina's preoccupation on several previous occasions. He thought he now understood the source of her anxiety.

He was feeling some anxiety himself.

He decided to pour himself a stiff one. In the kitchen, in the cabinet near the refrigerator, he located the half-empty bottle of Jack Daniel's. However, a glass did not come as quickly to hand. No matter. He drank from the bottle.

Better, he thought, and drank some more. After a while, a pleasant, welcoming attitude warmed his heart. Good old Bob! He liked the boy, after all!

But Bob could not live here, no, no, no.

He looked again for a shot glass. This drinking from the bottle seemed suddenly rude. Finding a souvenir from Caesars Palace at Tahoe, he filled it and downed it.

But he was hungry. It was dinnertime. All is flux, people sleep at five in the afternoon, plans go aft agley. . . .

He checked the microwave, in case some plate was in there, still warm. Empty. He checked the refrigerator. Also nothing. The uncooked fish filet in there looked disgusting.

On the counter, nothing but an ancient wrapped turkey sandwich and a sandwich bag full of pennies and acorns and loose, discolored peppermint Lifesavers and blackened scraps of paper. He discarded the sandwich, fiddling with the bag.

Various things fell from the baggie onto the counter. They appeared to be the property of Wish Whitefeather, student, or so it seemed according to the filthy student ID he found. Finding nothing of redeeming value in the stuff, he tossed most of Wish's bits in the garbage below the sink.

But what was this?

He examined a plastic card of electronic material, no more than a few inches long, narrow. Familiar, he thought, squinting. Oh, yes, but why here?

He knew that he had drunk too much when he stumbled slightly leaving the kitchen. He would have some coffee, he promised himself, just as soon as he checked this out.

Opening a cupboard by the television, he pulled out his camera, opened a small compartment, and pushed the thing into place.

A memory card, perfect fit.

He clicked through twelve pictures, all orange-and-yellow, flames, underexposed because Wish must have been using the automatic functions of the camera, which would not be able properly to process the brightness of the nighttime scene. Three showed people, men. Two men.

He woke Nina up.

28

In the harsh light of the fire, the whole forest around Wish was revealed, bit by bit, as he had spun around, twelve pictures in all. In nine of the pictures they saw nothing but creepy-looking bushes and trees, and whiteouts of smoke.

"*Blair Witch* stuff," Paul said. After sneaking into the den to retrieve it, he had moved the pictures from his camera to his portable computer screen. The bigger pictures made the faces of the men easier to see. He double-clicked on his photo program, and began doing some easy enhancements to see if there were any details he had missed on first perusal. He brightened the pictures of the men, compensating for the poor exposure.

They now sat together on the couch in the living room, two cups of coffee steaming on the table, the warm body in the den behind the closed door nearby lurking between them like a monster under the bed. Nina had changed into jeans and a T-shirt. Paul now wore shorts.

They were not touching.

Wish had taken one photo of Danny in his spinning, the very first shot on the memory card, and now they saw the man who had brought Wish up the mountain, Wish's dead friend, at last. Danny's hand was up, shielding his face from the light, and he was grimacing. He wore a dark T-shirt over black pants. He must have flung off the Army jacket. His face was handsome, planed, stark in the light, and he had a thick neck and shoulders.

He looked directly at the camera and his parted lips were arrested midword. He looked familiar to Nina, as though she had met him before, and she had indeed met his type before, strong young men who ought to be building families or serving in the military but instead drifted into purposelessness.

"Good-looking dude," Paul said, keeping his voice low. He clicked to the third and fourth shots and manipulated them so that they were side by side on the screen, and Nina saw that Wish had done it, managing in spite of his terror to take two shots that linked Coyote forever to the fire.

In the third shot, they saw mostly Coyote's lower body as he hid or stepped out from behind a bush. He wore a long white T-shirt and jeans, and his long dark face was somewhat shadowed.

"Nothing in his hands," Paul said, disappointed. "A can of kerosene would have been good."

"It's incredible just to have the shot."

In the fourth shot he had stepped fully out and was advancing toward Wish, holding his hands up and looking scared and angry. He was built like Danny, muscled, tall, dark, and young.

"Wish was lucky," Nina said.

"To get these pictures?" Paul's hand moved to her thigh. They had both leaned back to study the three shots, now side by side on the computer screen, their necks stiff with the effort, as if the shots were Picassos. Which they were, lawyers' Picassos, strong, timeless, and irrefutable.

And as mysterious as a Picasso. The two shots still did not reveal why this young man had killed three people and almost killed another.

Nina accepted his touch. "Yes, Wish was lucky to take the shots, but also to still be alive."

"So, after tucking the memory card into his pocket, Wish drops the camera and runs at this point, and Danny gets lost for a while but catches up to him on the trail. But

Coyote has followed Danny. He kills Danny and grabs Wish, who manages to escape."

"That's how Wish says it happened."

"Why didn't Wish mention this memory card? How the hell could he forget it?"

"He must have popped another one in before he ran. When the sheriff's office found the camera on Robles Ridge it had a memory card with no photos taken."

"That's it, then. Why are you grinning?"

Nina said, "I've got something Jaime doesn't have, and it helps Wish. Of course I'm grinning."

"Danny couldn't have been in on it either. If he was, Coyote wouldn't have had any reason to kill him."

"I know. That's how it must be, and Wish won't have it any other way. But Britta said Danny was in on it. She heard him plotting with Coyote, for Pete's sake."

"She's lying?"

"Anyway, look at how a jury will see this. Wish up on the mountain, taking photos. Coyote caught in two of the shots. I don't understand what part Danny may have played, but I do know this, it's going to look like Wish was trying to catch an arsonist, and the rest is a tap dance. I don't have to explain everything."

Paul got up and stretched. "You going to give the photos to Jaime?"

"I have to in order to use them at the prelim. I'm going to have Wish take the stand, Paul."

Paul shook his head. "You are the only lawyer in the whole world who would do that. Then the D.A. has months to go over what he says and twist it into anything he wants. It's a murder case. Are you sure?"

Nina ticked the points off on her fingers. "First, he's led a clean life, Paul. No ugly character evidence or prior felony convictions to come in and slime him if he takes the stand. They can't mention any juvenile offenses. Second, he's got a simple story and I think he can handle the cross-exam. Third, he's innocent, and I think it'll come across.

Fourth, I need him to authenticate these shots and explain what he was doing up there. If he doesn't take the stand, his story doesn't come out, the prelim becomes a pro forma exercise, and Wish stays in jail for maybe a year."

Paul thought about this. "But—"

"Mom?" Bob stood in the doorway in his rumpled skivvies, rubbing his eyes. Nina took in again his height, his long narrow feet, a slight shadowy hint of whiskers above his upper lip. The light fell on his face in a way that made her think of Kurt. "What time is it?"

"Seven. At night. You had a good nap."

"Hi, Paul."

"Hi, kid."

"I am so hungry. Is there any food?"

Nina jumped up. "Sure, honey. What would you like? Cereal? I could fix you some scrambled eggs. Or do you want a sandwich?"

"Oh—whatever. Anything edible."

"Come on in the kitchen." Nina went over to Bob and gave him a quick hug.

They went into the kitchen and Nina got out the frying pan. It was seven in the evening and she and Paul had just found an important piece of evidence and Bob was sitting at the table drinking orange juice.

She broke the eggs in the pan and put toast in the toaster. In the other room Paul had passed through the duffel area and sat down at his computer. Bob looked out the doors to the deck and said, "Check that foggy night. In Stockholm it's summer. It stays light until midnight."

"It's summer here too, silly."

"What'm I gonna do now?"

"Eat. Bob—"

"Yeah?"

"I have to work tonight."

"On Wish's case?" She had told him on the phone about Wish.

"That's right. We have a prelim in his case starting next week."

"I'll help you. Sign me up."

"That's a nice thing to say, honey, but—the best thing you could do is give Hitchcock lots of love right now and help him get better. Could you take on that responsibility? I would really appreciate your help."

"Sure." He petted the dog, who lay at his feet. Poor Hitchcock's bandages were soiled already. The vet had given him painkillers, which made him drag around and sleep a lot. Nina patted the dog too, and tried without much success to restick the gauze on his neck. "What happened, anyway? Did Hitchcock get hit by a car?"

"A dogfight."

"Hitchcock fought with a dog? Who won?"

"Hitchcock," Nina said. "How are you feeling?"

"Like sh—not so good."

"Don't worry, everything will be fine," Nina said, too brightly. She served him the eggs and toast and watched him eat. "Do you want to talk?" she asked.

"No, you're busy."

Nina dropped into the chair beside him. "Not that busy. You've just come from a far country. I'm sure you've had a million adventures, and I want to hear—"

"You have to work tonight, and we've got plenty of time to talk later. I have stuff to do. I have to call Taylor and Troy at Tahoe. Call Dad and tell him I made it."

"Call your grandpa too," Nina said. "He'll be happy you're here in town."

"Yeah, I want to see Isaiah."

Nina left him eating and went into the bedroom to get her jacket. From the kitchen to the bedroom she had to go through the living room, where Paul was now sitting on the couch talking on the phone and leaning over at an uncomfortable angle to look at the photos again. Bob's open duffel lay in the corner, and his carry-on knapsack lay in the middle of the floor.

She picked it up and set it inside the den, saw the sofa sleeper with its roil of blankets taking up most of the room, and got busy.

Kitchen, bedroom, living room, and study. The place already felt like a tiny box, now that Bob was in it.

Isaiah, Angie, Harlan. Family who had been comfortably distant, moving in fast on her radarscope, now that Bob had come. Her father, big, filling up emotional space she couldn't spare right now.

She sat down on the bed. Between Paul and Wish, she had thought the motel was full up. But now Bob was here. For a moment, she panicked. But following this, she thought of Bob in the kitchen, eating eggs, and inside her, something that had been tense and anxious and incomplete soothed and smoothed itself.

The Boy was back. She was complete again. And happy.

Paul, one finger looped in the top of his shorts, observed. "You'll be going, then," he said.

"Not necessarily," Nina said, punching in Elizabeth's number.

"Yes, you will. And you will avoid the inevitable confrontation."

She held the phone to her ear, desperate for an answer.

"Can't put it off forever, Ms. Reilly," he said. He drank some cold coffee, making a face. "Things have changed. Must reevaluate options. I'm going if you go. Protect and serve."

"You can't, Paul. You've been drinking."

Elizabeth answered. "Nina? You're coming, aren't you?"

"I was wondering if we could make this tomorrow?" Nina asked.

"I'm leaving for the weekend. I have to get away. You really ought to make it if you can."

She let her brown eyes rest on Paul's bloodshot hazel eyes. "On my way," she said. He looked away.

Nina drove out Carmel Valley Road listening to the Cal State station blasting hip-hop. She didn't want to think. Sometimes, and this was the human condition, wasn't it, sometimes she relied solely upon emotions to inspire her next move.

The human condition, irrational, unpredictable, people just trying to scrabble through life—the truth is, we don't think very well.

Eminem's song about cleaning out his closet came on, and she remembered the Boyz cleaning house to that very tune. She turned it up to make it so loud, the people in the car passing her illegally on the right could hear the earth-shattering bass. She sang "I never meant to hurt you-u-u" along with the chorus. Son home, lover drunk.

Fine. Go to work. She felt quite alert after the nap.

At Southbank Road, she turned and climbed up the hill toward Elizabeth Gold's. The house, larger than she would ever have dreamed, had that expensive up-lighting that turned greenery and home into a movie set.

Elizabeth, luminous in a clingy bamboo-spangled robe, answered the door promptly. Not exactly trained sociologist attire, which caused Nina to think again, she's in danger of turning into Virginia Woolf.

She took Nina into a living room that resembled the inside of a cathedral. Gigantic, sparkling windows curved along one whole wall, pines and oaks fluttered beyond.

"Wow," she said, starting off with some especially articulate lawyer talk.

"Thanks," said Elizabeth. "Want to try some lapsang souchong?"

"Whatever."

Elizabeth left Nina to admire the scenery, returning after some time with a tray loaded with teapot, honey, noncaloric sweetener, and a colorful tin tea canister.

"I'll bet you see deer out there," Nina said, stirring honey into the tea.

"They eat everything." Elizabeth hadn't sat down, but had gone to the window, looking dreamily out. "If they don't, the gophers do. One year I planted three Japanese maple trees. The gophers ate the root balls. They just toppled over one fine day."

"But it's beautiful," Nina said.

"Yes," Elizabeth agreed. "I wanted a fortress. A nunnery of one. I found an architect who specialized in women like me." She smiled. "He enjoyed building to the absolute limit allowed by law. The size is obscene, I know. One time the Cat Lady came up to me as I was getting into my car in the driveway and she whispered, 'Obscenely wealthy people should have their wealth taken.' "

"The Twelve Points," Nina said. "That was only one of her pillars of wisdom."

"She was right. If you don't use your surplus money to help others, you ought to have it taken for that purpose. I've given so much away, I may have to actually start working for a living." She laughed. "But the house . . . it's my security. I'm trying to decide if it's my prison too."

Elizabeth stirred honey into her tea, her movements as exquisite as a geisha's. It irritated Nina, how much time she seemed to have to pay attention to small things, to be sensitive, to think about herself. She realized she felt envious of the young woman sitting in her luxurious home. She knew from the Siesta Court party that Elizabeth inspired that reaction in others too.

"So what's on those tapes?" she said abruptly.

Elizabeth sipped. "I don't know if you've studied sociology."

Nina shook her head.

"I'm working on my Ph.D. thesis. In my branch of study, we look at group dynamics and power struggles."

Nina said, "You taped those people as a research project?"

"Well," Elizabeth said, "for years my sister, Debbie, talked about these get-togethers she hosted. I listened, feeling like I was listening to a weekday-afternoon soap. The characters seemed like cardboard. The conflicts between the locals and the newcomers were so aptly illustrated they almost seemed contrived, you know? When I moved here, I really thought it would be interesting to take an objective look-see. I decided to write my thesis about gentrification on Siesta Court."

Nina said, "How does your sister feel about that?"

"Debbie doesn't know. None of them know. It would affect their behavior and ruin the study."

"But—you're part of it. You affect the parties and their behavior."

"Not really. I keep a very low profile. You're smiling. You don't think I'm sufficiently objective. I can compensate for these problems." She sighed. "Actually, you're right. I have just developed a rather significant objectivity problem."

"And his name is Ben," Nina said. "We ladies do have a grapevine."

Elizabeth tensed, then smiled back. "I can find something else to write about," she said. "I won't find another Ben. If you know about Ben, I suppose you also know how Darryl Eubanks has been harassing me."

"That too."

"I've taken care of it."

Nina said, "You know, Elizabeth, I'm interested in sociology and psychology, and I can't wait to hear what you've discovered in connection with your thesis. But what I'd really, really like to know right now is how you've taken care of Darryl."

Now they were both smiling. "I called Tory, his wife, and had a chat with her," Elizabeth said. "I took the bull by the horns."

"Wow," Nina said again, impressed.

"I explained that Darryl was having a problem, and I suggested counseling."

"How did she react?"

"She slammed the phone down in my ear. I believe she'll calm down quickly and have a rational discussion with him and that he will stop bothering me."

"No doubt."

"You're making fun of me?"

"Not at all. I just have less faith in the rule of reason than you when it comes to human beings."

"Maybe when this is all over we could have lunch together," Elizabeth said. "I'd like to make some friends. What do you think?"

"Sure." They nodded at each other. Nina felt as though she had been handed an unexpected gift. She liked Elizabeth, and she also needed a friend.

"I promise not to tape you," Elizabeth went on, and laughed.

"Speaking of tapes . . ."

Nina received a ten-minute lecture about the classifications Elizabeth had assigned to each of the neighbors, and her hypothesis that the newbies, though fewer in number, were winning the power struggle, not only because they had a monetary advantage, but also because they possessed what Elizabeth called a "timely" advantage.

"Different groups of people develop at different rates," she explained. "The newbies live in the twenty-first century. The locals live in about 1960. I have surveyed both groups informally. The mores of the locals haven't stopped developing, but the rate of development has been slower because they stayed in their enclave and didn't experience as many upheavals as the newbies. The newbies move all the time. It speeds them up."

"I never heard this idea before," Nina said.

"I made it up. It explains so many things. Of course I will have numerous references to other authorities who have said something similar. But no one has put it exactly this way."

"So never the twain shall meet? The newbies and the locals are fated to slug it out, and the locals will fade away?"

"And then the newbies will become entrenched, and slow down. And they will become locals. If they're lucky, they will have some time before the next wave of newbies arrives."

"What happens to this ongoing power struggle if an outside threat comes along that threatens both groups?"

"That's exactly what happened."

"That's exactly what happened? You mean on Siesta Court? When the Green River development started?"

"Obviously."

"And all this has to do with your tapes?"

"Yes. For all this time I have been quite sure that the core group issue was gentrification. The subjects aligned according to their newbie/local status as predicted.

"But then about two months ago, I noticed a change in the dynamic of the block parties. I would listen to the tapes afterward, and in the middle of the usual hanky-panky and drinking and skinned knees on the kids, I realized that a surprising new set of alliances had formed and most of the group energy had transferred there."

Nina waited.

"Very sudden and very powerful, this shift. Different people became leaders, and some people became irrelevant. The dynamic changed utterly."

"Go on."

"The alliances solidified and secrets developed."

"You're too general," Nina said. "This is interesting, but I know you asked me here to tell me something important about my client's case. It's late, Elizabeth."

Elizabeth said, leaning forward, "I'll make it simple. The men allied. And the women allied. Across the newbie/local lines."

Nina considered this. "They broke into gender-based groups over the conflict with the subdivision?"

"Precisely."

"Secrets developed?"

"The men began holding private conversations. I should mention that Ben was the exception throughout. He was kept outside."

"Why?"

"I think—I think they knew Ben wouldn't want to get involved."

"Involved in what?"

"I'm not sure. Now. Remember, at this time Danny was still alive. He had always been an outsider too. Suddenly he was talking a lot and being listened to. He was an integral part of this new alliance.

"I could only catch bits and pieces of their conversations during the parties. They always came back to the Green River development. I'm quite sure that they began holding other conversations outside the parties. Away from the women, whom they didn't trust."

"And you say the women began doing the same thing? Meeting secretly?"

"Not exactly. They had always used that extremely fast and efficient telegraph called gossip, but they talked as a group more than they used to. I was curious as to why they tolerated Britta at all. But then I realized that Britta had an important role as the transgressive woman in the group. They all had the same issue—the men were shutting them out, and they all felt resentful. Actually, the men had always shut them out in various ways—George keeping Jolene from their money, Darryl shutting Tory out emotionally—but this was a conspicuous exacerbation."

"You mean they tolerated Britta because she caused so much trouble?" Nina asked, amazed.

"Oh, yes, Britta helped all the women vent their frustrations. Did you notice how muted Debbie's response was to Britta's transgression with her husband, Sam?"

"You mean the lap dance?"

"Yes. It reminds me of the custom in a certain African tribe. It's called 'sitting on a man.' The women go to the hut of a man who has violated some social custom and compel him to submit to the very same obscenity. It's a sexual attack. Humiliating. Degrading."

"You're kidding," Nina said. "The women despise Britta."

"Consciously, they do. Unconsciously, they admire her."

"You know, I think you're right. It was like a—a rape," Nina said. Elizabeth nodded.

"Then Danny died. The last tape I made—at the party you went to—contains a few bits of conversation from one of those male groupings. I want to play it for you." She got up and led Nina into a book-lined study, green-walled and octagonal, like the tower of a princess in a fairy tale. She had already inserted the cassette into the player, and she switched it on and off at each phrase, watching Nina's reactions.

"This is Britta," she said.

"What're you guys talking about, hmm?"

"Sam answers her":

"Danny. We're toasting Danny."

"They all laugh here, you can hear it, and I don't know who says this":

"Good riddance."

"Now another group response":

"Yeah."

"And that's what I thought you should hear," Elizabeth concluded. They were both standing, and both very excited.

Nina said, "They were glad Danny was dead."

"They were toasting his death," Elizabeth said. "Fascinating, no?"

PART FOUR

And folks who put me in a passion
May find I pipe in another fashion.

29

ON WEDNESDAY MORNING, Nina was eating her breakfast when her father came to the door. Paul had just gotten up and was pouring himself his first cup of coffee, and Bob had been up for hours E-mailing on the computer and playing with Hitchcock.

"Grandpa!" Harlan hugged Bob and followed him into the kitchen.

"Figured I had to come to you," he said to Nina, and sat down. "Long time no see."

"Well, Dad, what a surprise."

"When I got the call from Bob last night, I decided to drop by. Okay with you?"

"How about a cup of coffee?"

"Sounds good, Paul." Harlan, hale, red-faced, and loud-voiced as always, was wearing a Pebble Beach Company golf shirt and creased pants. At sixty-four, he had already been retired for years and he lived for the putting green. "My own daughter moves here and doesn't come to see me. I have to come to her. Hard to imagine, isn't it, Paul?"

"I'm sorry, Dad, I've been so busy—" Harlan ignored her crummy excuses and turned to Bob.

"So you've been chatting up Swedish girls in the Land of the Midnight Sun?"

"Not exactly," Bob said.

"What brought you back so soon?"

"Stuff."

"You talk just like your mother at your age, which is to say, not at all. You okay, though?"

"I'm okay."

"Glad to be home?"

"Yeah. I guess this is home."

Harlan accepted the coffee and began telling them about his new house in Pacific Grove and how Angie and Isaiah were doing. He made it all sound so normal and homey that Nina began thinking to herself, How come I've stayed away?

Still, she never felt comfortable with Harlan's new family. Her stepmother, Angie, was younger than Nina, and Nina's half-brother, little Isaiah, was more than thirty years younger than she. Nina didn't feel that she belonged in this new family constellation.

And, to be unfair, she still thought Harlan had remarried too soon after her mother's death. But Bob had none of these reservations, and was asking a lot of questions about his Uncle Isaiah, age three.

"We got him this electric-powered toy loader. Tot size, but he can raise and lower the loader and pick up dirt. He's a hoot. He rides up and down the driveway all day in it."

"This I gotta see," said Bob.

"Come on over this morning and you can. I'll take you boys to Cannery Row for pizza and drop you off later."

Bob said, "Mom?"

"Your mom can come too. You too, Paul."

"Sorry, Dad, but I have a prelim on Monday."

"As always. How about it, bud?"

"Is that okay, Mom?"

"Sure," Nina said. "Clean clothes in the laundry room. Hustle now." When Bob had left, she said, "I really am sorry, Dad."

"I'd like to spend some time with you, Nina-pinta."

"I'll try to do better. We'll have dinner soon."

"Where's Bob sleeping?" Harlan was looking around.

"In the second bedroom. Paul's study."

"That's all you have? Two bedrooms? Angie and I have four. He ought to stay with us. He'll drive you two crazy in this little place, and Angie likes to make nice dinners. Not that you couldn't make a nice dinner if you had the time," he added.

Before Nina could respond, Paul sat down across from Harlan and said, "That's a mighty nice offer, Harlan."

"I'd love to have Bob for the summer. I'll teach him to play golf. While you people figure out what you're doing."

"Isn't that a great idea, Nina?" Paul said.

"It's very nice," Nina said. "I'd have to give it some thought. And talk to Bob about it."

"Sure, sure. I know Angie wouldn't mind a bit, though. And he hasn't spent much time around Isaiah. He's Bob's uncle, after all." And my half-brother too, Nina thought. Dad, why does your life have to be so complicated? This thought was followed by a chastening realization: She took after Harlan in that respect.

Bob came back in with his backpack.

"You ready to roll?" Harlan asked him.

"I just wanted to ask you something first, Mom. In private," Bob said.

"Sure, honey." They closed the door to the main bedroom.

Bob said, "I was listening to you guys. About living with Grandpa."

"Oh."

"What did you think of his idea?"

"What did you think, Bob?"

"I think it sucks," Bob said. His blue eyes blazed out of his face. "I want to live with you, Mom. We're the family. You and me and Hitchcock. I like visiting Grandpa but forget it—it's us, right? Right?"

"Right," Nina said. "Don't worry, honey. Go visit Isaiah and we'll talk later."

———

She and Paul drove together to the office. Paul hadn't broached the subject of Bob again, though she felt the pressure of his patience, and Nina had already moved into work mode.

They stopped at the photo shop to pick up blowups of Wish's photos, which had come out well, and carried the manila envelopes upstairs to the office. Sandy hadn't come in—it was visiting hours at the jail—and Paul began telling Nina about his visit to the Robles Vista facility. The director had spent a long time with him and Paul was of the opinion that none of the residents had the physical ability to carry out the arson fire on the hill below them.

"These people are severely disabled," Paul said. "Blind or wheelchair bound, almost all of them. One of the blind guys is very independent and works out, but the director thought it would just be impossible. Besides, as he pointed out, to torch their hillside could result in having Robles Vista burn down too. The handicapped facility is right above that model home."

"Has Crockett talked to them?"

"Every resident has been interviewed. I talked to Crockett, and he says none of them could be a suspect, even if he didn't already have Wish. Most of them seem to be resigned to moving, though there is a great deal of anger and insecurity."

Nina said, "Okay. Scratch them. No jury's going to buy them as alternate suspects. We're back to Siesta Court."

"Danny and Coyote and the Moneyman."

"Elizabeth played me an interesting tape last night. From the Siesta Court block party I attended."

He was on the computer. "About Elizabeth. I meant to say, uh, sorry about getting juiced last night. I don't even know why I did that. So what about this tape?"

"I think Elizabeth just wanted to talk to me anyway. And I know you don't drink that much, but Paul, with Bob around, we're going to have to straighten up in general."

Paul swiveled around so he was facing her. He looked like he was thinking that the good times were over.

Nina said, "I really want that chair, Paul. That is the most comfortable, coolest chair in the world."

He leaned back and let a beatific expression cross his face. "It is."

"So that's a no? You won't let me use that chair? I have to use this director's chair?"

"Honey, without my chair, I'm nothing."

"Not very chivalrous."

"I'm much nicer to my wives. But let's not go there this morning, we have work to do."

Nina fidgeted uncomfortably, just to make him feel bad, but he was pretending not to see it. So she went over to him and sat down on his lap.

"A compromise," she said as he put his arms around her. "Anyway, she taped a conversation in which several men were standing in a group apart from the rest of the party, having a quick conversation. Their voices were lowered, but you could hear some of it. They were toasting Danny's death."

"They were what?"

"I'm telling you. They said, 'Good riddance.' "

Paul thought for a moment, then said, "They must figure Danny was responsible for the fires. Even so, it's damn cold."

"I think it might be more than that, Paul."

"What do you mean? Who are we talking about, anyway?"

"Darryl Eubanks, George Hill, Sam Puglia, David Cowan, and Ted Ballard."

"You think—what? One of them is the Moneyman?"

"One of them? Or all of them?" Nina said. "If it's all of them, you see, there wouldn't be six thousand two hundred fifty dollars missing from anybody's account. They each could have pitched in part of the money to pay Coyote."

"I don't know. First of all, who's going to set all these

fires for a little over six grand? Ben already told me that Danny hadn't had an influx of money. So was he not involved after all? It doesn't make sense."

"No, you're right, but we have to start untangling this somewhere and I still feel this money in Coyote's bank account is hard evidence of something."

"Okay. What now?"

"I'm glad you asked me that, Paul."

"What are you up to?"

"I'm going to call Debbie again. And ask her about the sum of twelve hundred fifty dollars, whether that rings any bells for any of the women."

Paul was nodding. "Twelve-fifty times five. Six thousand two hundred fifty. I get it, even if it sounds extremely far-fetched. Can't hurt. Meantime, I'm scheduled to go talk to the Boyz again and get them ready to testify. Maybe they'll remember something else."

Debbie was out on the deck, if the birds chirping madly in the background were any indication. "Just thought I'd check in," Nina said.

"Sam wants to know if you're going to subpoena any of us," Debbie said. "For this court proceeding."

"That's not the plan at the moment. A preliminary hearing is a lot less thorough than a trial. There will only be a few witnesses, and at the moment I don't see you and Sam as involved." She added the lawyer's private asterisk: But that could change.

"What with Britta still in intensive care and Danny's death and the Cat Lady, I just can't seem to get to the gardening or the housework. All I do is worry. I wish I knew what was going on."

Nina felt a jab of conscience. She had told Britta, not Debbie, about the threat to the children. Maybe Britta hadn't spread the word before she was assaulted. "Debbie," she began, but Debbie was ahead of her.

"We had a prowler a few nights ago. Behind David's house. Now we're all wondering about this guy Coyote you told us about."

"Debbie, I think you should worry. I think you should be careful." She told Debbie about Donnelly's death. Then, taking a deep breath, she told her Nate's words about the children.

"Our children?" Her voice was tremulous. "Here in the neighborhood? What is he doing? Why would he hurt Britta and set fires and threaten the children?"

"I just don't know. But, you know, I don't agree with the police that there isn't a possible danger."

"I think Nate doesn't make things up. He does get confused, though."

"That's true."

"But—someone hurt Britta. I need to talk to Jolene and Tory. And David." Now she was in a hurry to sign off, but Nina said, "Wait. There's one more thing. You know how I told you about the money Coyote received from somewhere?"

"Yes, you got us in a tizzy and nothing came of it."

"I made a mistake," Nina said. "The amount was twelve hundred fifty dollars."

There was a long silence at the end of the line.

"Okay, then, gotta go," Debbie said, feeding her a big tablespoonful of phony cheer.

"Call me if anything comes up," Nina said.

"You bet. Oh, absolutely. Bye now."

When Darryl got back from the hardware store, Tory didn't seem to be around, and the kids, who had been playing in the backyard when he left, must be with her. When he opened the back door, though, he heard them next door and he went out into the backyard.

Tory and Debbie were chattering on the deck and the kids were trampolining. "Hey, ladies," he called. They looked his way and Tory called, "Be right there." So he put away the paint in the garage for his Sunday project and settled down in his La-Z-Boy to watch ESPN. He didn't feel so good and he just wanted to be left alone, so of course Tory came marching in a few minutes later and, would you believe it, picked up the remote and turned off the tube.

"I want to know what you've been up to," she said. "You better start talking." She stood right in front of him, arms folded, face white, wearing her gardening jeans and one of her old flowered cotton pregnancy tops that gave her lots of room to grow.

"What's the matter?" Darryl said. He set down his beer. "What happened?"

"You ask what's the matter. Britta's in the hospital, Danny's dead, the hills are alive with the sound of crackling, the Cat Lady was murdered—murdered, Darryl. You don't love me anymore. And you ask me what's the matter? I'm going to pack up the kids and get out of here. I'm not staying here. We're going." Her voice sounded strange. He'd never heard her so angry. He stood up and tried to put his arms around her to calm her down, but she shook him off.

"You better listen this time," she said. "I've had it."

"But what did I do?"

"I don't know what you did yet. I'm going to go check our bank records and find out some of what you did, but even before I do that, I'm going to tell you, Darryl, you better make up your mind if we're going to stay married. I'm not putting up with it any longer. With you chasing after Elizabeth, jealous about her." She burst into tears.

"Oh, sweetie, don't get so upset." Darryl felt helpless. "Where are the kids?"

"Debbie's watching them so I can talk to you," she choked out, and Darryl had that terrible sinking feeling that this was it, he was going to have to really talk to Tory. He wasn't ready.

"We're leaving you, Darryl," Tory sobbed. It felt like getting hit with a ninety-mile-an-hour fastball. Darryl sat down. He couldn't breathe. "I'm packing up. All because of you being so stupid. You don't care about anything but your big stupid self. You just sit home and wait for your girlfriend to come to you. I doubt she ever will, but that's the way you've decided to live."

"But—but Pastor Sobczek—tomorrow—"

"Too late. Too late." She was crying like her heart was broken, and all of a sudden Darryl realized it really was. This was serious. She was thinking the unthinkable.

He cleared his throat. "Sweetie, can we sit down? Please? Let's sit down." She let him take her hand and they sat down on the couch. He took her chin and tried to get her to look at him, but she wouldn't. Now he was really alarmed.

"Well, you love her, right?" Tory cried.

"I—I—"

"Putting me through hell. For what? She doesn't love you! Me and the kids, that's who used to love you! Well, it's over. You keep your secrets, all of them. I don't even care what you've been doing."

"What brought all this on?" Darryl asked, his alarm making it hard for him to hear, making his ears ring.

"Debbie says the kids are in danger from the man who hurt Britta. I'm not staying here, Darryl. And I found out you went to see her."

"How?"

"Who cares how? You think I'm stupid old Tory, I'll put up with anything! I'm leav—"

"Tory," Darryl said as calmly as he could, "listen to me for just a second. You're very upset and I—I understand. But you can't just take off."

"Watch me!"

"We have five kids!" The thought that he might lose his kids was new and so frightening he could barely say that.

"Four. I'm not keeping this one, Darryl." Stunned, Darryl let go of her. His mouth fell open. She too seemed stunned by what she had said. Then an expression of the most awful sadness and hostility all mixed up came over her face.

"I'm going to have an abortion. I am."

Darryl's eyes filled up. He couldn't say a word.

"I don't want to, but what am I going to do with five kids? Society doesn't support motherhood, not really."

"No. Please, no, Tory. Please listen."

"To your lies? You and your secrets. All you men. Something awful is going on around here." She spun around and ran into the bedroom. Darryl stood there a second, panic knotting his gut, then he followed her in. She had pulled open the dresser drawers and was setting clothes on the bed.

"Tory—Tory—"

"Go away, Darryl." She was crying again.

"We'll go see the pastor tomorrow."

"No."

"I'll do anything. I love you. I do. I'll prove it. Please don't leave." He grabbed her and she tried to struggle free, but he wouldn't let her. They fell onto the bed and thrashed around and she got one arm free and hit him in the face, hard. She fought so hard he had to let her go so he wouldn't accidentally hurt her. She was yelling and screaming the whole time.

She rolled away and got up on one elbow, trying to catch her breath. Darryl felt something wet on his face and wiped under his nose and saw his hand covered with blood.

"I think you broke my nose," he mumbled. She jumped up and came back in with a bunch of tissue and said, "Stuff it under there." Then she went back into the bathroom and a minute later came back with some wet washcloths. He sat on the edge of the bed and she wiped the blood from his lip and mouth carefully. She had stopped crying, but her eyelashes were wet and her face was all flushed and he felt the most tender and sad feeling come over him. He had made her cry.

"Just a nosebleed," she told him.

"You have a hard right."

"You deserve that and more."

"You're right. I'm stupid. I don't believe how stupid I am. But please don't leave me. Please. Let's go see the pastor tomorrow. Then if you have to go, all right. Tory, I can't make it without you and the kids."

"I don't know," Tory said. "I'm very mixed up. And afraid for the kids. And you're no help at all. No support at all. Worst of all is that you don't love me."

"But I do. I do. I just forgot it for a while."

"I don't believe you."

Darryl got down on his knees and buried his head in her lap. He broke down like a little kid.

And after a minute he felt her hands stroking his hair. It was like crashing a car and then, finding, thank God, you're still alive.

30

THE BOYZ GAVE notice the next day.

"We're leaving tomorrow, but we'll pay the rent until the end of the month," Dustin said on the phone. Nina, on the floor in Paul's bedroom, files and books and papers spread around her in a semicircle, tried to wrap her mind around this new domestic disturbance.

"You sure will," she answered. "Care to give me a reason?"

"This whole thing with Wish."

"I don't see how—"

"Wish's mother. Mrs. Whitefeather. She's here right now. Know what she's doing?"

"What?"

"She's scrubbing the bathroom. She's putting my razor in the cabinet above the toilet where I'll never find it." Dustin must be on a cordless phone because he seemed to be watching Sandy's movements. His voice, hushed, went on, "She's sniffing the towels."

"Put her on, would you?"

"It won't change our minds. We're leaving. Sorry, Nina."

"So that's it? There's nothing I can do? Even make Sandy go stay somewhere else?"

"Something else will happen. Tus and I need quiet to study. If Wish gets out he'll come back here and—no offense, but who knows what'll happen next? We need quiet.

Quiet, man." Nina heard the sound of the toilet flushing. "There goes the roach that lived in the medicine cabinet," Dustin said. "He was kind of a pet."

Nina said, "Okay, Dustin. But I'll still need you in court next week."

"We're still on. I owe Wish that." Sandy came on the line.

Apparently Dustin hadn't told her the news yet. When Nina told her she was about to become the sole tenant of the cottage, Sandy said, "I wasn't going to say anything. But there were things in the freezer that would make your hair stand on end. So what now?"

"The rent's paid for a couple of weeks. I'll rent it out again when you leave."

"It'll be a lot better-looking around here by then. They're nice boys, they just never heard of Ajax cleanser."

Nina returned to her work. She was writing down points to cover during her cross-examination of the medical examiner when Bob knocked on the door.

"Mom? I'm going for a hike."

"A hike? Where?"

"In the hills out back."

"I don't think that's such a good idea. There are tarantulas and snakes and poison oak and—"

"I'll watch out. Hitchcock hasn't been for a good walk since he got hurt."

Yes, but there's a fugitive hiding somewhere out there who wants to take some children, Nina thought. "I'll go out with you about four."

"But I want to go now."

"Go swimming at the condo pool. Okay?"

Bob's eyes had fallen on a book that lay open in front of her. "What the heck is *that*?"

"Don't look at those, honey." Nina hastily closed the book.

"What happened to those people?"

"It's a book by two medical examiners, both named Di Maio, called *Forensic Pathology*. It's about trying to figure out how people have died."

"You have to read stuff like that? Look at those cracked-up skulls? That one guy looked like a mummy. His skin was hanging in flaps!"

"I'm sorry you saw the pictures, honey. This book is a reference book for doctors and lawyers. Not for you to look at."

"Remind me not to be a doctor or lawyer!"

"I've got to get back to work now, Bobby."

"So when are we gonna have our big talk?"

"In the next couple of days."

"Is Paul mad that I'm here? He's staying away a lot, isn't he?"

"Paul likes you just fine," Nina said. "Don't worry about a thing."

"You always say that."

"Bob, I—" I don't have time to talk right now, I have a prelim tomorrow and I have to get to work, kiddo, she wanted to say. And managed not to say it. "So go have a swim and get some sunshine."

He also hesitated. He was growing up and she couldn't always read his mind anymore. "Okay. See you later."

"I'll be knocking off around four. We'll take a hike and later we can eat at Robata and we'll stop at the Thunderbird Bookstore." And then she would work some more.

He closed the door and Nina opened her text again. The caption under the photo said, "Scalp burned away, exposing cranial vault." Outside the window, it was summer.

At Ben Lomond, Ted and Megan stopped for more water and granola bars, twenty hard miles from where they had started cycling. Ted's hair, when he removed his helmet, curled in tendrils above his brow and made him look like a Roman emperor. They sat on a bench in front of the general store, drinking water and sweating it out almost as fast as they took it in. The tourists drove along Highway 9, gawking like they were exotic or something.

"I never liked these mountains around Santa Cruz," Megan said. "They're too dark. Too thick. Too many murders too. I think the hippies who never grew up came here and some of them stagnated for a long time and then they got rotten."

"They're dying off now," Ted said. "The music was pretty good, though."

"Sex and drugs and rock. Do you think they had more sex than the current generation?"

"Oh, crap. Are you on the sex thing again?"

Megan looked at him, tall, hard, sucking down his water, wet hair, black spandex cycle shorts, hairy legs. "I've got a theory," she said. "About the sex thing, as you call it."

Ted groaned.

"I think it's your bicycle seat. And all the time you spend on it. It injures your testes."

Ted ate some of his granola bar. He said, "I thought that just made you infertile."

"If it can do that, it must be cutting back on your testosterone production."

"Stop it, Megan. You're starting to really bug me."

"It's that, or have an open relationship," Megan said. Ted groaned again.

"You never quit."

"Because you won't be straight with me. Yes, I am straightforward. I don't make three hundred thousand dollars a year pussyfooting around. But remember, Ted, I am also nonjudgmental. I want to solve this problem of us not making love."

"Maybe it is you," Ted said. "Maybe you're cutting my balls off talking about all the money you make."

"You're stronger than that."

"Maybe I need a seventeen-year-old honey who blindly adores me."

"I adore you. In my way. But I won't let you keep secrets from me."

"Megan, I—"

Megan waited.

Ted's face contorted. "All right!" he said in a low, intense voice. "You asked for it! I don't like to have to be the one who does it! I want you to do it to me!"

"Do what?"

"You know! I need you to—I've been feeling so guilty about some things I need to be—I don't want you to go easy on me—"

Megan finally understood. She had been obtuse, very obtuse. "You mean, you want to be the passive one in—"

"Don't say it! Don't say it out loud!" Ted looked embarrassed now.

"Thank you," Megan said. "That wasn't so hard, now, was it?"

"Let's go. Let's get out of here. I need to ride."

Megan put her lips close to his ear. She said, "After our hot tub tonight, I'm going to—are you listening?—tie you—to the bed—and—punish you severely." His ears flamed. He filled out his shorts in a whole new way.

31

WISH HAD THE flu. He snuffled into a handkerchief beside her at the defendant's table. He had a generic prisoner's look about him with the shorn hair and the orange jumpsuit.

Behind him, in the audience section of the court that Nina thought of as the pews, Sandy sat in her purple coat, her purse in her lap. They had whispered a few things to each other. Then Wish had folded his hands in front of him on the table and gone mute.

Paul sat next to Nina at the defense table, reading the Monday morning paper. He had arrived home late the night before and had been sleeping when she headed for his office at 7:00 A.M.

In the second row she recognized two newspaper reporters, farther back Elizabeth Gold and Debbie Puglia, and, sitting together, two drifters who enjoyed going to court proceedings. She also saw David Cowan in the back row. Cowan looked anguished. His wife had had some sort of setback over the weekend and had barely pulled through.

The witnesses for both the prosecution and the defense came in one by one. For the prosecution, they were Davy Crockett and Gertrude Rittenhauer, the chief medical examiner for the county of Monterey, and also the county deputy sheriff who had located Wish at the condo, Deputy Grace. Crockett sat down at the prosecutor's table on the right, looking spiffy in a blue suit.

For the defense, Nina had subpoenaed Dustin Quinn, dressed up in a sport coat and giving Wish the thumbs-up. Wish would testify too. The hell with received wisdom, this defendant would take the stand.

Jaime came in from the side door, arms full of books and papers. He said "Hi, Nina" in that low-key way he had, and started getting organized. At the same time, Judge Salas's clerk, a blond woman of about fifty, had taken her chair and was writing on a form. To the side of the room, by the empty jury box, the bailiff leaned back in his chair in his tan uniform.

Wish was extremely nervous, and she thought again about this decision to have him testify. Yet how else could they explain what he was doing on the mountain? The burden of proof in a preliminary hearing was so minimal that if they left it with Jaime, Wish would certainly be bound over for some distant trial date.

But Wish had to be credible. He had to stop looking so guilty. "Sit up straight," she whispered to him as Judge Salas appeared at the judge's dais.

"The Superior Court of the County of Monterey, State of California, is in session, the Honorable José Salas presiding as magistrate."

Judge Salas had shed his role of Superior Court judge for this proceeding and become a mere magistrate, for arcane legal reasons that Nina, in a discussion in bed on Friday night, had been unable to make Paul understand.

"It's a legal fiction," she had told him finally. "Don't worry about it. A Superior Court judge can't conduct a preliminary hearing, because the appeal from the prelim is to a Superior Court judge, and an appeal always has to be to a higher court. So they just change the name of the judge when he's doing a prelim, to magistrate. So technically a lower court has conducted the prelim, and the law is satisfied."

"What about the defendant? Is he satisfied? What about reality?"

"Reality? Vat is dis ting you call reality? This is law we're talking about."

"Okay, why should the appeal be to a higher court?" Paul said persistently. Sometimes they did this now, instead of making love, lay close to each other and talked softly, endlessly, about very unromantic things. Sometimes Nina enjoyed this pillow talk so much that she kept Paul awake long after his silences lengthened as he fell into drowsiness.

"Several underlying policy reasons. So the judge's close colleagues on the bench aren't passing judgment on him or her by reviewing the decision—"

"Okay."

"And, obviously, an appeal by its very nature is a request for some higher authority to review a decision made by a lower court—it's a matter of constitutional due process—"

"So how does calling a Superior Court judge a magistrate satisfy these policy reasons? His Superior Court colleagues still review his decision, and the defendant still doesn't get a higher-court review."

"That's true. But it satisfies the letter of the law. That's why it's called a legal fiction."

"And that's why I don't trust lawyers," Paul had said. "Twist, twist, twist." She lifted her head off his arm and looked at him. His eyes had closed and he gave no sign of realizing how he had casually pushed into her territory and butted into her thinking. Once again, he was openly challenging her assumptions about her own work. She flushed, annoyed and surprised. Then she thought about it. He was right, but you have to pick your fights. You can't take on the whole system. Other lawyers will consider you naive for wasting your energy on a hopeless cause.

Then again, life was a hopeless cause. Which didn't mean you stopped fighting.

Nina said, "You talked me into it. I shouldn't take this for granted. It's a denial of due process. I haven't protested because it seems like it's too big an injustice to take on. I guess I get inured."

"Is that like getting inert? Like we are now?" They were indeed flat on their backs in the bed, talking at the ceiling.

"I guess, now that you bring this up, I'm going to have to object to having this matter heard by any Superior Court judge, no matter what name they give him. Judge Salas is going to hate me. Oh, well, he doesn't like me right now anyway, so . . ." Her eyes closed and she slept.

"*People* v. *Whitefeather*. State your appearances," Salas said in his absurdly young voice.

"Jaime Sandoval, Monterey County District Attorney's Office, appearing for the people of the State of California. Detective David Crockett of the State of California Special Arson Investigation Unit is my designated investigating officer." This meant Crockett could sit in on all the proceedings even though he was a witness.

"Nina Reilly, law office of Nina Reilly, appearing for the defendant, Willis Whitefeather, Your Honor. Paul van Wagoner is my investigator in this case. The defendant is present."

"Any new motions this morning before we begin?" Don't you dare, Judge Salas's jaundiced eye told Nina.

However, she had decided otherwise. Sometimes you have to do it, for your own self-respect and because of your respect for the law, even if you're going to lose and know it. Salas wouldn't like her any more, but he could hardly like her any less, so there was no strategic ground to be lost. She stood up and said, "One new motion, Your Honor."

"Paperwork?"

"Right here, Your Honor. Filed just before court this morning."

Jaime looked hypocritically regretful, as an Olympic skater might look watching a competitor execute a triple axel, only to land hard on her ass. He had read her motion and knew what she was in for. Salas was skimming the papers.

"Proceed," he said.

"The basis of this motion is that this court has no jurisdiction to conduct this preliminary hearing." Nina launched into her motion, which essentially said that Salas should step down until some real lower court could hear the case, on grounds that the defendant would otherwise be denied his right to appeal to a higher court. "A conspicuous and egregious denial of due process, I would respectfully submit," she finished.

Salas knew she was right. So did Jaime. So did every criminal lawyer in the state of California.

The judge flipped through her points and authorities, which relied heavily on the United States Constitution, looked at Jaime, and said "Is she for real?"

"She is," Jaime said, nodding.

"Counsel, do you know how many preliminary hearings are conducted in this state each year?"

"No, Your Honor," Nina said.

"Thousands. Tens of thousands. Do you presume to know better than all the county courts, all the legislators, all the lawyers who have never raised this in any preliminary hearing to my knowledge since the act permitting consolidation of lower and superior courts was passed?"

"I don't presume to be anything other than a lowly defense lawyer, Your Honor."

"Then why do you raise this in my court, at this time? Is it to persecute me?"

"No, Your Honor."

"Your motion is denied."

"Very well, Your Honor. Thank you, Your Honor."

"Feel free to appeal my ruling to the Superior Court," Salas said, and gave Jaime a sideways glance. Jaime let out an obsequious chuckle.

With the Constitution out of the way, they moved along swiftly. Judge Salas asked about the witnesses and how long the hearing might last, and cast an incredulous look at Nina when told Wish would testify. The witnesses trooped out after being admonished to wait outside and not talk to one another.

Ten minutes later, all other legal detritus cleared away, Jaime called Deputy Clay Grace to the stand.

His complexion had, alas, not improved, but he was alert and responsive. Nina had no beef with him. She let Jaime get through the preliminaries efficiently.

"The Carmel Valley EMS advised they had a male subject who was DOA at Community Hospital. The subject had been found the day after the fire lying near some rocks about a quarter mile up from Hitchcock Canyon. Badly burned and no quick ID possible."

"And what was your assignment with regard to this victim?"

"To determine who it was. We had what we considered to be significant information in this regard. The Carmel Valley police had been contacted by the defendant's roommates the morning after the Robles Ridge fire and told that he was missing."

" 'He' meaning Willis Whitefeather, the defendant?"

"Correct."

"What else did these roommates say in their report?" Deputy Grace was testifying as to hearsay, but Nina couldn't object. In another sleight-of-hand, prosecutors had managed to get a law passed that allowed hearsay in preliminary hearings, as long as it came from a law-enforcement officer with five years of experience. She contented herself with rereading her copy of the handwritten report made by Dustin Quinn.

"They told the Carmel police that the defendant had gone up to Robles Ridge the night before—"

"The night of the fire?"

"Yes. Carrying a backpack with equipment, accompanied by another young man named Danny Cervantes. Based on that, we were working on the theory that the burn victim was either Willis Whitefeather or Danny Cervantes. Also that these two gentlemen had perpetrated the arson fire on the ridge."

"What did you do next?"

"Well, we advised Mr. Whitefeather's mother that we needed her assistance in viewing the body, but she couldn't fly in right away. It took another day to get ahold of Mr. Cervantes's uncle here and he was the one who made the final ID, but as of the day after the fire, we didn't know which one of them might still be alive. Neither of them had local dentists and we would eventually have been looking for those records at Lake Tahoe, where both of them were originally from."

"While you were waiting for a family member to make this ID, what, if any, other avenues of investigation did you pursue?"

"We started calling every hospital and clinic in Monterey County. The CVPD was continuing to search the fire area, so I was assisting by trying to determine if the other individual involved in the fire might have also been burned and needed medical help."

"And did you locate anyone in this way?"

"No. I then made the assumption that the one who survived might have been able to flee the jurisdiction and I put out a request to surrounding counties up to Santa Clara County for information as to hospital and clinic admissions."

"Object to the characterization implied by the use of the word *flee,* Your Honor. Lack of foundation," Nina said.

Salas looked up, displeased. "You'll have your chance to cross-examine. There's no jury here, Counsel. I can separate the wheat from the chaff. Overruled."

"And did this inquiry bear any fruit?"

"Almost right away. I got a call on Thursday evening from the Las Flores Medical Clinic in San Juan Bautista, about fifty miles from the fire site. The admissions clerk advised that Willis Whitefeather had checked in there on the morning after the fire and had just checked out. Apparently he had fled the county and was hiding there. I had her fax me the admissions form—"

Nina's finger moved to her copy of that form, signed in Wish's crabbed hand—

"And he had given an emergency name and number of his employer, Paul van Wagoner Investigations. I determined Mr. van Wagoner's home address—"

Paul whispered, "Ask him how he did that!"

"Shhh!"

"—and my partner and I proceeded immediately to the address in Carmel Knolls, with a CVPD car for backup. I knocked at the door.

"The door was answered by this lady here, Ms. Reilly. She would not let us enter and she returned a minute later with Mr. van Wagoner. They were putting us off, and I became suspicious."

"Then what happened?"

"I continued to ask if Mr. Whitefeather was in there and finally he came to the door. He was wearing a towel and I saw burns on his arms and legs. He said he would cooperate and had nothing to hide and agreed to come to the station to meet Detective Crockett. Ms. Reilly insisted on coming along and showed me a State Bar card and said she was his lawyer, so I said okay. Mr. Whitefeather was taken to the station with Ms. Reilly following in her vehicle."

"What happened then?"

"Detective Crockett interviewed the defendant. Then I was called in to place the defendant in custody pursuant to Detective Crockett's arrest. By then it was almost midnight. I then took the defendant to the jail facility, where he was booked."

"Thank you. Nothing further."

"Your witness," Salas said.

"Good morning, Deputy Grace." Nina spoke from her place at the table.

"Good morning." The deputy crossed his legs, maybe to show she didn't unnerve him at all.

"You were trying to determine the identity of this burn victim found on the ridge?"

"Correct."

And you assumed it must be Mr. Whitefeather or Mr. Cervantes?"

"Correct."

"What made you assume it had to be one or the other?"

"Because we had the report that the two of them went up the ridge that night."

"And so you were also assuming no one else did?"

"Not necessarily. We just had this report on these two."

"So it's possible one or more other people were up there?"

"There's no evidence of that."

"But it's possible?"

"Sure."

"Now, you also assumed Mr. Whitefeather and Mr. Cervantes set the fires, is that correct?"

"That was our working theory. We had a witness report on a previous fire that two men were involved."

"Did you consider that someone else might have set the fire, and these two young men were trying to catch him?"

"No. We didn't have any evidence of a third party, as I have stated."

"Other than a report from some other incident that there might be two men, what evidence do you have that these men set the fire on the ridge?"

"The witness report in the second fire reported that one of the suspects was dropped off on Siesta Court in Carmel Valley Village, which is where Mr. Cervantes lived, which in my mind linked him to at least the second fire. Mr. Cervantes died in the third fire. So he was present. He went with Mr. Whitefeather. I have read Detective Crockett's report and I am aware that the defendant admitted he was there. Bottom line, it was late at night on a deserted mountain and an arson fire was in progress and the defendant was there. He exhibited burns consistent with flame burns, as if he'd been caught in a wildfire."

"Any other evidence?"

"Detective Crockett's interview—"

Jaime intervened. "Your Honor, since Detective Crockett is the next witness, it would be better for him to testify directly regarding additional evidence developed by the Arson Investigation Unit."

"Counsel?" Salas said.

"Sounds fine to me," Nina said. "Oh, by the way, Deputy, when you came to Mr. van Wagoner's door, did you have an arrest warrant?"

"No, ma'am. We only wanted to question—"

"Was I obligated in some way to allow you inside the home?"

"Not legally, ma'am, no."

"And did Mr. Whitefeather in any way attempt to resist or flee?"

"No, ma'am."

"And was he in any way uncooperative?"

"No, ma'am. You were the one who was uncooperative. You advised him not to say anything." Nina heard a ripple of laughter behind her.

"How did you get Mr. van Wagoner's home address?"

"We have it on file."

"Now, you said that you got a call from the Las Flores Clinic that Mr. Whitefeather had been hiding there?"

"Yes, ma'am."

"You assumed he was fleeing police?"

"It was my working theory."

"How do you know he was hiding?"

"Well, there were plenty of places to get medical treatment closer than fifty miles away."

"Is the Las Flores Clinic a private clinic?"

"No, ma'am, it's part of the San Benito County system."

"Did Mr. Whitefeather use an assumed name?"

"No. He used his real name."

"Did he use a fake emergency name and number?"

"No, since it led us to him."

"Did he have genuine injuries?"

"It appeared he did."

"Is there any indication he stayed unnecessarily long at the clinic?"

"Not that I know of."

"And as soon as he was discharged, he returned to the county?"

"Yes, ma'am."

"Is that the usual behavior of a fleeing felon?"

"Objection," Jaime said. "Calls for a conclusion. Calls for an opinion. Speculation."

"He can speculate all he wants about why the defendant was on the mountain and why he chose this clinic, but he can't speculate about the behavior of a fleeing felon?" Nina said.

"I get the point," Judge Salas said. "Objection overruled. Let's move it along."

"Your answer?" Nina said to Deputy Grace.

"No, it's not what I would expect from a fleeing felon." Grace was still relaxed. He had told the truth without any fuss, and Nina respected that.

"Thank you, Deputy."

"No redirect," Jaime said, and Deputy Grace stepped down.

They took a short recess. Paul was fuming. "On file," he said. "I guard my home address like El Al guards its ticket counter. No way could they get my address."

"So that's why we don't have many visitors," Nina said.

"Why didn't you follow up some more on how he got my address?"

"Because it has nothing to do with this hearing, and it would add a confusing bit to the transcript, and because you can call him and ask him."

"They're keeping a file on me, Nina."

"They're keeping a file on everybody," Nina said. "I'm going back in and get ready for Crockett."

32

"Good afternoon, Detective Crockett."

"Good afternoon." Jaime had already taken Davy Crockett through the story of Wish's arrest and interview at the station. Methodically, he had then obtained an outline of the series of arson fires that had occurred, the Cat Lady's statement about two men, Wish's burns, and had even attempted to bring in Wish's juvenile record for setting a fire. Nina had objected, of course, but Judge Salas had absorbed it even as he sustained her objection.

Now it was her turn. The object of all this was to show that Wish's actions and statements were consistent with innocence, and that Coyote had also been on the mountain.

"Now, Mr. Whitefeather told you at the interview that Danny was only trying to stop the fires?"

"That's about all he said, yes. You advised him to remain silent but he did say that, in addition to admitting he was on the ridge that Tuesday night."

"All right. Now. There was a reward for information leading to the arrest and conviction of the arsonist in the previous two fires, am I correct?"

"I believe so. It was put up jointly by two corporations that suffered property damages due to the arsons."

"And the amount of this award was?"

"A hundred thousand dollars, I believe." Judge Salas stroked his chin.

"You had received numerous tips from the public about who the arsonist could be?"

"Yes."

"Ruth Frost asked for that reward, did she not, after she signed her statement?"

"Doesn't mean she wasn't telling the truth."

"Right. So there was great public interest in this reward? It had been well-publicized?"

"Yes."

"Would a photograph of a man, accompanied by a sworn statement that the photograph was taken at the time and place of an arson fire, be evidence that the man was an arsonist?" The question was clumsy, but Crockett understood and Jaime made no objection.

"Possibly. It might be a firefighter, or an innocent bystander."

"Right. But your office would follow up to determine if this person was an innocent party or not if presented with such a photograph?"

"Sure we would."

"Now, you have testified that the murder weapon was found to be a camera."

"Dr. Rittenhauer will go into that further in her testimony, I believe."

"But that's your understanding?"

"Yes."

"And you have identified the camera as belonging to the defendant?"

"Yes."

"Speaking as a highly trained and experienced arson investigator, why do you think the defendant brought the camera up the mountain with him? You think he did that, right?"

"He was up there and so was his camera. There are several possible reasons for bringing it up there. The first one I would think of is, he wanted a souvenir. It was an ego trip. Can I make a comment about why the fires might have been set?"

"Go right ahead." She had been hoping Crockett would go into his lecture mode. Let Salas hear about all the many reasons others might have set the fires.

"Juveniles set most of the fires, probably fifty percent of the fires in this country. They love the colors, the excitement, the destruction.

"Adults don't get that same kick. Maybe they want to do something grandiose, something that will make them famous. We call that a vanity motive.

"Then there are the revenge arsons. Love stories gone bad. Feuding relatives. These people aren't worrying about being caught. They're too busy being drama kings and queens.

"Of course, there are always the insurance fires. The list goes on. Lately, we've seen an increase in arson that is used to commit homicide or to cover up a homicide.

"Now, we don't know exactly why these fires were set. But in any of these scenarios except the last, the arsonist might have wanted a photo to remember it by."

"Isn't it true that the last scenario is actually what you believe at this time was the motivation for the third fire? To cover up a homicide?"

"We can't be sure—"

"You've testified that Mr. Cervantes's death was no accident, that the camera was the murder weapon. Mr. Whitefeather is charged with premeditated murder in one of the counts of the complaint. Which of the scenarios you have mentioned is the most likely scenario explaining the third fire, based on your experience and training?"

"For the third fire, it seems that at least one purpose was to commit a murder," Crockett said, because he had to, or else the premeditated murder count would have to be dismissed.

"And, as you've just said, it is actually not at all likely that a suspect would bring a camera to record that?"

"You never know."

"But it's unlikely?"

Crockett pursed his lips and said reluctantly, "Pretty un-likely. They might take a souvenir, but usually some physical item, not a photo."

"So the first reason for bringing the camera up the ridge, an ego trip, doesn't work in this case. What other reason might there be to bring a camera up a hill, assuming that a hundred-thousand-dollar reward has been offered?"

"Presumably to try to get the reward by documenting the arsonist."

"Ah," Nina said.

"Pretty stupid way to go about it, though. And it doesn't make sense in light of the other facts."

"Why don't you remind us of those facts again."

With exaggerated patience, Crockett said, "Fact: The defendant went up the ridge with Mr. Cervantes. Fact: Mr. Cervantes was linked with the previous arson. Fact: There is no evidence anyone else was on the mountain that night."

"Let's look again at that third fact." Judge Salas looked at the clock on the wall, stifled a yawn.

Nina took the photos recovered from Wish's memory card from an envelope on her table. The memory card looked like a tiny disk and held digital memories of photos, taking the place of the roll of film of yore. She showed them to Jaime as a courtesy. He already had his set, and nodded, not particularly perturbed.

"You've seen these photos, haven't you, Detective Crockett?"

Crockett looked through each of them and said, "Yes, your investigator gave me the same set."

"He explained that these were developed from the memory card taken from the camera of Mr. Whitefeather?"

"He didn't know where that memory card came from."

"He told you I found it in clothing worn by Mr. White-feather during the fire, didn't he?"

"Maybe you ought to testify, Counsel. I know nothing about where these photographs come from."

"You have attempted to match the memory card to the camera, haven't you?"

"Haven't had time due to the prelim taking place so quickly." It's all your fault, his eyes said. He wasn't happy about being rushed into the prelim, and now she was paying a price.

"What do the photos show?"

"Some people running around in some woods."

"Recognize any of the people?"

Jaime got up and said, "Your Honor, this has gone far enough. This witness has testified that he can't authenticate or identify the photographs. I object on grounds of lack of relevance and competence. The pictures could have been taken anytime, anyplace. Let's not waste any more time."

Nina said, "Offer of proof, Your Honor. Mr. White-feather will testify that he took these photographs during the Robles Ridge fire. He will identify the two other men pictured."

"I look forward to that, I really do," Jaime said. "It'll be the first time in my legal career that a defendant has taken the stand in a prelim involving such serious felonies. I can't wait. But, until he does, I object to questioning this witness further on this subject."

Salas took his time. Finally he said, "This witness isn't competent to testify about these photographs. You haven't laid any groundwork. You have to assume too many facts not in evidence. I will sustain this objection."

Salas was right, but she had had to try. The photos had at least reared their ugly heads. She took the set of photos back to the table and took a breath. Onward.

"All right. Back to your contention that there is no evidence of any third party being present during the third fire. My investigator, Mr. van Wagoner, also came to your office and signed a statement regarding a child-endangerment case in the Arroyo Seco area about a week after the third fire, is that correct?"

"Ye-es." Crockett, puzzled, looked to Jaime for help, and Jaime shrugged his shoulders.

"The suspect in that case was a man named Robert Johnson, also known as Coyote?"

"Yes."

Two could play at the hearsay game. Nina could make Crockett testify about Paul's statement and keep Paul off the stand.

"You recorded the interview and later provided a copy of the statement to Mr. Sandoval here?"

"Yes."

"And in the interview with you did Mr. van Wagoner tell you about anything he saw at Robert Johnson's, uh, home?"

Crockett looked surprised. "A couple of conchos. Silver medallions. He also reported kerosene and weapons on the premises. We took all these items into custody pursuant to a search warrant executed that same day."

Turning to the judge, Nina said, "Your Honor, I have previously requested that Mr. Sandoval bring to court today the conchos under discussion and I would now request to have them given to the witness for examination."

Jaime said, "I have them right here." Two small chased silver medallions lay in the evidence bag Jaime passed to Nina.

"Let's see," Judge Salas said. She gave it to the clerk and the clerk passed it to the judge. He turned the bag to and fro and held it up to the light, then passed it back.

Now Crockett had the bag, and pulled on a pair of latex gloves and emptied the conchos onto the witness stand.

"Seen those before, Detective?"

"Yes, I have marked the bag. These are the conchos Mr. van Wagoner reported."

"Have you attempted to match the conchos to any other conchos in police custody?"

"Yes. Our evidence technician did find a match. The conchos matched conchos on the belt worn on the body of Mr. Cervantes."

"Was Mr. Cervantes's belt missing any conchos?"

"Two. I can save some time here and state that our evidence tech examined the conchos and belt with a microscope and reported that the conchos were from the belt of the decedent. There were marks showing they had been torn off. It says here that he found one print of an index finger on one concho matching records on file for Robert Johnson."

"Yes. I have that report. And what conclusion did you draw from this?"

"No real conclusion. The belt had been in the possession of both men, or Johnson found the conchos after a bar fight in Cachagua. They may have known each other." Crockett was reading the technician's report as he spoke. A deep frown came over his forehead. He had had a lot of work to do, and little time, and he had missed something. He was realizing that now.

Time to ram it home. Nina found herself turning and looking at Paul as she said, "Your evidence technician found traces of soot on the two conchos from Mr. Johnson's home, isn't that correct, Detective?" Paul winked. Nina tried not to smile.

"Appears he did." Crockett was still reading. "It does mention that."

"Soot? The product of a fire?"

"A wood fire."

"So now we have conchos torn off from Mr. Cervantes's belt, with Mr. Johnson's prints on them, which have been in or near a fire. That's what we have, am I right?"

Salas was tapping his lip again, interested at last.

"That's what we appear to have," Crockett answered.

"What inference do you, based on your experience and training, draw from these facts, Detective?"

"You might infer that he got these conchos during or after the fire."

"Come on, Detective, how could he have gotten them after the fire? The belt was in police custody, wasn't it?"

Crockett gave in. "Could have gotten them during a fire."

"Could have torn them off Mr. Cervantes's belt during a struggle during a fire?"

"Objection, calls for speculation." Jaime had finally woken up.

"Overruled."

"That would be consistent with the report from our evidence tech."

Nina paused. Paul was nodding, Salas was tapping, Jaime was scratching his head. She felt focused and in control.

She moved closer to Crockett and said, "That links Mr. Johnson to the time and place of the third fire, doesn't it?"

"It's interesting. It's very interesting. It could."

"Now, let's back up to our previous discussion, about ego trips in arsonists. Detective Crockett, in your experience, do murderers ever take souvenirs from their victims?"

"Yes."

"Why do you think Mr. Johnson might tear off a couple of conchos from Mr. Cervantes's belt during the fire?"

"During a struggle. Or trying to save him, maybe. Or—"

"Or for a souvenir?"

"Maybe."

"But he was there?"

"I can't say for sure."

"You can't say for sure? Did you find any evidence of kerosene when you searched Mr. Johnson's place?"

"Yes. Three empty gallon cans with kerosene residue."

"You're a well-experienced arson investigator, Mr. Crockett. Please give us the benefit of your expertise. What if anything would you conclude from the facts we've just gone through, that Mr. Johnson was in possession of several empty kerosene cans, that kerosene was used in the Robles

Ridge fire, that Mr. Johnson was an associate of a victim of that fire, that Mr. Johnson had in his possession items matching those worn by the victim, with his fingerprints on them, and *with soot on them from a fire*? What do you make of those facts?"

"Objection," Jaime said. "Not a proper hypothetical. Lack of foundation. Misstates the facts set forth in the testimony."

Nina argued, "He's an expert, and I have a right to ask for his opinion."

"I'll draw the appropriate conclusions of fact and law in this proceeding," Salas said. "The facts are as stated. It is my function to interpret them."

"Detective Crockett is here to assist you in that regard, Your Honor," Nina insisted. She didn't want to, but she would have to get in Salas's face.

"Overruled."

"I ask that the court reconsider in light of the established body of law on the subject of expert testimony——I ask that the ruling on the objection at least be deferred and I be allowed to brief this point."

"Overruled."

"I'll file a writ."

"To one of my Superior Court colleagues. Good luck."

"I'll object to use of one of your colleagues too," Nina said. "I'll take it right out of this county to a real appellate court."

"I don't like your attitude, Counsel. I think you disrespect this Court." Salas was blinking hard, angry and trying not to show it.

"For the record, I do not disrespect the Court," Nina said. She left it to Salas to decide if she disrespected him.

Night fell upon the central coast. Debbie had made a lasagna and put out some red wine, thinking they could have a little talk about some big things on her mind.

But about ten, after their TV shows were over, just when she turned off the TV and said "Sam, I need to talk to you," he got a phone call. He might have been expecting it, because he jumped for the phone.

"Yeah?" he said. Debbie didn't go into the kitchen. She sat right on the couch and listened.

"Yeah. Okay. On my way." He hung up and looked at her. What's he feeling, she thought, and then, it's regret, that's what it is. He's sorry about something.

"What's to talk about? Are the kids okay?" he asked her.

"They're fine. Jenny called today from L.A. and she had just talked to Jared. He's fine too. That's not what I wanted to talk to you about."

"It'll have to wait." He went into the bedroom and came out with his shoes on. "George is up at Kasey's and not feeling too good. He doesn't want to alarm Jolene so I'm going to go up there."

"We should call an ambulance."

"He says it's not that bad. He's resting out front. I'll just run up and check on him."

You do that, Debbie thought. She heard the car start up.

In the bedroom, she pulled out the bedstand drawer and she'd known it somehow, but it was still a shock—the Smith & Wesson he kept there was gone. So he had to bring his gun to help poor old George, that clinched it.

"Jolene?"

"Hi." Jolene was washing dishes, judging by the noises on the phone.

"Where's George?"

"He had to go out and get something."

"What?"

"Whadda you mean, what? Razor blades or something."

"He make any calls first?"

"A couple. From the bedroom. I couldn't hear. What's up?"

"I'm calling Tory, then I'll call you back." She dialed the Eubankses' number.

"Where's Darryl?"

"He's taking David over to Mid-Valley to get some cough syrup. Poor David has the flu, I guess, and he's such a mess he asked Darryl to drive."

"How long ago did they leave?"

"Why, I can see the car pulling out of David's driveway right now."

"Stay by the phone."

Debbie grabbed her purse and ran out to the pickup. The men drove by as she shut the door and pulled herself down in the seat. Then she revved 'er up and headed up Esquiline, their taillights faint in front of her.

With so little traffic, it was easy. She was kicking herself for not bringing Jolene along, but there hadn't even been time to think, and Jolene had the little girls. Darryl and David pulled into the Kasey's parking lot and she saw her pistol-packin' husband had beat them to it, and there was George's old sedan too.

She was very upset. She was mad, mad at everything, mad at being patronized and blown off and kept in the dark by Sam. But she drove right on by like they did in the cop shows, then parked over by the travel agency. She sneaked back over to the convenience store. They were leaning against the wall away from the road and the streetlight: George, Darryl, David, Ted, and her Sam.

She didn't round the corner. She heard them talking and she rested behind a flower bush not fifteen feet from them, trying not to breathe. She pushed her hair back behind her ears and cupped a hand behind the left one and listened harder than she had ever listened to anything in her life.

Finally, after about ten minutes, they broke up. Debbie heard cars start up and leave the lot.

She was alone, sitting in the flower bed hugging her knees like a little girl. She let out a moan that could be heard from here to San Francisco.

33

EARLY THE NEXT morning, David sat close to Britta's head in the hospital room, his head in his hands.

The flowers people had brought the week before drooped in their cheap vases. The neighbors came, and the women Britta worked with at the travel agency. That was it. Britta had no friends in the Valley. The people had come out of duty and the flowers were duty flowers.

He had taken her away from her whole life in New York, the flying, the laughter, all the things she needed, and made her a prisoner of the luxury he offered.

She had retaliated. He had known they couldn't go on living in the Valley, that he had made a mistake.

He had married her quickly and taken her to a place where he would be comfortable. As time went on, she never flagged, but her brashness turned to recklessness and her gaiety took on a bitter edge. It happened gradually and he tried not to notice. He was enjoying wallowing in his depression, feeling sorry for himself, the way he had gotten what he wanted since childhood.

But now, in this sterile room with its wilted flowers, he had to notice that hardly anyone cared besides him that she was hurt. It made the fact that he had set in motion the attack on her all the more dreadful.

She hardly seemed to breathe. Her head was wrapped in bandages and under those bandages was the frightful wound that had been inflicted on her. Probably a baseball bat, the doctor said. Her pretty face was drawn and white.

He hadn't called her parents in Reykjavik. He would, soon. He just couldn't stand to talk to them, the guilt in him was so sharp and acrid.

". . . David . . ."

Was he dreaming?

Another small noise from the bed. He lifted his head and saw that her eyes were open.

"Britta, Britta, my darling . . ."

She was trying to whisper something. He put his ear close to her mouth and heard her say "So I'm alive?"

"Yes, you're going to be fine, you've had a terrible . . . a terrible . . ." he jabbered.

"My God. Alive." Her chest heaved. She was trying to laugh. ". . . I remember everything. . . ."

"Oh, my God, I'm so sorry, I . . ."

". . . David?"

He began stroking her forehead, trying to calm her. She still gazed at him with such open eyes, as if she had never seen him before.

". . . Take . . . me away."

"Oh, yes. Where shall we go?"

"I . . . don't know. My wonderful . . . idiot . . ." Her eyes fluttered and closed. For a moment he thought she was dead.

But she had only gone to sleep. She will live, he thought in wonder, and he ran out into the hall, calling for the nurse passing by.

Debbie was pouring out margaritas for the four of them, her hand shaking so it made the crushed ice rattle in the frosted pitcher. The sun beat down right through the canvas umbrella onto Jolene's frosted hair and worried expression. Tory had moved under the eave of the house for the shade.

"Sit down, now," Megan said. She pulled out a chair with padded blue patio cushions and Debbie sank into it. Under her makeup her face was distraught.

"You said it was important," Megan reminded her.

"Oh, yeah, it's important."

"Well?"

"Don't push her, Megan," Tory said. "You always push too hard. It's something awful bad, isn't it, Debs?"

"Yes," Debbie said, and tears began to flow.

"We're gonna help, whatever it is," Jolene said. "Is George involved in this trouble?"

Debbie nodded tearfully.

"Is Ted part of this?" Megan said sharply, taking her cue from Jolene.

Another nod. Megan sat back in consternation. Debbie took crushed ice out of her glass and rubbed it into her forehead. "So's Sam. And David." She took Tory's hand. "So's Darryl."

"Well, lay it down for us," Jolene said in her practical way.

"They met last night. At Kasey's parking lot. Around the side, away from the Valley Road. They gave you all some excuse like Sam gave me."

"They met? Why didn't they just get together at one of our houses?" Tory said.

"Just wait. I followed them. I wanted to know what they were doing."

Jolene said, "Why, you sly thing." She was holding her glass tightly.

"And I heard—"

"Uh huh, uh huh—"

"Listen." So she told them what she'd heard from the bushes.

". . . in," somebody said. Maybe David.

"We turn him in, we're turning ourselves in."

"I don't care, Sam. He almost killed my wife. I can't let him get away with that." That was David for sure.

"He's taking us on one by one," Sam said. "You guys have that figured out yet? Ted, who you think that fire on Robles Ridge was aimed at?"

"Megan and me?" Ted said. "Our house site? Really? He could have burned down half of Southbank Road!"

"He told me forty-eight hours to pay up or he's gonna do something worse," Sam said.

"Well, I'm not paying a thing." David again.

"That's fine, you turn us all in. Then when Britta gets out of the hospital, who's going to take care of her?" George said. "I got my family, you got Britta: Darryl, he's got four little ones. Think about that before you go running off—" David made a strangled noise.

"If we pay him off, will he go away?" Darryl had started talking now.

"If we'd paid him way back after the second fire we wouldn't be in this fix," George said.

"We all agreed," Sam said. "He had no right. All he was supposed to do was set a little brushfire, scorch up the model home a little—he could have hurt somebody burnin' down the café. That was right in the heart of town! We couldn't pay him after that!"

"We can't pay him now either," David said. "It's just piling another crime on all of us."

"But he'll go away if we do," Darryl said.

"He's only hanging around out there waiting to collect. He doesn't want to be here, he's hot. We're keeping him here," Ted said.

"We have another problem," Darryl said. "Tory asked me why I withdrew the first twelve-fifty." The other men groaned. "She knows something."

George said, "So that's what Jolene's been up to! I thought the kids were playing with my desk. It's her. I'll be damned."

"Look. We have to pay him," Sam said. "You should

have heard him on the phone. He's not reasonable. He said forty-eight hours and that's it."

"But, Jolene—"

"Be quiet a second, George. I want to ask David here a question. Now, David. You could pay out the twenty thousand balance we still owe him right now, end all this, save us all. It's the simplest way, right?"

"That's good. That's good," Darryl said.

David said in a tight voice, "He hurts my wife like that and I'm supposed to pay for all of you? No. No."

"David, listen—"

"Hey, don't go—"

"David!"

Debbie heard a car door slam and the car peeled out of the lot.

There was a long silence. Then Darryl said in a disbelieving voice, "He had my car keys. That was my car he drove off in."

"Great. Now we're totally in the crapper," Ted said.

"Ted—"

"Don't look at me, man, Megan knows all our finances and most of it's her money and she'd figure it out in ten seconds."

Darryl said, "Sam, what are we gonna do?" He sounded desperate.

"Keep your shirt on, Darryl, I'll think of something. I'll call him and tell him we need more time to get the money together."

"He'll do something else to us."

"I said, I'll take care of it. Now listen, all of you. The women can't know about this. Don't say anything or we're all going to prison. Darryl, you hear me? Huh? Darryl?"

"What'd you bring that gun for anyway, Sam?"

Sam said, "I don't know. I just feel like killing somebody." Debbie had forgotten about the gun. She held on to a branch and closed her eyes and said a little prayer.

"Don't scare him, you jerk," Ted said. "I have to get home."

"I'll call you. Stay cool," Sam said.

Megan said, "Is that everything, Debbie? All you can remember?" Maybe she spoke too sharply, because Debbie put the pitcher down and propped herself against the table and started blubbering again.

"Now, honey," Jolene told her, "stitch yourself back together, because we need your help. Not a one of us can afford to have a nervous breakdown right now."

"I'll start," Megan said. "They're a bunch of selfish little boys. I checked our books. Twelve hundred fifty dollars withdrawn by Ted two months ago."

Jolene said, "Mmm–hmm. George did the same. Tory?"

"Yes. He told me it was for something else."

"Debbie?"

"Yeah." A big tear fell into Debbie's salt-rimmed glass. Her mascara was streaked all the way down to her lips.

"I think we can figure that David paid too. Serve 'em right to go to jail," Jolene said. She looked around the table. "I know, I know. Now, George, he'll die in jail. He's sick."

"I don't know where to start. All the harm they've caused," Tory said. "I decided to have the baby after all, and now this. Who's going to buy the food for five kids?"

"None of us wants to turn them in, but what else can we do? There's a man killing people left and right out there, it's all their fault, and—"

"We could urge them to turn themselves in," Tory said.

"I am not able to raise this with Sam, not alone," Debbie said, still sniffling. "He won't listen."

"We could all meet with all of them—" Tory was still trying.

"They've already made up their minds what they want to do," Megan said. "But they're going to fart around until somebody else gets hurt. I could just pay the money."

"After how he hurt Britta? How he—he sneaked up on poor Ruthie—"

The women were silent. Debbie poured them all another round.

"No way," Tory said, and they all nodded.

"But—the kids? What about them?" Tory said. "What if—"

Jolene looked at her watch and said, "The girls get off that bus at two-thirty, and I'm going to be right there to meet them. So we better make a decision."

"He gave the men until tomorrow," Debbie said fearfully. "I think."

"And then you know what he threatened to do. Take the children. I'm sure as hell not taking any chances. Now I have two more minutes, girls. Callie's got her soccer practice after this and I'll be right there on the field. Here's what I think. I'm as mad at the men as anybody. But I'm not calling the police. I won't do it to George."

"We can't trust the men to handle this," Tory said.

"Call me," Jolene said. She patted her hair and picked up her purse. "I'm so damn mad I can't think."

When Jolene had gone, the women kicked back for a couple of minutes. Finally, Megan said, "We need a lawyer. To advise us."

She was thinking about the business she had built up, the clients, what would happen if Green River got a judgment against her and Ted's community assets. She was feeling humiliated about the night before. Ted had wanted to be punished—if she had it to do all over again, she'd have punished him for real when she tied him to the bed, she'd have beat the shit out of him.

She had never felt so wounded. "My boon companion," she said, choking up, and put her hand over her eyes.

"Not you too, Megan, we need you to stay strong," Tory said. "I think you have a good idea. If we could get somebody right away. Because our children are in danger."

"How about the lawyer who's defending Danny's friend?" Debbie said. "She's a criminal lawyer. I liked her."

"But—wouldn't she have a conflict of interest? She already has a client—"

"Maybe not," Megan said. "She could consult with us confidentially, and if she can't help us, she'd at least have to keep her mouth shut about the consultation."

Tory said, "I vote we call her."

"Me too," Debbie said. "She's probably in court right now."

"We'll leave an urgent message," Megan said. "Now, meantime, if any of us talks to the men, it'll all blow up even worse. *Capisce*, Debbie?"

"I'll just watch TV and go to bed. I can do it."

"I'll pretend I'm sick. I am sick. Sick of Darryl not growing up," Tory said. "Do you want me to talk to Jolene?"

"Yeah. I'll call the lawyer," Megan said.

The medical examiner, Dr. Rittenhauer, took the stand after lunch on the second day of the prelim. She was young, with a pleasant face and a practical haircut, and a recent medical degree from Columbia. She gave Wish a curious look and then turned to her papers. A very well-prepared lady, Nina thought. Nina hadn't found much wrong with the autopsy report either, but she did have a couple of subjects she couldn't wait to explore.

After the preliminaries, Jaime asked, "Did you perform the autopsy on the decedent later identified as Daniel Cervantes?"

"I did." Nina pulled out her copy of the autopsy report, and Dr. Rittenhauer kept a hand on her own copy.

"Please summarize the autopsy findings for the court."

"Certainly. The most conspicuous feature presenting externally was massive flame burns over about eighty percent of the skin. The burns penetrated very deeply into underlying musculature and internal organs in places. As I noted, this made it impossible at first to determine ethnicity, weight, nourishment, or age. We were able to tell that the body was that of a male over six feet in height. Almost all the clothing was burned away. However, we had an immediate break. As we turned over the body I noted that the posterior side had not been burned."

"Go on."

"The body, when I first saw it, was on its left side with the arms drawn up in a pugilistic attitude, common in burn victims. However, Monterey County sheriffs reported that when found on the mountain, the decedent lay on his back in that position. There had been a fire that had passed over him, but it didn't burn the body so severely that it could get to the back. Therefore, when we turned it over, we saw clothing and skin. I was then able to identify the decedent as a young male, probably Hispanic, no particular identifying marks on the skin. He wore the remains of an army camouflage jacket, a white T-shirt, and jeans. Also the remains of a pair of steel-shanked boots were still on the feet. Around the waist, under the jacket, we found the remains of a black leather belt with silver conchos attached."

"What kind of condition was this belt in?"

"In the back, good condition. There were six conchos still attached in back. In the front, the belt was burned but was still in one piece. There were four conchos, and two more were missing. CVPD did not locate those in the vicinity."

Salas, Nina, and Jaime all scribbled a note.

"What else could you determine from the exterior of the body?"

"The hair in front had burned away. However, in back there remained hair on the scalp that was long and black. No scars, tattoos, moles in back. In front, impossible to determine. You have the autopsy photos, correct?"

"Yes, thank you, they are in evidence by stipulation. What did you do after this initial evaluation?"

"We attempted to take fingerprints, without success. We also took photos for identification. I then began a detailed examination of the body. Charring from direct contact with flames was extensive in front. We are talking about fourth-degree burns, which are incinerating injuries extending deeper than the skin. In general, however, the skin was burned away in front, with muscle exposed and ruptured. Unburned skin had a seared and leathery consistency. There was a partial skeletonization of the face due to soft tissue being burned away. Portions of the outer table of the skull had fallen away in the right frontal region."

"And the clothing had been destroyed in front?"

"The camouflage jacket was made of cotton, which transmits more thermal energy than polyester, and provided almost no protection. The undershorts were of polyester, which protected the genitalia to some extent."

"Which is how you knew immediately it was a male." Paul was grimacing.

"Yes. Our dental consultant came in at that point and prepared a dental chart and took X rays of the remaining teeth to attempt to identify the body. When he was finished, I began examining the skull area. I observed some heat fractures on the skull."

"What else, if anything, did you observe with regard to the skull?" Jaime said.

"I observed a severe linear skull fracture in the parietal area, obviously an impact injury. The fracture was several inches long and the skull had been slightly deformed by the impact of the object. I took photographs and called Detective Crockett to see if any objects near the body had been collected that might have been impact objects. Detective Crockett brought over a Canon camera with the remains of a long strap, a surprisingly heavy camera. I tried fitting it in various ways and found that the base fit the injury. At first I was puzzled because even though it was heavy I wondered how hitting the skull with a camera in your hand could cause such a severe injury. Then I tried swinging the camera by a portion of the strap. This added considerable impact velocity."

"And what, if anything, did you conclude regarding—"

"Before I could come to any conclusions I completed the autopsy, including weighing and examining the internal organs. I was interested in the possibility of carbon-monoxide poisoning, what is sometimes referred to as smoke-inhalation injury, but the skin in back didn't exhibit the cherry-red coloration I would expect and the subsequent lab tests confirmed there was very little CO in the blood. I also checked very carefully for soot around the nostril and in the trachea. There were only traces."

Dr. Rittenhauer sat back. Her face said, There you have it.

Jaime said, "Those were your major findings?"

"Yes. I can go into much more detail if you have particular questions."

"I think we have enough of a factual basis. I would now like to ask you some of the conclusions you may have come to pursuant to the autopsy."

"Very well."

"Could you identify the body?"

"Not as a result of the autopsy. I was informed that a report had been made of a missing person and for the first two days was working on the assumption that the victim might be Mr. Whitefeather. Apparently the shoes were a match to Doc Martens Mr. Whitefeather was known to wear. However, the next day, I believe it was, the uncle of the victim came in. He was able to make the identification based on the remains of the camouflage jacket, the concho belt, the long hair, the general build and height, the color of skin in back, and other factors."

"And that identification was?"

"That the victim's name was Daniel Cervantes."

"All right. Could you determine whether the victim was alive at the time of the fire?"

"That's difficult. It's hard to tell if burning occurred before or after. There was no inflammatory reaction, which might tend toward an assumption that the burns took place after death. I would expect soot and perhaps some evidence of internal burns to be found around the breathing passages if the person was breathing at the time of the burn and for the CO level to be higher. I therefore concluded that the burns occurred postmortem."

"What, in your opinion, was the immediate cause of death?"

"A skull fracture caused by blunt-force trauma."

"Nothing further. Thank you, Doctor."

The Court took its afternoon recess. "You had a call from Megan Ballard," Sandy told Nina from the office. "She says it's very urgent. She wants a consultation."

"What about?"

"She won't go into it."

"I'll give her a call after court. Call her back and let her know."

"Okay. I checked the hospital. Britta Cowan is conscious."

Nina put her hand over the receiver. "Paul, Britta's awake. Can you try to go and see her?"

"You don't need me this afternoon?"

"I'll bring you up to date tonight at dinner."

"Okay. I'll go over there right now."

"Sandy, call David Cowan and see if Britta has said anything to him about who struck her."

"Will do."

"Anything else happening?"

"A couple of German tourists got into a fight at the Hog's Breath. They knocked over a couple of tables. The cops came."

"Stay with it."

"I'll be here."

Nina returned to court without Paul, already missing his comforting presence.

"Your witness," Judge Salas said. Dr. Rittenhauer had already taken her seat.

"Doctor, isn't it true that no fingerprints were found on the camera?" Crockett had told her that in the beginning, so Nina felt she could make a point here.

"Not immediately," Dr. Rittenhauer answered. "However, I just heard from Detective Crockett this morning. There was in fact one fingerprint found. Fortunately, the camera was found partly under the body, where a portion of the lens was protected from the flames."

Nina turned to Jaime, who stood up and said, "I just heard about it myself. I had no intent of surprising Counsel with this new information. As we all know, one of the problems inherent in holding the prelim so quickly is—" While he went on excusing himself Nina was performing a lightning-fast calculation. She saw clearly that Jaime had let her walk into this trap. He could have told her right up to five seconds ago. No problem for him—if she hadn't raised it on the cross-exam, he'd have slipped it in on the redirect. Therefore it was harmful to her case.

Therefore, the print was Wish's.

"I will withdraw the question at this time, as the district attorney has apparently not shared new discovery with me," she said.

But Salas wanted to know about the print. He said, "If you refuse to waive time, these things happen. Not everything can be finalized in ten days." To Jaime he said, "You only received this information this afternoon? You have not withheld this information?"

"Absolutely not, Your Honor."

"I am here as an examining magistrate to make a determination, and I wish to know this information. Counsel, any objection?"

"Most definitely, Your Honor. There is no question pending. It is a breach of the discovery rules—"

"There is good cause for the breach. The prosecutor didn't know about it either. Are we searching for the truth here, or not?"

Nina didn't have time to explain how she was not necessarily there to search for the truth, she was there to defend Wish. "Objection overruled," Salas said. Huh?

"I withdraw the question," she said again stubbornly.

Salas gave her a look and said to Dr. Rittenhauer, "Has this fingerprint been identified by a certified fingerprint technician?"

"Yes—"

Nina said, "Objection. Hearsay. Dr. Rittenhauer is not a law-enforcement officer with five years of experience and therefore cannot testify as to hearsay."

"Overruled. What identification has been made?"

"The print on the camera matches that of the defendant, Willis Whitefeather." Wish gestured to Nina and she sat down, burning with rage.

"It's my camera, so of course it'll have my prints," he whispered. "But listen—"

"Just a second," Nina said, and rose again, and said, "To your knowledge, has Mr. Whitefeather ever denied he brought the camera up the mountain?" Jaime would hammer on the fact that there was no *other* person's print on the camera. That was the problem.

"No," said Dr. Rittenhauer. She was so admirable, so impartial and calm, so machinelike, she could be so helpful if Nina could just figure out a way to use her—Wish was pulling her jacket sleeve.

"One moment," she said to the judge, and he looked pointedly at the clock, then nodded his head. "What?" she whispered to Wish.

"What she said about the boots, it isn't right."

"What's wrong?"

"Something. I forget. It's all happening so fast."

"Well, let me know if you think of it." She said to the

witness, "Thank you. Nothing further at this time." If she needed Rittenhauer, she could call her in rebuttal later.

"The witness is excused."

"The prosecution rests," Jaime said. The air seemed to go out of him and Nina thought, He's as tired as I am.

"It's four o'clock," Judge Salas said. "I am going to adjourn until tomorrow—that is, if you still intend to put your client on the stand?"

Nina nodded. "As our first witness."

"Court is adjourned until 10:00 A.M. tomorrow." He rapped once, hard, with his gavel.

"All rise," the bailiff said as Salas went on to the next case.

Wish was still shaking his head. Nina said, "Are you ready for tomorrow?"

"After all the time you spent getting me ready, I feel pretty good about it."

"You remember the sequence? How you'll tell the story, then authenticate the photos I showed you?"

"I remember."

"We'll show them their third party," Nina said. "It might be enough."

"I can't wait to get out of here. Then somebody's going to pay. It's not enough to get free, Nina. I have to find him. It's horrible what he did to Danny. I'm going to have bad dreams tonight."

"Hi, Megan."

From her voice, Megan had lost her happy face. "Thank you so much for calling. I would like to make an appointment to see you as soon as possible."

"I'm in the middle of a—"

"I know that. But this will interest you. Perhaps even help you with your current case. The problem is, you have to assure me the consultation will stay strictly confidential even if you decide not to represent us."

"What's it about, Megan?"

"About the fires. Please, we really need your help. Debbie and Tory and Jolene and I. We are worried about the children."

"Megan, I'm beat," Nina said. "I'm washing dishes after a good supper and I need to talk to my son and then go to bed. I'm worried too. I suggest you call Detective Crockett and try to get some help out there."

"That won't work."

Nina said, "I'm sorry. If you were my client, I might try to meet you tonight. But you're not and for the sake of the client I have, I need to get some sleep tonight."

"We'll come to you."

"Tomorrow," Nina said. "At the lunch break. Twelve noon at the law library at the courthouse. I'll find us a conference room."

"All right."

"Meantime, I'm saying it again. If you have new information involving a threat to the children, please call the police."

"We're guarding them," Megan said. "That's all I can say right now."

"Good night, then."

Paul came in. "News from the hospital?" he asked, referring to Britta, who still hadn't made any statement.

"No. Something else. It's handled. What time is it?"

"Nine."

"What's Bob up to?"

"Passed out on the couch. Jet lag."

"Let's get him into bed and go to bed too."

"Sounds like a plan." He had moved in on her and begun kissing her. She led Bob into the study and said good night, then went into the bedroom. Paul had just taken his pants off.

"Am I mistaken, or are those polyester boxers you're wearing?"

"Silk is so flammable," Paul said. So Nina pulled off her jeans.

"What happened to the little cotton things?" he said. "Are you wearing polyester too? ' 'Ave you seen Polyester Pam,' " he sang, and reached for her underpants.

"In a minute." She managed to wiggle free and headed for the bathroom, and heard Paul exclaim ere she dove out of sight, "Well, I'll be darned. They do protect the genitalia."

34

"CALL WILLIS WHITEFEATHER." Wish was escorted to the stand.

Nina's turn to speak first had come. She had a five-page outline of questions to guide Wish gently through his story. The object was to let Salas see and believe him. Of course, if Wish was bound over for trial, Jaime would have months to go over every stutter in the transcript, the better to hang Wish with at trial. Inconsistent statements would naturally occur in the two proceedings, and Wish would look like a liar.

But Salas couldn't be left with a print on a camera and a picture of Danny's charred skull. They couldn't win the prelim without exposing the interior of Wish's own skull. Nina inhaled, exhaled, picked up her outline.

They started at ten-fifteen. By eleven-thirty they had gotten through the whole story of Wish's move to the Monterey Peninsula, his studies, his work for Paul, his interest in criminal cases, his history with Danny, his visit from Danny at Aunt Helen's house, and the subsequent events on Robles Ridge. The court reporter ran her machine, which turned each word to stone. Nina kept Wish on a short rein, never letting him say more than a couple of sentences.

Jaime sat back and enjoyed the show. He made not a single objection. The more Wish said, the longer the rope. The transcript could be gone over, at leisure, for months between prelim and trial, and every detail of Wish's background checked. Any exaggeration of his accomplishments, any denigration of his failures, could be thrown back at him to attack his credibility.

But Nina needed Wish to tell the judge about himself, based on a gut-level judgment: that Salas would find points of commonality with Wish that might develop into sympathy and understanding. Salas didn't like her much, but for all his possible bias she felt that his intentions with regard to his responsibility were serious.

The judge paid attention and took notes. She had surprised him by making the hearing real, not just a pro forma exercise. Part of her calculation had involved the fact that he was new on the bench and still capable of being surprised. He also was not as detached as he would become; he still took some things personally, she had noticed. If she could involve him in Wish's story, show him someone telling the truth—

And now he was involved, listening intently. Wish was explaining why he had driven all the way to San Juan Bautista for medical treatment.

"All I could think about was getting away. I decided not to go home because he might follow me there, so I headed the other way, toward Salinas. Then I thought he was behind me and I got on 101 and kept driving, but I think I was getting faint or delirious or something. I had been feeling very blurry, but now I started feeling a lot of pain all over. I realized I had to go to a hospital. I was at the turnoff for San Juan Bautista so I went there and stopped at the gas station to ask where the hospital was."

"And you subsequently checked in at the Las Flores Clinic?"

"They admitted me overnight and kept me there the next day. They were worried about infection on my leg and thought I had a concussion. Turned out I did have a concussion."

Nina showed him photos marked in evidence showing

Wish's injuries, which Paul had taken just before his shower on the night of his arrest, and he authenticated these. Now Salas had in-your-face evidence that Wish also had an impact injury.

It's coming together, she thought with gathering excitement, and she brought out the photographs taken by Wish's Canon. She passed a set out to Jaime, then handed a marked set to the clerk. Up they went to the judge.

"Now, Mr. Whitefeather. You testified that in the course of the fire you took photographs at the moment you believed you saw the arsonist running down the trail?"

"Yes." Wish sat forward in the witness stand, fanning out the photos. "Then I popped out the memory card and stuck it in my pocket, and then I popped in another memory card before I started running and dropped the camera."

"Are these the twelve photos you took numbered in the sequence in which you took them?" Don't dither, she prayed, don't say I think so or that's what Paul said. She had given Wish the set as soon as she had prints and Wish had told her he could identify the shots.

She needn't have worried. "Yes," Wish said positively.

"Nine of these have no people in them?"

"Correct." Nina paused to let the judge and prosecutor confirm this for themselves, and to see the flames, the forest, the night.

"I direct your attention to Photographs Number One, Three, and Four. Would you pull those out, please."

"Okay."

"Are all three of these photographs of the same person?"

"No. There are two people here. One person in Number One, and then two shots of another person in Numbers Three and Four."

She had done it, provided hard evidence that someone else was on the mountain. Jaime was still looking from one photograph to the other. Salas was nodding. A lot of hard work was paying off.

"May I approach the witness?" Nina asked Salas. He nodded, and she went up to Wish at the witness stand and took the first photo, Number One, Danny holding his hand up to shield his face, saying something.

"This first photo? Do you recognize the man?"

"Yes."

"Who is it?"

"A man named Robert Johnson," Wish said. Nina shook her head and tried again.

"Look again, please. Tell us who this man is."

"It's Coyote. Robert Johnson."

"B–but that's Danny Cervantes, isn't it?"

Wish looked hard at the photo.

"No, that's Coyote."

"Well, let's take a look at Numbers Three and Four," Nina said, to give Wish a chance to get his head straight. He had been doing so well! "Those are photos of the same person, you said. Do you recognize that person?"

"Yes. It's Danny Cervantes."

"Don't you have it backward?"

Jaime was up. "I must object. She's cross-examining her own witness at this point. He's made the identifications." Nina rolled her eyes at Wish, trying to get him to wake up from whatever dream he was in. But Wish just looked back at her, wide-eyed.

"What's the problem?" Salas asked her.

"Well, it was my understanding—it's clear that—let me just confirm this identification, Your Honor."

"Go ahead. It's important. Objection overruled."

"Let's go back to Photo Number One. What is that person wearing?"

"Dark shirt and pants. Doc Martens."

"And who is that person? Look carefully, Wish."

"That's Robert Johnson."

"But—look at Numbers Three and Four. Please notice what that man is wearing on his feet."

"Jeans and a white T-shirt. He must have taken off the

jacket, it was so hot. And black Nikes. Nikes! That's Danny. That's it! I knew something was wrong about the shoes the doctor was talking about! Remember yesterday, Nina? She said Danny had Doc Martens on his feet! Now, how could that be! How? How?"

"Take it easy, sir," Salas told Wish, who had half gotten up.

"One moment, please," Nina said, and walked back to the counsel table where Paul was waiting. "Help!" she whispered.

"You got me," Paul said. "Maybe Wish is all mixed up. Go back and try again."

She stood up straight again and said, "Mr. Whitefeather, did you specifically notice the shoes Mr. Cervantes was wearing when he came to your home to ask you to go to the ridge that night?"

"I sure did," Wish said. "He wore black Nikes. I remember up on the ridge he got mad at me because his shoes were so much quieter than my boots."

"But you've heard the testimony that Mr. Cervantes was wearing Doc Martens when he was found?"

"Yeah. And I think I know where they came from. That's what Coyote was wearing. You can see, here, in Number One. Black Doc Martens."

"But that can't be," Nina said.

"But it is!"

"I'm not following, Counsel," Judge Salas said. Jaime was shaking his head, baffled. Nina was not following either.

Coyote wore Doc Martens. Therefore the body was Coyote. But the body wore a white T-shirt, jeans, Danny's concho belt . . . therefore the body was Danny . . .

Wish said, "Can I say something?"

Salas spread his hands. "Can you shed some light on this?"

"Those boots take a long time to unlace."

"So?"

"So the feet in the boots were Coyote's feet. That's for sure."

"Ah-ha," Salas said, tapping his pencil on his dais. "So—"

Wish was pounding his fist into the palm of his other hand, blinking as he tried to figure it out. Jaime's eyes were shut as if in prayer. Paul was staring fixedly at his shoes.

But it was Nina who got it clearly into her noggin first. "So the feet in the Nikes are still running around somewhere, Your Honor," Nina said. "Which would mean that Danny Cervantes is alive."

"Wow," Wish said. "I can't believe it. That is so—that is so—maybe it isn't."

"Wish," Nina said, "is it your testimony that the man in Photos Number Three and Four, who is wearing shoes that are obviously not Doc Martens boots, is Danny Cervantes?"

"Absolutely."

"Thank you. I have nothing further. Your Honor, I move for a dismissal of all murder and manslaughter charges in the complaint, on grounds that there is no probable cause to believe that the defendant committed any crime against Daniel Cervantes."

"We're all pretty excited," Salas said. "But I'm not so excited that I won't let Mr. Sandoval cross-examine. It is now the lunch hour. We will resume at one-thirty. Jaime, why don't you and this lady talk to each other."

Jaime and Davy Crockett came up as soon as they were adjourned and Jaime said, "I can't figure out if this is some scam you guys are trying to pull or if we ID'd the wrong man." Paul stood next to her.

"Did you do the DNA test yet? Or the dental records comparison?" she asked Crockett.

"We haven't had time. We relied on the uncle," Crockett told her. "I'll call the uncle. I'll talk to Dr. Rittenhauer some more."

"I have to go," Nina said.

"See you after lunch." The prosecutor and his investigator left quickly, and Nina repeated to Paul, " 'Those boots take a long time to unlace.' Is it really possible? You know, sometimes you think you have this huge surprise in a case, but then it whiffs."

"The foot bone's connected to the leg bone. The medical examiner said it still was. And the leather boots were practically welded to the burned feet. And the photos don't lie. Coyote's wearing the boots. Wish ought to know. Didn't you have him explain who was who in each picture?"

"No. I gave him the pictures and told him he'd be authenticating them and that we were going to show that both Coyote and Danny were at the fire. I didn't go through each one with him. I blew that."

"So the man in Arroyo Seco—the man who chained Nate—"

"Was Danny!" Nina clasped her hands together and said, "Nate wasn't as incoherent as he sounded, Paul. We should have given him more credit, questioned him more closely. I remember—he said his brother was gone or something."

"We missed some bets," Paul said, "but I forgive us."

"Maybe Coyote and Danny exchanged shoes during the fire."

"You lost me there. Why—"

"It doesn't make any sense. The body was wearing Danny's clothes."

"Maybe Coyote and Danny exchanged clothes during the fire. That's more likely than switching shoes, because—"

"—the boots take a long time to unlace," Nina said again. Nina smiled, spread her hands, and said, "Wish has such a way with words. He loves his boots too."

"What now?"

Nina looked at her watch. The Siesta Court people

would be waiting in the law library. "There's so much I still don't understand, Paul. Maybe Danny's dead."

"Then who killed Ruth Frost and Brian Donnelly? Who attacked Britta Cowan?"

"Right. It has to be Danny. But why bring Wish up to the ridge that night? What was Danny's relationship to Coyote?"

"You go to your meeting," Paul said. "I'm going to help Crockett, whether or not he wants my help. Try to get something to eat at some point so you don't keel over in court."

The Siesta Court deputation waited in the law library: Debbie Puglia, Megan Ballard, Jolene Hill, and Tory Eubanks. Nina shook hands and led them into one of the drab conference rooms nearby. They sat down around the table quietly. Jolene opened her bag and took out sandwiches and Snapples.

Nina took a moment to adjust to these women, who seemed so different from her impressions at the party and the talks on Debbie's deck. Extracted from their family lives by whatever grave business had brought them here, dressed in business clothes, they had taken on the look of serious adults. Megan, in her suit coat and slacks, seemed to be the leader of the moment. The block party—had it only been ten days or so ago? It seemed to have been years ago.

"I'm very sorry," Nina said. "I have to tell you that I don't have very much time right now."

"We understand," Megan said. "But this is so important we had to see you. This is a consultation that is protected by the attorney-client privilege?"

"Yes. Even if I don't represent you, this initial consultation is protected."

"What is your fee for this consultation?"

Nina said, "I don't charge initially."

"What if we give you information about a crime that has been committed?"

Nina thought about her answer. "That's a complicated

subject. What I can do is this. I won't take notes. If in our discussion there comes a moment when I feel we're getting into an area where it's my duty as an officer of the court to break the privilege, I will immediately stop you from speaking and tell you. But understand that I'm a criminal lawyer. If my client has committed a crime, I can defend him or her and the conversations are privileged."

"I don't know about this, Megan," Tory said.

"We're out of time, Tory," Debbie told her. "We have to talk to somebody."

"I know."

Jolene said, "I suggest we get down to it. Okay, everybody?" They all nodded.

Megan said, "Debbie overheard the men talking night before last. Our husbands conspired to start a fire on the Green River land. George, Darryl, Sam, and Ted. They hired a man to do the job and they each put in twelve hundred fifty dollars as a down payment. David Cowan paid the same amount too."

"A total of six thousand two hundred fifty dollars," Nina said. "The amount in Coyote's bank account. A down payment."

"This man—Coyote—did the job, but he went farther than he was supposed to and burned down the model home completely. The men got scared. Then, Coyote decided on his own to burn down the new café in the Village. The men got even more scared and mad, and they decided not to pay the rest of the money."

She stopped and waited for Nina to react. Puzzle pieces were falling into place in her mind. "Go on," Nina said. "So the six thousand two hundred fifty dollars was just a down payment."

"Yes. They were each supposed to put in another four thousand dollars apiece after the job was done. But they told him no, that's all you're getting.

"So, what we think happened then is, he started taking revenge on the men, one by one. First he went after Ted.

He set the fire on the ridge because that's where our construction site is. He almost burned it but the wind changed
and the fire came down the mountain instead."

Nina nodded slowly. "I think he had another purpose
also the night of that fire. Anyway, go ahead."

"Then he hurt Britta, to get David."

"He's cruel and vicious," Debbie said. "We think he
killed Ruthie in her car because she might identify him."

"Yes," Nina said. "Yes, I think you're right, Debbie."

"We don't know why he would kill the artist."

"I do. His cover was blown and he needed money. It
was a robbery-murder." Debbie started to ask more questions, but Nina said, "Let's hear the rest of what you need to
tell me."

"He told the men he'd take the children if they don't
pay. This was night before last. He gave them forty-eight
hours. The men couldn't agree what to do. Debbie heard
them talking about all this. Finally Sam said he'd call and say
they needed more time, but that they would pay the
money. Is that right, Debbie?"

Debbie said, "David wanted to go to the police, but the
rest of them wouldn't do it."

"Then what?"

"Then we met and decided we needed to talk to a
lawyer as soon as we could."

"What did you think I could do for you?" Nina said.

"Tell us what to do," Megan said. "These are our families we're talking about. The men are in jeopardy of going
to jail or maybe getting killed. Our kids aren't safe until
Coyote is found."

"Where are your children now?"

Jolene said, "George picked up the girls at noon at the
bus stop. They had an early day today. Britta's kids are at a
day-care center in Carmel. Debbie's kids are in Los Angeles. Tory's kids are—where are they, Tory?"

"My sister's place on El Hemmorro. I told her not to let
them out of the house."

"That's not good enough," Nina said. "He's too dangerous. That's not enough protection. You can't just watch the children and pray for somebody else to resolve this. Do you understand that?"

Jolene sighed. "I think we all know that. But if we call the police, our husbands are involved in all these terrible things. They'll be put in prison. We need them, but, more importantly, we—well, we love them."

"You could talk to them."

"Not one-on-one," Debbie said.

"I agree," Nina said. "It would be better for them to come forth as a group. Why can't you talk to them as a group?"

This got responses from everyone. "They'll just say to butt out," Jolene said.

"They'll be so humiliated that we know, they might do anything," Megan said.

"They'll refuse to go to the police and get us to agree not to go either. Then we'll all be conspirators," Debbie said.

Tory asked, "Would you do that for them, Nina? Talk them into surrendering and helping to catch Coyote?"

"Do you think they would hire me to handle their surrender? I'm not at all sure I could represent all of them together in any other way, but I could represent them for that purpose," Nina said. "I could smooth the way for them. I would consider it part of my representation of Wish Whitefeather, because it would be a way of resolving his case."

"Can you keep them out of jail?"

"I don't know. It would help if they started cooperating fully right now."

"What about just paying the money ourselves?" Megan said. "We did talk about that."

"The men are going to be arrested soon anyway," Nina said. "Detective Crockett will figure out the money trail. And there has been a change in the case you don't know about yet. The police have been hunting the wrong man."

"What do you mean?" Jolene felt in her pocket and said, "Excuse me. It's George." She pulled out her cell phone and went into the corner.

"Let's not worry about that right now," Nina said. "It's still not certain. Anyway, here is what I can do. I can meet with the men. If they choose, I can arrange the circumstances of their surrender and represent them in the questioning process. I have to say that their interests as individuals are not precisely the same and I doubt I can represent them as a group any further than that."

"Can't we hire you to represent them without them knowing?" Debbie said.

"No."

"I'm so afraid."

Megan said, "We'll handle it, honey. Now then. We'll have the men on the deck at six tonight. Can you make it, Nina?"

"Court usually adjourns by five at the latest," Nina said. "I think I can."

Jolene came back to the table and leaned on it, her face drained of color. "Callie didn't get off the bus."

"Oh, no! No!" they all cried.

"April told a crazy story. She said—she said Danny took Callie for a ride in a Jeep and didn't bring her back. George told her Danny's dead—there's no such thing as a ghost—"

"He's not dead," Nina said bluntly. "He killed Coyote and assumed Coyote's identity. He stole a Jeep from the artist in Cachagua."

"Oh, my baby," Jolene moaned, and Debbie rushed around the table to hold her.

"It's Danny?" Tory cried. "But he's our neighbor! How could he!"

"It's Danny." As Nina said this, watching their stricken faces, she thought, How can they be anything but Furies, the way they have been betrayed? But instead they were still trying to save the situation, and in time, Nina knew, they would absorb some of the guilt. It is an ancient role of Woman.

"But the kids all know him. They like him. They wouldn't go with a stranger, but—"

Megan said, "What shall we do, Nina?" She looked Nina right in the eye and Nina thought, It's all on me, is it? She didn't want to take on this crushing responsibility.

Then she thought, Well, if not me, who?

"Megan, help Debbie and Tory get home right away. Collect all the children and keep them at your house, Debbie. Don't let them leave the deck. Tell them Danny is dangerous and to watch out for him. Debbie, call your kids in L.A. and tell them what's going on. Jolene, you come with me. I'm taking you over to the police station right now and we're going to make a report about Callie. All of you. Do not tell anyone about the conspiracy until after the men have their opportunity to obtain legal representation tonight."

They all got up. Debbie was crying. Before she left with Debbie and Tory, Megan took Nina's hand and said, "Thank you. At least it's clear. We couldn't see straight. I don't know why. But you made it clear."

"It's your families. It's hard to see straight."

"You won't let us down?"

"Have the men at Debbie's house at six. Come on, Jolene."

35

"WHAT ARE YOU doing?" Nina found Sandy at Wish's desk in Paul's office, only a pool of light from his desk lamp lighting the room. "It's late. Go home."

"You're here," she said.

Nina dumped the contents of her briefcase on the small table in her corner. No longer skimpy with a pad and paper, it now stored a library of paper. "I have to think."

"Maybe you should be sleeping. You've been a busy bee. I get your calls all afternoon. You call from court, but the judge still won't dismiss the case—"

"Jaime got a three-day continuance. I couldn't get Wish out quite yet. Jaime told me afterward that if the judge had dismissed he would have kept Wish in custody as a material witness until he gets this straightened out anyway. I'm sorry."

"—you call from Crockett's office—"

"Another child was kidnapped this afternoon. Mikey Eubanks."

"—and then you went out to the Valley?"

"I had a meeting I couldn't miss. And then, yes, back to Crockett for the past few hours. That was the hardest job I ever had, Sandy, persuading Crockett and Jaime Sandoval to let my new clients be released on their own recognizance."

"How about we start over?"

Nina went over to Paul's chair and stretched out in it while she explained it all to Sandy.

Mikey Eubanks had left his aunt's house at twelve forty-five, while Nina was still talking to the women at the courthouse. He had run down the hill to his house to pick up a video game.

That was the last anyone had seen of him. No ransom note.

The meeting with the men of Siesta Court took place at four instead of six. It was chaos at first. Darryl Eubanks was practically beating his head against the wall. George Hill, Callie's grandfather, wept throughout.

They agreed to turn themselves in. Nina put them all in her Bronco and drove them to the police station, where they made limited statements, were booked, and then declined to talk further upon advice of counsel. After her lengthy palaver with Jaime, they all went into Judge Salas's court at nine o'clock. He came in specially and heard them out.

"He would definitely have jailed them, but Jaime said he thought they'd be more use outside," Nina said. "I owe Jaime."

"Where's Paul?" Sandy had taken all this in with unblinking aplomb.

"In Carmel Valley. Talking with Ben Cervantes. Trying to find Danny before he—"

"He was the one who was trying to kill Wish, wasn't he?"

"I suppose," Nina said. She went to the bar refrigerator and pulled out some cold bottled water, which she used to chase the three ibuprofen she swallowed.

"You should go home, Sandy."

"I have some calls to make," Sandy said pointedly.

"Then don't mind me," Nina said, putting her hands behind her head and her feet on Paul's desk. If Sandy needed privacy, she could go home and make her calls. She picked up a folder, leaned back in her chair, and read, quickly becoming absorbed in the paperwork. She reviewed the autopsy of the body found on Robles Ridge, examined the discovery materials Jaime's office had provided, looked over her notes on Elizabeth's tapes, tasks she had done before, and would do again until something startling leapt off these dry pages.

Sandy made a number of phone calls, punching with vigor, but talking in such a low voice, she made a soothing background hum. In the night, the busy street outside quieted, the crickets that hid in the picturesque Carmel alleyways awakened and sang. Nina yawned and flipped through her papers. She yawned again.

"Wake up!" Sandy had her by the shoulders and was shaking her.

Nina opened her eyes, sighing. "I fell asleep."

"Uh huh."

"Guess you were right." She started stuffing her papers back inside her case. "Guess I should get home and get some rest. Maybe all the answers will come to me in a dream."

"You need to call Paul."

Nina looked at her watch. "Wow. Two o'clock. Sandy, he's sound asleep."

"He'll want to hear this. I just spoke to Danny's mother. I think she knows where he is."

"Fantastic work, Sandy! We have to notify the police right away," Nina said. "Back to my favorite people for the third time today."

"Not yet."

"Sandy, he's taken two children!"

"They won't be able to do anything unless we go up there and talk to her and find out where he is. She won't say anything more on the phone. She didn't even say she knew where he was," Sandy admitted. "I just know she does."

"How?"

She did not like the question, but she answered anyway. "I used to know her pretty well years ago, when Danny and Wish were friends. And I'm a mother." Sandy folded her arms, and Nina knew the look meant, no justifications, no proofs, just unadulterated belief. "You understand that."

Strangely, she did. "Did you talk to Danny's father?"

"No. He's working, and I remember Danny being closer to his mother."

"What's she like?"

"Weak. That's how I know he went there. He depends on her when things get tough. She always loved him, but she's kind of a hopeless character. She never really knew how to handle him."

What a mess, Nina thought. Sons and mothers. "She wouldn't help him hide, under the circumstances."

"She isn't convinced he took any kids. She doesn't want to believe he would hurt anyone."

"Did she say she saw him?" Nina asked.

"No."

But Sandy knew she had, and by extension, so did Nina. She called Paul and woke him up. He packed up a bag for himself and one for her, and met her half an hour later outside on the street, wipers going because the fog had grown so thick.

Sandy roared up in Wish's brown van.

"You're coming, Sandy?"

She wore her voluminous purple coat and clutched a small suitcase. "Yep. She'll talk to me."

Paul steered Nina's Bronco onto Highway 101 and started the long haul over Pacheco Pass, through the central valley, and up the mountains. Nina and Sandy slept.

He had left a message for Bob on the kitchen counter saying that he should call his grandpa and stay with him for a few days. No doubt the boy would find it when he was looking for cereal in the morning. Good that Nina's son was old enough to be left alone for a short time, bad that he lived in the study.

This late at night, the truckers ruled the highways. At the interstate heading to Sacramento, Paul got into the slip-stream of a big semi doing seventy and let himself relax and think about what all this meant for him and Nina.

He had worked so hard and for so long to have Nina here with him, and here she was, entangled as always in problems, far removed from the peaceable kingdom he imagined for them both. He glanced at her, snoring lightly on the seat beside him, brown hair balled up under her neck, cheeks flushed. He wanted life to be easy for her, but it never would be.

He couldn't accept that he couldn't protect her. He thought of her on a sunny summer day, back in those days of the Bucket, sixteen or so, hanging with the local hood-lums, skimpy or nonexistent swimsuit, maybe a little grass blowing in the wind.

If he'd met her then, before the baby, the broken heart, the law school, the years of grinding work, and they had gotten married—what would she be like? What would they be like? Maybe he would still be a cop. And she . . . an artist, a teacher maybe.

He let himself daydream another existence, because this one was so full of problems.

Because it was so late at night, they made the six-hour trip in five hours, the Bronco flying up the long slog through the foothills as lightly as a flag in the breeze. The mountains, usually a daunting prospect, offered clear sail-ing, twinkling stars, and a polished moon to light the way. They arrived just a little after seven-thirty on Thursday morning.

Located at the end of the highway from Truckee, stopped cold by the big lake, the road split at King's Beach to circle Tahoe in both directions, the eastern branch taking the Nevada side to the casinos of North Lake Tahoe, and the western branch moving along the California side of the lake past Emerald Bay until it reached the South Lake Tahoe casinos.

At the junction, a shadowy blue in the early-morning light, Paul turned right, then right again into the first gas station. Nina and Sandy stirred, murmured, found their shoes, and coughed a few times, complaining about the dry mountain air. After several minutes, while Paul pumped gas into the Bronco, they emerged, fresh-skinned, hair brushed into place. They drove a little farther along to the supermarket, where Nina told him to stop.

While they bought hydrogenated treats for breakfast, water bottles, and coffee in large containers, Paul moved into the passenger's seat, looked away into the mirror, and realized he had forgotten his razor. But instead of running in to buy another to make himself presentable, he put his head back and closed his eyes.

When he woke up, they were parked in front of a crudely built log cabin with a weedy flagstone pathway leading to a door with a single step up. No porch or over-hang softened the furious winter's passion or this morning's mountain sun. Sandy got out, motioning them to remain behind.

"You drove?" he asked Nina. They were parked on a slight rise on the northern part of the little town.

"You got a solid ten minutes' sleep. That plus what you got before I woke you up ought to keep us going for the day. Sandy's inside with Danny's mother. Want some coffee?" She handed him a cup, which he eagerly slurped. After drinking half the cup, he ate a sticky roll without examining the ingredients.

Nina rolled the windows down. "See the white pines?" she said, her voice nostalgic. "The scent of Tahoe. Oh, Paul. I've missed Tahoe."

As they watched the cabin, a yellow porch light came on. "You think she'll tell Sandy where he is?"

At that moment, Sandy appeared in the doorway and beckoned them inside.

"So you came." An unusually tall woman, made taller by the lowness of the ceilings, Connie Cervantes stepped back into the gloom of her cabin and allowed them to enter. "I was hoping you wouldn't."

"They had to," Sandy answered. "This is Nina. And this is Paul." They all shook hands.

Across from the front door on the opposite wall Nina saw a stone fireplace with an efficient insert for holding the heat in winter, and wood in the wood box even now, because June at Tahoe still meant cool nights. Over a mile high in the Sierras, people around the lake could find themselves in the midst of a snowstorm any month of the year. Sandy went straight to a table and chairs under the single window in the room; they all sat down and looked through it at the rocky yard with its low stone wall. A couple of blue jays squabbled in the pine tree by Connie's gate.

"Snow's all melted," Sandy said.

"For the next three months anyway." Sunken-eyed and older than she had first appeared, Connie wore blue jeans and a sweatshirt. Black hair now going gray flowed down her back. She hadn't looked again at Nina and Paul; her expression wasn't exactly hostile, but she was struggling with some inner turmoil, which preoccupied her so totally that she had little interest in her visitors, and Nina felt sure she never would have talked with them at all if she hadn't known Sandy. Nina folded her hands and listened while Paul rocked a little in his chair and kept his eyes down.

Sandy said in her matter-of-fact voice, "Where's Gary?"

"Staying with his sister in San Diego for a while." Danny's parents had been married for thirty years, Nina knew, but Sandy hadn't mentioned a separation.

Sandy and Connie seemed to be continuing some old conversation. Sandy said, "You remember my husband,

Joseph? Well, he went and broke his foot. He was cutting down some limbs behind the house and tripped over a rock. He's home in Markleeville right now."

"Left all this trouble for you to clean up."

"Now that's not fair. He'd help if he could."

"He ran out on you before."

"He came back. What about Gary? Is he coming back?" Sandy asked.

"Let me know when you find out," Connie said.

"Oh, so that's how it is."

"I'm workin' at least. In the cashier cage at the Cal-Neva. Right up the road at Crystal Bay. Gary has the car, but the bus goes right there."

"Good money?"

"Enough to keep this place going. When you comin' back to Tahoe?"

"Pretty soon. I'll see you at the powwow in August." Connie got up and went into the other room, returning wearing a shawl over her sweatshirt. The little room was cold and dreary, and Nina wanted to gather the information and leave, but forced herself to stay patient. She imagined the older woman returning from her job day after day, sitting at this table, looking out, as the snow came and the heat of summer and then the snow again.

"So you're chasing my son," Connie said to Sandy as she sat back down. "You didn't say anything to the police, like you promised?"

"Nobody knows but these two," Sandy answered, waving a hand at Paul and Nina. "They just want to stop him."

"He loves kids. You're crazy if you think he'd hurt a kid."

"Maybe," Sandy said.

"He kidnapped two kids? You're sure about that?" She paused, then went on, "I guess you wouldn't drive all the way up here if you weren't sure."

"If we find him and there aren't any kids, that'll be great. But see, the kids are gone and it looks like Danny."

Connie closed her eyes and pinched the bridge of her nose with her fingers and said, "I thought something was wrong when he got here. He likes it here a lot when Gary's not around, and he would normally stay a few days if he came up. But he was in a big hurry. He didn't look right, and he didn't talk right. I thought maybe he was on drugs, but now I think he was just very scared."

"He let everyone think he was dead," Sandy said. "How did he explain that?"

"It wasn't a big plot. I asked him, and he said nobody really cared one way or another. I told him I did, and he just said, 'Well, you.' " She swallowed and put one bony hand over the other, as if to hold it still.

"I hate to say it," Sandy told her, "you know I hate to say it. But if we don't find him right away somebody really could die."

Connie frowned deeply. In the back room Nina heard a clock ticking. Apparently Sandy had spared Connie the details of all that Danny might have done.

"Tell us what happened when he came," Sandy persisted.

Connie, who seemed to be still deciding whether to steer them toward Danny or not, said, "That time when they're nineteen, twenty . . . it's the hardest time for a boy. Figure out what you're gonna work at, figure out who you're gonna marry. They don't realize they've got time, they can go slow, the weight of all of it crashes down and they feel like they can't do it, growing up is too hard. Danny tried. He went to Ben's and tried to work, tried to do it right."

"He did," Sandy said, nodding.

"He was always lonely. We moved so much. Two months here, six months there . . . Danny never had a chance to stay put and have real friends, except that year or so we spent in Markleeville, living near you and Wish, Sandy. The happiest times Danny had growing up were with Wish," she said. "You know, Danny was a little older . . . he felt like a leader with Wish."

"Led him straight into trouble," Sandy said, "that time they set the tree on fire."

Nina bit her lip. So Danny had been with Wish during that first prank involving the stump of a tree. She should have known!

Connie did not look offended at the comment, taking it as Sandy offered it, as fact, not as criticism. She played with the fringe of her shawl and said, "Normal life never seemed exciting enough. He started playing with explosives and fire, always getting up to something he shouldn't. I tried to keep better track, to stay through one entire school year in the same area, but there's a time with kids, a right time, and I had missed it being busy, working all the time, trying to keep us in food. He wouldn't talk to me anymore.

"Ben found that job for him at the car-repair shop in Carmel Valley. He was good at that. He loved cars. I really thought things were looking hopeful for him finally."

"I hear he was good at it," Sandy said. Her calm kept them all calm, especially Connie.

"Then the business got sold. But Wish had come to town by then, and Ben says he was happy to have a buddy again. But then Ben says Wish decided to part ways with Danny."

"He did. I won't say he didn't."

"Another time things that could have gone good went bad," Connie said half-angrily. "Danny made me promise not to tell anybody he came here, and now look at me, I'm breaking my promise to him. His whole life is one broken promise."

"Stop. Stop it. You took the best care of him you could. You're still taking care of him by helping us get ahold of him. That's being a good mother. You know it."

"He'll hate me."

"Don't—"

"It's all right. He will hate me, because he's got a soul-sickness, but that's how it has to be. You know, we had a funeral for him. Flowers and speeches. Twenty-one years old, and we thought he was dead. We laid him in the ground. I suffered through my boy's death. I can't quite believe he's still alive. But seein' as how he is, I want your word that you won't bring in the police if I tell you what I know."

"I can't swear that, he's so far gone," Sandy said. "But tell me anyway."

After a long silence, Connie said, "He needed money."

"How much did you give him?"

"Everything I had. Three hundred dollars."

"What was he driving?"

She thought. "I thought he came in his car. It was overcast, and he must not have parked right out front."

"You didn't see any children with him?"

"I guarantee when you find him, you won't find any kids with him. Not unless they wanted to go along," she added, in a testament to her own uncertainty.

"Did he take anything besides money?"

"He keeps a lot in that closet." Connie pointed to a painted cupboard. "He grabbed a few things."

Paul got up quietly. "Mind?" he asked as he opened the door to the cupboard. Clothes and bed linens were wadded and stuffed into every shelf. Paul searched for a few minutes while the women watched. He emerged with a lantern and a ball of netting. "Camping gear," he said.

Connie examined the closet. "A couple of sleeping bags are gone. And a pup tent he used when he was a boy. Lamp fuel."

"Kerosene?" Nina asked.

Connie nodded.

"How much?"

"Half a gallon."

"Mrs. Cervantes," Paul said, "where is he?"

She didn't resist the entreaty in his voice any longer, but pulled out a creased map and showed them Danny's favorite camping spot. "I think maybe in the mountains above In-cline Village, an area near Rose Knob. He loves it there, and we have some old family friends with a cabin they loaned us a few times in that area, so it's familiar."

Paul got the address for the cabin.

"You think that's where he's gone?" Nina said.

"He wouldn't stay in the cabin. He never liked being inside when he could be outside. Also, he talked like he was going camping. Took wood from the stack behind the house for campfires. I really don't know. I'm guessing where he might be. He also likes to camp above Cave Rock, and over by Spooner Lake." She showed them two other spots. "Go ahead," she said, "track him down like an animal." Now Nina could hear the anger coming up in her, the anger at herself and Danny and her husband and Sandy for pressing her.

"Are you coming with us?" Sandy asked, standing stolidly in front of her. Nina hadn't thought of that possi-bility.

"No."

"It might help."

"Oh, I know I should. Just leave me alone. Go get him if you have to. I still can't figure out if he's really alive, if I really saw him." Nina and Paul exchanged worried glances.

"Okay, then." Sandy opened her bag, pulled out a box of doughnuts, and set them in front of Connie. "Chocolate-covered," she said. "Remember how we used to eat them back when the boys were little? Those were good times, and none of us are going to forget them. Nina, why don't you and Paul wait in the car."

Nina took Paul's hand and led him outside, Paul grab-bing the map as they passed the table. Lying back against the seat as Paul started the motor, she closed her eyes and thought that Bob would be passing through this dangerous transition to adulthood in a few years. She hadn't cared about Danny Cervantes as a person until this moment, the slow-burning match who had found only dried-up tinder in his search for a life, and had become a conflagration. Now she hoped that somehow he could be saved. But Callie and Mikey came first.

In a few minutes Sandy came out to the car and opened the door. When they were moving again, she said, "Danny took a bottle of pills from the medicine cabinet before he left. Thirty pills. Ambien."

"It's a very powerful sleeping aid," Nina said. "My God! We have to find him."

"He let her think he was dead. He was already a ghost, all the ties with this world cut. I don't think he can come back. She knows that."

36

BACK IN THE car, they regrouped. "Do we call the sheriff's office now?" Nina asked. "Shouldn't we tell them where we think Danny Cervantes might be? What's he going to do with those pills?"

"We still don't know he's there, Nina," Paul said. "I wish we had more to report. Give Crockett a buzz. See what he says." He knew what he wanted to do: Go to Rose Knob Mountain. He knew it well. He had hiked that section of the Tahoe Rim Trail traversing the summit the day the trail opened a year ago. But he was willing to let Crockett make the decisions.

She called Crockett, who sounded very anxious at the news, especially when she told him about the pills. "He's frustrated, Paul. He wants us to keep in close touch," Nina said, closing her phone. "He's going to talk with the local police and get back to us."

They drove for a few minutes more before Nina's phone rang. She talked briefly, then hung up. "They don't feel they can do anything with Connie's information yet. They are sending someone out to talk to her right away. Apparently, Crockett is also pursuing a credible report that Danny's hiding out with the kids south of Cachagua in the mountains near Big Sur."

Paul took a deep breath. "Damn. Those kids . . . do you think Danny's mother told us the truth?"

"I do."

"Drop me at the TART stop in King's Beach," Sandy told Paul as he swung back toward the road that ringed the lake.

"Say what?" Paul stole a glance into the back seat at Sandy, who was looking out the window, hands tight on her bag. He refrained from making a wise-ass addition to the question, terrified he would laugh and alienate her forever.

"Tahoe Area Rapid Transit," Nina explained. "The bus goes around the lake to South Lake Tahoe."

"You don't want to help us decide what to do?" Paul asked.

"I know what you'll do, and I'm not dressed for hiking. You brought what you need to go up the mountain and try to find him, I assume," Sandy said.

"Yes, we have what we need in the back of the truck."

"Well, then."

"Shouldn't we call Joseph to come and get you?"

"I already did from Connie's. He'll have somebody pick me up at the bus station. Don't waste any more time worrying about me. I know how to get home. You have mobile phones, both of you?"

"Yes."

"Charged?"

Nina checked her phone, then Paul's. "Yes."

"Don't forget them for a change."

"Okay, Sandy."

She had a few more instructions and edicts for them, which they listened to all the way down to the bus stop. When she got out, she held a hand up. "He's a kidnapper and a murderer," she said. "Paul, take your gun."

He patted his shoulder holster. "Check."

"And remember," she said, "he's still Wish's friend. I used my friends to find him and now we're trusting you with his life."

"Here we are," Paul said, stopping.

"Thanks, Sandy," Nina said.

"For what?"

"For coming to the party."

"We beat Crockett," Sandy said. "Now you do the rest."

Nina watched Sandy grow small in the rearview mirror as they drove back around the lake toward Incline Village. "How do you think she really feels about Danny?"

"She remembers him when he was innocent. Probably wiped away a few tears for him once. Now, could you check the map? Do I turn onto Mount Rose Highway or not?"

Directed by Nina, Paul made a left up the highway that eventually led over a nine-thousand-foot pass to the high Nevada desert and Reno. After a short distance, they turned left again and wound through some high-altitude residential streets set in landscapes that looked like they had been transported from the Alps. The asphalt dead-ended in patches of sprouting mule ears, white lupines, and penstemon getting ready to bloom. "Park here," Nina said, pointing. "This is it. The end of Jennifer Lane."

On the left, a few large houses crawled over the edge of a downhill slope. "That's his friend's cabin," Paul said, consulting a number he had written down. "Let's go look."

The smallest home on the block, it was very quaint, a gingerbread model, with filigreed blue shutters and painted flower boxes, obviously empty, given the pulled drapes and windblown pine needles all over the entry deck. They knocked. They rang the bell. They waited. When there was no answer, they tried again.

"An old door-to-door solicitor trick," Paul said. "You assume only a friend would have the nerve to ring twice."

Still no one came. Paul reached above the door to feel for a key but came away empty-handed. He proceeded to wander the front deck, turning over pots, fingering things around the edges of the deck.

"Got it," he said, fiddling with what looked like a rock.

"You make me so nervous," Nina said.

"Worried the neighbors are watching?" He turned

around with a big smile, waving the key. "Now they think we're visiting friends."

"Forget the neighbors. I'm worried about breaking and entering."

"We're not breaking anything. Besides, a friend of a friend said we could check it out for a possible rental, remember?"

"I'll remember," she said, "and I'll wait here."

Paul disappeared through the front door. "Have a seat there. Do your best to look innocent. I'll just be a second." He was true to his word, returning quickly. He placed the key back into the fake rock and put it back where he had found it. They walked back to the car.

"What did you find?"

"Kitchen raided for pots and pans. Bread crumbs and peanut-butter-and-jelly stains on the counter. Couldn't tell what all was taken, but the place on the whole was incredibly neat, so it was obvious that someone in a hurry tromped through."

"He was there with the kids," Nina said.

"Has to be him. Crumbs so fresh the ants hadn't even noticed yet."

"Anything else?"

"Just this." He pulled a wadded-up map out of his pocket that had pinholes in each corner. "Found it stuck to the wall in the living room. Favorite trails of the Gerdes family, marked in various colors. There's blue for easy hiking trails, red for steep ones, and yellow for four-wheel drives. . . ."

"Crockett told me he dumped the Jeep in Sacramento and stole an SUV. Less conspicuous."

"Yeah, he would once he had the kids. Nina, would you try to hike kids up that ridge?"

They looked up a steep hillside on the left, moist, loose gravel dotted with thick brush, and looked down to their right into an almost-vertical gully that led up to the ten-thousand-foot peaks of Rose Knob and its neighbor mountains on the ridge. "A waterfall!" Nina pointed. "It's really rugged here."

So where would Danny go from here, with two presumably reluctant children and camping gear in tow?

Paul put a finger to the topo map. "There's the nearest jeep trail, back to the highway, and then no more than two miles before you turn back this way. I'm guessing, but I think he'll want to stay around here, on familiar ground, but he can't hike far with gear and those kids, he really can't. Your car's four-wheel drive. Let's get going."

The day before, just about noon in Carmel Valley, Danny had had no trouble luring Callie into the black Jeep. He knew just where she'd be waiting for her bus home at the school—he used to drive her there for Jolene now and then—and she climbed right in when he said Jolene had sent him.

He cruised with her right down Carmel Valley Road, every nerve on edge, and turned down Esquiline to see if he could find one of Darryl's kids. And he saw Mikey, his good little buddy, throwing stones off Rosie's Bridge.

"You're supposed to be dead," Mikey said. The kid's hair was so short it made his ears stick out at right angles. His mouth was hanging open in puzzlement and curiosity about the big open vehicle Danny was driving, but he didn't seem all shocked that the ghost of Siesta Court was back haunting him. He just instantly figured out, hey, it was all some bullshit adult mistake. Danny liked that.

"I got lucky at Vegas. Bought me this Jeep. Wanna drive it?"

No problem. They went back and got on the Los Laureles Grade toward Salinas, Mikey driving like a little champ, just barely hitting the pedals. Danny had let him tool around some nights in his own old car back in the days before it all went wrong. When Danny finally kicked Mikey out of the driver's seat, Callie begged to drive.

He let her sit in his lap and spin the Jeep around an

empty parking lot in North Salinas a few times, then took over. "We gotta get started. We want to make Tahoe today."

"I can't go to Tahoe," Mikey said. "My parents will worry."

"That's a long way," Callie said, "isn't it?"

"Oh, not so far. Don't worry. Your parents know all about this. They're meeting us up there. Yeah, the whole neighborhood's clearing out because of the fires, taking a Fourth of July holiday. We're gonna have a big party. I had extra room for the trip so they sent me to pick up you guys, that's all."

"What about clothes?" Callie asked. "What about summer school?"

"Well, this fire thing scared 'em, and they all needed a break. I heard—yeah, Callie, your grandma said she called your teacher, didn't your teacher tell you?"

"No. I guess she forgot."

"You ever been to Tahoe?"

Mikey said, "It's cool. Maybe we can swim in the lake."

"That's it. There are little lakes high up in the mountains. A place called Ginny Lake like a blue jewel—right, like a jewel . . ."

They were loving the adventure, and all the good sense in the world went bye-bye temporarily. He played the radio stations they liked, and for a while, they pretended to shoot out the window with cocked fingers aimed at enemies all around. He knew they stood out and the Jeep was a gas hog, so as soon as he could, he switched it for an old Ford Explorer at a rest stop while the kids and the owners were in the bathroom. Luckily, the kids came out first and off they drove. The SUV had leather bucket seats, bottled water, all the conveniences.

Danny felt like laughing, though the money front was pretty dire. He'd killed Donnelly over seventy-five bucks in Donnelly's wallet. He'd been sure Donnelly would have a lot of cash somewhere at his place, but before he could find out anything Donnelly came at him and—and—

And Donnelly lost. Dumb speed freak, he only weighed about a hundred fifty, what made him think he could take Danny?

"We need something that'll take the bumps up in Tahoe," he said. "My friend switched with me for a few days. You ever fished before?" Neither one had fished, and they were both eager to try it. So they accepted what he said the way kids sometimes did, whatever, shrugs, after a few more easy lies.

In Dixon, they stopped for shakes and burgers at the Carl's Jr. They fought over what channel to listen to on the radio, but after a while, the carbs and fat did their dirty work, putting both the kids out for the rest of the count. By the time they woke up, it was morning. He had already stopped at his mom's for his fishing gear, some sleeping bags, and traveling money, and they were at the Gerdes cabin, hungry again.

"Best way to catch fish in most of the lakes up here is with Power Bait," Danny said. "Orange. For some reason, that works." Maybe the fish up here were deprived of the bright colors fish in warmer waters saw every day. They saw the orange bait as something unique and maybe especially tasty, like candy.

They were sitting by what was really nothing more than a dammed-up part of a stream, but it was big enough to excite Mikey, and Danny needed something to get the kids off his back until he could dope them both up good for the night. He was running on adrenaline, scared, thinking how the whole state would be alarmed by now, thinking about the turning lights on the tops of the sheriffs' cars. But the kids couldn't see his fright.

Having them around comforted him. He had always liked stories about mountain men, off in the woods surviving on the land, but always knew he couldn't stay out for long because he couldn't stand being alone. Sitting on the damp new ground cover, looking at the mule ears pushing up from the ground the snow had finally left, he could rest for a second. Mikey swished his little pole through the water and Callie wandered around, and Danny wished like hell that none of it had happened.

He should have thought up a better cover story. Like, a kidnapper was after them and their parents wanted them to hide out with Danny for a few days, that would have been so much better. But he never seemed to have time to plan right. He'd get the germ of an idea about how to handle something and the next thing he knew, it blew up into something awful.

They had spent the morning hours finding and setting up a camp. He liked this location, with the tents butted up against the rocky caverns that kept hibernating bears cozy in winter. He got on his dead phone twice and pretended to check in with George and Darryl. "Yeah, we gotta stick it out tonight all by ourselves, something came up," he had told them.

He'd give old George a real call pretty soon, when it was convenient. Good old George, called him a loser, then begged him to do his dirty work, then stiffed him.

"But we don't have anything orange," Mikey was saying, peering into the small fishing kit.

"We got worms, though." Danny brought out the night crawlers he had picked up in town, and showed Mikey how to thread one up the shank of a hook, leaving some dangling over. "Use a number six hook for this bait, and blow 'em up with a worm blower." He showed the kids how. "Another trick is using sugar cubes on a bigger hook," he said. "That's the method in clear lakes like Emigrant and Margaret. You fix 'em on the line with rubber bands. You got to cast real carefully, but when they melt in the water, the rubber band comes loose and the worm looks real natural. Or you can always try grasshoppers."

"I'm hungry," Callie said.

"That's why we're catching fish, Callie. To eat. This is Outdoor Camp," Danny said.

"I'm cold." She hugged her little sweater tight.

"You can't be cold. It's eighty degrees!"

"I am."

"Well, sit down here in the sun. That'll warm you up."

"No."

"Then go back there in the tent and get your bag to wrap up in," Danny said, working to keep the meanness he felt out of his voice. "Go on."

"No."

"Fine." He ignored her and worked on getting Mikey set up. After a few minutes, she went back to the tent. She came back wrapped up in an old sweater of his mother's he had brought along.

You would expect that the one who would be hard would be Mikey. Although he was little, he was nearly thirteen and seemed on the ball, but he bought Danny's every story. Callie was something else. She doubted every word, and wouldn't let up, wanting to call Jolene. He let her drive the big black Explorer a few feet up the jeep trail, but even that just scared her. She cried when they came to a big rock and he made her go over it anyway. She had to learn, didn't she? Fear was no protection. You had to do what you had to do.

He felt sure this time, he would get action. They had food, bait, and plenty of fuel. All the Siesta Court Bunch had to do was pay him what they owed him and he would go to Arizona or Montana and get lost. If it took the kids to get their attention, okay.

He didn't want to think about what would happen if he didn't get his twenty thousand. He had been stupid, giving the whole down payment to Coyote. But Coyote knew the ridge mountains, Coyote could get the kerosene in a way that wouldn't point at Danny, and Coyote was company, like the Lone Ranger and Tonto.

Coyote turned dangerous with his loose lips, though. The whole thing would have been much more fun with Wish. But he had known early on that Wish wouldn't follow him anywhere anymore.

A chill settled over the stream and around them. Callie went a little way away to pick wildflowers. "Remember what I told you about the bears. Stay in sight," he reminded her. Working bait on a hook, with Mikey happy beside him, butt firmly embedded in the loose dirt, Nikes kicked off, Danny couldn't help thinking about when he first arrived in Carmel Valley to live with his *tío* Ben. Why, he had been happy, it was incredible to think that now. He had loved the parties, hanging with the guys on the deck, shooting the shit, even taking his turn with Britta, a kind of initiation rite.

You did everything right, you tried to be a friend to people, someone they could call on for help. In return, you got cheated and put down. Those chiselers on Siesta Court had reeled him in with their grand plans, acting like his good buddies, not a single one with the balls to see the thing through except him!

And then they turned on him. Stiffed him. Whined, Oh, we never asked you to set those other fires! We never meant you to kill anyone!

Well, they had put toes over the line when they had hired him to burn across the river and decided to break the law. They went from being respectable to being criminal, and there was no way to go back ever again. You couldn't wipe the slate clean once you took that first little step over.

Not that they understood that at first. Those developers made these guys feel little, and they didn't like the feeling so they broke the law and felt like big shots all of a sudden. There was plenty of celebrating about that!

But when things got tough, and one crime led to another, then everything was Danny's fault, right? They had wives, kids, jobs. No need to pay what they owed! No, they were just bastards and hypocrites.

His dad used to say people were no damn good. Danny never believed it when he was a dumb kid. Well, he didn't have enough experience with friendship then to understand how right his dad was.

That was before Wish turned up in Carmel. For a few weeks Danny was happy. They did everything together.

This thought made him clear his throat and spit. Wish turned against him like everybody did and tried to leave him flat in the dust, more alone than ever.

Wish was always bragging about his classes, how hard they were, or his great job working with a detective. He could never understand that Danny's life was different, and headed somewhere different. School was not for him. A long, slow drudge life working at the auto shop wasn't going to cut it either.

And then suddenly, one day, no auto-repair shop job.

While he was still looking for a job, he would see ads in the paper sometimes and would think, That job's perfect for me. Well, this job was perfect.

Set a fire.

He knew something about that. He liked the work.

Tell that to smug Wishy-washy, who didn't want to talk to him anymore. Or don't tell it, a smart decision after all. Danny had wanted to call him a few times and let him know he had it in the bag. He had worked things out. Great things were in store, etc. But something made him hesitate, maybe a sense of self-preservation. Wish wouldn't approve. Danny knew that. He didn't like thinking he cared about Wish's approval, but he did think about how good he would feel showing up with a new car and a pretty girl beside him someday at that run-down old house Wish lived in in Pacific Grove.

"Go get another job, Danny," Wish had said, after the repair shop closed. Same old conversation a hundred times

until one day Danny looked into the eyes of his old friend
and former admirer and saw—

Disgust. Yeah, disrespect and contempt for everything
he was. Old Wish couldn't hide his feelings from Danny.

That was when Danny got the idea that Wish could die
in his place up on Robles Ridge. He would lure Coyote up
there the same day, two birds, one can of kerosene.

Okay, a couple cans.

Wish looked enough like him to pass for a few days so
he could stay off the scope until he made the men pay his
money, and Wish was handy, and Wish wasn't a friend, not
anymore. He had entered the world of Danny's enemies.

What did Wish know, with his cushy existence, that
mother of his always there to back him up instead of dying
slowly in a rotting cabin with her wasted husband? In real
life, Danny didn't waste his time pointing unloaded fingers
at his enemies. When old friends turn on you, that's such a
big hurt, you do stupid things.

In real life, when George and the rest announced after
he set the second fire all by himself, Hey, you've gone too
far, blah blah blah, and said they wouldn't pay him, he put
on the pressure, real pressure.

When he heard Wish survived the fire, he got anxious
and confused. He had set things up right and it should have
worked. The police, finding the two bodies, would be satisfied that they had their two arsonists. He thought back to
that day, convincing Wish to go when he didn't want to go,
getting that drunk, Coyote, up there so he could shut his
big mouth at the same time.

He should never have hired Coyote to help him on
those first two fires in the first place. He'd given him the
whole down payment so he could keep it clean and keep all
the rest. Then, up there on the ridge that day, the fire went
the wrong direction when the wind came up. He took too
long whacking Coyote and changing clothes with him and
then he couldn't get the Doc Martens off Coyote's feet.
How he'd managed to get the pants on him over those

boots he'd never know. And he'd really hated sacrificing his concho belt.

By the time he got back to Wish, the fire was so intense he had a few bad moments thinking he might not make it out himself. So he hadn't hit hard enough with that rock, or been thorough enough, checking to see Wish was dead or near enough. He flashed to grabbing Wish for just a second from behind, the terror that Wish might somehow turn around and look him in the eyes.

Still, all he needed was his money now, and he'd go find some big mountains far away, and it wouldn't matter that a few things went wrong.

One thing for sure, he'd keep on with the fires.

Fire was the most intense, rushing gusher of relief. Fire filled the emptiness inside him, and he felt fulfilled, caught up in his destiny, active, happening. Productive, destructive, unbelievably powerful.

Born to burn, Danny thought to himself, but he felt hollow and terrified and thought again, now they're all after me. And there was this surprise that kept pushing up from inside, this dismay, that he had killed Coyote and Donnelly and that woman; if he thought a lot about it he'd hate himself. Later for that, he'd get crazy at some motel out in the desert when he was safe and cry and shout it out and find a way to live with himself.

Next to him, Mikey thought he caught something and in his excitement, tangled the line on a log. They spent a long time disengaging the line and getting him set up again. Danny took the opportunity to mentally talk himself down.

"I don't think there are any fish in this stream," Mikey complained.

"Well, we won't know if we don't give it time, will we?" Danny asked, proud of how patient he acted with these two pains in the ass.

They moved downstream and Mikey started fishing again. Now Danny was jumping out of his skin with boredom. He hated waiting, but waiting was what was called for right now, and his patience would be rewarded, he was sure of that. He would sneak out later that night and make some calls . . . get things arranged, finish with the kids, and be on his way to the Big Sky Country. Lots of Natives there. He'd go to powwows and get with the People: he was half Washoe, he would be accepted.

Callie chose that moment to return, both grubby little hands holding bouquets. "Smell this," she said, shoving some yellow flowers under Mikey's nose.

"Coconut," Mikey said, eyes closed. "Tropical."

"They look like some primroses Grandma planted," Callie said. "They aren't open yet. Maybe they open at night like jasmine?"

"I'm hungry," Mikey observed.

"You didn't catch any fish?" asked Callie.

"No problem," Danny said, reeling his line in. "We've got other food."

"I thought you said you knew how to fish," Callie said.

"The fish just don't know how to get caught," Danny said, and Mikey laughed, but Callie just stared steadily at him, and he could see she had a little of her no-nonsense grandma in there, which scared him into giving her a big smile.

Callie, sticking the flowers one by one into an empty Gatorade bottle full of stream water, kept up an incessant, nervous chat that had everybody edgy while Danny and Mikey put the fishing tackle away.

"What's for lunch?" Mikey asked.

"You can't be hungry. We just ate. You had two sandwiches."

"I am. I have to eat now. What have you got for us?"

"Hey, I'm the scout leader here." Danny grabbed the fishing pole from him and picked up the tackle box. He walked back toward the tent, feeling anger popping like boils all over his body. Damn kids. Who was the boss here anyway? Well, he guessed they would find out soon enough who called the shots.

The kids trailed behind him. When he could speak, he said, as calmly as he could manage, "We've got canned Vienna sausage, bread, mustard, Chips Ahoys. A real feast."

Callie looked interested. "What's a Vienna sausage?"

"Camp food," Danny said. "I promise, you're gonna love it."

"Do we have to stay here all night?" she asked.

"Yeah, but it'll go fast."

"I'm not used to sleeping without my blanky."

"You're too old for a blanky," said Mikey disapprovingly.

"I know, but Grandma says whatever gets you through the night," Callie said.

"If you'll just shut up for one second," Danny promised, "I've got a plan for after lunch, an activity we're going to do together. Then, a little later on, when it gets dark, we're gonna have some real fun." He jumped up and put his Nikes on.

"I'm gonna teach you how to build a fire."

37

PAUL SHIFTED THE Bronco into four-wheel drive and turned left at the jeep road.

"There's a gate," Nina said.

"That's why I have an assistant."

She got out, wrestled the gate out of the way, and got back in. They bumped slowly along the mogul-strewn dirt road for a few minutes. Going around the first wide bend, they saw an amazing vista of Lake Tahoe swept with wind like a heavenly vision, as insubstantial as an enormous blue cloud below them. "How far do we go? We don't want him to hear any engine noise."

"Not far," Paul said. "He would get far enough from the highway so that the kids couldn't easily find their way back, but the road isn't that long."

They rode a little farther, until, at a spot offering one of the few level borders beside the road, Paul pulled off the road. He drove the Bronco over small logs and up a slight incline, then down into a gully. He got out and opened the trunk. Nina followed him.

"You insist on coming along?" Paul asked.

Nina didn't bother to answer.

"In that case, we leave the Bronco behind, instead of having one person drive it out. If he comes back up this road, we don't want him to see there are any other people around. Don't want to scare him. People like Danny are full of fear. You know that? Full of bravado, not bravery."

"But . . ." Nina said, puzzled, "he sets fires. That's dangerous. If he's so scared . . ."

"Scared he'll get caught. Scared he'll get hurt. Scared he won't be respected. We're going to do nothing that will set him off. Your pack," Paul said, handing it to her.

She put it on her back.

"Hope we don't have to go too far," he said, handing her a jacket, which she tied around her waist. They sat on the bumper lacing their hiking boots. "Prisons are full of Dannys. Some of these guys are terrified of heights. Some are scared of water. Some won't go on airplanes. They're superstitious and they're skittish. That's why we don't want to get near him. We scare him, he reacts. Problem is, we can't predict how." He finished, stood up, and adjusted the pack on his back.

"We have got to find him," Nina said. "Paul, we have to be so careful. Those kids . . ."

"Right. So we sneak. We've got to be very quiet, and we have to travel pretty slowly because we're going to be listening. And he is too. If he's here, which is a long shot."

Nina nodded.

They locked up the car and hiked back to the road. The road narrowed and switched back and forth. Before every curve, they held back until they were certain they weren't going to run into any nasty surprise around the bend. Progress was very, very slow, because they wanted to travel in silence, and afternoon faded into dusk.

Callie would not allow them to toss the trash or even bury it. "We have to hike it out. I saw this show at school."

The kids had eaten very little. They weren't really hungry. They just needed their routines.

"Go ahead and bag it," Danny said, feeling magnanimous. He went into the tent and came out again with a tiny recorder. Mikey, who had been looking unfriendly ever since refusing a second cookie, got curious and came over to see what he had. "That's old," he judged. "I had one of those years and years ago."

"It'll do the job," Danny said. "Now, here's what we're gonna do. Instead of writing letters, we're going to talk to them."

"To Grandma?" asked Callie skeptically.

"Yep."

Mikey looked even less sure. "What do I say?"

"Say, hey, Mom, Dad, I'm here, all's cool. That kind of thing."

"I thought they're coming tomorrow," Mikey asked. "Why can't I talk to my dad?"

"This stupid phone is almost out of juice is why. Just say you can't wait," Danny said. "Tell 'em about fishing. Tell 'em you miss them. I'll play your messages real fast so we get it all in."

"I do miss them," Callie said stoutly.

"Well, then say so."

"Why didn't you charge it on the car charger?" Mikey said suddenly.

"My friend's charger won't fit my phone." He glared at Mikey.

Callie was first to take hold of the microphone. "Grandma," she said formally, "it's awful pretty up here in the mountains today and camping's great but I miss you."

"That's exactly right," said Danny, taking the microphone from her and putting it into Mikey's face.

"Mom, Dad," said Mikey, "I almost caught a fish! I never knew camping could be so fun. Hurry and come."

"Great," said Danny. "They're going to love hearing from you."

"How will they hear it?" asked Callie. "Aren't we too far away?"

"They'll hear it," said Danny. "We're up high and the reception is better than at home. That's a promise." He switched off the microphone. "You guys like marshmallows?"

Turned out, they did.

"I'm going to show you how to make a fire that can't be beat," Danny said. He took some dry wood from the pile he had borrowed from his mother. He showed them how to stack the branches like a pyramid, how to get the fire really hot. They roasted a few marshmallows to perfection, toasty brown.

Danny got up and found three cups. "I've got a pot full of water here, and a couple packets of hot chocolate. Who wants some?"

They practically jumped over each other, wanting some.

While the water heated, he prepared the mixture.

"I want this side of the tent," Mikey said to Callie, who looked nervous, watching the night creep along the landscape.

"You can't see the lake anymore," she said, her voice small. "Are the bears going to come out?"

"I'm going to lock every crumb into the truck," Danny said. "They won't be able to smell it." That was a lie, but Danny had enough worries without adding on bears.

"I get this side!" Mikey put his sleeping bag in place to cement the deal.

The afternoon breeze had gone for the day. Watching the small fire flick in the wind, Danny waited for the darkness. When the water in the pot got hot enough, he poured the liquid into the prepared cups.

"I can't drink this," Callie pronounced, making a face. "It's way too hot."

Mikey gulped the chocolate. "How come things taste so good when you are outside!"

Danny blew over Callie's cup. "I can make it right," he said. "Cool it down just the way you like it."

For the first time that day, the little girl looked happy. "Okay," she said.

"We need a story, though," she said when Danny tried to get them into their bags.

"Sure, I'll tell you a story. You finished up all your hot

chocolate? There was the time I was down in Antigua and went out ocean fishing. You can catch fish there that are so big they can pull you right out of the boat!" He had never been to the Caribbean, but he had talked to a guy who had. He talked on, embellishing what he'd heard, making himself the hero, fabricating a lot of lore about marlin fishing he didn't really know. Actually, as a way of passing the time, storytelling was something he enjoyed.

Both children fell asleep. Danny piled wood on the fire, thinking about his little buddies. If•only it were real and they were just on a camping trip. He didn't want to hurt them. He'd played with them and had some fun with them and they'd never called him a loser. They weren't like sneaky Nate with his weird talk.

He looked into the dark forest, wondering if he was being hunted. He would never go to jail. The kids could go out in a blaze of glory with him and never grow up, always be happy and fishing and roasting marshmallows.

"It's dark," Paul said. He took his pack off and sat down on a fallen log.

"Yes." Nina joined him. They had crawled up and back on the jeep trail several times, foraying beyond wherever they thought a car might break through the trees and brush to a hiding place. They took water bottles out, and drank.

"Just remember, if a bear chases you and follows you up the tree to eat you, it's a black bear. If it knocks the tree down and eats you, it's a brown bear," Paul said.

"There aren't any grizzlies up here," she said, "only black bears that like berries a lot. They're big bluffers, and would much rather eat your garbage than you."

"You know they can get to six hundred pounds?"

"Are you trying to scare me or comfort me? Anyway, until you mentioned them, I wasn't worrying about bears."

"I know."

They wolfed protein bars. "The question is, should we head down to Spooner Lake, even though it's dark?" Paul asked.

"I've been thinking. I just could swear I saw something in Connie's eyes," Nina said. "Just there at the end. Remember when she was talking about how Danny thought nobody cared if he lived or died and she said she did?"

"I remember."

"She said, 'Go ahead, track him down.' I think she wants us to find him," Nina said. "All that other information was to convince herself she wasn't giving him away." She got up, stiff-legged, and put her pack on her back. "I think she knows he's here."

"I think he couldn't have brought these kids so far up," Paul said. "We should try Spooner Lake."

"No, Paul, he's here!"

In the moonless night, she could just make out his shrug. "Up we go," he said.

Danny closed the flaps down on the kids' tent and tied it shut. Considering the number of pills he had ground up in their chocolate, they wouldn't bother him until noon.

He felt like a ghost, cold, lifeless.

He went over to the pitiful fire and began tossing wood on it, all the rest of the wood he had taken from his mother, and made his own personal bonfire. After he got it burning big enough, and had drunk his fill of it with his eyes, he found the tape recorder. He pulled out a cell phone and dialed up Jolene and George.

George answered.

"I got someone here wants to talk to her grandma," Danny said, enjoying the cry he heard on the other end. The phone clattered, and Jolene spoke next. "Danny? Where is she, Danny?"

He played the tape. Jolene started crying right after

hearing the word *grandma,* so it didn't matter that Callie didn't talk much.

"Now put George back on the phone," he said. Damn the woman. She couldn't hear him through the wailing. He repeated himself, louder this time, and she let go of the phone.

"It's me," George said.

Danny put his face closer to the fire. "I got such a big fire going, George. Wish you could be here to experience it with me. But you don't like hanging with losers, do you?"

"I'm sorry I said that, son. Now you—"

"Callie's okay. She wants to go home, but that's up to you."

"Don't hurt her," George said. "We've talked. We'll pay you the full amount. Twenty thousand. Just bring the kids back safe. Or leave them somewhere so we can come get them."

"I'm going to need more money."

Silence from George.

"I asked for the twenty. But you all thought, he set the fire, how's he gonna collect? You forced me into all this mess."

"It was just—you kept on setting fires—"

"So?"

"I—I won't argue with you. I'm just waiting to hear how much."

"An extra fifty grand."

A pause, then George said, "Okay. On top of the twenty."

"Get it," Danny said. "Cash, unmarked, nothing over a fifty. I'll call you in the morning about where all to leave the money and where to find the kids. This whole thing could be over by one o'clock tomorrow. It's up to you."

"Son, tell us where you are."

"I'm not your son." Danny punched End and looked around, paranoid again. The wind was rising, so the licks of fire flared out and blew sideways.

"It's just possible," Paul said, pushing a branch back for Nina, "that he's dumb enough to build a fire." They stumbled through brush that in the daytime would have been daunting, but at night was nearly impossible. Wind had blown in intermittent bursts for the past hour, so the pines shook and whipped above them, and dry leaves rained down. They reached the top of a rise, but had to march around for quite a while before they could see any distance through the thick black forest.

"No fires," Paul said, disappointed.

"Keep looking," Nina said. She did not let herself think about what the children might be feeling in the darkness of this night, because she knew knowledge of their fear would paralyze her.

She took Paul's arm and pointed upward. She reckoned they had climbed to over nine thousand feet and still hadn't hit treeline. "There!" she whispered.

He peered. "I can make out rocks . . . white . . ."

"Smoke," Nina said. "It's a pretty big fire. And the wind is coming up again."

He watched for a long minute. "Controlled, Nina. At the moment. Let's go."

They began traversing along a steep slope to the left, toward a wooded gully where two hills came together, keeping well below the white plume. They were bushwhacking and it was hard to be quiet as they made their way across the talus slope. When they finally edged into the gully they found a swift meltwater stream and a gentle slope leading up.

They were on a huge ridge of mountains that flanked Lake Tahoe, looking down at the flat forests of Incline along the shore and out upon endless, distant, shining water. They moved even more cautiously now, until they judged they were within earshot. Then they slowed to a crawl.

"What do we do if it's them?" she whispered in Paul's ear.

"The minute we see them," Paul said, "we get the cops up here. We are not going to mess with this guy, Nina." She nodded.

The gully flattened into a saddle cleft by the spring. They slowed even more as they approached what appeared to be a campsite, bordered at the back by huge boulders of fallen rock. They heard a voice—Danny Cervantes.

"I never liked you either, Darryl," Danny was saying into a mobile phone. He looked like John Walker Lindh fresh out of Afghanistan, hair out of its customary ponytail, clothes dirty and disheveled, lit by flames that played over his skin like dancing demons. They had to move in close to hear him say, "Oh, they're sleeping good tonight, Darryl. I drugged them. You know I'm no doctor, though, I had to guess how much would keep them out of my hair for the rest of the night." He then spent a few minutes assuring an apparently frantic Darryl that he was "ninety-nine percent sure" they were still alive before shutting the phone.

To their surprise, after hanging up, Danny left the campsite, heading directly around a nearby bend.

"Where'd he go?" Nina whispered.

"My guess is, he wants a bigger fire."

Nina ran over to the campsite and tried to open the tent flaps, but they were tied shut. "Callie!" she hissed. "Mikey, are you there?"

Paul was by her side. He helped her fumble with the tent ties, and they both called to the kids.

"Rip them off!" Nina said, tearing at them. She was trying to locate her penknife, when they heard a sound in the woods.

Within two seconds, Paul had hold of her, had run her out of the camp area and back into the dark forest.

He looked back toward the clearing. They could hear Danny now, but they couldn't see him. Taking her by the arm, Paul walked her quietly farther from the campsite, although they could still see it, and could hear Danny, who was apparently gathering more dead wood, judging by the sticks and branches that flew roughly toward the fire.

Paul called Crockett. He ran down the situation and their location as well as he could, then shut his phone. "He patched me through to the local police. It will take them a while, Nina. It's a good thirty minutes up from Incline Village if they go slow along the back road, and there's no other easy way in. They don't want to scare him off, or scare him into doing anything to the kids. They'll have to go slow, like we did."

Nina made a call to the poison center and was told exactly what she thought they would tell her about the Ambien—get the kids to throw up and get them to a hospital. Now.

"I'm going back there."

A log as thick as a lamppost flew into the camp.

"Nina." Paul took her in his arms. "Listen to me. You'll put everyone in danger."

"They may be dying! I'm not afraid of him."

"Be patient, Nina. We'll watch over them until the police arrive."

"You don't understand!" she said. "You . . ."

"Don't have kids?"

She could feel his eyes on her, beams from his soul shooting through the dark.

"You think I'm making the wrong decision because I can't appreciate how serious the situation is? You think I don't care because I don't have kids of my own?" His voice had leveled to flatness.

Heart pounding, breath coming in bursts, Nina shook her head. "No, of course not. Paul, I'm sorry. . . ."

They waited for some time. Nina leaned against Paul and took comfort from him. She checked her watch frequently.

No sound came from the campsite.

Then they heard a crash as Danny broke through some bushes by the tent, bottle of whiskey in one hand, and a can of kerosene in the other. He had obviously already made headway on the bottle, because he was humming.

Nina and Paul crouched down. Paul had his gun out, Nina noted, and felt relieved at the sight. At least no more overt harm could come to the kids while they were watching.

"This is good," Paul said in her ear. "Maybe he'll pass out."

But as the minutes ticked by, Danny got drunker, and seemed not at all inclined to doze off. At one point he stumbled directly toward them, stopping at the first line of bushes, and let loose a gurgling flow of vomit. After that, he seemed livelier than ever, collecting more wood to keep the bonfire going, keeping it big, and keeping it under control. Nina thought a forest fire was not in his plan for the evening, and was thankful.

The sheriff's officers did not come, and did not come.

Danny's happy song turned into muttered cursing. His face, scratched and lined by firelight, drooped as his mood shifted. He peed into bushes. He drank some more.

He picked up the can of kerosene. At first, he contented himself with splashing a few drops toward the fire. It blazed up. Once he made a small fire next to it, and stomped it out.

"He could kill himself doing that," Paul whispered, his face grim. "That can could explode in his hand. Damn, he's so close to the tent."

She heard indecision in his voice. She, too, couldn't decide whether to rush him now—the dangerous can of fuel he was wandering around with could burn the tent—but a moment later, Danny, apparently overcome by his foul mood, made a move they could not ignore. He had been gesturing wildly, and now slopped the kerosene in a long stream that stretched all the way to the tent.

And it caught. A spark, something, set the whole stream of fuel alight.

Paul ran out into the clearing, gun in hand. Danny screamed as the fire hit his hand and dropped the can, saw Paul, and grabbed a burning limb. He brandished it at Paul, who moved around him in a circle pattern, looking for a way in.

The tent was in flames. Running past the fire, Nina grabbed a burning torch and ran behind Danny and then lunged at his back and bedeviled him with the flame.

Danny screamed again and turned to face her. She threw the fiery limb at him. Paul tackled him from behind, but he kicked out and had a second to stand up. He should have run into the forest where he might have escaped.

But he ran toward the tent and disappeared inside.

And Nina knew then that he had come to the end of his line and decided to burn with the children. Paul was up but he couldn't get inside the low doorway, it was a sheet of flames. She was pulling at the lines, trying to pull the tent anchors away. The anchors popped up and she could pick up the whole side of the tent—

Danny pushed her hard from inside the tent. It felt as though the tent fought her. She fell and her shirt caught fire. Tearing it off, she ran back to the canvas-covered form in the tent and picked up her leg in the hiking boot and gave Danny the hardest kick she could.

The whole tent fell down. Now it was only burning sheets of canvas with two children and a murderer lying trapped inside.

For a moment she and Paul just stood there and looked at each other, horror in their eyes.

Then Danny began crawling out of the collapsed tent, dazed and burning, and Paul tackled him.

The forest around them came alive. Police in uniform, firefighters burst into the campsite. Three cops rushed Paul and Danny, and at almost the same moment a crew of firefighters came running in and used handheld extinguishers to spread foam on the fire.

And Nina ran through the burning half-circle of fire to the one side of the tent that wasn't already engulfed, ripped through the fabric with her knife, and found the children.

EPILOGUE

One Month Later

A BIG BANNER, hung across the entrance to Jolene's new business, said WELCOME TO THE CAT LADY CAFÉ! BEST LATTES IN THE UNIVERSE! Through the front window, Nina saw a big crowd of adults and children talking and laughing.

"Go ahead, Wish," she said. Wish had twenty thousand dollars thanks to his cut of the reward, which had been shared with Connie Cervantes, Sandy, Nina, and Paul, and he looked self-confident and happy again. As he dipped his head and disappeared inside, she held Paul's hand and stopped him.

"You okay?" he said.

"It's the first time back in this town since—"

"It's just good old Carmel Valley Village again, and the party goes on," Paul said. "I think the Cat Lady would approve of this tribute. She was a tough character and so is Jolene. Look in there. See Jolene behind the counter?"

"I like the cat ears."

"I've been hearing at the Carmel post office that this is the best lunch place on the central coast. The place is jammed. She's a hit."

"Thank goodness. I had heard she found a start-up stake somewhere. She moved fast. There's Debbie and Nate. He looks happy. Isn't Debbie a remarkable woman? She had to work hard to get the foster-care certificate."

"She wanted another child," Paul said. "She's going to take good care of Nate, and then she'll find other foster children when Nate goes back to the Washoe tribe. I wonder how her husband took it."

"Like a man, I hope," Nina said. "Tory told me that Nate and Mikey are getting to be friends. Oh, there he is, behind the counter."

"Ah, I see the ex-cons drinking coffee at the table in the corner. How many hours of community service did they get?"

"Six hundred hours apiece. They'll have to testify against Danny in a few months too. And they all have records. And then there's the payback to Green River."

"You did a great job keeping them out of jail. They know how lucky they are."

"Keeps them busy," Nina said, smiling. "I hope they're only talking about golf. I wonder if they miss David and Britta."

"I doubt David and Britta miss them. Britta's going to be happier in New York. She made an amazing recovery, didn't she?"

Nina nodded. "And Tory's looking very pregnant. I'm glad she didn't throw Darryl out. Check out Elizabeth and Ben by the cash register. He has an arm around her waist. Very interesting. Jolene did mention something about that when she called to invite us. Ben decided he didn't want to live on the same street as the men who toasted his nephew's death and Elizabeth had extra room."

"Are you ready? They're not going to bite you, Nina."

"One more minute. It's going to be intense," Nina said.

"Here comes Megan. I noticed the bikes in the rack." Megan came outside and said, "Hi! Why don't you come in? I saw you out here."

"Oh, we're just enjoying the sun. It's so foggy today in Carmel. Be right in. Looks great."

When they were alone again, Nina said, "Paul?"

"Mmm-hmm?"

"It's really all right? About Bob and me moving into Aunt Helen's?"

"I told you, I can live with that. If I can't live with you, I'll live with that."

"It's better for all of us. I don't have to be the girlfriend with the suitcase, we're together, Bob isn't in your face—"

"It's progress," Paul said. "On the whole. Up, down, but I do detect a gentle forward movement."

Nina laughed. "Hey, there's the lady in the wheelchair, helping Jolene. The handicapped folks on the hill are still fighting. I forgot to tell you, Paul, the director called me a few days ago and asked me to look into their legal situation."

"Really. Now I'll never get my office chair back from you," Paul said. "Can we go in now? You'll just get more nervous putting it off any longer."

"I guess."

"They'll give you a hero's welcome. You're a legend. The one who stopped the Pied Piper of Siesta Court. Come on, Counselor, don't be shy."

"I didn't do it alone, I enjoyed working with you, partner," Nina said.

He held open the door for her and offered her his arm. She still held back, thinking about the Cat Lady's Twelve Points, and wondering what her crossed-out Conclusion had been.

Jolene came to get them, her cat ears bobbing, her nose painted black, little black whiskers on her lip, smiling broadly. Nina smiled too and took Paul's arm.

They walked in and the clapping started.

ACKNOWLEDGMENTS

WE WOULD LIKE to express our grateful appreciation to Nancy Yost, our lovely, cheerful, brilliant agent, of Lowenstein-Yost Associates. The opera world lost a star, but we gained a guide and bulwark over the past ten years who has brought us only good. We also thank Danielle Perez, Senior Editor at the Bantam Dell Publishing Group, who, with this book especially, has shown her rare ability to catch the lags, the vagueness, and the illogic of our manuscript, while continuing to encourage the spirit of our work.

To Irwyn Applebaum, that hardworking, helpful, and astute presence who is our publisher, and to Nita Taublib, Deputy Publisher, the skilled and enthusiastic supporter who works behind the scenes to bring out the best in all of us—we hope you know that we are aware of your importance to our success. We also appreciate the hard work on our behalf by Susan Corcoran, Shannon Jamieson, Glen Edelstein, and Jeffrey Ward. Thank you all.

We would also like to recognize and thank the many people who answered fact questions and rode shotgun with us as we wrote, including Andrew "Drush Bobx" Fuller, Patrick O'Shaughnessy and Meg O'Shaughnessy and Brad, June, Connor, and Cory Snedecor. Peter von Mertens read our manuscript and provided many helpful comments. Thanks to Cheryl Mikel and Hazel Shaw for their kind support, and the many wonderful readers who have written us words of encouragement at our Web site, perrio.com.

The lyrics our guitar player sings at the party are from a song titled "Green Eyes and White Lies" by R. C. Cole and R. J. Masters, copyright 2000. We can't play the tune of this beautiful song in a book, but if any reader wants to hear it, please contact B. C. Cole at *rccole@comcast.net*.

Couplets quoted at the beginning of each part come from Robert Browning's poem "The Pied Piper of Hamelin." All other song lyrics, doggerel, and poetry, except the John Keats quote before the prologue and a few words from "El Paso," are ours.

Our characters are completely fictitious. There is no Siesta Court in Carmel Valley. Although we like to talk about real places for the reader's enjoyment, if it's connected with the plot, we probably made it up.

ABOUT THE AUTHOR

PERRI O'SHAUGHNESSY is the pen name for two sisters, Pamela and Mary O'Shaughnessy, who live in Hawaii and on Lake Tahoe, and in California and on Lake Tahoe respectively. Pamela graduated from Harvard Law School and was a trial lawyer for sixteen years. Mary is a former editor and writer for multimedia projects. They are the authors of nine other Nina Reilly novels: *Unfit to Practice, Writ of Execution, Move to Strike, Acts of Malice, Breach of Promise, Obstruction of Justice, Invasion of Privacy, Motion to Suppress,* and *Unlucky in Law,* on sale in July from Delacorte Press.

Don't miss the next exciting
Nina Reilly novel

UNLUCKY IN LAW

BY PERRI O'SHAUGHNESSY

Coming in hardcover from
Delacorte Press
In Summer 2004

UNLUCKY IN LAW

ON SALE JUNE 29, 2004

<u>Prologue</u>
Christina's Story
Monterey, California, 1966

Her friends called their fathers "Dad" or "Daddy," but he wanted Christina and her little brother to call him Papa because he had called his father Papa. His mustache drifted below his mouth at the corners, tickling her when he kissed her cheeks. When he was sick and lying on the couch in his study, he liked to sing to her. At bedtime he read her stories, like Masha the Bear, which was a lot like Little Red Riding Hood, and the story of the Crow and the Crayfish. Sometimes she persuaded him to read her favorite.

"The Snow Maiden story again, Papa."

He groused and teased, finally pulling out a tattered book and finding the page. "Everyone else was building snowmen. 'Why not build a snow maiden?' the old lady asked. And so they did. When they were finished, they stepped back to admire her."

"She came to life," Christina said, excited. "Like Pinocchio!"

"She smiled!" he said, "and she began to move her arms and legs. How her grandparents doted on her. White as the snow was Snyegurochka, with eyes like blue beads. Blond hair dangled all the way down to her waist. She had no color in her cheeks, but cherry red lips made of shiny ribbon. She was so beautiful!"

He read on. Finishing the story, he leaned over to touch her cheek. "You, my little princess, have pink cheeks, nothing like this pale girl made of ice who melts in a bonfire."

"Why did she jump over the fire?"

"She didn't want to hide by the icy river anymore. She forgot she was made of snow, and dreamed she could be something she was not."

"I'll be like her. Brave. Jump over the fire."

"No," Papa said. "Remember, she lost her life for this dream."

He shut the book. "Tomorrow, I will play some music for you, something you will like."

"What is it?"

"Music for the snow maiden, based on the story you love so much," he said, "by a man named Rimsky-Korsakov."

"Okay." Her eyes drooped. "Papa?"

"Yes, my princess."

"I can't sleep."

He kissed her forehead. "One last story," he said, "the true story of a boy in Russia. Then if you can't sleep, you will have to count sheep." He thought for a moment. "I warn you in advance, it's tragic."

"Does the wolf tear the goat to bits?"

"Yes and no," he said.

"Is it sad?"

"Yes, some of it is sad."

"Put your blue egg in the story, the one you keep in your study."

"All right." He laughed.

"Does anyone die in it? I don't want them to die."

"In true stories, people die, Christina."

"Not me!"

"Everyone."

She digested the information silently, then said, "Tell me your story, Papa. I promise not to cry."

1

SEVEN A.M. ON the first Monday morning in September. Nina Reilly and Paul van Wagoner snoozed in his king-sized bed in the sole bedroom of his Carmel condo. As the sun came through the shutters, striping the rug with light, Paul kicked off the covers on his side and, as Nina opened her eyes, turned over so all his long naked backside was displayed, the blond hair, the smooth, well-muscled back, strong legs, and narrow feet.

As if he felt her attention, he turned back to her. Eyes closed, he grabbed her around the waist and pulled her tight to his body.

Nina was naked, too, the way Paul liked her. Herself, she favored expensive silks or shabby cottons, but since she had gotten involved with Paul, she had learned to appreciate what he called his simple needs. He liked skin, he liked the smell of her, he wanted nothing to come between them, so nothing did, at least not when they were in bed together.

This time with Paul was precious. Her son, Bob, fourteen, had spent the previous night with his grandfather. She had "freedom," in the way all mothers had freedom, meaning contingent freedom, but at least Bob was safe enough for the moment. She stretched in Paul's arms so her toes reached his calves, and kissed his stubbled cheek.

"Mmm, coffee time," Paul said, smiling, eyes closed.

It was her turn. She didn't have far to go in the compact condo. When she came back with the mugs, Paul was sitting up in bed, legs crossed.

"I feel suspiciously elated considering it's Monday morning," she said.

"Ben Franklin would call us slackers. He would have been up since five, making a kite."

"Progress means we get to do whatever the hell we want this early in the morning," she said.

Nina had moved to the Monterey area from Tahoe in early summer to be with Paul, just to see how things would play out for them. She had gone to law school here, at Monterey Peninsula College. Her father lived here, and she had other old ties. But now, after her move from Tahoe and after a brief vacation of sorts, she had signed on for her second murder case in three months.

Her part started today, though the poor client had been counting the days at the Monterey County Jail for four months. A new case, a new chance to test herself and show her stuff, was always a thrill. So she felt good right now, enjoying the smoldering looks she was getting from Paul.

"Get back in here," Paul commanded. He patted the bed beside him.

"Be polite or you won't get this coffee. Triple strength fresh-ground French roast. You'll never get better."

"All right, I'm begging you, please, get back in here. Or is the plan for me to admire you standing there with your hip cocked like that?"

She climbed into bed and pulled up the sheet, and they both sipped their coffee. Paul seemed to have something on his mind, so she held back the impulse to jump up and throw her clothes on, waiting to hear it. He ran a very successful investigation and security business. Selfishly, she hoped he was worrying about work and not anything that would slow her down.

He set his cup on the bed stand and drew her close. "Back to the grind for our girl. I hope Klaus is paying you a whole lot to compensate you for putting your life in such an uproar."

"I'm just glad to have a paying gig again, even though I'm coming in so late. It's going to be very demanding. But I've got you, and I've got Sandy to back me up, so I'm wallowing in a pleasantly fuzzy false sense of security."

"What about this case snagged you? You told me you weren't going to accept any more work until you made some decisions about the things that really matter. Remember?"

She knocked back some of the coffee left in her mug, remembering a distant time when she made decisions with only her own future to consider. But she had Bob to worry about, too. "Klaus called. He needed my help. And then the case . . ." she stopped. "I don't know much yet, but Klaus is ready to go all the way with Stefan Wyatt. He says Wyatt is accused of stealing a skeleton and strangling a woman in Monterey named Christina Zhukovsky. I'm going to meet the client today and start going through the files."

"Fine," he said, so absorbed in his own thoughts he probably hadn't heard hers, "but what is it about this case that has you looking so damned"—he paused to run his hands through the tangle of her long brown hair—"gorgeous?"

She laughed and hit him with a pillow. "That's your eyes giving you trouble. I've heard that happens as a man ages."

"You don't fool me," he said, pulling her into a full-bodied kiss. "You like distinguished. Aged red wine, ripe bananas, men with faces that show they've lived a life of excess and pleasure, flaky cheeses . . ."

"Shall I compare thee to a flaky cheese? Do you really want that?"

He laughed. "Anyway, have you considered this? Maybe this case will lead to a partnership opportunity. How would you feel about that?"

"Would you like that?" She knew the answer. She asked to avoid answering.

"Yep. You know I'd love to tie you down right here on the Monterey Peninsula. I'm always on the lookout for opportunities."

She smiled at him. "I guess I'll deal with a partnership offer when and if the time comes." Life felt easy here in his arms. Protected. But she was starting to notice something after this time she had spent away from work and from her own solo practice at Tahoe. She felt smaller, younger, less able.

Criminal defense work had always been her big place, her New York City. Good at her job, getting better all the time, she helped the hapless, damn it. She had a calling to go out and save miserable souls who could not save themselves, help them through the labyrinth, make sure the rules were followed and that they had their defense, even if they were guilty. She liked a large life. She wasn't sure yet how big her life could be with Paul.

He looked at her now, considering something, stroking her hair. Then he reached beyond her and pulled open a drawer to the bedside table. "Maybe the time has come," he said.

"What? Nobody's made me a partnership offer," she said.

He pulled out a small, ornately decorated enamel box. "Oh, but I have."

"Ah." She pushed her hair out of her eyes and looked at the box.

"Right. Marriage."

"We should have talked about this last night, at dinner, when we had time."

He shook his head. "Last night was chaos."

She remembered. Bob had forgotten his red hat, essential for reasons known only to him, but he had been so insistent on her bringing it that they interrupted their dinner date to drive back to her house to get it, and then drive it to her father's to deliver it. Paul had done it all so patiently, even though she had been fuming.

"Anyway, I don't want to talk, Nina. We've said it all and now's the right time for this. Mornings with you are so beautiful." He took her left hand and turned her to face him, popping open the box to reveal a twinkling square diamond ring, with two tapered baguettes flanking it.

He has asked her to marry him before but the ring was a new, serious development. Nina held up her side of the sheet, gazing at the ring, her lips parted. The band, sleek platinum, held the big stone between elongated prongs so that the light could dance around it in all directions.

"It's called an azure-cut—four equal sides. It was my grandmother's," he said. "A bluestocking in the early nineteen hundreds, I'm told. Seemed like the symbolically perfect thing for you."

"It's gorgeous," she said, stammering a little.

He took the ring from its box. "Nina, will you marry me?"

He had been patient with her. He deserved an answer. "I think . . ."

"Don't think."

She took her hand out of his, and covered the hand holding the ring with both of hers, feeling tears coming to her eyes. "I really love you!" she said.

"Then say yes."

"Marrying you means what? Staying here? Or would you come with me back to Tahoe?"

"I want you with me, Nina, forever and ever." Blond hair fell over his forehead and his bare flat stomach creased delightfully at the waist.

"There's Bob," she said.

"He's a kid. He'll adjust."

"My work. Matt, Andrea, their kids. My whole life is in Tahoe."

"Unless it's here with me." He pulled the ring out and turned it in the sunlight, watching it twinkle. "Wear it?" he said. "Be mine?"

"I am yours."

"Yet, I get no answer." He said it lightly, but she could hear his disappointment.

"I just . . ."

"Okay. Bad timing, trial comin' up. So here's what we'll do. You try it on for size. See how it feels on your finger. Take some time. Think if you must. Sound like a plan?"

She let him slip the ring on her finger. She liked the way it felt, and how pretty it looked there.

They kissed for a long time, languorous, loving.

"Maybe I should wear it on a chain around my neck," she said, "or everyone will assume we're engaged."

"Wear the ring. Maybe you'll discover you can't take it off."

She glanced toward the clock on the bureau. Well, if she was a little late, so be it. Her client wasn't going anywhere. "Paul, I have questions."

"Okay."

"Being together," she said slowly, "what's that mean to you?"

He leaned back and laughed. "I don't want a Stepford wife, okay, or why pick you? There's a babe out there somewhere who is ready to bake a rhubarb pie for me, and even wash my dirty laundry once in a while as part of the deal. I hope you will sometimes. Maybe I'll do the same for you, in a pinch. I'm willing to go untraditional. I just want us to take the next step. It would be beautiful to marry you."

She rubbed a finger against his rough morning cheek. "What I'm trying to say is, how about a counteroffer? I don't see why two people who love each other, two strong people, have to . . ."

"Marry? It's not a bad word. Go ahead. You can say it."

She nodded. "Marry. It's not as if—you always said you don't want kids."

"I do say that."

"So that's not an issue. I mean, you have such a fine life here, your business, friends. And I've got another one up in Tahoe. I miss it. I think all the time about my little house and my brother's family, and I check the weather up there every day. When it's foggy here, I think about how sunny it probably is in the mountains. When it rains here, I wonder if they're getting snow."

"Is this a no?"

She shook her head. "Just, I have questions. Isn't what we have good enough? Isn't it excellent?"

"I don't know what to expect. I don't know if you're coming, going, staying."

"I'm not sure I know what you mean by 'marry.'"

"Enough discussion, okay?" He fiddled with the ring on her finger, centering the stone so that it glittered. "You know what I mean when I ask you to marry me. You know. Don't start quibbling. Now come closer, you're making my brain ache with all this talk."

Her thoughts whirled. Only his touch brought them to a screeching stop. "Is this close enough?" she asked.

"No."

"This?"

"No."

"You always know exactly what you want and you aren't afraid to make your wishes known," she murmured. "I have to get to work. I have a meeting."

"Fifteen minutes."

"I really can't. Five."

"Five isn't enough for what I have in mind."

"Okay, ten, if you can convince me you'll make it worthwhile."

"Damn lawyers! Everything's a negotiation."

Later, his body wrapped tightly around her, he said, "Nina?"

She was busy covering his neck with tiny kisses. "Yes, Paul?"

"I love you."

"Ditto," she said.

"I await your final verdict."

Carnival Elation

7 Day Exotic Western Caribbean Itinerary

DAY	PORT	ARRIVE	DEPART
Sun	Galveston		4:00 P.M.
Mon	"Fun Day" at Sea		
Tue	Progreso/Merida	8:00 A.M.	4:00 P.M.
Wed	Cozumel	9:00 A.M.	5:00 P.M.
Thu	Belize	8:00 A.M.	6:00 P.M.
Fri	"Fun Day" at Sea		
Sat	"Fun Day" at Sea		
Sun	Galveston	8:00 A.M.	

TERMS AND CONDITIONS

PAYMENT SCHEDULE:
50% due upon booking
Full and final payment due by July 26, 2004

Acceptable forms of payment are Visa, MasterCard, American Express, Discover and checks. The card-holder must be one of the passengers traveling. A fee of $25 will apply for all returned checks. Check payments must be made payable to **Advantage International, LLC** and sent to: Advantage International, LLC, 195 North Harbor Drive, Suite 4206, Chicago, IL 60601

CHANGE/CANCELLATION:
Notice of change/cancellation must be made in writing to Advantage International, LLC.

Change:
Changes in cabin category may be requested and can result in increased rate and penalties. A name change is permitted 60 days or more prior to departure and will incur a penalty of $50 per name change. Deviation from the group schedule and package is a cancellation.

Cancellation:

181 days or more prior to departure	$250 per person
121 - 180 days or more prior to departure	50% of the package price
120 - 61 days prior to departure	75% of the package price
60 days or less prior to departure	100% of the package price (nonrefundable)

US and Canadian citizens are required to present a valid passport or the original birth certificate and state issued photo ID (drivers license). All other nationalities must contact the consulate of the various ports that are visited for verification of documentation.

<u>We strongly recommend trip cancellation insurance!</u>

For further details call 1-877-ADV-NTGE or visit www.GetCaughtReadingatSea.com

---

For booking form and complete information
go to <u>www.getcaughtreadingatsea.com</u> or call 1-877-ADV-NTGE

Complete coupon and booking form and mail both to:
Advantage International, LLC,
195 North Harbor Drive, Suite 4206, Chicago, IL 60601

From *New York Times* bestselling author

PERRI O'SHAUGHNESSY

"Move over, John Grisham."—*BookPage*

___0-440-22068-8	*Motion to Suppress*	$7.99/11.99
___0-440-22069-6	*Invasion of Privacy*	$7.99/11.99
___0-440-22472-1	*Obstruction of Justice*	$7.99/11.99
___0-440-22473-X	*Breach of Promise*	$7.99/11.99
___0-440-22581-7	*Acts of Malice*	$7.99/11.99
___0-440-22582-5	*Move to Strike*	$7.99/11.99
___0-440-23605-3	*Writ of Execution*	$7.99/11.99
___0-440-23606-1	*Unfit to Practice*	$7.99/11.99
___0-440-24087-5	*Presumption of Death*	$7.99/11.99

Please enclose check or money order only, no cash or CODs. Shipping & handling costs: $5.50 U.S. mail, $7.50 UPS. New York and Tennessee residents must remit applicable sales tax. Canadian residents must remit applicable GST and provincial taxes. Please allow 4 – 6 weeks for delivery. All orders are subject to availability. This offer subject to change without notice. Please call 1-800-726-0600 for further information.

Bantam Dell Publishing Group, Inc.
Attn: Customer Service
400 Hahn Road
Westminster, MD 21157

TOTAL AMT $_____
SHIPPING & HANDLING $_____
SALES TAX (NY, TN) $_____

TOTAL ENCLOSED $_____

Name _____

Address _____

City/State/Zip _____

Daytime Phone (_____) _____